David L. McDaniel

Quarterstars
AWAKENING

Black Rose Writing | Texas

ISBN: 978-1-68433-370-7
PUBLISHED BY BLACK ROSE WRITING
www.blackrosewriting.com

Printed in the United States of America
Suggested Retail Price (SRP) $18.95

Quarterstars Awakening is printed in Andalus

To Brittany and Mitchell, my Alpha and Omega
beta readers of the roughest of rough drafts.

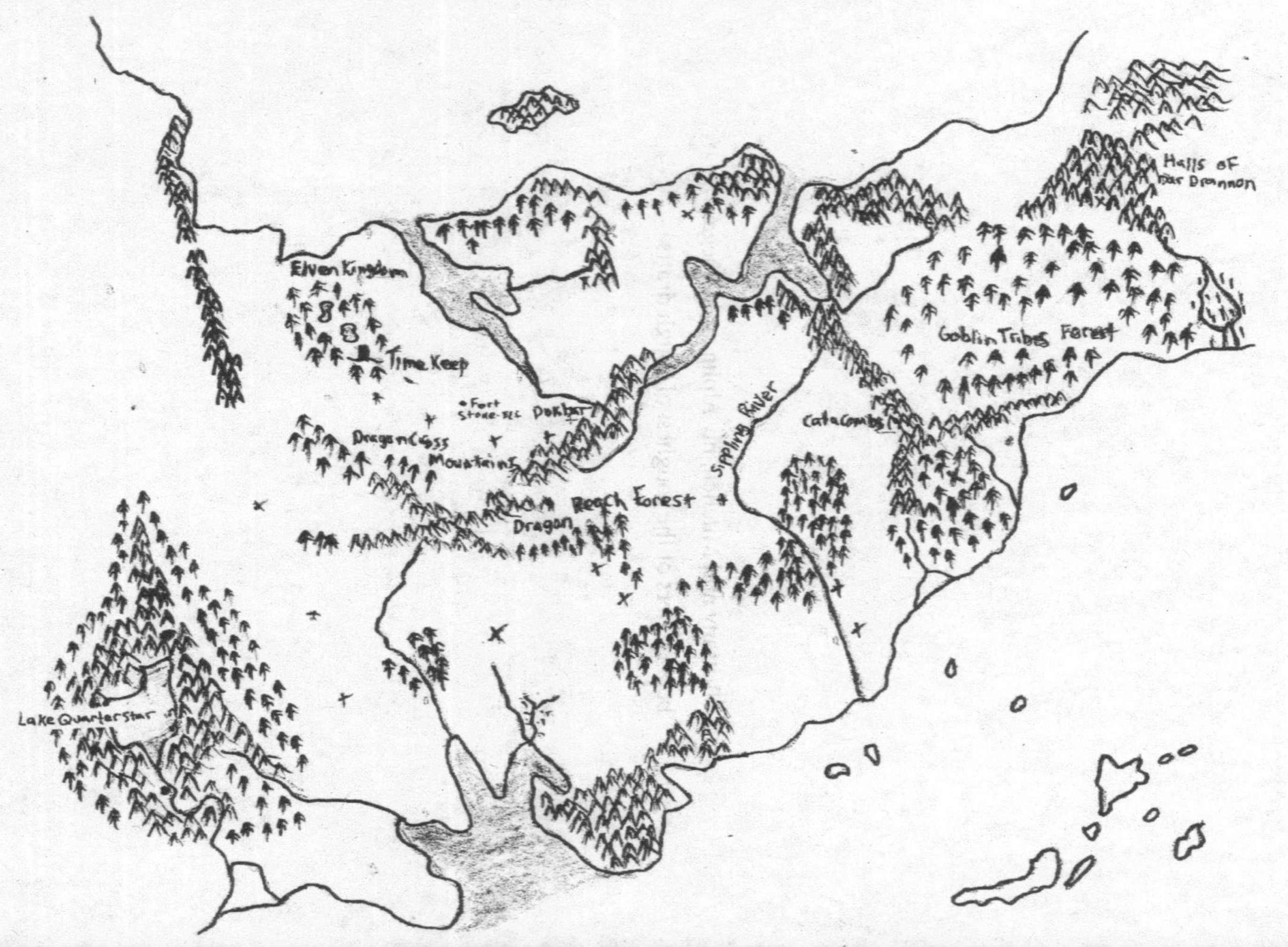

Halls of Dar Drannon
Goblin Tribes Forest
Catacombs
Sipphing River
Elven Kingdom
Time Keep
Fort Stone-Hal
Dorbar
Dragon Pass
Mountains
Dragon Reach Forest
Lake Quarterstar

Quarterstars Awakening

Author's Introduction

This series, The War for the Quarterstar Shards will be a five-book series. One book for each Quarterstar and this Quarterstars prophecy book. I wrote this book that you now hold in your hands after The Warrior's Bane, but it isn't necessarily the second book in the story, in fact, I have written it so that it can be read at any time during the series, full of hints of events that will be revealed in all four of the books. Even though this book is an origin story, Alaezdar Kerlethian is not one of the characters, yet it has absolutely everything to do with him.

The Weathered Old Man

The weathered old man walked down the trail that led to the rocky cliff that faced the Rae-Om Sea. The children followed until he reached the edge and stood unflinching on the edge of the precipice. The sea slammed into the cliff face causing gusts of sea spray to climb up the steep face and ruffle his robe.

"Look far beyond the horizon," he said pointing outward with his wrinkled and spotted hand. "Use not your eyes, but your mind to see the land that is not there."

One by one, the children sat down. The kids knew they could not realize this vision as he wanted, but they knew that another great tale was about to begin.

"All of this land used to be frozen. Icy frozen tundra; no trees, nothing green, only silvery white, blinding landscapes. This realm had no life, save one man; a hermit."

"The Kronn man!" they cheered in unison.

"Close, but not quite, at least not yet. He did not become the Kronn man until after the battle between the gods. A battle that happened on the other side of this sea."

The old man then lifted himself above the cliff and drifted out above the sea. The children's eyes widened in amazement, for they had heard that he was capable of such wondrous feats, but this was the first time they had witnessed him doing so. They stood up and ran as close to the edge of the cliff as they dared, and watched the old man weave his tale.

"The hermit was not a man, elf, or dwarf. He had no real shape or form. He merely existed as part of the land, because he was the land. He lived alone, he cared for no one, he had no life other than to exist, but that changed one day when two elves and a dwarf came through the portal. They were not expecting to find the hermit. The hermit tried to use his magic to turn them away by blinding them with snow and confusing them. However, the elves and dwarf persisted and continued to search out and destroy this mysterious barrier to their mission.

The old man floated above the cliff's edge and turned the scene into a snowy landscape. The children no longer saw the ocean's horizon in the background. All was white and crystalline, and they saw that where the weathered old man was floating, appearing as a hunched-over, nearly crippled old hermit standing in the snow facing his adversaries.

"It was a magical battle between them. It went on for hours with no one gaining any ground on the other until one of the elves cast a spell, changing the hermit into a black evil beast with huge horns growing out of his head and thick leathery wings."

"A dragon?" the kids gasped.

"Oh no, much worse. The birth of the Markenhirth!" he exclaimed loudly and then went back to his tale. The children then saw the whole battle being performed before them as the old man told his tale.

"The Markenhirth flew to the air just as a star exploded into the atmosphere, crackling and screaming towards the surface, but the Markenhirth unknowingly jumped into its path. The star cut through its chest, slicing through his heart and splitting the star into four equal parts. The Quarterstar shards flew to different corners of the land as the hermit and the newly formed Markenhirth fell to the ground, becoming trapped in the frozen underworld.

"The hermit, now as the Kronn man, disappeared, and with no adversaries to stop them, the elves and dwarf made the land green and became gods to the thousands of people that would soon populate the land.

"For many years the elven gods Val-Eahea, Raezoures and the dwarven god Har-Ron ruled the land in peace, but what they did not expect, was a new powerful race that rose out of the dirt of the land. The humans inserted themselves into this land and became a complex thread to this tale of Wrae-Kronn."

The old weathered old man then turned back into his normal form and the icy landscape disappeared. Floating back to the children, he landed softly before them and smiled. We are descendants of those humans, and you will soon learn the Tale of the First Human King Dar Drannon.

Chapter 1
Year 566

Traelyn's ancient body ached. Her ankles, hips, even her slumped shoulders hurt as if her body would crumble to the ground in pieces. Even with all this pain, she still felt the compelling urge to keep walking. She had not been outside of her small but active village for many years because she was too old and too frail to travel any farther than her gardens. Today she did manage to braid her long silver hair back before she left, as she felt she might be taking a long journey, even if it was only a long walk through the forest. Her hair was wiry and brittle, but it felt good to braid it again, as it was something she had not done for herself in such a way for many years. She almost felt young and beautiful again, which made her smile to herself at the absurdity of the thought.

She really had no idea where she was going, or why she was doing this; she just felt the urge to walk, and walk she did. The trail before her was nothing more than a deer trail of crushed weeds meandering in between the shrubs, ferns, and clustered pine trees. She had to stop numerous times to catch her breath when the trail sloped uphill.

She had been walking for hours until she came to a massive clearing. The meadow before her was vast and she had no idea that it was here. Three sides were surrounded by thick forested woods that covered three large cliffs on each side that towered high above the evergreen forest, but what impressed her more was what occupied the large meadow. Men. More men than she had ever seen. Her son Daegon and a few of his top warriors could be seen atop a rock shelf on a low portion of the cliff, high enough to give him a complete view of the valley below, but close enough for his men to see him. The soldiers practiced fighting with sword, axe, mace and shield. Her son Daegon was the commander of a few small bands of raiding forces that had changed their mandate from fighting against other human tribes in the area, to hit and run tactics against the large elven forces to the north, but she had no idea he had this many men.

Walking into the meadow she marveled at the strength and amount of energy the men displayed. They were all so preoccupied with their training that they didn't notice her watching at first, but as she inched her way in between the fighting, they began to take notice and stopped their training, bowing to her as she walked passed them. Some even took a knee, eager to show their respect and take a break from their training while doing so.

"Great Mother," they all gasped or mumbled under their breath.

By the time she reached the face of the cliff, all of the men had taken the position of one knee bowing in reverence.

Daegon, realizing what was going on, grabbed a rope that allowed him to repel down the cliff face and hurried down to the bottom. Angry at the distraction by the Great Mother, he threw the rope against the cliff and allowed it to dangle so the others in his company could follow him.

"What are you doing here Great Mother?" he asked, giving her a mock bow. He then reached out, gave her a hard hug, and held her tight.

"Where did all of these men come from?" she asked, breaking his embrace and putting her hands behind her back attempting to rub out the pain that was beginning to scream at her from her long walk.

"These men," he began smiling, showing his slightly crooked teeth behind his rough and splotchy facial hair "are my latest achievement, as they are the last of the tribes to have finally joined us after generations of intertribal warfare."

Traelyn smiled. She hated the elves as much as Daegon did, and he hated the elves with such unmatched passion that few could ever surpass it. The elves had been a painful thorn and major irritation to the human race for generations. When the humans migrated north in an attempt to escape the constant dragon attacks, the elves aggressively turned them away, sending them scattering back to their home under the shadow of the Dragon Cross Mountains.

Even in peace, their pleas were ignored, and the elves flaunted their superiority over the scattered and disorganized human tribes. Infuriated by the elven arrogance and lack of sympathy, the humans tried to aggressively break into the elven defense system at the southernmost keep, Fort Stone Elf.

Every attempt to storm the fortress failed.

They tried many times to send scouts around the keep to reconnoiter the area, looking for a weakness in the fort. They found themselves wandering the forests for days only to return weary, hungry, and scratched head to toe from traveling through the thick forest foliage, leaving them to believe that elven magic was at play to keep them lost in the tangle.

She assessed the men under her son's command. "This is such a large force, but is it large enough?" she asked.

"You are correct, Great Mother. This force is not large enough to take those wicked forest creepers, but what you see is merely the last of the tribes to join our cause."

"They have magic. How do you plan to stop the elves from using their magic?"

"We will hit them hard and fast and then retreat, just as we have always done, but this time, we will not stop like we always have. We will stop, overrun them, and make them beg us to kill them."

Traelyn smiled and nodded. "I think you are still being a bit over-confident, but I like your enthusiasm. Tell your men to continue on."

"As you command, Great Mother. I will have Traegon take you home."

"No, I do not want to interrupt your training. I can find my way back."

"Traegon is not needed here," he insisted.

"He is your son, he should be by your side."

Daegon's face turned red; as he knew his next words needed to be placed very carefully, as he did not want to anger the Great Mother. "He is not needed here. I do not plan on taking him with us."

"My son, Daegon, why? He looks up to you, he wants to please you, he wants to prove his worth to you, when are you going to allow him that opportunity?"

"Never," he said as he turned around, yelling for someone to find his son.

Traelyn turned around to walk back home. Traegon would find her soon enough, she could find her way back easy enough and so could he. If Daegon truly intended to send Traegon, and she was not completely sure he would, he would catch up to her in quick fashion.

She had just wandered into the forest from the meadow when the sky began to turn purple. This caused her to look up at the sun and witness the red hazy blur that was blotted out by orange clouds. This made her curious because it was a sight she had never seen in all of her ancient years. She had never seen the sun look so peculiar. Shrugging it off as something new to add to her long list of memories, she continued to walk on, but immediately her vision began to shimmer with sparks forming in her peripheral vision. She tried to keep walking, but had to stop when her old creaky knees began to shake.

"Oh my," she said as she thought she was about to lose consciousness, but before she fell to her knees a figure stood in front of her and wrapped his arms underneath her arm pits, propping her up.

"Don't be afraid Traelyn," the man whispered in her ear.

"Father!" she screamed, more like a hoarse shrill of excitement that came out, barely louder than a loud whisper.

"Yes, but I am not really here. I am only here to tell you it is time. Something has happened in the future to allow me to contact you in this way. One of your children has made this happen, but because of this new event, I know things are about to happen that will shape coming events."

"What do you want me to do?" she asked breaking free of his embrace and sitting in the dirt sobbing, unable to contain her emotion.

"It is time for you to find the king of the elves," he said, smiling the exact same smile that made her ache for his return. Her brain scrambled to bring back memories of so long ago. Her memory was such a fog, three hundred long, unnatural years she had waited for his return. She wondered how she knew he would return. She believed it so deeply for her whole life, but she could not remember why. Then it came to her as clear as it was yesterday. Yes, it was simply because *they* said he would. The elves had told her this.

"What is going on?" she asked, trying to remember more. The more she tried to remember the more it seemed she would forget as soon as she remembered. "We will, we will be attacking them soon."

"No. That is not what I mean. You must find King Jaerick. He needs you, he wants you."

"That cannot be. What does he want with me? The elves, they hate us, they kill our people, and they deserve to die."

Her father, Dar Drannon, knelt down beside her, took both of her hands, and stood her up, holding her tightly in a loving embrace that made her feel young and safe again. She wanted to go home. He pulled her away, wiped the tears from her weary and wrinkled face and continued. "It is time to put that aside. Go north and find the elves. If you go with aggression and not compassion, you will find a hard and tragic end to you and your children, and your children's children."

"I don't know if I can do what you ask."

Dar Drannon pulled away from her and smiled as his form began to dissipate. "You must. You will remember everything very soon. Once, very long ago, you were in love with the prince of elves. That prince is now their king. Find him. Find him in peace. Also, know now that I am not far from you. I am not dead, but I am trapped in a place that will not allow me to return yet. Only you can help me someday return. If you do as I ask, it may happen soon, but you must do as I ask."

As he spoke his last words, he faded away, the dark sky brightened again, and she found she was standing on the trail facing a tree. She looked around and shook her head.

"Now this old woman has resorted to talking to trees," she said blankly as she wiped her tears. Slowly she began to remember a little more of the details. It was still foggy, but she remembered when Jaerick was still a prince, his father, King Keiyann Krowe had told her that her father would return someday.

The only thing she felt she could do now was continue back home. She had not walked too far when Traegon appeared from behind her, out of breath as he had been running to find her.

"Great Mother!" he gasped. "How did you get so far so fast?"

"I don't know dear boy. I just walked. Did you see the peculiar sky just now?"

"No, what did you see? There isn't a cloud in the sky."

"Oh, never mind, don't listen to me, I'm just an old woman rambling on," she said.

Chapter 2

The dark leaf-colored curtains of the elven king's quarters rustled from the evening breeze as it blew in the crisp scent of Flamespan waning at the coming of the Doreal season. The moonlight glimmered in the room, illuminating it with a soft lustrous glow that showered the room with a silvery haze. The evening seemed peaceful enough to provide restful sleep for the king and his people, but instead, the king tossed in his sleep, dreaming dreams of terror and tension that worried the high elven king of Wrae Kronn.

King Jaerick Krowe endured his fitful slumber. He groaned and cursed leaving his sheets wet with sweat with every toss and turn. Uncomfortable and anxious, he awoke with a start for at least the tenth time, and sat up in his bed. He looked around the room and gathered his bearings. Shaking his head, he looked at the door and saw that it was closed, as it should be. He ran his fingers through his long blond hair, and in a frustrated grunt clenched his fists, grabbing a handful of hair. He yanked at his hair as though he were attempting to remove the visions his dark dreams had left him. He flopped backwards onto his pillows. He cursed incoherently again. Feverish, he pulled the heavy cover off his bed, then grabbed the thin sheet, pulled it over his head and turned over with a grunt.

Even in his frustration, he was still able to fall back to sleep within minutes. But as he feared, his dreams did not end, promising only to continue their horrible cycle.

It was all so clear. He stood on a northern hill overlooking an intense one-sided battle, a battle he knew he would not win: a battle so fierce, that as the leader of the whole elven people, he could not bear to witness. A battle so violent that total annihilation was the only possible outcome. Surrender was not an option, nor was retreat possible.

To the South, the rival commanders stood on the opposite hill watching the battle below them. Jaerick had foolishly committed his whole elven battalion into a choke point, trapping them in a deep ravine where they were surrounded by steep rocky hills on all sides. Human archers stood on top of the hills mercilessly picking off the elves one by one. They showed no mercy in shooting the arrows into the ravine, peppering them as if they were dogs in a pit. The human commanders stood atop the hill laughing, and barking orders to hurry, and kill them faster.

King Jaerick watched in horror as his son scrambled, attempting in vain to give the orders that would save the lives of his fellow elves. The prince, in all his bravery and honor, circled his warriors on his horse giving shouts of courage and direction. In a final act of desperation, he tried to lead a charge up the steep ravine toward the humans. The ravine was too steep for he and the dozen other brave warriors that followed, and in doing so took two arrows in the rib cage. He arched backwards and fell off the back of his horse, landing on his head and left shoulder, knocking him unconscious and leaving him seriously wounded. His subordinates scrambled to take him to a safer position.

The human commanders raised their arms and cheered in exhilaration over wounding the great king's son. As they cheered, a dark cloaked figure appeared from the shadows, and went directly to the human commander and whispered into his ear. The other commanders then surrounded the hooded figure and conferred in secret for a while. They talked and plotted for many minutes until the dark figure stepped away and pulled his hood back.

Jaerick watched in terror as he realized that the cloaked figure looked like him, except that this Jaerick had no eyes on his face. He knew that the other dark, hooded version of himself could not be witnessing the battle the way it was actually happening. He was plotting his own destruction, but could not see it as it happened.

The dark Jaerick now turned behind him and grabbed the hands of a person that had just come into view. The person walked forward, and even from this distance, he could tell it was Traelyn. He was amazed at how young and lovely she looked. She was as beautiful as the day when he first met her. He had not seen her in years, and had long since totally forgotten her, yet in the moment he remembered her as if he had just seen her yesterday.

She was the love of his youth, so long ago, but somehow, he had forgotten her completely. *How was this so?* He wondered as he dreamt. How could he forget her? She was so beautiful, how could he forget such beauty? He watched her from the distance, longing for her, fires rekindled. He wanted to hold her again so badly, and even as he watched the demise of his son, nothing else mattered. Memories flooded his mind, soul, and being. He watched her intently and barely noticed her smiling grimly as with one arm she cradled a baby to her side. They made eye contact, but instead of feeling the shared love they once had, he saw that she was full of rage and hate. So much rage that she seemed happy to see the death at her feet.

Then he saw in her possession something he had not seen in years. She held the Quarterstar Talisman, with the Val-Eahea Quarterstar Shard firmly clasped in the center as she dangled it above the baby's head. This should not be, he thought. It cannot be; the talisman and shard cannot be joined. The last time they were joined was before his father's time. Their god Val Eahea had forbade the shard to be united with the talisman out of fear that someday all four shards might be united into a single talisman. The Val Eahean Shard currently resided in the guarded Wayerman Crags, and the Quarterstar Talisman, an elven family heirloom, was locked in the vault in the deepest portion of the castle.

Jaerick awoke again. "Naemyn!" he shouted, sitting up in a start. "Naemyn! It is gone! Where is Naemyn! I need Naemyn now!"

The guards entered the room to console their king. Only this time he demanded his spiritual advisor. "We will get him; he will be here shortly my king," they reassured him.

Chapter 3

South of the Elven Kingdom, nestled at the base of the Dragon Cross Mountains, rested the human fortress of Dokbar. Overshadowed by the rocky, forested mountains, a fortress made of blackened stone and wood from the massive redwood trees nestled tightly in a small valley below, protected from any elven attacks. Traelyn slept heavily after her long walk back home, and on this quiet night, only the human guards at their posts were awake to feel the evening late-Flamespan-turning-to-Doreal breeze that meandered between the towering pine and redwood trees.

The moon lifted shadows over the fortress and into the private room where Traelyn slept. Her aged and brittle body ached as she tossed and turned feeling every square inch of her body. She woke many times only to fall asleep and dream the same dream over again.

She was young again. It was of a time long ago, before she was given the elven root of life to sustain her health, and to help her live as long as she has. She had lived over three hundred years: three hundred years of slow aging and brutal waiting. In the dream, she was saying goodbye to her love, Prince Jaerick. Traelyn felt confused, the memories rushing back. The dream was almost exactly as it had happened, so long ago.

They stood on a small footbridge that spanned a small babbling brook, and Jaerick held her tight as she cried on his shoulder. He was shaking as he told her that he loved her, and that was why she had to go. He assured her that he would return for her soon. Still, she did not want to let go. She was willing to hang onto him indefinitely, and listen to his heartbeat for all of time. She did not want to leave. Left all alone in a world in which she had no stake. She needed him, and she loved him. She would not, could not leave him; it hurt too badly to even think about leaving, much less to be forced to do so against her will.

She would have stayed with him holding him in the pre-dawn morning.

They were quiet for many minutes until she heard someone approaching. Her memory told her that it was King Keiyann Krowe, but when she turned around, she saw her father instead. He approached her with his familiar, loving smile. When she saw him, she felt that everything would be all right, and her father would take her home at long last. She waved at her father and ran to him, leaving Jaerick standing at the footbridge.

She ran to her father and embraced him so tightly that she felt his heartbeat against her ear, and cried even harder, letting all the anxiety escape her. Her worries replaced with joy and happiness. Dar Drannon stroked her hair and told her everything would be all right, but he was not returning to her yet, she still had to be patient and wait for certain events to pass before he could come back.

Shocked, she released him, but instead of explaining his intentions, he left her and ran to help Jaerick who was in great trouble. She turned around and watched in horror as a cloaked figure appeared from behind Jaerick and attacked him. The attacker quickly overtook the elf and had him on his back. The cloaked entity sat on Jaerick's chest, and began strangling him over the bridge. The prince's neck and head hung over the edge of the bridge as the cloaked figure began to choke the life out of him, shaking the elf with a fury Traelyn had never seen before. Jaerick squirmed to save his life, his eyes bulging, and face red. Jaerick was close to losing consciousness, powerless against the brute strength of his attacker.

"No!" Traelyn screamed as she ran passed her father to save Jaerick. Just as she reached him, the ground began to shake, and the cloaked figure stopped choking Jaerick for a second to get his balance against the rumbling ground. He shifted his weight and returned to the coughing and gasping prince to finish squeezing the life out of him. Traelyn corrected her balance, but before she could reach Jaerick, the ground split and fell away from her, causing her to fall into an open crevice in the ground. Somehow, her forward momentum allowed her to grab the top of what had now become a cliff face and she hung on for her life.

Trying to pull herself up, she could hear the figure choking Jaerick, and guessed that he was only moments away from losing consciousness. Still holding on for her life, her father suddenly appeared and stared down at her and emphatically shook his head, then looked to Jaerick as he clung onto the last moments of his life. He had to make a decision. "I have to save him honey," he said to her as his eyes began to swell and turn red. "I love you, but I have to do this."

"But daddy, I'm slipping. I cannot hang on much longer," Traelyn cried. "Father! Please help me, I'm slipping!" she screamed as she lost grip of one hand and hung on only by her fingertips of her other hand.

Dar Drannon left her, ran to the footbridge, grabbed the cloaked figure, and pulled him off of Jaerick. Jaerick then rolled over and grabbed at his throat, gasping for much needed air. Dar Drannon then yanked the cloaked figure up by the waist and heaved him over his shoulder like a mere straw scarecrow into the open crevice. Traelyn watched the figure fall deep into the foggy depth of the crevice. As the figure fell, tossing and squirming into the darkness, the cloak fell off its body. Traelyn saw that the cloaked figure was her. In despair and confusion, her grip gave out and she fell.

Screaming, she awoke, and once again found herself alone in her bed, again an old woman in the calm evening moonlight.

Chapter 4

King Jaerick, Naemyn, and a handful of elven soldiers sped down the spiral stone stairwell, their footsteps echoing through the dark tunnels as they raced down to the deep levels of the tower to reach the sacred vault. The tower was in the center of the elven fortress, hidden in the northern forests of Wrae-Kronn. The sacred vault held all of the precious elven artifacts, including the Quarterstar Talisman.

The Talisman was forged before the recording of time, and was made to hold all four of the shards of lore that fell from the sky at the beginning of the creation of Wrae-Kronn. The elves had only ever found one shard, the shard that landed near the catacombs, which they called the Val-Eahean Quarterstar.

It was told that the first elven king carried this talisman with the Val-Eahean Quarterstar Shard around his neck at all times, but the magic of the Shard was never mentioned in the early tales. Legends persisted through the years, that the Shard, when placed into one of the four slots on the talisman, had magical properties beyond imagination. The talisman was then given to the line of elven kings that would one day see the two rejoined.

One in the line of kings fearing its power if it fell into the wrong hands, placed the Shard back in the exact spot where it fell to the earth, deep inside the catacombs. An elf was then appointed, or more accurately, sacrificed, to live in a small room where the Shard was housed to guard it from being stolen until such time when they required them to be joined.

In return for the sacrifice, the guardian elf would protect the Shard until it was to be removed, at which time he would die, his body withering to dust. Elven prophecies told of a day when the Quarterstar Shard and talisman would be re-joined by the son of the Great Bringer of Peace whom would be born down the bloodline of the first human king. Most elves loathed the idea.

The Shard was nearly beyond reach. The Val elves had long since left the dangerous and increasingly goblin-infested forests. King Jaerick knew how important it was that the Shard remained where it was until the time to be joined with the talisman. He had faith that Val Eahea would come to him and tell him when that time would be. Maybe this dream was a sign that the time lay near, but right then, the only thing that mattered was determining whether the talisman was where it should be.

The king held a stern and worried frown as he neared the final steps to the vault. Naemyn looked worried as well, but also had a look of confidence, as it was his nature to be the solid rock companion and advisor to the king. Naemyn was the leader of the Elven Sorae, a council of Val and Sor elves that worked to keep the unity of the two races of elves as well as advising the king in spiritual, prophetic, and mystical matters.

One of King Keiyann Krowe's final commands from his deathbed was to make Naemyn, Jaerick's childhood friend, the leader of the Sorae to aid in his son's rein.

The Sorae had groomed Naemyn for this position from the very beginning. Many years earlier when Naemyn came to the castle, he was put under the tutorship of the wisest of the Sorae to learn the ways of prophet and seer. The current Sorae, with the help of the spirit of their gods Val-Eahea and Raezoures, had granted Naemyn purpose.

The two elven races, though both peaceful in nature, were still historically separated and two very different races. The Val elves from the mountains in the south-eastern valley, ever the invader to the Sor, controlled the new combined race through population and position. The Sor elves, undyingly loyal to the god Raezoures, had small rebelling factions that peacefully made known they did not welcome the new race of elves. In an effort to bridge the races, the king of the Val elves formed the Sorae to help all of the Sor elves have a voice in the new elven kingdom.

The small group pressed on toward the vault. King Jaerick eyed Naemyn with a strange sense of wonder and doubt.

The Sorae consisted of all views of elven lore, prophecy, and worked to keep a balance in the elven political direction, because the Val elves were often ambitious and needed to slow their advance. The Sorae helped guide the king to help the elven kingdom remain strong, peaceful, and prosperous, yet move slow enough to include the Sor elves in this great directive from their now common god Val Eahea.

Jaerick and Naemyn grew up as friends, as was the plan from the beginning. Someday Jaerick would become King and Naemyn would be his advisor, prophet, and next in line to lead the Sorae. This was thought to be a good plan from the beginning by both Keiyann Krowe and the Sorae, to continue the success of the elven races. Both Jaerick and Naemyn grew up knowing the prophecies of the Shard and Talisman, and of their importance.

They continued down the stairs until they reached the bottom of the tower to a circular antechamber that opened up to the vault. A single guard stood in front of a large iron door to the chamber. Jaerick paused and stared at the sentry at his post before asking, "How long have you been on guard here?"

"Two hours," the young soldier answered.

"And how long are your shifts?"

"Three hours."

"How many years have you been a guard of these chambers?"

"Two hundred years."

"So you were also a guard during my father's reign?"

"Yes, my king."

"During your time of service, how many times has this door been opened."

"Never, my king."

Jaerick looked to Naemyn and said nothing. He then looked back at the elven soldier and commanded him to open the door.

The soldier went to a table on the opposite side of the hall and moved a few small stone figurine statues of ancient elven sages, which revealed a small handle imbedded into the wall, and slid it open. He grabbed a single key from the indenture, and walked back to the door and slid the key in and unlocked the door, which revealed a small, dark and nearly empty room. The smell of ancient mold carried on the stale air escaped the room as the soldier entered, went to a table near the door, and opened a box containing torch supplies. He quickly grabbed them and lit the six torches in the room.

The torch fire flickered as it chased away the musty darkness revealing a room that contained rare and precious artifacts, many of which Jaerick had never seen before, but had known they existed through the tales his of father and high-ranking elves of this land. Jaerick knew what he wanted, and what it looked like. He went straight to a small box covered with leaf shaped jewels that sat on a shelf centered on the back wall. Above it was an historic painting of Val Eahea holding the Sword of Valkilye as four shooting stars fell to the ground from the dark sky. The painting depicted the epic battle against the Markenhirth on the day of creation of Wrae-Kronn. It was the day that they not only sent the Markenhirth to the underworld, but when the Star of Rae-om, the mother of their creation, split into four pieces, creating the three races: the two races of elves, the race of dwarves, and the last piece falling to the west contained the heart of the spell and the heart of the Markenhirth.

In another painting to Jaerick's left, Val-Eahea wore the talisman around his neck. The Quarterstar Talisman lay on top of his leaf armor housing the Quarterstar Shard in its place in the Talisman. This painting depicted the future of the return of Val-Eahea and how he would retrieve the Shard and place it in the Talisman. Prophecy written by Val-Eahea and Raezoures predicted how one day they would both return and secure all of the Shards and reunite them in peace.

This elven god, Val-Eahea, came to a young Keiyann Krowe, while he was yet in his youth, to give him a sword that he would eventually give to the human king, and he also explained to him the power of the talisman and how the shard and talisman must not be joined until a time of great need. The key to the prophecy was the human king. The talisman could only be used to defeat the Markenhirth. The shard joined with the talisman will give the wearer everlasting life and the power to travel anywhere in the land instantly and at will.

Jaerick picked up the box, instantly knowing by its weight that it would be empty, but instead of opening it immediately, he said a small silent prayer to Val Eahea. Naemyn placed his hand on Jaerick's shoulder, interrupting his prayer. Jaerick raised his head, looked at Naemyn accusingly, and then swung open the lid. As he feared, all he saw was an empty velvet liner. The Talisman was missing and had been for some time. Naemyn took two steps back in shock. "How did you know it would be missing?"

"A dream."

"We will search the castle! Every person and their possessions will be searched. We will search the land for this. No stone will be left unturned. We will find it."

"No need for all that, Naemyn. I know who has it."

"How could anyone have possibly stolen our precious symbol of elven existence when it has been so guarded?"

"Not stolen, but *given* away."

"Who has it and who gave it away?"

"Traelyn has it, and my father gave it to her."

Naemyn winced, revealing to Jaerick that Naemyn knew this was the truth.

"She must be long dead by now. How will we find it?" Naemyn asked as he rubbed his chin, recomposing himself.

King Jaerick shook his head. "No, she is not dead. I do not know how, but she is alive."

"How can you know?"

"I can feel it within; something has changed, and it is not right. My memories of her had been completely erased until now. I do not know why or how this has happened, but it has, and something has set the wheel in motion. I intend to find out why I have forgotten all about her. My father knew this would happen, triggering the prophecy to be set into motion long before she left; we know the prophecy, but I am just now beginning to believe that she is part of the prophecy."

Naemyn straightened his robe and looked back to Jaerick. "But that prophecy changed when she left our kingdom."

"I do not yet remember everything that happened, in fact, for many years I have had no recollection of her. It is as if she never existed until now, and I have only a foggy memory of her life here and why she left, but I do know that she did not leave on her own accord, but rather was sent away." Jaerick thought carefully before he spoke again. After a few silent moments, he looked at his friend and boldly stated. "I also think you have a part in this."

Naemyn said nothing, but stared into his friend's eyes disconcertingly.

Jaerick let the matter drop for now, and continued with the matter at hand. "We must seek her out and find the Quarterstar Talisman."

"Then I will find it for you, my friend. I will personally search all of the known lands for you."

King Jaerick forced a smile. "My friend," he repeated his friend's response. "I cringe whenever you say that."

"It is because you know that I mean business."

"It is also because it means that your decision is final, and that I know I cannot talk you out of anything once you say that."

The two friends stood gazing at each other as in a duel of the mind for a few moments before Naemyn spoke. "I await your command."

"I want you to find Traelyn and bring her here, but first I want you to travel to the catacombs and assure that the Quarterstar Shard is still in place and that she does not have that as well. While you are there, I want you to inform the Guardian what has been discovered tonight, and ask him what he knows of the prophecies and most of all, instruct him to keep the shard where it is until I can figure this out. It is also very important that I know it is still there and will not be removed until I can get there. I cannot rest until I know that it has *not* been joined with the talisman.

"Should she have both, Traelyn may already have them joined. It is crucial that we know whether we are off our prophetic course. I will begin studying the texts we have here and I will talk to the Sorae. If you find that the Shard is no longer at the catacombs, then we must assume that Traelyn has the shard and the talisman…" Jaerick paused to consider the possibility. "No, she must not have both. If she does, we, the whole elven race, may be in grave danger of extinction. The human clans will surely have the power to overrun and destroy us."

"Shouldn't I just bring the shard back here so that we can make sure it never falls into human hands?" Naemyn asked.

"No. If it is there, then it will be safest there. The joining of the two is not for you, anyone, or me yet. And…" Jaerick paused, deliberating if he should mention his thoughts any further. "I want to see her again. I suspect she has the talisman, and for some reason I believe that she is going to show herself, and when she does, we will find the talisman. If you have the shard and the talisman so close to each other, I believe the temptation will be too great." King Jaerick paused in thought. Then his brow wrinkled, and he added. "Naemyn, as much as I trust you, I cannot afford to send you on this trip, it is too dangerous for you to go. You will have to cross through the heart of our enemy's territory to get to the catacombs. We need to appoint another."

"No, my king," Naemyn objected. "I'm going. Who else could you trust with our most precious artifacts if not me?"

"I suppose, once again, that you are right. I trust no one else, and you are the only one I would trust to not be tempted to put them together. Then, if you must, take fifty of my personal Elven Pathfinders with you."

"But my lord, this mission will require that we move with stealth, not force."

"Then take twenty-five."

"I will take twenty regular cavalry, with five of them being scouts."

King Jaerick shook his head and knew he was not going to win against his stubborn, thickheaded friend. "Fine, take twenty, but leave before dawn, and hurry back.

"If you find Traeylnn before I do, bring her back, I want the talisman back and I want her here. I need her here. She belongs with me. She should never have left in the first place."

"Very well, my king, but promise me one thing while I am gone."

King Jaerick smiled at his friend. "What is it?"

"Just inform the Sorae for me. I will not have time to brief them on our task."

King Jaerick frowned slightly, but immediately recovered, hoping that Naemyn did not notice. "I will inform them of everything as I will also seek knowledge to the meaning of my missing memories."

"Thank you Jaerick. Now I will take my leave and prepare for my journey. Have your elven cavalry ready for me at predawn. And I mean regulars, do not try to sneak any of your Elven Pathfinders in with them. They need to be here to protect our kingdom."

King Jaerick smiled. "Yes Naemyn. Do you always have to be right?"

"Always," Naemyn said with a wink as he left the room.

Chapter 5

"Great Mother?" Traegon whispered as he entered the garden sunroom where Traelyn tended to her flowers and spices. Quietly, she prepared to harvest certain fruits and vegetables.

"Yes Traegon, come in my love," she responded, straightening up, feeling the pain in her back stab and crawl up her spine as she did so. Her whole body ached, and it frustrated her that she could not move like she used to.

Traegon entered the greenhouse, he was a young man just recently maturing into manhood, and was eager to prove he was mature to his peers and elders. He wore the simple clothes of a servant. His loose, baggy, tunic hung on his body more like robes than the well-fitted clothes most of the villagers wore. His shoulder length brown hair matched the color of his clothes. He grew a soft, scruffy beard only because he could, not because it looked good, as it did nothing to mature his soft features. It was not thick, little more than stiff peach fuzz, but he liked it just as well.

"Do you know what this plant is Traegon?" she asked as he walked toward her.

"No."

"It is a Drodennum plant, it is an elven plant that grows wild around lakes," she picked up a flower and pinched it off the stem. "See this flower," she said as she straightened out a small flute-like white flower that had a single, long yellow pistil shooting out of the middle. "They bloom once a year in the fall, but the blooms only last two weeks."

"It's a pretty flower," Traegon said feigning interest as politely as possible.

Traelyn noticed and released the flower and straightened herself again, but groaned as she did so. Her age was showing, though she was in perfect health, and no one in the village was healthier. By first appearances, people would see a tall, but very frail looking old woman. Her wrinkles were pronounced, but her eyes sparkled with life. However, today her eyes did not sparkle and her body ached from her shoulders to her many joints, and her pain had been increasing over the past few days. Grabbing the flower, she twisted the center and plucked out the pistil.

Traelyn looked at the pistil and ran it in between her fingers before she slowly placed it in her mouth, and chewed the reproductive part of the flower for a long while before swallowing. Traegon watched patiently as she did this, not interrupting, nor speaking before being spoken to, as was the custom when speaking with the Great Mother.

"It is not because of its beauty as to why I grow the Drodennum plant," she said as she closed her eyes and waited for the effects of the flower to begin. "It is for its life-sustaining qualities." She continued after she swallowed. "One bloom is intended to extend your life for up to twenty years, and my body has been aching so badly the last month waiting for this bloom." She paused again, and Traegon noticed that her skin began to change color from the pale unhealthy, almost corpse-like color, to a rejuvenated healthy pink skin tone. Though her skin was still aged and wrinkly, it began to give the appearance of healthy life.

"Let's sit, my son. I am weak from the shock to my system."

Traegon took Traelyn's hand, and guided her out of the greenhouse to an open courtyard. They walked under a large maple tree that left a huge shadow over a lush grassy yard. Small buildings surrounded the open area that looked upon the perfectly landscaped shrubs, flowers, and small trees. Small birds happily flitted from one tree to another.

Traelyn had spent her life caring for and grooming this area underneath the shadow of the Dragon Cross Mountains. Traegon guided his frail grandmother to a bench made out of the wood from a massive fir tree, and helped her to sit comfortably - and with a slight bow, he took a seat beside her.

"Thank you, my child," she said, feeling the flower's curing power in full effect.

"Great Mother, your eyes, they have brightened, like life has just passed anew in you."

"That is exactly what has happened," she said with a faint, satisfying smile.

"Has the flower always done that for you?"

"No," she paused, closing her eyes, thinking back. "No, when I was young I didn't feel anything; in fact sometimes I did not eat the bloom every year. I would just forget and skip a year. When I was given the seeds to the flower, I was told I could skip even twenty years, but the less I used, the faster I would age. It was recommended that I continue to eat one bloom a year, but just as eating less had consequences, eating it more often also had its drawbacks. Eating it too often would be toxic, and be too much for my body to handle, and would, in essence, poison me. As it was, my body still aged, though it was progressively slower, but I have nonetheless aged. The older I got, the more intense the curing feeling. Now I crave for the fall so that I may eat the single bloom."

"How long does it last, this feeling?"

"Only a few hours," she smiled and touched the top of Traegon's hand. "A few hours of feeling twenty-five again, but alas, the aches and pains of being three hundred years old slowly return. Time is indiscriminate in the end. It takes us all eventually. Elves who live hundreds of years can extend their lives into a thousand by a steady diet of this flower, but it is not so kind to us humans. I have slowly continued to age no matter how often I take the pistil, and by mid-summer, I am feeling my true age, and each year the intensity of the pain increases. That is partly why I'm telling you this," she paused to take a deep breath to smell the fragrant air of her garden while looking to the sky, and then looked back at Traegon. "This is the last time I will take the bloom."

"But Great Mother, won't you die a very painful death from being so old?"

"Most likely," she said laughing at his sweet innocence, "and that is why I want you to take me to the elves."

Traegon stood up and looked at her with his brown eyes wide open in shock. "But Great Mother, they are our enemy! We are at war with them!"

Traelyn looked up at him. "I have finally determined that this war is wrong; the elves have done nothing to us. We are the ones who started the fight so many years ago."

"Because they hate us. They have done nothing to help us! They watch us die as the dragons shrink our population, they laugh at our misery. I wish they all would die, just as they wish us all to die!"

She paused so that she could repeat her command to have the proper effect of urgency. "Take me to not just the elves, but to the *king* of the elves."

Traegon's mouth opened, and his eyes widened, then reddened with fury.

"No! I will not!" he blurted out disrespectfully.

Traelyn remained calm, and responded in her most soothing, yet firm voice as a mother reprimanding her young child. "Are you disobeying my command?"

Traegon dropped to one knee and bowed his head. "Please forgive me Great Mother; I will not do this task." She placed her hand on his head. "I will find my father. He will know what to do," he said, not looking up.

"That will be acceptable. If you cannot take me to the elves, then you must take me directly to your father."

Traegon took a deep breath almost choking on it. He did not understand why she was being so persistent.

"You cannot travel in your condition," he finally spoke, finding the courage out of his fear not to sound disobedient. "Besides, I am sure he has already left north with his force to fight the elves. It will be too dangerous."

"It does not matter. You will take me to him and *he* will take me to the elves."

Traegon smiled as he felt that he had won the debate as he stood up. "I don't think that will ever happen. He fights the elves almost daily; he sees all of their evil. I know he will not take you to the elves, and definitely will not take you to see their king."

"He must," she said sharply.

"Then you stay here while I go to look for him and bring him back."

"No, do not take him from his duties. I will go to him, but you must find him first because, you are right, I am too weak to travel the many days it will take you to find him. But once you find him, tell him that I'm coming and that I command him to stay where he is so that you can come back to me, and bring me to him. That will be the quickest route to deliver me to him."

"This I will do," he said lowering his head in submission.

"Then leave now. Gather your things and seek him out."

"Yes, I know. I know his mission, and where he was going. I tried to go with him, but he would not allow me. He told me he was going to gather a force large enough that no elven army could withstand," he said excitedly. "But then he then told me that my place is with you," he finished, downtrodden.

"As it should be my young eager son. Do not worry, your time will come sooner than you think."

"Yes, Great Mother, but I'm eager for more."

Traelyn smiled. "You are so young, there is so much you do not know. You have not seen war as I have. My father, your Great Father, disappeared in a brutal and very bloody battle."

"I know Great Mother, we all know. We know that is why you live so long. Waiting for his return."

"Yes, you are right," Traelyn said as she leaned back and drifted into thought with a sad smile upon her face. "Go, and go quickly for I am dying. Tonight I will destroy all of the Drodennum plants, and their seeds."

"But, Great Mother."

"Go. And go now."

Traegon did not wait. He turned and ran away as fast as his legs would take him. Traelyn smiled as he ran away, he was so much like her father, his grandfather of many generations before. She was not much older than the young Traegon when she lost her father. Dar Drannon's final days were also a beginning, for it was in his last days when she had met Jaerick, prince of the elves, for the first time. Her father disappeared soon after.

She remembered the day she had seen elves for the first time. They came to her home, a fortress her father built, nestled in a cliff face in the farthest northeastern mountains in the land.

Dar Drannon, Traelyn's father, had organized the most intelligent of the human race and moved them away from the more primitive goblin tribes to form a new advanced civilization. It was a time just before their forced move westward, fleeing the goblins as the elves had done hundreds of years earlier.

The elves arrived in grand procession. It was late in the afternoon and the sun was beginning to set behind the Ogregash Mountains to the west when the horns sounded. Soldiers atop the battlements of the large rocky human fortress scrambled to meet their guests. The Halls of Dar Drannon was aptly named, due to the many halls tunneled throughout the side of a giant cliff face.

The human soldiers stood erect and silent in respect as the first of the elven entourage came out of the wilderness amongst the trees that were shedding their crimson leaves. The first group was led by two elves on horseback; each displaying the banners of the individual elven tribes, followed by large horse drawn chariots, and surrounded by hundreds of elven foot soldiers. Though this was a peaceful meeting, the elves did not want to take any chances travelling through the dangerous woodlands whose creatures had chased them out of what had once been their home.

The elven king was not visible from the view of the castle, but there was no mistaking which chariot carried the king. Three chariots total, two smaller than the first, the larger one decorated with the finest elven woodwork, soft colored metals and grand laces.

Finally, the tail end of the procession filed out of the tree line. Three battalions of elven warriors, both on foot and on horseback marched in perfect order and cadence. King Dar Drannon was immediately summoned as the elven leaders were allowed into the staging area at the foot of the mountain cliff. The elven leaders assembled tightly in an enclosed perimeter of chiseled stone and towering pine trees.

The main force set up just outside of the inner perimeter while the leaders waited for a few moments before a handful of human soldiers led them up the long winding stone stairs up to the castle proper. When they reached the top, the elves walked into a large expansive hallway of pillars on each side that filed to the back of the room where Dar Drannon and his advisors stood. Banquet tables were set up in between the pillars and servants stood erect at their positions.

As the elves walked forward, they noticed the servants bowing as they walked past.

"Greetings, and welcome back my friend," Dar Drannon spoke as they approached him.

King Keiyann Krowe bowed before his host. The elven king stood taller than the other six elves standing beside him, but was still a foot shorter than Dar Drannon. They were dressed in white breeches lined with silver thread, and wore a white overcoat that reached to the knees. The back had a slit like an upside down V designed to cover over the horse's back while riding. The elven king wore no crown, as was customary for the elves when away from their kingdom, but by his clothing and stature anyone could pick him out from even the finest of dignitaries.

"I have come at your request, but only with a small and humble force," Keiyann began. "I have brought today for your introduction my son, Jaerick, the prince of the Elven Kingdom and heir to my throne. Lord Meztrae, the commander of my armed forces, and Kroejin, my spiritual advisor. Along with them, I have brought their aids to discuss all the matters at hand."

"And I am glad you have traveled so far to discuss such matters. I will reward your travels with information that could affect both humans and elves, but first I will introduce to you some of the people who are important to our cause as well." He then introduced a number of men to the elven entourage while Traelyn stood proudly at her father's side as these formalities proceeded. "Lastly, but most important to me is Traelyn, my daughter."

The elven king stepped up and greeted all of the men, and then came to Traelyn, took her hand and kissed the top of her soft, young hand. The prince did as his father had done, but when he took Traelyn's hand he held it for a few moments longer than what was customary, and looked into her eyes while smiling, but said nothing.

"Now we feast," Dar Drannon said, breaking the awkward silence.

After a short period of small talk and when they had their fill of food, the two kings and their top advisors went into King Dar Drannon's council chambers and discussed the matters at hand. Traelyn watched Jaerick enter the room with them, but did not follow. Her father liked to keep her protected from such political and military matters, so she knew it was not her place to follow.

Traelyn learned at a young age of her father's protection. Her mother had died when she was eight years old. Long before Dar Drannon built this fortress, they were part of the same hideously morphed human–gront tribes that now attacked them frequently. Though they were a part of those tribes long ago, Dar Drannon was different. His ideals stood him apart from the rest of the tribe. He was far more advanced for what the tribal leaders at the time were comfortable with. After many years of his elders punishing him, and his persistence to continue enhancing his ideals, he was scorned and encouraged to leave.

The tribes had begun to mix with some of the tamer goblin tribes, and in short were evolving away from human traits and becoming more goblin and barbaric than human. Dar Drannon, for fear of his life, took his wife and a small group of followers to start a new tribe.

Dar Drannon shared his ideals with this group while they traveled to other tribes trying to increase their numbers and at the same time find a new home. His ideals were often much too advanced for those other tribes as well, but he did always leave a tribe with a small handful of new followers. It was during this time that Dar Drannon's wife began to show her dislike to this new nomadic lifestyle. At first, it was minimal, even when Dar Drannon had found the site for his new home.

It was not until he had begun to build the Halls of Dar Drannon into the cliff face that she began to show her opposition by disappearing into the wilderness for weeks at a time. Traelyn was young, but old enough to remember unhappiness and discomfort. They had been separated from their tribe for two years and her father had accomplished much. A fortress was being built, a security force was organized, farming and trading began amongst them, and small vale communities grew just outside of the wilderness.

However, they did not flourish without deterrents. Soon they found themselves the target of raiding attacks from the surrounding combined gront, goblin, and human tribes, which aided in the bolstering the defenses of the fortress as they built it.

When the fortress was complete, Traelyn noticed that her mom was homesick, and gone for longer periods. But when weeks turned into months, and months turned into a year Dar Drannon was forced to accept the fact that his wife was not coming back. She had either died in the wilderness or found herself a new tribe. Either way, to Dar Drannon, she was dead, and explained it as such to his young daughter.

Shortly after that, the community crowned Dar Drannon as their king. Dar Drannon then absolved Traelyn from all work duties, chores, and responsibilities, therefore leading a life of boredom and seclusion. This had Traelyn the most frustrated. Moreover, today the king of elves and his prince were here to help their growing problem, and she was shut out, not even allowed to sit and observe. Therefore, sit outside she would. Not happy about it, but she would wait. Someday she would be important enough to be considered a leader among men. She smiled at that thought, and thought it silly, but knew one day it could be true.

* * *

Inside the council chambers, Dar Drannon seated everyone at the large stone table in the center of the room. The sun shone through the massive open windows surrounding every wall in the room. Dar Drannon had his back to his guests and looked out the southern window overlooking the forest as his guests took their seats. He continued to gaze looking to the towering and rocky Goblin Ridge Mountains to the south while his servants catered to his guests, serving them ale and bread.

"I often see them creeping in the woods from here," he began, still looking out the window pointing past the forests, to a clearing miles away. "It looks so peaceful from here, but I know better. I was born out there, right there at the foot of the Goblin Ridge Mountains."

"The Waerymyn Crags," Keiyann Krowe interjected.

"That's right," Dar Drannon said turning to face the elven king. "We changed the name from your elven tongue because the goblin hoards now infest that whole area, and I believe they are preparing to launch an assault together with these gronts very soon."

Dar Drannon paused, and then began again. "I see them coming, crawling and scurrying through the forest. I sometimes see them assembling, gronts and goblins, together. For years, I never thought the two would ever ally, but somehow they have. My scouts have reported that the goblins have a mighty leader, a demon-lord. He is stronger and smarter than any goblin, orc, ogre, troll, or gront, and they worship him as a living god and call him Gralanxth."

General Meztrae stiffened, and looked at the kings' prophet, Kroejin, but made no comment or gesture.

"Gralanxth?" the prince questioned as if the name seemed familiar.

"We know of Gralanxth," the elven king finished. "At least we know of the prophecy of his coming. His arrival has been prophesied by many cultures. All with horrible occurrences. Until now it has been doubted that it would ever come to pass because they are only goblins—easily fooled by such myths."

General Meztrae turned sharply in his chair to face his king on his left and whispered. "This is trickery, my king. We have no proof of this demon; he may just be using this prophecy against us. How can you trust him?"

Keiyann raised his hand to silence the general. "Please forgive my obstinate military advisor," Keiyann Krowe apologized to Dar Drannon. "He has a lot at stake at home and abroad." Then he turned to Meztrae. "Please hear him out commander."

"Have you seen this Gralanxth yourself?" Prince Jaerick asked.

"No, I have not, but as I said, my scouts have seen him, and I have seen increased activity with the goblins and the gronts."

"What do you expect us to do?" General Meztrae blurted out. Then realized that he was speaking out of turn when everyone in the room locked their eyes upon his. Dar Drannon stiffened and looked at the elven king. "I humbly ask for your gracious support by sending troops to help support our very small and lacking defensive force."

General Meztrae squirmed in his seat, and opened his mouth, but said nothing, closing his mouth.

"I have little to offer in return right now," Dar Drannon continued. "But your troops will not only be paid well, they will also be boarded well. Your common soldiers will be treated like officers, and your officers will be treated like ambassadors."

King Keiyann Krowe stood, and faced his general on his right, then turned to his prophet on his left giving him a look of understanding before addressing Dar Drannon.

"We have been friends for a few years now, and as you know I have said before, I commend you on your separation from the gront tribes. This is truly a monumental task, if not prophetic and a historical evolution to the human race. This makes you a true credit to the humans, and if the rest of the tribes evolve to become like you there may be hope for this world. But, unfortunately,

I do not know how I can sacrifice even a small force to help you."

Dar Drannon nodded his head and smiled politely. "Then I would like to ask if you would consider keeping an elven garrison between here and your kingdom. We have recently built it, but it has never been occupied.

Keiyann thought for a second, and then tilted his head. "This could be a possibility, slight, but possible."

"But my king," General Meztrae interrupted. "We are spread out thin enough without sacrificing any troops. We are still building and maintaining our own garrisons, and many of our soldiers are barely trained in the art of combat since they are so new."

"I realize this commander, but I have an obligation to my friend," Keiyann then turned back to Dar Drannon. "As to your offers we will consider both, but I cannot give you a final decision today."

"This is fair, and all I ask of you is to consider our plea. Now, as to my promise that brought you here, I would like to go over all that I have learned about the gronts and goblins, and more about Gralanxth."

Dar Drannon called for his servants to bring forth all of his maps, books, and logs. He then showed the elves everything he knew. Using the maps, he showed them all the locations of every known gront tribe, and movements of the goblin tribes. He explained to them how they have attacked and how often. He showed them where Gralanxth had been sighted and the frequency of the attacks since the initial sightings of the goblin demon god. They spent most of that evening sharing information, and possible battle strategies until the moon had moved from the north window to the southern window.

After the meeting, Dar Drannon went to his daughter's room. Traelyn had been in bed for a few hours, but was awake when she heard a soft knock at the door.

"Come in father," she said recognizing his knock.

Her father entered with a smile.

"What have you learned?" she asked.

He walked over to her bed, sat on the edge and put his hand onto hers, leaning over to kiss her cheek. "Not much really. I spent most of the evening going over our history, why we left and where we want to be in the future, and where we will be without their help."

"Do you think they will help?"

Dar Drannon took a deep breath before answering. "Maybe. They seemed concerned, but not too eager to agree to such a commitment as sending troops for our defense."

"Do you think they will eventually help, or will they turn a blind eye toward us?"

"Oh, honey, I am not so sure. Try not to trouble yourself with these matters. That is my job," Dar Drannon stood up, walked to the door, and put his hand on the door handle. "By the way, the prince asked about you."

Traelyn smiled and sat up, but then leaned back again feigning disinterest. "Really?" she said sarcastically. "How so?"

"I think he is attracted to you. He wants to see you tomorrow."

"What did you tell him?"

"I told him that I needed to talk to you to see if you wanted to spend time with him."

"Good. But I don't care to see him."

"Ok. I'll tell him that."

"No, don't," she said quickly, and then regaining her composure began again. "What I mean is, if I see him I'll see him. Just don't make special plans for me."

Dar Drannon smiled, walked back to her, moved a lock of her long auburn hair, and kissed her forehead.

"What happens if the elves don't commit daddy?" she asked.

Dar Drannon smiled and shook his head. "Don't worry honey; I will protect you, even if it means that I send you back with the safety of the elves."

"No! Don't do that! I will never leave you! Besides, why would you do that anyway? Mother is gone, and you are all I have left, I will not leave you here to die."

"Not to worry. I will not be dying any time soon. Everything will work out for the best."

Traelyn looked sternly into her father's eyes. "I will never leave you father."

Dar Drannon smiled, leaned over and kissed his daughter good night, then stood up and walked to the door. "We will be fine," he said before blowing her a kiss and leaving the room.

* * *

Traelyn's old and frail body ached as she rose from the bench. Tonight she would destroy the Drodennum flowers. She would pull them all and burn them in a quiet and private ceremony, beginning the final phase of her life.

Chapter 6

The elves travelled south, staying on the road, taking the quickest and most direct path. The dust from their traveling could be seen from miles away, including the human warriors that saw them from a hidden watch in the foothills below the Dragon Cross Mountains. They had just passed the Ronlorle River when the soldier on watch alerted Daegon, the high commander of the human forces.

"How long ago did they pass the river?" Daegon asked as he reached the final rung of the ladder leading up to the high tree post. Their post was perfectly hidden amongst a clump of high fir trees. It was built beside a tree fastened to two other trees forming a triangle base. From a distance, the post was completely camouflaged.

"Not long," the soldier on watch answered.

Daegon walked up to the edge of the post and saw the dust rise up like a brown puff of lingering fog.

"They are moving fast," the soldier commented.

"Very fast. Too fast, in fact, something's not right," the commander agreed.

"Look closely just in front of the dust. You can see their nasty flat-back vedoes."

Commander Daegon pointed to the carriage that was not being pulled by horses, but by four creatures the size of large dogs with flat backs upon which the carriage was carried. They had wings on their feet and were lightly touching the ground as the carriage moved at a great speed.

"Now look just ahead of that, and you will see a few scouts a few miles ahead of them?"

"No, not quite, look at the trees a few miles off of the road to the north and the south of them, more scouts."

"I don't see them."

"You will. Just train your eyes. Elven scouts are the best at not being seen.

They are smaller in frame than us and can hop from tree to tree quicker than a horse travelling on the road below them, but because of their speed they get careless and they can't stay concealed for too long. Just watch the trees. Always watch the trees."

They watched for a few more minutes before the soldier spotted a scout leaping from tree to tree, occasionally exposing his head out of one of the treetops and then disappearing again into the canopy. "There. I see him," he said pointing. "Where do you think they are going?"

"Not sure. It is too small for a combat force of any kind, yet their numbers are too great for just a routine a patrol. One thing is for certain, that wherever they are headed, they are in a hurry to get there."

"And they're mainly in the wide-open space, not even attempting to travel off of the road," the soldier added.

"Very true," Daegon paused, "maybe they know about our force here and want to draw us out."

Daegon spun around and charged down the ladder as fast as a lizard climbing down a rocky slope. He ran to the encampment where seven hundred soldiers camped and had been training for weeks, awaiting their orders to move out. He went to his command tent and moved open the flaps so hard that they slapped the side of the tent with a crack. "I want our best scout now!"

The watch officer sped out of the tent leaving Daegon alone with his highest-ranking officer. "What is wrong Daegon?" he asked as he stood up from behind his desk.

"The elves are on the move."

"Coming for us?"

"No, I don't think so. They are skirting around us; around the eastern side of the Dragon Cross Mountains."

"I don't understand."

"That's just it. Neither do I."

"Do you think they know of our plans to attack them?"

"I don't see how they possibly could, but I don't want to assume that they don't. They may be trying to draw us out."

"Draw us out? Impossible! They cannot possibly know we are here, as we have been travelling so slowly and discreetly. We have been joining our forces only in small groups and only regrouped three times since we left two weeks ago."

"It doesn't matter. We must consider the possibility that they have indeed spotted us. These elves are cunning, and after all, this is their terrain, not ours."

"I know, but we have worked so hard."

"Don't fear. We will succeed, no matter what the set back. If this even is a setback, it may present us with a perfect opportunity to strike."

The two commanders looked over maps, and discussed their options while they waited for the scout to arrive. After a few minutes a man in full lightweight leather armor appeared. He carried his helm of green and black with a painted red horse on the side signifying that he was a leader in one of the tribe's cavalry.

"Captain Voll reporting!" he shouted with a brisk salute. "I am honored to be in the presence of the high commander!"

He had such a strong and intimidating appearance, that even Daegon was taken aback by his confident demeanor. Voll had shoulder length dark hair and stubbly facial hair. Evidence of the lack of personal time or rest during the weeks of hard training they had suffered through at the makeshift encampment.

"Captain Voll, we have a mission for you," Daegon said as he returned his salute. "A small group of elves is heading southeast at a brisk pace. They don't seem to be aware of us, nor are they headed our way. They will be out of reach soon and I want you to follow them until they reach their destination. Reconnoiter their intentions and return. Stay at a safe distance and use caution, for they have scouts to their rear and flanks. Don't worry about losing their trail as they are making no attempt to conceal their position."

"Where are they now?"

"A few miles passed the Ronlorle River."

"Understood, I will search them out and find you to report my findings."

"No need. We will not be leaving until we know what they are doing. Simply return here to report."

"Anything else?"

"That is all. Go, and return swiftly."

Captain Voll saluted and left the tent.

Chapter 7

Naemyn pushed his patrol hard for five straight days, not caring if he was spotted by any pesky human patrols. He knew they were out here somewhere, as the humans were always active during the summer, but for some reason their attacks were limited this season. He feared that he might run into a patrol or more, but he had brought some of his best elven warriors for this mission. He did not choose from the king's elite Pathfinders as promised, but he did hand pick his warriors for the mission.

Midnight of the fifth day out Naemyn decided to set up camp on a hillside at the edge of the forest just a few miles off the road. The clouds had been rolling in for most of the day and a foggy blanket shrouded the tops of the Dragon Cross Mountains. The elves needed some much overdue rest after rushing towards the human territories at a forced, quick pace. Naemyn felt confident that the rest of the journey would be uneventful, for the rest of the road between them and their destination was on mostly plain lands, and they had quickly skirted passed the human claimed territories, which meant that the threat of humans and even the dragons lay mostly to the rear of their position.

"Send the scouts to secure the perimeter," Naemyn commanded to the highest-ranking officer.

"The hawks are already in flight," the scout answered.

Naemyn winced at this response. Hawks were a crucial element for the success of the elven scouts. Scout trainees were trained with experienced Hook-feather Hawks so that training would be fast and efficient. As soon as their initial training period was over, the scouts would be assigned a hawk chick to train as their own. The chicks would grow to become theirs for life in order to form a bond between the pair so strong that they become inseparable.

The bond was often so strong that if the scout died, the hawk would be rendered useless, and would not be able to recover. The hawk would therefore be released into the wild. Conversely, if a hawk dies, the scout would be pulled out of commission for service until a new bird could be assigned, and retraining completed. The connection so strong the hawks could communicate all they saw to the elves.

Naemyn knew the importance of these hawks, and he heavily depended upon their use, but he also had a great fear and hatred of them to the point that just mentioning them made him uneasy. Turning on his heels, he decided to take a short walk in the woods.

The hillside oaks and sporadic evergreens covered the low rolling hills under the evening overcast. The moon was high in the sky, but a few clouds were moving in, periodically blocking the moon, which created intermittent shadows on the ground. The smell of fresh dew was in the air as the evening temperature dropped. The oaks were beginning to shed their leaves so a thin layer lay scattered on the ground. Nothing seemed to be alive in these woods, which had Naemyn's senses piqued, both in curiosity and caution. He reached a small stream with a wide rocky bed that showed watermarks on the banks from when the snow caps melted and ran off into the valley below. Naemyn knelt down and listened for any sounds, he still heard nothing but the sound of the stream splashing by. He began to think he should not be here by himself when he heard something.

A loud thrashing sound reached his ears as if a huge animal was tearing in between the trees snapping branches as it ran. Naemyn stood and listened intently. His sensitive ears picked up sounds that helped him determine that the sound was moving away from him. Feeling confident, he ran toward the sound. The other side of the stream was rocky and uphill, but Naemyn charged through the rocks, bounding from one to the other like a jackrabbit, and grabbing limbs and bushes to pull himself up the steeper portions of the hill.

The thrashing was louder when he heard a scream, followed by a deep guttural growl, almost like a roar. The scream was elven, but the roar he suspected might be a beast of some sort. Realizing that the beast might be a dragon, he froze and knelt down and waited so that he could determine what to do next.

There was a short thrashing, followed by silence. He waited many moments before his curiosity got the best of him. Standing up, he ran toward the last sound he heard.

After running a few hundred feet, he came upon a small clearing of only low-lying bushes and shrubs. Then he saw what he had heard. First, he only saw the backbone of a dragon that led to its head devouring something. Sneaking around to its side he saw that it was tearing into the carcass of a freshly killed horse. It ripped through its belly, tearing muscle and flesh into large bite-size chunks. It raised its head slightly, tossing its head back as it swallowed the large chunks after only a few, quick chomps.

It was swallowing its meal as if it had not eaten in years, but Naemyn knew that could not be the case. He knew that the dragons had been feasting on humans and their livestock ever since the humans had made their home near the Dragon Cross Mountains, and starvation was never a problem for the dragons.

Naemyn crouched down behind a clump of bushes and watched the beast eat. He wondered what happened to the elven scout, if he had been eaten first, or if he had gotten away. However, what he saw next answered his question.

A hawk flew straight down towards the dragon's head and began dive bombing, hitting the dragon on the crown of its head. The hawk flew up, and back down again at the dragon many times before it began to recognize the hawk as a nuisance. The dragon snatched up the horse carcass by its breast and took flight at a speed that Naemyn found incredible. It stayed low to the ground and sped in between the trees and bushes like a snake weaving in and out of the bushes while keeping the horse carcass dangling from its mouth.

The sound of the dead horse hitting and snapping the top branches of the oak trees as it flew was almost too much for Naemyn to bear. Meanwhile, the hawk continued to pound the backside of the dragon's head as they flew together. Eventually the dragon tired of this distraction and dropped the horse carcass to concentrate on this nuisance. The dragon flew in a circle searching for an angle to attack the small hawk, but the hawk continued to pester the dragon hitting it in the head and flying out of the snapping range of its massive jaws repeatedly. The dragon tilted one way, then the next, trying to get sight of the hawk, but the hawk was too small for the dragon to see clearly as it flew.

The dragon, in frustrated desperation, flapped its sleek wings and ascended straight up before stopping in mid flight, then floated almost weightlessly for a moment before turning downward. Spotting the hawk, he puffed his throat, arched his head, and spit a stream of fire at the hawk, incinerating the valiant hawk instantly.

Naemyn saw the hawk's life extinguished, and beside all the fear of seeing the dragon, he could not help but to smile at the hawk's demise.

He knew the dragon would be back for its meal, so he turned and ran back toward the camp. As predicted, the dragon did indeed return, but it saw Naemyn running down the hill, bounding in between the rocks heading back to the streambed. The dragon, now active and excited, was encouraged to play chase.

The dragon landed in the stream in front of Naemyn, who stopped suddenly upon jumping atop a rock, and stood on its hind legs before lowering its head level to his. Frozen, and not willing to move a single muscle, or even breath, he saw its yellow eyes as they glared deep into him. Oddly, the dragon appeared to be smiling, as though it were in a playful mood. Sensing this, Naemyn knew he had to get away, so he did exactly what the dragon wanted him to do, and ran.

Naemyn jumped from the rock he was standing on, but slipped and fell in between two boulders. The dragon jumped above him straddling the two rocks and stuck its snout just inches above his head. It exhaled a tuft of smoky breath that filled the crevice, causing him to cough. At the sound of his coughing, the dragon backed away and twisted its head in curiosity. Naemyn took this advantage to leave the spot, scurrying forward to exit the crevice, and ran down the rocky hillside before the dragon regained itself. Losing his footing, Naemyn slid on his butt the rest of the way down, landing feet first into the rocky streambed.

The dragon jumped, flapped its wings once, and again landed facing the frightened elf. This time Naemyn was flat on his back in the stream. Water began to roll over his legs and chest as the dragon made a temporary dam, and the water began to rise. Naemyn slowly lifted his head out of the water, propping himself on his elbows.

The dragon lifted a claw and tried to grab him, but Naemyn stood up and attempted to make a dive for the dry ground. With lightning speed, the dragon pinned him down before he could make it. He felt the padded palm of the dragon on his back, and was surprised that he felt little pain, only the weight pinning him down upon the rock bed of the stream.

Counting down the last moments of his life, Naemyn wondered how long the dragon would play with him before killing him. Water began running into his mouth and nose as he struggled to lift his head, and he contemplated drowning as a way of dying. A death far better than the torture he was about to endure with this dragon.

The dragon gave a long, low growl, it sounded almost like a purr. This beast truly was enjoying himself, Naemyn thought. He spat water, using what breath remained to push the water from his nose and mouth. Then the dragon roared so loud that the water vibrated violently, splashing over his body. Shockingly, the paw lifted. Sensing this as a possible chance to escape, he crawled away toward the rocky slope. Turning quickly to take a curious glance, he noticed that the dragon was in pain. It roared again and twisted, turning its body around.

That was when he understood what was happening, for the dragon's back had a few dozen arrows lodged beneath its thick scales. Many arrows fell into the stream, but a few had found their target under the dragons slick but near impenetrable scales. Within the trees, a dozen elves relentlessly pelted the dragon with their arrows.

Not wanting to tolerate this annoyance any longer, the dragon jumped and lifted into flight, heading back to the Dragon Cross Mountains. As the dragon flew away, the elves rushed to Naemyn and helped him to his feet. "I'm fine. Let me go!" he snapped.

"You shouldn't have wandered off alone," one of the elves said, reprimanding him.

"I know. I was concerned for one of our scouts. The dragon got one of them."

"We will know for sure when all of the scouts report."

"Don't get your hopes up. I know it got at least one."

"Well, regardless, we have to get you back to safety. The dragon may return."

"It may. Let's move on. Break camp, and move a few hours down the road and set up camp again," Naemyn commanded, walking away and feeling confident in grabbing his authority and confidence back.

•••

Voll saw a flash of light in the darkness and knew instantly that there was a dragon nearby. He had seen many dragon blazes in his lifetime to know one by sight and by smell, when he was so unfortunate to be that close to one. This one, he figured, by its brightness, was maybe five miles away. "So, now the elves get a little taste of dragon-fear," he said to his horse patting it on its neck. "Let's wait here and see if he finds elves as tasty as humans. If we're lucky, maybe he'll like elven flesh better," he said, smiling.

Chapter 8

Destroying the flowers made Traelyn reflect on how much she enjoyed gardening. It was flowers and plants such as these that she attended to at her home when her father was alive centuries ago. She found herself thinking of the elven prince as she pulled the plants and re-worked the soil, and it reminded her of the first time she spoke to him. She found him attractive, and was fascinated by the fact that he was an elf from a distant land.

It was later in the evening when he came out of the meeting with her father that she saw him again. She was standing atop one of the battlements watching the sun as it dipped behind the green-forested mountains, when Jaerick, the elven prince, walked up behind her. "Beautiful country," he said.

Traelyn heard him coming before he spoke, but did not turn to face him. When he spoke, she felt his breath upon her neck. "It is," she said flatly.

"Much like my home, but this land is much more dangerous."

"It is," she repeated.

"What do you enjoy the most?" he asked, attempting to force her into a conversation more than the short, cold sentences he was receiving.

She turned to face him and tried to stay staunch, but when she saw his face, she smiled and looked down and blushed. "I like it because it is my home."

Jaerick put his hand under her chin and lifted her head so that she would look into his eyes. "Your home is beautiful, though beauty is almost never as it seems. Much like you, very pleasing to the eye, yet wild and untamed."

Jaerick smiled, winked, then turned and walked down the battlements, returning from where he came. Traelyn stood speechless at his bold actions, but smiled in spite of herself.

"Wait!" Traelyn called. "Where are you going?"

"For a walk," he said, stopping and turning to face her. She then walked toward him and stopped before him like a shy child, unsure of her actions, but then straightened herself with a surge of new confidence.

"Come with me, I want to show you something." Traelyn said, then just as he had done moments before, she smiled, winked, turned, and walked away from him. He stood and watched her leave shaking his head at her, and then watched her walk away until she was almost out of sight when she went downstairs into the courtyard.

He started to hurry after her, but caught himself and changed his pace to a brisk walk. Following Traelyn downstairs, he passed the courtyard through an archway that lead to a walled flower garden. As he caught up to her, they walked through the small garden and Jaerick noticed the care taken in the plants and flowers.

All four walls surrounding the garden were painstakingly covered with so many flowered vines that the exit on the other side of the garden was nearly obscured. The smell of the various flowers in full bloom permeated the dusky evening air. As they walked amongst the flowers and various colorful plants, Jaerick grabbed Traelyn's hand. To his surprise, she took his hand into hers and cupped it tightly. Jaerick was still looking at the various multi-colored flowers, shrubs, and vines when she broke his awed silence.

"I brought you to this garden for two reasons. One, for the quietness of the garden, and two-" she paused and turned to looked into his eyes, "-to get away from everything. But, this is not all I wanted to show you. Follow me, and I will show you what I mean." She let go of his hand, still facing him, and began to walk backwards. Once he began to follow her, she turned away and ran.

The prince ran in pursuit, following her through the rows of flowers, and then immediately turned to the right and the end of the row, rounding the backside of the archway to a clump of bushes where Traelyn was standing. She then walked into the bushes and stopped as she was surrounded up to her chest in the foliage, and motioned Jaerick to follow. She then inched her way to a spot between the bushes and the wall where a small clearing exposed a square wooden cover on the ground completely concealed by the bushes so well that it could only be seen by standing directly above it. She reached down and picked up the cover, revealing a downward spiraling stairway.

Traelyn nodded to the prince and stepped down into the dark and damp entrance. Jaerick followed her down the steps and saw through the flickering torchlight mounted on the walls what unveiled to be a long hallway tunnel through solid, painstakingly chiseled rock. The torches were already lit as if they never ceased to burn and condensation dripped from the walls in the dark shadows. She continued walking down the spiraling steps at a brisk pace, saying nothing while Jaerick followed. They continued downward for several minutes until they came upon a long hallway-like passageway where they passed many corridors that forked left and right. The passageway had a distinct downward slant to it and it felt to Jaerick as if he was still going deeper and farther down into a cavernous tunnel.

Finally, she stopped at a the bottom of the stairway that led to a large open circular room. She turned to face Jaerick and saw the confused and amazed look on his face.

"What now?" he asked.

"Beauty. Wild and untamed," she said with a wide grin, repeating his words.

"I don't understand."

"It's a bit of an illusion." Traelyn then moved a few stone blocks that revealed a latch. She lifted the latch and a door opened, revealing another stairway steeper than the others. They continued down a few hundred feet until they came to the base of the stairway that ended in a wide room with a large iron door on the other side. Traelyn walked to it and opened the door. Outside light from the sunset flooded the room as she allowed Jaerick to exit before her.

He stepped through the door, looked around, and saw huge majestic pines towering high above. A small brook prattled away in the distance. He turned around to look at the surroundings, and saw a steep rock cliff looming over him. He had to crane his neck straight back, to see that the top of the castle was chiseled into the face of the cliff. Traelyn closed the door and watched as the seams to the door disappeared, the illusion returning.

"Is this not amazing?" she asked, beaming.

Jaerick did not answer, but continued to gawk at the beauty of the surroundings, including the splendor of the size of the cliff.

"Now try and find the door."

He looked at the cliff wall before him, and could find no door, no seams, nor any signs of any door, but only saw a rock face.

"No one knows of this door, other than my father and his engineers. Father doesn't even know that I know. This is the eastern side of the castle. I come here to escape the trapped feeling I have within the confines of the castle walls from time to time. Sometimes my father can protect me too much."

"But it's, –" Jaerick began, but she put her hand to his lips.

"I know. You even said it yourself, that beauty can be deceiving. It is beautiful, yet wild. I am also attracted to this type of beauty."

"How long do you stay?"

"Long enough, never too long, sometimes I even take a walk. I will walk to the brook and think."

"But the door is impossible to see from here, how do you find your way back?"

Traelyn smiled at her cleverness. "I have planted this Scillia tree to mark my return," she pointed to a small, five-foot tree that was nestled in-between three large pine trees. The tree had a small wispy trunk but stood firmly in the ground. It had many thorny branches and upon each branch had many leaves – beneath each leaf was a bright pink flute-like flower.

"The tree is like my situation. Not only does the tree mark my way, but also these large trees in the wilderness protect the tree. It is like my father, who smothers me with his protection. I love him dearly, but I am enticed by the danger that he shelters me from."

"I don't like it. Your father is right to protect you, but he is also wrong to keep you here at all."

"And what would you have me do? Leave?"

"Yes. It is not safe. Your father has told me of the gronts and goblins here. They are so desperate to destroy you and everything you have here. Do you not understand that?"

"Please don't worry about me," Traelyn said sternly, shaking her head. "We are fine here. This is our home, it is *my home*."

"You are not fine here, and I do worry. I want to know you better, and in order for me to do this, you have to be alive."

"I will be alive long enough for you to know me," she said softly, moving a step closer to him.

Jaerick reached out and touched her hand. She accepted his hand over hers and smiled as he looked into her eyes. "Don't you long to see new places, to see what is outside of your castle walls?"

"No, I love my father, we are here to stay. He knows this land, and I do not long to see anything else."

"My ancestors lived in this land for many years, but it is no longer safe for any of us to stay, including you, your father, and his dwindling defensive force."

"Maybe so, but I choose to stay. This is my home, no matter how stifled I may feel at times, or as dangerous as it may be."

Jaerick brought her close to his body and held her tight. As he did so, she trembled as if she had a slight chill. They remained there for an hour beneath the darkening shade of the pine trees as their conversation changed from the dangers and cares of the moment to talking about the little things of daily life. When the stars had reached the brightest point of the night they decided to return to the castle, hoping no one had noticed their absence.

•••

Early the next morning the elven king and his entourage met with King Dar Drannon for one brief and final time. The elven king promised to keep in contact, but no other promise was made. Keiyann Krowe emphasized that maintaining this kingdom in the wilderness was a certain risk that he deemed unnecessary. The elves did not wish to see the humans slaughtered, but he doubted he could commit any of his elven forces to such a dangerous environment with so little to gain in return. The elven king gave Dar Drannon a sincere promise that he would talk with his advisors to consider the human king's request.

The elves then left in the same manner in which they came. They filed in their formations in the courtyard, then left single file through the tunnels, then regrouped at the foot of the fortress. Jaerick sat mounted on his battle horse and saw Traelyn watching from the top of one of the battlements. Traelyn waved goodbye to Jaerick. The prince looked at her only one time as he rode away. He did not return the wave but looked at her for a long while before turning his horse and falling back into formation. Traelyn stood unmoving until the last elf was out of sight.

•••

Once the elves returned to their kingdom, King Keiyann Krowe called his leaders together for a secured meeting. His chambers were not as elaborate as the human king's, for the elves were still in the midst of settling into their new home on the northern coast. The last of his people had only crossed into these borders just forty-two years prior from the same wilderness that Dar Drannon called home. They settled in the temperate northern coastal area and began to build in the tangled forests where the coastal breezes offered a pleasant climate for them. It took time just to clear out a defensible area to effectively build their fortress.

Val Eahea, the founder of the Val Elves, once walked amongst the elves when they were nothing more than scattered tribes near where the Halls of Dar Drannon now stood. During this time, he sought out a young Keiyann

Krowe. Even though Keiyann was just a young boy, the elven god knew he would be the elves' first king and he gave Keiyann the Sword of Valkilye, the sword of kings.

This sword, he told him, must one day be given to a human king, and that human king would later return with the sword to unite the whole world in peace. He also told Keiyann to begin the elven migration to the west, because this land would soon turn too dangerous for the elves to thrive.

Keiyann would begin but would not finish. Under this direction, he traveled first northwest and found the northern coastal areas perfect for what they needed. He knew Val Eahea had directed him to go farther west, but this land was fertile, the temperature mild, the trees of the forests were plentiful, and the area proved to be free of hostile creatures.

They also found another race of elves, the Sor elves, which were receptive to their people. Keiyann, at first, found this race of elves much inferior to them in intellect and society as they were still in the tribal stage of understanding. Though they did discover that they were much more magical than the Val elves were, and that it was a different type of magic. Where the Val elves relied more on an outward magic to manipulate events to their advantage, the Sor elves were quiet, withdrawn and worked, lived, and breathed the land, in essence, using magic to become the land.

The rebuilding and unification phase had proven to be exhausting, but not without its rewards. The capital city Aalararae was built within the first five years. The Val elves accepting the Sor elves animistic ways intact, decided to join forces and together built Aalararae to its living breathing magical splendor. The surrounding communities began to form shortly after.

Keiyann Krowe stood at the head of the table ready to address his advisors while they took their seats. Kroejin, his spiritual advisor, Jaerick, General Meztrae and the general's top commanders, and the rest of the king's advisors who had remained in Aalararae took their seats and waited for him to speak.

"Most of us here have just returned from the human kingdom and have witnessed how isolated they are from any civilized race. I want to discuss his dilemma with you before I make any decision to his requests."

"My king," General Meztrae stood as he spoke. "I think you know where your military stands. I don't see how we can spare even a single warrior."

"I understand your concerns to the here and now and our rebuilding, but we need to consider the bigger picture. That is why Kroejin was part of our journey, so that he may witness first hand the possibility of Dar Drannon being the one prophecy speaks of."

Kroejin stiffened, but did not speak.

"What of the prophecy, and why should it matter?" Meztrae said defiantly.

Kroejin now stood, but General Meztrae, still standing, spoke before he could answer. "The prophecy must be ignored, my king. There must be some other way."

"There is no other way other than to allow the prophecy to be fulfilled," Kroejin finally said, reasserting his position of authority in the conversation.

King Keiyann Krowe looked directly into Kroejin's eyes and paused before asking the question he had waited many years to ask. "Is Dar Drannon the human king the prophecy speaks of?"

"It does not matter!" Meztrae shouted, now walking towards the king.

"It does matter!" Keiyann responded. "Our entire race depends on it! Ever since our creator Val Eahea came in physical form and gave me this sword that I now carry by my side, I have also carried the burden of our people."

"The burden does not need to be yours alone," Meztrae said, grabbing the king's shoulders with both hands, and looking to him with sincere compassion. "The sword is powerful, it belongs to elven kings, and I beg of you, pass it down to the elven kings, starting with your son Jaerick."

Keiyann unsheathed the sword, and raised it with both hands, pointing the sword towards Meztrae's head causing him to jump back in surprise. Keiyann then laid the sword on the center of the table with the point of the blade pointing towards Kroejin. The blade itself was polished silver, without a single blemish, save the etchings of elven language on the blade. The grip of the sword was ivory white with a twisted twine-like handle leading to a single purple gem on the end of the sword. "I want everyone to read the words on the blade that is inscribed upon this sword by Val Eahea when the sword was forged in our eternal home." All eyes were fixed upon the sword in awe as if this was the first time that they had seen it, and for some it was. Keiyann put his arm around Meztrae, and instructed him to read it.

Meztrae looked at Keiyann, reluctant to comply, but did so obediently. "It reads . . . The sword of Valkilye; the sword of elven kings, device for delivering the human king, and erecting the mighty elven kingdom."

"I repeat my question to Kroejin, and I would expect no interruptions this time. Is Dar Drannon this human King?"

Kroejin did not look at his king, but instead looked at Meztrae and muttered in a low voice. "Yes. Yes he is the one."

"Good! Now we need to get to business." Keiyann picked up the sword and sheathed it. "Val Eahea promised me that our road ahead would not be an easy one, in fact, it will take us to the depths of darkness before we prosper again. It will also involve moving one more time. We will know where this land will be when the final Quarterstar shard is found. So then our next and final move will be to the west to our promised land. We must continue the path set before us."

Meztrae spoke to the king while looking at the prophet. "I do not believe in this weak interpretation of our future." Meztrae then stood back up and addressed the king respectfully. "I beg of you my king, let us take the elven kingdom to the highest, most powerful reign it deserves. The good elven people do not deserve to be oppressed and treated like transient beggars moving from land to land searching for a mystical homeland."

"I hear your request, and again I defer to our spiritual advisor, whom I have noticed has been far too quiet in this matter." Then the king pointed to Kroejin and asked, "Tell us. Is there any other way out of this?"

"If you wish to follow the path of Val Eahea, then there is no other way."

"But your response suggests that there is another way," the king pressed.

"Yes, but it is of my own opinion, and I am very much divided as to if it truly is the will of Val Eahea."

"Tell me, I do indeed wish to hear it."

"It is simply by letting the human kingdom be destroyed instead of preserving it, but instead bring the human king here to the elven kingdom. I believe there is a chance that Val Eahea will smile at our strength and be forced to bless us."

"No!" Keiyann announced slamming his fist to the table. "Years ago Val Eahea spoke his intentions to me, and now I question why he must speak to me through another person when long ago he spoke to me directly. But regardless to whom he speaks, you or I, we must not speculate what Val Eahea will think after we disobey his commands. Your job is to simply tell me what his wishes are, and from there I will choose what action to follow."

"Father," Prince Jaerick interrupted after an awkward silence of fuming emotions filled the room, stifling rationale. "What about his daughter?"

Keiyann directed his attention to his son, slightly perturbed and impatient. "What of her?"

"What if the two kingdoms unite through marriage?"

Keiyann stood silent for a few seconds. "You and the human princess?"

"Yes."

"I am not sure how that will make a difference. Do you have affections for her?"

"I'm beginning to, yes, I believe I do."

Meztrae and Kroejin looked on dumbstruck, as if they had just been slammed against the wall.

Keiyann saw the shocked faces of everyone in the room. "Do you see how everyone in this room has just reacted to this option?" Keiyann said pointing to Meztrae and the others with a wave of his hand. "Our people would never accept such a maneuver, even for the gain of the kingdom."

"I am also concerned, for her, and their safety. It is only a matter of time before they are completely overrun. Traelyn unknowingly showed me a weakness in their defense, if this weakness is discovered, they will not be around to even host further conversations."

"Do you suggest that we don't have much more time for debate?"

"Exactly that. That weakness is a door at the foot of the cliff, and if found, the gronts could shatter it with two hits of any makeshift battering ram."

"Then we should get busy. I will move to fulfill the prophecy, and it sounds like we may not even have any time left, for if the human king dies, the prophecy will never be fulfilled. General, earnestly, I need your support on this."

"My glorious king, I highly disagree with your actions, but you are my king and I will carry out any and all of your wishes with my life, and you know this."

"Very well, assign three detachments to go with us back to the Halls of Dar Drannon. We will secure the fortress and hand over the sword of Valkilye when everything is safe and secure."

"Yes, my lord."

"Now Jaerick," The king continued, " When we get close, I want you to show the general where that door is so that he can secure and or seal the door for good."

"Yes sir."

"When we leave, we will leave behind two of our detachments to keep their fortress secure."

"My king," Meztrae interrupted. "You do realize that you will be leaving two detachments to their eventual death don't you?"

"I am confident in our forces. Two detachments will be plenty, but just to be safe, we will leave all three."

"Father, may I make a request?" Jaerick spoke breaking up his father's focus.

"Ask it, and we will see," he answered, a bit annoyed.

"Can we bring Traelyn back with us to the elven kingdom?"

"Why? Do you fear her death as well?"

"Yes, I do."

"Why should I save her life when I am committing many elven soldiers to their deaths to defend her father?"

"Because, whether or not you agree on the reactions of our people, you made a commitment to the human king, and you should hold true to that promise. And if you choose to abandon that promise, I urge you to do so not because I have feelings for her, but for the simple fact that the line of human kings might continue with her survival, should the Halls of Dar Drannon Fall."

Keiyann shook his head in disbelief and looked at the others seated around the table and rubbed his chin. "What does the prophecy say of this Kroejin?" he said, now smiling.

"He is right. In order for the prophecy to be fulfilled, her line must continue."

"Then I will allow it. The elven people will most definitely not understand, especially if you two wed, but we will have to deal with that later. There is so much in the near future that they will not understand."

After the surprise by the prince, King Keiyann decided to end the discussion. He then dismissed the assembly and left the room in expedient fashion. The committee also quickly left the room, whispering avidly amongst themselves. Meztrae and Kroejin were the last to remain. When everyone had left, Meztrae went to the door and closed it. "What happened to you these last few days?" he said.

"I'm sorry, things have changed. When I saw the human king, I knew then that he is the one the prophecy speaks of."

"We had a deal!" Meztrae shouted shaking his fist in the air.

"I know! That is why I tried to persuade the king differently."

"Oh, I see, with your personal opinion, not your spiritual one. The king does not have you by his side to hear your personal opinion."

"I could not lie to him," Kroejin said quietly looking down at the table.

"Then die with him!" Meztrae said as he marched out of the room.

* * *

Traelyn did not hear from the elves again for many weeks until her father came into her room with a letter that was sent by an elven courier.

"News from the elves," he said as he handed Traelyn an opened letter hand stamped by the elven king. "They are returning. They will bring a small force to help us."

"The prince?"

Her father smiled. "Yes, he will come as well."

The elves arrived a week later. While the elven force mustered their forces near the fortress at the base of the cliff, General Meztrae steered his mare away from the side of the kings' entourage, and went two rows back to the prince.

"Now show me this entrance."

Without a word, the prince turned his steed eastward and skirted along the edge of the sheer rocky cliff. As Jaerick rode away, the general assigned twenty soldiers to follow them.

Within a few moments, the prince had found the Scillia tree hidden within the cluster of tall pine trees. "This is the spot."

General Meztrae stopped and looked up to the face of the cliff, and stared for a few moments before looking back to the prince. "But where is the door?"

"I will show you."

The prince dismounted his horse, groped at the cliff face for a few seconds before finding the crease exposing the door, and opened it for the general.

"Very good, that is all I need you for," General Meztrae said to the prince. You should go back to your father. He needs you by his side."

The prince rode back to the king, but as he did so, he heard the general barking orders to his troops to enter the forest and to secure the immediate area.

Meanwhile, at the main entrance to the Halls of Dar Drannon, the humans escorted the elves inside. Once they reached the top, the two kings immediately went into the council chambers. Jaerick and the soldiers stayed mounted on their horses in the courtyard, while Traelyn stood on the upper hall looking down to the courtyard, her eyes on the prince. The prince did not move, but held a somber look on his face.

Jaerick looked up and saw Traelyn. Immediately he dismounted, ran across the courtyard and up the stairs to the hall. He was out of breath when he reached her, and in an urgent tone he said, "I'm glad I found you first."

Seeing the sense of urgency in his expressions, she backed away a few steps. Jaerick reached for her face and ran his hand from her chin to the back of her neck, feeling her soft auburn hair between his fingers. "I missed you so much Traelyn."

She smiled and began to speak, but Jaerick put his other hand to her lips.

"But I have more to tell you –" he stopped to look into her eyes, brought her head closer, and kissed her while wrapping his left arm about her waist and holding her tight.

Traelyn returned the kiss but pulled away abruptly. "What must you tell me Jaerick?"

Jaerick, holding her waist with both hands, looked into her eyes and began to tell her the news he knew she would not want to hear. "We have come to take you back with us."

Traelyn pulled away, shook her hands downward as if attempting to shake something off of her.

"I will not," she stated, before turning and running down the hallway. Jaerick stood still for a few moments and then followed her. Traelyn ran to the end of the hallway and spoke to the two soldiers standing watch, and then continued downstairs and into the courtyard.

Jaerick walked to the soldiers, and attempted to walk past them, but they blocked his path. He thought briefly of forcing his way passed them, but instead he turned around and walked back to where his father and King Dar Drannon were meeting.

As he walked back, he looked down at the courtyard and saw Traelyn slip out of sight into the garden where she had taken him when they were together. He remembered their time together through the garden and to the outside of the fortress. He knew she would be heading out there to the Scillia tree where she felt free.

He began to wonder what would happen now if she would run away and no one could find her. His father would undoubtedly be upset that he had told her their plans prematurely, but he could not wait, as much as he wanted her to be with him, he cared too much for her to simply take her by diplomatic force. Sure, she would be in safe hands, but she might not care for him the way he would like her to.

He wanted her unconditional love and he did not want to be selfish and take what was not his to take. Jaerick stiffened as he approached the door to the conference chambers where his father and King Dar Drannon were meeting. Four soldiers stood at the entrance, two elven, and two human. All four stepped aside as he approached. He had just put his hand on the door when he heard loud screams and clanging of swords from behind them somewhere within the castle.

"What is that?" Jaerick said to the human guard. The guards looked at Jaerick with a surprised look and shook their heads not knowing the answer.

"Tell your king that something is wrong, and call for help. I think we are in for a fight and will need as many soldiers as we can muster!"

Chapter 9

Jaerick ran in a panic. He had to find Traelyn before it was too late. Running back to the open hallway that overlooked the courtyard he saw that many soldiers were already battling gronts below as they poured out of the garden area into the courtyard. The gronts outnumbered the surprised soldiers at least two to one. Jaerick yelled for his elven warriors to engage in the battle as he drew his sword and charged into the courtyard.

He ran into the courtyard and could not stop thinking of Traelyn, whether she was safe, or if she had been overrun and killed during the beginning of the raid since he saw that the gronts had entered from where he saw her last. The human soldiers were already in close combat by the time Jaerick reached the battle, and many soldiers had easily cut down a number of the poorly skilled and poorly armored attackers. Still, the gronts, who outnumbered them, fought onward, causing the defenders to slowly lose ground.

A handful of elven soldiers came running down the stairs and joined in the defense of the fortress. The elven charge attacked with a fresh fierceness that knocked some of the gronts back initially, but they regrouped and tightened up their ranks enough to gain the little ground that they had lost. Jaerick noticed this, and commanded his soldiers to charge again, while he and his guards slashed, cut, and hacked their way into the middle of the pack. This onslaught dropped a number of gronts to die a bloody and mangled death on the sandy ground. Despite this successful charge, many of the gronts slipped passed the elves and humans and charged up the stairs where Dar Drannon and Keiyann Krowe were leaving their chambers to enter the melee.

Dar Drannon saw five gronts charging towards them, and withdrew his ceremonial sword, which was used for decoration and not sharpened for fighting, as Keiyann Krowe drew the Sword of Valkilye and prepared for the charge. They did not have any shields or protective armor, but the two of them stood firm to defend themselves alone, for the door guards were already down below in the courtyard fighting.

Both of the kings blocked the center of the aisle-way as three gronts charged shoulder to shoulder while two more followed behind. They barked as they charged feeling the blood rage run through their feral veins. Dar Drannon and Keiyann ducked as two of the gronts charged. Dar Drannon used his shoulder and stood up as fast and as hard as he could, hitting the gront below the rib cage. The force threw the gront over the rail and into the courtyard, twenty feet below. The gront screamed and flailed his arms right before landing on his head, breaking his back and neck.

At the same time, Keiyann stood from his crouch and slammed the other gront into the wall, pinning him against it. The third gront that did not jump, now charged into the fray and aimed his blow for Keiyann's head with an overhead swing, but missed his mark when Keiyann moved to slam the gront against the wall.

The gront was hunched over with both hands on his sword attempting to regain the initiative, but only looked up in time to see Dar Drannon swing his sword downward with a killing blow to his neck and shoulder.

The two remaining gronts, sensing a new advantage, charged the preoccupied kings. Both attacked Dar Drannon who had just struck his blow to their fellow warrior. In a maddened rage, one dropped his sword and dove at Dar Drannon's mid section tackling him to the hard stone floor. Dar Drannon landed flat on his back and lost all the air from his lungs. The last gront, not expecting his partner's rage, swung his sword high and wide and missed both the king and his partner. Keiyann, realizing the confusion, stabbed the unsuspecting gront in the side of his ribs. The wounded gront lay on the ground groaning and writhing in pain.

Keiyann then looked over and saw Dar Drannon wrestling with the other gront. The gront was reduced to using his bony fists as his only weapon and was doing a fair job of pounding Dar Drannon's face in a fierce rage of numerous blows. Dar Drannon lay unconscious as the gront let out a guttural yell with each blow. Keiyann ran to the gront and kicked him off his friend, causing the gront to roll on his back just as Keiyann's sword was plunged into his exposed chest.

Down below in the courtyard, Jaerick battled the gronts from every side. He stopped long enough to see one of the gronts fall from the upper hallway. He noticed his father and the human king engaged in a heavy fight. The gront fell a few feet beside him landing on his head. He heard his neck crack and saw a small trickle of blood escape from the corner of his mouth. Jaerick looked away and saw one of his lieutenants waving at him to follow. "This way!" he yelled, motioning toward the open hallway that led to where Traelyn was last seen.

The battle had raged with no single group gaining any ground, even though more gronts than elves were giving up their lives. Hoping for a change in strategy, Jaerick ran from the battle to join his trusted lieutenant. He was surprised at how easily he had slipped away from the fighting. "Follow me. We need your help over here."

"We?" Jaerick questioned and followed behind his lieutenant as they ran through the gateway. They ran through the garden and down through the wooden door in the ground, the same one Traelyn showed him. It was eerily quiet inside, but he continued down the stairway, still hearing the now dulling sounds of battle above them.

They continued down the steps that led down under the depths of the castle. When they reached the bottom to the final iron door, he saw five of his own elven soldiers standing side by side with five gronts. General Meztrae stood behind them in front of the iron door. One of the gronts held Traelyn in front of him. Her hands and feet were bound with a strong woven vine, and he held an oversized dagger to her throat.

"What's going on?" Jaerick demanded, as he looked at Meztrae. Meztrae stepped out from behind his soldiers, and without a word charged the prince, shoving him into one of Jaerick's soldiers who was just now arriving. His soldiers caught him and held him upright as they stripped his sword from his hands, then shoved him back to Meztrae.

Prince Jaerick, flushed with frustration, shuddered from the betrayal of his own soldiers. More confused than ever, he stared at Meztrae as he felt his face turn hot. Without thinking of the consequences, Jaerick lurched toward Meztrae and wrapped both hands around his throat pushing him back a few steps.

"Harm me and she dies," Meztrae managed through gasping breaths, holding his arms out wide in mock obedience and submission.

Jaerick tensed his fingers, hands, and arms, but could not finish what he wanted to do. He wanted to squeeze the life out of this betrayer to the king and elvenkind. He wanted so badly to watch his lungs scream for air until they finally give up on life. He wanted to see Meztrae's eyes mist over as he slipped into unconsciousness and enter into the slow breathless dark of death. Reluctantly, he pulled his hands free from Meztrae's neck, turning him loose. He then looked at Traelyn, who to Jaerick's surprise, showed no signs of fear, or emotions.

"Are you hurt?" he asked, but before she could answer, Meztrae struck the prince in the jaw.

"Shut up and listen! We don't have much time. I do not intend to hurt you, but you need to control your father. This need to help the humans will only bring the fall of our elven kingdom."

Prince Jaerick rubbed his chin and glared. "If you hate these humans so much, how can you justify in helping these barbarians kill your own people upstairs in the courtyard?"

Meztrae shook his head as if shaking snow out of his hair. "You don't understand the severity of our cause do you? What is happening now is only the price we must pay for your fathers' stupidity. A small price to reverse his actions and to assure that the elven kingdom does not fall during his reign."

Jaerick remained silent while he looked at Traelyn, the gronts, and his fellow elves betraying him and his father. All their eyes were on him, but when he looked to his own soldiers, they immediately looked to the floor and would not look him in the eye. "You all will be executed for your treason," he blurted, knowing he did not have any say in the matter at this point, but had to say something.

"A price we are willing to pay, my young prince, now call off the battle upstairs. Send the elven soldiers home and let the gronts finish this battle with the humans."

"Why would I do that?"

Meztrae smiled. "For her life," he said, pointing to Traelyn. "If not for her life, then for yours," Meztrae nodded to one of the gronts who then opened the iron door.

Outside Jaerick could see legions of armed gronts and goblins awaiting entrance to the rocky fortress. Their numbers were incredible. The forest was crawling with these ugly beings of ignorance and brutality. Jaerick now knew that the human-elf defensive coalition would not stand an attack from a force of this size. He felt the hope from within melt away, and knew very little could be done to change the imminent outcome.

The gront then closed the iron door.

"As you can see," Meztrae began. "The battle is nearly won. What you decide now will only determine how great the loss will be to our people."

"It seems that you have this all planned out already. What would you have me do?"

"You have the power to influence the king. We both know that he has only returned at your request, because of your love for this human." Meztrae said, looking at Traelyn as if a putrid smell had just wafted from her being." Tell the king to leave these humans alone. Let them fight their own fight and die their own deaths. It is that simple. That is all we ask. Do this, and she will not die. Do this, and the gronts will give us safe passage out of here, and then you and the king can punish us for our loyalty to the elven race, and we will submit to the punishment knowing our cause to be true."

"A promise is all that you ask."

"Your word, yes, because I know you have always been and will always be loyal to your word," he said with a smile and a legitimate bow.

"Traelyn, if I do this, will you come with me?"

Traelyn, still bound by the vines, did not speak, but only looked to the ground. Jaerick knew then that the love for her father was stronger than her love for him and that she would not leave her father.

"I cannot do as you ask Meztrae."

Meztrae, not blinking, took two steps toward the prince and punched him in the jaw again. "Are you that love struck with this ugly human that you would corrupt our elven people? I have no problem in letting her die. In fact, it will be easy. It is you, my prince, that would break my heart to see die in this corridor."

"Still, I cannot do as you ask, without the will of the one I love."

Meztrae stiffened. "You would love a human more than your people. You do not deserve to lead them."

Jaerick stood firm and stared deeper and harder into Meztrae's eyes. Hate swelling in his chest, and helplessness filled his heart. He then looked to Traelyn and knew that the choice was easy for her to die for her father and what they believed in. Her resolve gave him strength to believe that he could also die for her love. Without thinking any further, because there was nothing more to think about, and nothing else to lose, in an act of desperation, he dove for Traelyn and the gront holding her captive. He slammed into the both of them with such a force that they all toppled sideways to the ground.

As they fell to the ground, the dagger flew from the gronts' hand, but not before slicing Traelyn from her throat to the bottom of her right ear. Blood squirted from her neck and onto Prince Jaerick and the gront. Traelyn screamed as she fell and then rolled off the gront realizing that she was cut. She covered the wound with her hand, and even though blood wetted her hand, she knew that she was not too seriously injured.

As Jaerick landed, he saw Traelyn go down with him and knew he had only a few seconds to react to his surprise attack before he would be overtaken, so he drilled the gront with the back of his fist, crushing his nose and upper jaw. Jaerick then reached over its now unconscious body and grabbed the dagger, then moved to Traelyn and cut the ropes binding her feet.

"Run!" he yelled to her as the bindings fell to the ground. Two gronts and three elves, seeing this attempt to escape, were quicker than Jaerick, and tackled him, pinning him down to the cold stone floor before he was able to make any ground.

Traelyn stood up as they wrestled with Jaerick. Her hands still bound, she ran up the stairway and disappeared into the dark cavern hallways.

"Chase her down!" Meztrae yelled to the elf not holding Jaerick down. The elf disappeared up the stairs, chasing after Traelyn. Meztrae then looked to Jaerick who was now being stood up by his captors.

"Bring him here!" He commanded. Meztrae walked to meet them as they brought Jaerick to him. Meztrae did not stop until he was very close and punched him in the mouth. Blood drained from Jaerick's split lip. "I will not deal with you anymore, son of a weak king! With the help of Kroejin, I will be the new king. You and your father are a disgrace to the name of Val Eahea." Meztrae turned around. "Take him outside and let the gronts kill him!"

At his command, Jaerick started yelling and squirming trying to break free of his captors' grips. General Meztrae walked to the iron door, pulled the latch open, and was about to swing the door open when an arrow sunk into the side of his ribs. Stumbling, he grabbed his side and looked back to the stairs. There on the steps stood a dozen elven and human archers who had just let loose a second barrage of arrows. The elves holding Jaerick loosened their grip, and Jaerick taking notice, jerked himself free and ran to retrieve his sword from the grip of an elf that had been killed in the barrage of arrows.

Meztrae, recovering his balance, found that now it was his turn for a final act of desperation. He stumbled over to the iron door to open it and escape. Once Jaerick had his sword, he ran to the safety of the elven archers.

"Shoot them all!" He commanded. The archers loosed their volley as General Meztrae swung the iron door wide open. The arrows flew across the room with all of them finding their mark. The elves and gronts fell dead or wounded, except for Meztrae. Though an arrow pierced him in the back, he continued out the iron door and into the sun.

The army of gronts waiting outside saw this as their cue to charge inside the fortress, and with a loud battle cry, they rushed toward the door. Meztrae saw the massive charge coming in and instantly realized his grave error, yelling in horror as the army of gronts trampled over him, crushing him as they began squeezing through the door.

The battle inside lasted only a few minutes as the gronts tumbled two at a time through the bottleneck. The elven archers had easy aim at each one of the gronts, and picked off twenty gronts before they stopped coming through the door, having realized their disposition, and retreated into the woods.

Prince Jaerick ran to the door and watched the gronts retreat. They scattered aimlessly into the woods, and as they did so, Jaerick looked down and noticed the bloody corpse of his father's military advisor. The gronts had trampled, kicked, and stabbed him so severely that there were no recognizable features left to distinguish him between an elf, human, or gront.

Jaerick closed the door, but as he did so, he noticed a large green skinned, misshapen figure coming out of the woods. He swung a massive spiked wooden club and howled in a terrible massive roar, exposing an overly large mouth with twisted teeth as he ran towards the opening. The retreating gronts ran in every direction except toward this lurking creature. A massive assembly of goblin warriors stood ready for battle behind their goblin lord. Jaerick quickly shut the door and then faced his loyal soldiers and human allies. "We'd better get ready, Gralanxth is coming!"

Jaerick paused, and then listened for any signs of the battle going on upstairs. "Is the battle over upstairs?" he asked when he could not hear any fighting going on.

"Yes, the enemy forces above have been routed and executed," said the soldier.

Prince Jaerick straightened his composure and smiled. "Let's regroup with the others, for the battle is far from over."

•••

Traelyn found her father in the council chambers. The elven king was tending to the human king's wounds. Dar Drannon was lying on the table while Keiyann applied simple elven healing ointments. Dar Drannon was conscious, but groggy.

"Father!" Traelyn shouted as she ran into the room and fell onto her fathers' chest. "I'm ok, daughter. What about you?" he said as he touched Traelyn's neck. The blood still trickled down her neck and over some already dried blood that was collecting under her chin.

"I'm fine."

Keiyann walked over to Traelyn, grabbed her hand, and led her over to the table where he had his bandages and ointments then closed and dressed her wound.

Jaerick stormed into the room and smiled at Traelyn, not knowing until just now that she had made it to safety.

"Father, Meztrae betrayed us," Jaerick announced as Keiyann finished bandaging Traelyn's neck.

"What happened?"

"He showed the gronts the door, and let them in."

"But now they know of the door?" Dar Drannon croaked while sitting upright.

"Yes."

"It's all my fault." Traelyn sighed. "I showed Jaerick the lower vault door."

"No, it is not." Keiyann said abruptly. "No one is to blame but the elves. Your secret with Jaerick would've been safe, but one of my most trusted soldiers betrayed us all."

"They will be coming back then," Dar Drannon said, stepping down from the table and reaching for his sword lying near.

Keiyann looked at Jaerick, then at Dar Drannon. "It is time. Jaerick, find a horse and escape, take Traelyn with you."

"No!" Traelyn shouted. "You're not taking me anywhere! I am not leaving!"

"Yes, honey, you are," Dar Drannon said as he approached his daughter, taking her hand in his.

"I cannot leave you father," she sobbed, tears welling up in her eyes. "Please don't make me leave."

"You must. It is time for you to leave me here."

"How can I?"

Dar Drannon pulled Traelyn close to him and held her for several minutes before whispering in her ear. "I love you more than anything in this world."

"Then let me stay," she said, the tears rolling down her cheek. She fought, knowing somehow that there was no other option but to leave.

"You have to go. You have your full life to live, and I cannot take the chances of you dying here today."

"What about you?"

"I have to stay. The people are counting on me."

Dar Drannon gently pushed her away and held her at arm's length. "Go, and go now. You can go with Jaerick through the south tunnel, take as many of our people as you can round up."

"We have to hurry to do this," Jaerick responded.

Dar Drannon looked at Jaerick. "Take as many of the horses in the stables as there are riders for."

Traelyn hugged her father and squeezed him tight, not wanting to let go. Jaerick stood behind her and put his hand on her shoulder. He waited a few more seconds before whispering to her. "Let's go Traelyn."

She stepped back, still looking into her fathers' red and watering eyes. He mouthed the words 'I love you' and raised his hand as a gesture for her to go.

Two soldiers entered the room and announced that the goblin and gront armies were charging up the tunnels. Jaerick grabbed Traelyn by her hand and led her out of the room.

"Daddy, I love you!" She screamed with outstretched arms as if she could pull him back to her. Jaerick left the room while ordering a human soldier and an elven soldier to find as many people as they could gather to come with them.

Human and elven soldiers scrambled while Jaerick and Traelyn ran through the hall around the courtyard and down to the south tunnel, hoping to make their exit. When they reached the tunnel, they stopped and stared in horror. The entrance to the fortress that was normally secured by a wide iron door hung by only the top hinge and squealed as if it would soon break under the weight of the heavy door. It had been forced open and leaned upon its own weight on the hard ground.

Jaerick and Traelyn waited while the soldiers came with fifty of the residents. Jaerick turned to face his loyal elven soldiers and motioned the ranking sergeant to take a squad to scout out their exit. The soldier dutifully did so. With his sword drawn and ready, he walked outside through the gate, bringing behind him his squad of ten elves.

Jaerick looked around and could see nothing of the gronts or goblins that had obviously broken through already, but could hear the screams and shouts of the soldiers fighting behind them in various winding tunnels of the fortress. The screams were becoming louder and closer behind them, but they still could not see any of them. Jaerick, not wanting to waste another minute, motioned the others to follow him out of the fortress when his sergeant and three soldiers came running back inside. "Run!" He shouted as arrows flew past them. "There are too many of them!"

Jaerick, with the grim realization that they were trapped, grabbed the sergeant, and shouted in his face, "Push the people back into the stables in the courtyard, make yourselves an elven shield, and then protect them with your lives."

Jaerick took Traelyn's hand and began to lead her back to the courtyard, but she stiffened.

"No. I know another way. Follow me," she said jerking her hand out of his, and then ran up a flight of stairs to their right. Jaerick followed and commanded his soldiers of the change of command and to grab all of the others and to follow as well. As the group charged up the stairs, the goblins rushed out of the south tunnel, attacking the tail end of the group and slaughtering them one at a time as they caught them.

Traelyn led the group back into a hallway, made a sharp left turn that took them further upstairs. They could hear the fighting closing in on them. The sound of soldiers and goblins fighting and dying was even closer, in front of them now as well as behind them. Then Traelyn made an abrupt turn into an empty round room with a gravel floor, she lifted a large wooden hatch on the floor exposing a large hole. The sound of rushing water could be heard far below. She looked at Jaerick with fear in her eyes. "We have to jump."

"How far down?" Jaerick asked.

"I don't know. This is where we dump our liquid wastes. It goes straight into the Sippling River."

"I guess we have no choice," he said as a small group of commoners filed into the room. "The soldiers are all killed!" the last one shouted as he came into the room, then fell over as a sword tip came through his chest. His eyes bulged in shock and horror as the goblin behind him withdrew his sword and pushed the body to the ground. A dozen more goblins rushed in one by one, grabbing and killing the commoners as they tried in vain to escape.

They had no choice; Jaerick grabbed Traelyn's hand, and jumped. They fell straight down. They fell about fifty feet landing on a metal grate that snapped at the hinges as they landed, breaking their fall. Wooden buckets and metal tools caught by the grate long ago bounced, then fell with them into the water, still another twenty feet below.

Jaerick and Traelyn splashed into the deep cold water, and came up gasping for air. Jaerick looked downstream and saw Traelyn move through the swift current. Jaerick swam to her and caught her arm and grabbed her, held her tight, and did not fight the current, but let it take them downstream, and away from harm.

***

After Traelyn and Jaerick left Dar Drannon's chambers, the two kings rushed out to the battle only to find that they were much too late to make any difference in the outcome of the battle. The goblin and gront force was peppered throughout every crack and crevice of the fortress, like ants before a rainstorm. They slaughtered everything that moved and breathed. They set aflame anything that would burn. Hutches, work shacks, equipment, everything was being destroyed and burning. They screamed their victory cry as they scurried to find more things to burn and destroy.

Dar Drannon looked at his friend, Keiyann, and they both knew that there was nothing they could do, it was too late for last-minute tactics, no last great heroic charge to demoralize the enemy. In short, the fortress, the soldiers, and common people had been overrun.

"Dar Drannon," Keiyann said, not taking his eyes from the carnage of once brave soldiers and terrified common people who thought that the halls of Dar Drannon could not be penetrated by such a barbaric force. "There is one more thing left to do."

Dar Drannon looked to his fellow king in confusion. "What more can we do other than go down there and take a few to their deaths before they take us."

"No. My people have prophesied this day, and though it will end in defeat, it will be both a glorious, yet controversial day for many years to come."

"I don't understand."

"I don't expect you to. Follow me back to the chambers."

The two men went back to the council chambers and barred the doors. As they did so, Gralanxth charged into the lower courtyard. He had a sword in one hand and his spiked club in the other. He screamed as he ran, and in his rage of battle, he knocked two gronts off their feet with one wide swing of his club. The gronts flew ten feet to his left and fell to the ground dead.

The goblins in the area cheered as their fellow gront soldiers cowered and stayed clear of Gralanxth. Gralanxth then looked up at the upper causeway and saw the backs of the two kings. He yelled to all who would follow and charged up the stairs. Only minutes after the two kings closed and bolted the door, Gralanxth and his soldiers were there. Gralanxth began hacking the door with the sword and club simultaneously, while the goblins behind him began to chant their death march. Gralanxth slowed his rage and chopped at the door in tune with the chant. Thump, thump, thump, he pounded at the door, taking off shards and pieces of the door with every blow.

Keiyann began to say something, but Dar Drannon shook his head. "Wait.

Help me first."

Dar Drannon ran to the wall and started tearing down shelves against the wall. He threw artifacts, cups, and helms of honor to the ground. He then tore into the wall and removed a three-by-three piece of wood that looked like a stone block exposing a square hole in the wall. "Follow me," Dar Drannon said as he slipped through the hole and disappeared.

Keiyann lunged in headfirst and followed. They crawled down the narrow tunnel until they came to an opening that was a small fifteen by fifteen foot room. The room was solid stone and on the walls hung many weapons, swords, shields, bows, and boxes full of arrows. "We can defend ourselves for quite a while here," Dar Drannon said.

"Not long enough, I'm afraid."

"True, but they can only come in one at a time, and we will kill them all, one by one. I built this shelter for a day such as today. I had planned to put Traelyn here to protect her from harm if such a thing happened. Of course, I hoped it would never come, but here we are, and us instead of Traelyn."

Then they heard a large crash of the door in the council chambers coming down.

"Here, grab a bow and some arrows. It won't be long before they figure out where we are."

Finally, Gralanxth knocked the door off of its hinges and kicked it, shattering it into pieces flying across the room. The goblins, along with Gralanxth, charged into the room with a victory scream, but their excitement was soon silenced by Gralanxth's loud roar when they noticed that their victims had somehow escaped.

Dar Drannon and Keiyann heard some scuffling and crashing of the goblins destroying the room, but it wasn't long before they heard one of them crawling down the tunnel. Dar Drannon notched an arrow then shot into the tunnel. The goblin screamed as an arrow pierced his arm. Grimacing in pain, he crawled backwards out of the tunnel.

Gralanxth saw the retreating goblin, and grabbed him by the legs as he backed out, forcefully ripping him from the tunnel. He saw the arrow in his goblin soldier's arm and realized that he was retreating from an attack. In frustration, he growled even louder and looked at the fear in his warrior's face. The goblin wiggled as Gralanxth held him tight by his ankles then smashed his head repeatedly against the wall until he became limp in his hands before dropping the lifeless body to the floor.

Gralanxth issued further orders, and one by one, the goblins crawled into the tunnel. The two kings fired arrows into the hole, always killing the lead goblin. The goblins behind each dead warrior continued their advance by pushing their dead forward into the room. As soon as the dead goblins were clear, Dar Drannon and Keiyann continued to fire more arrows.

This tactic went on for many minutes, but only managed to fill the room up with dead goblins. Even so, the goblins grew weary of not making any successful advance, and backed out of the tunnel. Gralanxth could be heard issuing a new set of instructions as the goblins retrieved the bodies remaining within the small tunnel.

Once cleared, all became silent. The two kings stood with their arrows nocked and waited for the next assault. This time, instead of goblins, there came a barrage of lit arrows. Many hit the stone wall behind them and bounced to the floor, but some hit the dead goblins catching their clothes on fire.

Dar Drannon and Keiyann put out some of the fires before they became a problem, but so many arrows were coming through the tunnel that they could not reach them all. The smoke and the rancid smell of burning flesh permeated through the whole room. Soon, the smoke became so thick that Dar Drannon and Keiyann could hardly see each other.

Then the arrows stopped, and all was silent. The two kings took advantage of the pause to put out the smoldering clothes on the goblins, until a goblin crawled through the tunnel and into room. In his arms, he carried shards of wood from the furniture in the other room. Dar Drannon unsheathed his sword and easily skewered the unarmed goblin, but three more followed with more fuel for the fire.

Both Dar Drannon and Keiyann Krowe made easy work of the goblins, but as soon as they killed them, the fiery arrows began anew, this time catching the wood and starting a fire that quickly became uncontrollable.

Dar Drannon looked at his friend, fearing that the worst would come to pass.

"I told you earlier that I have a last resort, and now I will show you," Keiyann yelled above the crackling timber.

"Then I guess now would be a good time," Dar Drannon responded smiling, but looking as all hope was lost.

Keiyann withdrew his sword and gave it to Dar Drannon.

"What's this?" Dar Drannon asked, taking the sword and shaking his head.

"It is called the sword of Valkilye, and we are about to fulfill its prophecy."

"I cannot take the sword of your ancestors to my death."

"That's just it. You are not going to die, my friend. I may, but you will not."

"I don't understand. What does the prophecy say about me?"

"All you have to do is take the sword, and read the inscription. The future of this realm depends on this moment. Doing so will somehow bring this realm to unity."

"What are you talking about? We are about to die! Look around. The flames are getting closer and very soon we will burn to death."

"Read the inscription!" Keiyann said grabbing the blade and twisting it in Dar Drannon's wrist so that the inscription faced the human king.

Dar Drannon wiped the sweat off his forehead and looked upon the sword. The flames began to consume the whole room. "I do not understand it. It's in your elven language."

"You don't have to understand it, just speak the words written on the sword."

Dar Drannon looked at the sword again, read the inscriptions from the hilt of the blade to the tip, and back again to the hilt. As he spoke the last word aloud he looked up and saw his friend beating away the flames from his legs, but as he did so he noticed that the elven king began to get smaller and smaller and the flames seemed to be frozen in time. Then like a cardboard cutout he saw the shape of Keiyann Krowe lift out of the room and delivered back to his own kingdom.

In a hazy blur devoid of smoke, but in a gray dizzying effect, Dar Drannon was then also lifted from the room. He looked down and could see his fortress below him. The enemy forces were destroying everything in his home. He saw the fires, the dead soldiers—human, elf, gront, and goblin. The destruction of what he had worked so hard to build. He now saw from an even higher elevation the whole realm of Wrae-Kronn—the civilizations, kingdoms, trading routes, and he realized that there was so much more to this realm than he had ever imagined.

As he continued to rise, everything began to fade to darkness, he wondered how he was to fit into the elven prophecy, and he thought of his daughter and how he wished he could see her just one more time.

Then, as if a wish was instantly granted, he saw her. His last sight within this realm was of Traelyn and Jaerick climbing out of the Sippling River. They were still a great distance away from the elven kingdom, but he could see a legion of elven riders charging in their direction. His final thoughts of her were a little more comforted knowing that she would be safe with the elves.

***

Jaerick and Traelyn floated downstream until they were clear of the fortress and far away from the battle. Jaerick swam towards the riverbank and pulled Traelyn with him. As soon as he touched the dry gravel, he turned over on his back and looked to the sky in relief and exhaustion. Traelyn crawled out of the river, stood up, and kicked the gravel to the side of his face as she walked by. She turned and looked at her home as the smoke filled the sky above and around it. The smoky haze covered the fortress as if a death blanket was being laid over its massive walls.

"Father!" she screamed, then fell to her knees and wept. Jaerick hurried to her side and touched her back to soothe her, but she jerked her shoulders. "Go away!" She sobbed.

"Traelyn, we must continue. I don't think we are safe yet."

Traelyn turned to face him. "Why should I? Don't you see my home? My father? Look. His ashes are probably mixed within the smoke lingering above our home, and you want me to continue on?"

Jaerick sat down, crossed his legs, and put his head in his hands. "This is my fault Traelyn. My father may also be dead, but there is hope."

"What hope is there?" she snapped. "You saw those evil creatures, you saw the destruction!"

"There are things about this world that you don't understand. Elven mysticism can be a very peculiar thing. Things happen that have been foretold for generations, and this is one of them."

"No!" Traelyn screamed and ran away towards the woods. "I will not hear it! My father and I are not puppets of your people and your religion!"

Jaerick stood up and watched her run through the forest brush and onto the main road. He watched her until she was almost out of sight. The river's rushing water flowed behind him and the noise of the current slapped the shore, crowding his thoughts. He shook his head, miffed and dejected, then hurried after her.

***

Keiyann Krowe was near unconscious lying by a brook near his castle when his soldiers found him. His clothes were nearly burnt away and his body had minor burns in several places. His soldiers brought him back to the castle and tended to his wounds. He was still being cared for when Jaerick entered his chambers.

"Father. How did you arrive before us?" he asked.

"The Sword of Valkilye brought me home."

"I knew it! Then the sword belongs here and not with the humans."

"No son, you don't understand. I gave the sword to King Dar Drannon, just as the prophecy was written. As soon as he read the inscription upon the sword we both disappeared."

"Then where is he?" He asked.

Traelyn ran into the room, her face flush from running up the stairs after Jaerick had left her at the entrance of the castle.

"Father? Where is my father?"

Keiyann sat up and leaned his back against the wall. "I'm not really sure, but he will return. The prophecy says he will one day return."

"When will this happen?"

"I don't know. It may be tomorrow, or it may not be for hundreds of years. That part of the prophecy is unclear."

"Then where is he?"

Keiyann Krowe stood up and walked to Traelyn, grabbed her hands, but when he saw the pain in her eyes, he let go of her hands and hugged her. "I don't know, but I do know that he loves you very much and wants to see you soon, and if it is up to him, he will return to see you again."

"I hope so," Traelyn said, crying on Keiyann's shoulder.

* * *

Traelyn wiped her eyes. She had not realized the tears were flowing as she destroyed the last of the flowers. Her father had indeed returned, but not how she expected. There must be another way to bring him back permanently. Now that she had her memories returned to her, memories that she was sure the elves had somehow stripped from her, she was going to find a way. With a new determination to find Jaerick, she was going to find a way to bring her father back to this realm.

Chapter 10

King Jaerick entered the conference chambers. He was in a solemn mood and he had been putting off this meeting for several days for many reasons. Naemyn was the First Sorae, and had been the leader of the Sorae since the day Jaerick was crowned king, but this friendship still did not take away the hesitancy and distrust toward the group.

King Keiyann Krowe had created the Sorae to be the prophetic voice for the elven people, as well as the driving force in keeping the two elven tribes at peace. The quiet, passive, purist thinking Sor elves, which hold a direct link to Kronn and spiritual matters, constantly hold the intellectual Val elves at bay.

The Sor elves have been known to be a conduit of communication between the elven mystics directly to the high elven leaders. Even though his father's intent was noble and just, it seemed to Jaerick that the Sorae was nothing more than a political hindrance using the gods for their own faction's gains.

It was also because of the Val elves and their sense of duty, respect, and self-preservation that both tribes not only survived, but also thrived in this northern territory. The Val elves were not afraid to do whatever was necessary to protect their interests. If not for the Val Elves, the human tribes would have overrun the Sor elves long ago.

Six somber faced elves sat at the table. *Always smug and defiant,* Jaerick thought to himself as he sat upon the polished stone chair at the head of a table made from ancient cedars on the northern coasts. The six elves stood up, feigning respect, waiting until the king was fully seated before they would sit back down.

Jaerick, realizing this, frowned. "Be seated," he commanded in a voice announcing his displeasure.

The Sorae also believed that they were the only direct link to any communication with their deities. They often used this factor for leverage in every disagreement. It was with these pompous attitudes of putting their ideals first before the concerns of the people that made Jaerick distrust and dislike the Sorae.

"I called you here as a favor to Naemyn," he began.

"You should call more of these meetings my great king. As always, your word is revered and well respected among us," said Sahven, who was subordinate to Naemyn.

"Yes, I am sure it is," he said shaking his head, not surprised to hear such mock respect.

"Where has Naemyn gone to in such a hurry?" Laesting asked, bowing to Sahven for speaking out of turn.

"He has gone to the catacombs to assure that the Quarterstar Shard is still safely within its sacred place."

All six of the Sorae sat straight up, shifting uncomfortably in their seats. Some then leaned back in their chairs and threw their heads back, while the others remained perfectly still. Then, almost at once, not heeding what the other was saying, they began yelling at the king.

As king, he felt he did not need to consult the Sorae. In fact, the Sorae did enough consulting by making their opinions known without Jaerick having to ask for them. He worked with them, if only for the alliance. As much as he disliked them, he could not simply disband the Sorae, or else there would be immediate dissention within the two races, and Jaerick did not want that. He knew of the importance that the king and Sorae work together, if nothing else to give the impression that the two races could live in harmony. They had done so for hundreds of years, and he did not want to disrupt that harmony.

"Why would he go to our sacred burial grounds? He should not go there when it is dangerous to do so," Sahven said, as he stood asserting his authority.

"The Shard is dangerous! It cannot even be touched! It cannot be transported without the talisman. All who touch it, without it being housed in the talisman will die." Another responded.

"That's right, and there are traps deep within the catacombs to protect it!" spoke another. "Only an elven keeper can even touch the Shard. If Naemyn just attempts to touch it, horrible things will happen."

"You are right, and you know better than I do that according to prophecy, what originally the elven and dwarven gods could only do, now belongs to a descendant of Dar Drannon. I want to assure that none of his descendants have done this. I am certain that all of you would agree with my concerns." Jaerick said as directly as possible without coming across to harsh.

"You are still wrong to command him to go there! Among all the things mentioned, there are hundreds of human tribes along the way, including the goblin tribes surrounding the catacombs! You, most of all, know this. This is why your people left and why you now live here in ancient Sor land," Reprimanded Sahven.

Jaerick leaned forward, put his left elbow on his knee, and rubbed his chin. "This was not of my calling, and Naemyn is only obeying that calling. This mandate I have commanded comes from a higher source than mine," he paused to wait for their pompous reaction. He had their attention at this, because he was alluding to the fact that he had conversation with a higher source than a king, which can only be their deity Val Eahea. He smiled, as they remained silent and attentive.

"I had a vision from Val Eahea."

"Val Eahea would not speak directly to you without speaking to one of us." Sahven mumbled, sitting down, obviously disturbed, while the others spoke simultaneously.

"And he hasn't spoken to any of us," finished another.

"You speak blasphemy," said yet another.

"Think what you may," Jaerick said raising his hand to silence any more reaction from them, feeling a little agitated with their pious platitudes. "I have been having dreams of Traelyn and the Quarterstar Talisman with the Shard *embedded* in the talisman."

"But, my king, once again, the Shard can only be transported out of the catacombs if it is first put into the Quarterstar Talisman," Sahven commented looking at the other five Sorae in attempt to calm the emotions, and bring the meeting back into control. "As long as we have the talisman, we can be assured that the Quarterstar is safely where it is supposed to be."

"That is why I sent Naemyn away. We have found that the Talisman is missing," Jaerick said calmly, knowing that this new information would lay down yet another hammer blow upon their never-ending pompous attitudes.

Shocked silence filled the room.

"How can it be missing?" Sahven asked in barely more than a whisper.

"I don't know, and that is why Naemyn has left for the catacombs."

Sahven took a deep breath and realized the situation had just unfolded into something more ominous than he first anticipated. "Then tell us your vision," he said in a sincere, humble voice, knowing he had to give the king audience to his absurdities.

"Now that I finally have your attention, I am also confident that your prejudices against me won't get in the way moving forward."

"My king," one began, feigning insult. "You misunderstand us. We only serve you and the elven kingdom."

"Is that your true belief, your sole motivation?" Jaerick said noticing the mock reverence.

"It is, my king," he said.

"If you speak truly then listen and do not interrupt until I finish."

Jaerick then went on to describe his dream in detail from beginning to end. He explained his confusion as to how he could forget Traelyn from his memory so completely, and why now he had regained his memory of her through such a dark dream. He went into detail of his son's demise in the pit, and demanded that the Sorae take this portion of the dream in context when they make any rash decisions to their interpretations to the dreams. When he was finished, he looked at the six Sorae members and waited for a reaction or comment.

"My king, you have shared your vision with us, and even your fears, but what do you think this vision ultimately means?" Sahven asked.

Jaerick was surprised that the first question was actually a question of his concern, and a fair and honest question.

"I don't know for sure." He paused and thought a little deeper before answering. He was not sure what they might think of his completely honest opinion. "I suspect that Traelyn is still alive and her human children will attack our home and kill my son. I also think Traelyn has, or at least very soon will have, the Quarterstar Talisman. And we must do something."

"Some dreams are mere paranoia. Do you really believe Val Eahea has sent to you a vision in the form of this dream?"

Jaerick shook his head. He had told them too much, almost as if he fell into a trap.

"I know where you are going with this Sahven. My father had this problem with his own spiritual advisor. The Sorae are not the only ones that have communication with the creator. If Val Eahea wants to speak to someone directly, or through dreams and visions, don't you think he is capable of doing so? You are not so much more powerful than our creator that you can dictate to him that he must speak only through you so that you may interpret his meaning."

"Yes, we fully understand that our creators can do anything they please, but please remember that Val Eahea was originally your god. We are trained to understand and react on all such matters concerning all three of the gods. That is why you are talking to us now, is it not, my king?"

Jaerick shook his head, wondering how he continued to fall into their verbal traps, he was only talking to them because his friend Naemyn had asked him to, and for no other reason was he here. "So what is your interpretation, and suggestion?" he mocked, speaking as he exhaled.

"I do indeed believe that this is a message from Val Eahea, and he is trying to warn you of what could happen if you let these humans rally to their full strength. Send our forces and crush them before it is too late," Sahven said slapping his hand on the table as he spoke the last word.

Jaerick blinked twice in surprise at Sahven's reaction. He responded with a quick hand slap on the table. He shook his head, again not surprised at how aggressive these peaceful Sor elves respond when it comes to humans. "And what of the Quarterstar Talisman?" he added, getting them off of the path of destroying humans, at least temporarily.

"That is only a marker to tell you that it is Val Eahea who is speaking to you."

"But what of Traelyn, then why does she have it?"

"That is merely your subconscious working into Val Eahea's message and confusing you."

Jaerick stood up and became annoyed again. "Do you remember that the Quarterstar Talisman is missing?"

"Yes, but you will find it."

"On that we agree, but I also believe that I will find it when we find Traelyn. She will have it in her possession."

"No! Do not search her out! Do not bring her here. We sent her out many years ago to save the elven kingdom. Please my king, do not attempt to bring her back," Sahven said before he could think about his words.

Jaerick paused, and stared at the group as they collectively went silent. "What do you mean you sent her away to save the kingdom?" He asked slowly.

"You don't understand…" Sahven began, attempting to backtrack his error.

"No, *you* don't understand," Jaerick said, almost in a whisper, but loud enough for the others to hear. "I am just now finding out what events transpired when Traelyn left us. I will not allow such important events to pass against my wishes again."

"But my king, surely you must know that she is dead by now. Humans cannot live for three hundred years."

"Yes, reason tells me this to be true, but I also feel that she is alive and something tells me that it is important that I see her again. I honestly feel that the elven people cannot be so afraid of one human female that they would deny their king his wishes."

"We sent her away three hundred years ago to save the people from a possible civil war, caused by the possibility of a half-elf heir, not to mention her being the heir to the prophecy we have been speaking of today. To bring her back will only reactivate the prophecy and bring about those fears again. That is the true reason why your son dies in your dreams."

"So you sent her away to avoid a civil war, but for three hundred years we have been at war with humans because they now believe their sons are rightful heirs to my throne, and I am to believe that my son dies because of this influence."

"The humans have no real claim to the throne. The first human king was a blasphemer to the elven race and is dangerous to our existence."

"I refuse to believe it. Dar Drannon, her father, was our loyal friend. These humans may have been, and still can be, of service to elven kind."

Jaerick despised the human tribes, but he did not wish their complete destruction. They were simply a thorn in his side that he wished would disappear on their own volition. He understood their plight in that they were sandwiched between the elven kingdom and the destructive dragons from the Dragoncross Mountains. However malicious he or his elven counterparts thought the humans were, he understood that theirs was a need of survival.

"No! This is more blasphemy, my king. Do not speak in such way! These humans are the barbarians that followed us out of our original homeland, and they have been a nuisance to us ever since."

"What if fighting is not the answer?" Jaerick asked. "We have been doing it for so long with no just conclusion."

"My king, unfortunately, fighting them is the only option. This has been, and so shall be, as far as humans are concerned. They cannot be allowed to be part of our prophecy. Only you and your father insist that they are part of it for good. If these humans get a foothold, they will overrun us, we will slowly, but surely, cease to exist, and that is true even if they do not secure the shard and talisman together. Either way, it will mean our demise."

"That may be so, but what if we are not meant to be here in the first place? What if this is land was destined for humans, and what if we are supposed to be somewhere else, what if my father was supposed to take us even further, maybe to another place farther west?"

"What are you saying?"

What I am saying is, maybe this northern coastal area is not supposed to be our final home."

"Are you saying we should leave this homeland? Leave all that we have here? And what of Aaestfallia Keep? If the fact that we now exist here together isn't a sign that Raezoures and Val Eahea wanted us here and nowhere else, then I don't know what is."

"Maybe we should. I do not doubt that Val Eahea wanted us to find this place with your kind already here, but that does not change the fact that we may need to leave. We can dismantle and uproot ourselves and take away anything that is precious to us. It could be time to move on. Aside from the Aaestfallia Keep there is no proof that this is where we belong."

"No," Sahven said shaking his head. "I think it would be wrong to leave. It would also be wrong for the Val elves to leave and the Sor elves to stay, which is exactly the division that would create. We are one race, and it must stay that way. We must stay and simply rid the humans of existence by going on the offensive instead of always being on the defensive."

"Even Naemyn despises the humans and wishes them to be eliminated. Are you not in harmony with your closest friend and advisor? "Added Laesting.

Jaerick walked around the table. "I'm finished here. Naemyn asked me to tell the Sorae of what we have decided to do and I have done so. My decision is final, and Naemyn has already approved it. He is going to find the Quarterstar Shard, and find Traelyn and the Quarterstar Talisman if he can. Ultimately, I want him to bring Traelyn back, the motions are already in place. Thank you for your advice, I will consider all that you have said."

"I wish we could have spoken to Naemyn before he left."

"He had to hurry. There was no time for discussion."

"We just fear that he will not return, and we do not know what Naemyn's true intentions are."

"Well you don't know what he is thinking, so you are just going to have to put your faith and trust into your king for a change."

Chapter 11

A light breeze blew towards Traegon as he crested the hill and saw the massive army encamped in the valley. He had been riding solid for three days. The day was ending and the overcast sky hid the last moments of light that had been casting a dim shadow upon the land throughout the day. Riding down into the valley, he saw nothing but tents, all in a tight knit forest of brown and green canvas that littered the valley. When he neared the bottom of the hill, he began to make out the soldiers milling about. Some were sharpening and maintaining their weapons, while others were practicing their skills by sparring against each other. Many just sat around campfires drinking ales and talking amongst themselves.

They had been on a two-week road march, and during that time had only stopped twice to set up a full camp. They had been camped now for a number of days and were making the most of their extended down time.

As Traegon approached the encampment, he saw the banners flapping in the light dusky breeze. These banners symbolized and identified each individual tribe, signifying their regimental command. He knew there were hundreds of different tribes and regiments but he had never seen them together like this. When his father, Daegon, left two weeks ago, he left with five regiments of fifty men each with the intent of meeting the other commanders and their regiments at a designated rendezvous point. From there they must have mustered their large force together and headed north.

He had reached the first set of tents and was surprised that he was able to enter the perimeter without even a question or little more than a sidelong glance. Traegon then realized that it was the elves that they were suspicious of and not other humans, which to him was slightly odd, because as long as he could remember they not only fought elves, but they also had minor skirmishes amongst other tribes.

He walked his horse in a little deeper and approached a group of soldiers sitting in front of a fire near a circle of tents. They stopped their conversation and stared at Traegon with defiant distrust. Traegon took a deep breath and spoke.

"I'm looking for Commander Daegon of the Mothers Defenders."

"Big brown tent north of here. You'll see the banner," one of the soldiers said as he lifted his ale, took a swig, and then turned his head to the right.

Traegon nodded in return, and continued through the rows of tents, noticing the condition of the soldiers. They were tired, dirty, but still enjoying their rare time off. The banners he passed were creative and original as they all had some sort of glorious history to them. Daegon's originated from being within the true lineage of the Great Mother, and by being the son of many great leaders serving Traelyn, the Great Mother. Other banners represented the regiments' famous victories or overall attitude of their fighting abilities.

He passed the High Swords regiment, a simple red banner with a sword held high. He passed by many other banners and the men that grouped near them. After he made a few turns and switchbacks in between tents, he saw the Great Mothers' Defenders banner flapping in a light breeze from atop the brown and green commander's tent. Upon seeing the tent, Traegon trotted the horse, eager and yet hesitant to reach the tent and tell his father the news about the Great Mother.

Two guards stood in front of the tent and drew their swords as Traegon approached. Traegon pulled on the reins, stopping his horse. He dismounted and handed the reins to a servant boy who was standing obediently waiting for orders. He took two steps toward the tent entrance when one of the guards blocked his path. "Halt!" the soldiers commanded in unison as they pointed their swords towards Traegon's breast, both of their sword tips were planted firmly against his leather breastplate. Traegon raised his hands above his shoulders. "I need to see my father, Commander Daegon."

"What business do you have with the commander, boy?" the soldier said with an angry sardonic smile.

"Just get my father; I have news from the Great Mother."

The larger soldier of the two motioned with his head to the other soldier to go inside the commander's tent. Within a few seconds, Traegon and the other guard heard Daegon's booming voice commanding them to let Traegon enter. Traegon put his hand on the blade and moved it away from his chest. "Thank you for your obedient service," Traegon said, smiling as he entered the tent.

Daegon stood in the center of the tent. His staff sat around the edges of the tent. "What are you doing out here?" he shouted at his only son. "You had better have a good reason for being here, one for leaving the Great Mother, and two, for compromising our security by showing up here."

Traegon stood erect with both hands to his sides, but he looked straight into his father's eyes without fear, and answered. "The Great Mother has sent me here to deliver a message to you."

"What could be so important to the Great Mother that she would send you miles away from home that couldn't wait until we return?"

"She is dying," Traegon answered.

"What? That is impossible. She can live forever as long as she eats that nasty flower."

"That is just it. She has destroyed them all, and if that isn't bad enough, there is more ill news."

"Well don't keep me hanging, boy. Go on," Daegon pushed, becoming increasingly annoyed with the situation.

"Father, I tried to talk her out of this," Traegon continued, and for the first time since his adolescence years, he began to tremble while addressing his father. "She wants to come here with you so that you can take her to the elves."

Daegon instantly turned red and raised both hands, shaking his fists. "What kind of joke is this? What are you doing here? Why are you really here?"

"It's true father. She wants to see the King of Elves."

Daegon walked over to Traegon, grabbed him behind his neck, and pulled him closer so that their faces were less than an inch apart. "You do not understand what you are saying."

"Yes Father, I do. I begged her not to send me, because I knew that this would be your reaction. She wanted me to take her to the elves, but I refused, instead I said you would know what to do."

Daegon turned loose of his son, and turned to his staff. "Leave, all of you! We will resume our meeting later."

As the staff officers left, Daegon turned his back to Traegon and collected himself. Traegon stood silent and waited for his father's response.

"Do you know what this means?" Daegon finally asked his son.

"No, I don't. She said something about dreams, and the prophecy of Dar Drannon."

"I'm sure it does mean something to her, but I think she has finally lost her mind, and has forgotten what the elves have done to her."

"I think you're right father, because she said that the elves have done nothing to us, and she must see the elven king." Traegon said. "So what do we do?" Traegon asked after a long pause.

"I don't know yet. I suppose I will send you back."

"What do I tell her? Actually, all she wants me to do is find you and then bring her to you so that you can take her to the king."

"Well then I guess that is what you should do, she is after all, our supreme leader, but tell her I will take her only on my terms." Daegon smiled. "Maybe I'll take her as I march this army to battle and she will witness me killing this elven king."

Traegon nodded his head, but did not like the direction this was headed. "Then I will leave right now."

"No. There is no great hurry. We will be camped here for at least a few more days, maybe a week. So relax, spend some time with me tonight. Tomorrow at dawn you can leave."

Traegon smiled and exhaled a sigh of relief. "Fine, I'll leave tomorrow and then I will bring the Great Mother back with me."

"That'll work. When she returns, I'm sure I'll have a big surprise for her beloved elves."

Chapter 12

Voll awoke an hour before sunrise. The night sky was still dark, but the horizon had a slightly brighter tint as the sun neared the horizon. The night insects creaked and chattered as Voll rolled up his blanket into a tight ball and packed it away in the saddlebags. The morning chill had a calm, yet damp feel to it. It felt to him that today the sun was not going to bring anything more with it than the daily light. He then put the saddle pad on the horse, and placed the saddle on top. After he cinched it down, he pulled out a bag with corn and sugared oatmeal, and took a handful for himself. His horse eyeballed him as he chewed. Smiling, he filled his hand again and put it under the horses nose. The horse lipped it up and nodded his head back and forth, as he chewed his snack.

Voll looked to the south and wondered how the elves had fared against the dragon. He took the reins off the tree where he placed them for the night, removed the horse's halter, and put in its bit and reins. Mounting his horse, he continued southward, staying just off of the trail where the elves had traveled just in case there were any scouts to the rear.

The trail was still very easy to follow since the elves were traveling in such a hurried pace, but now it was getting harder for him to stay hidden since they were leaving the mountains and traveling the flat plain lands that lacked dense vegetation. Therefore, Voll decided to pick up the pace and use the last bit of mountain trees while he could.

The sun had risen and dark rain clouds were slowly beginning to roll in bringing with it a light breeze. Occasionally the sun would peak in and out of the scattered dark clouds. Voll's horse began to sweat from running all morning. He knew the elves would be moving even faster now that they were in safe territory, so he felt that speed was of the essence, and his attention was so focused on moving ahead that he almost ran over the dragon lying in the ravine at the neck of a draw in between two hills.

The dragon was nestled in between a clump of low bushes. Voll was hustling down the draw and did not see the dragon, but his horse did and stopped so fast that all four hooves slid nearly three feet down the soft slope. The horse then pulled his head back and tried to turn around. Voll yelled at the horse and pulled back on his reins to regain control still not knowing what had spooked him.

It was not until the dragon lifted his head that Voll had realized the extent of the danger he was in. He yanked his reins to the left and charged away from the dragon. Expecting to be chased and hunted down he did not even look back until he crested the top of the hill. When he did look back, he noticed that the dragon had not even moved.

Voll stopped his horse and turned her around so he could get a look at the dragon. It just lay there in the bushes. It had laid its head back down and all Voll saw was the top of the dragon's spine just cresting above the foliage. He stayed motionless for many minutes in fear and curiosity, but soon the curiosity took over since the dragon did not stir during the time he watched it. "Well Rox, should we check it out?" Voll asked his horse, leaning forward to whisper into her ears. As he did so, her left ear swiveled around while keeping her right ear attuned to the dragon.

"Then let's go," Voll said as he crept his horse down the hill and when he got within fifty feet of the motionless dragon, he dismounted and laid the reins on the ground so that they hung freely in front of the horse. "Wait here," he said as he stroked the horse's neck. Just feeling the soft fur of his long-time friend seemed to calm him briefly.

The dragon lay still like it was near death, and its breathing was slow and labored. Still being cautious, he approached from the backside of the dragon. Once he got close, he could see the blood was oozing down the side of the dragon from between many of its scales. Curious and enticed to learn more, he crept forward. He thought about drawing his sword, but decided not to, out of fear he might alert the dragon of his presence.

He continued on, step by cautious step, until he reached the tip of the dragon's tail. Something within him, his curious urge to touch caused him to reach out and stroke the end of the tail. He immediately stopped himself just as his fingertip was just about to touch the end of the tail. The dragon must know of his presence by now. He stood silent, debating whether to touch the dragon, until the urge overcame his fear of retribution.

First, he bent down to his knees, feeling the soft ground beneath him, pausing slightly to take a deep breath, he reached out and stroked one of the small scales on its tail. Expecting the dragon to lash out, he removed his hand, but to his surprise, the dragon did not respond. Feeling a little more confident, he reached out for the tail again. As he touched the dragon's tail, he noticed that the scales were rough and hard as rock, yet jagged like tree bark. This time, the dragon responded to his touch, not by moving or attacking, but by giving a loud snort that shook the bushes in front of him from the sudden burst of air.

Voll jumped back, but soon realized that the dragon was still not about to attack. He stood motionless, frozen in fear for many minutes before he realized that the dragon had as many as two-dozen arrows pelted underneath its scales.

"Just do it. If you're going to kill me, then do it now, and be done with it," Voll heard a raspy female voice say inside of his head.

"What?" he said aloud and feeling a little confused by voice.

"Aren't you here to kill me?"

"Are you talking to me?"

"Whom do you think I'm talking to, if not you?"

Voll's eyes opened wide with shock and wonder. "No, I won't kill you," he said as he walked around to the front of the dragon. The dragon's head was as big as the barrel of his horse. The nose of the dragon lay in the dirt and its upper teeth protruded over the bottom of its mouth and almost touched the dirt. Slimy brown saliva dripped into the dirt from the corners of her mouth as the dragon watched Voll with her dark yellow eyes. Bumpy ridges ran up the top of its nose leading to two dirt-brown horns above its eyes. The dragon closed its eyes after watching him for a few minutes.

"Did the elves do this to you?" Voll asked.

The dragon's eyes snapped open, and she lifted her head, letting out a gurgled, almost terrifying growl, and then dropped her head back down to the ground, making a slight thud in the soft soil.

"Yes. I just wanted a tasty snack. The first elf I ate didn't even satisfy that urge. I so much wanted that second little elf by the creek," The dragon went on, but then stopped and let out another puff of air that almost knocked Voll over. He felt the heat mist as it came from deep inside the dragon's inner body.

"Are you going to eat me?" Voll asked.

"If I wasn't so tired, I might. My back stings so bad and I am beyond being angry or hungry."

"Can I help you then?" Voll asked, and was surprised as he said it, for it came without any thought, or planning.

"How?"

"I will pull out the arrows and stuff your scales to stop the bleeding."

"I don't need help from a puny human."

"Fine, then lay there in your own pity and bleed to death. I don't care. You will only be one less dragon to raid my crop and home. I really don't know what I was thinking."

The dragon was silent, and did not stir for many moments before it responded. "I hope mother doesn't find out."

Voll froze. "Mother?"

"Yes, mother hates humans. She doesn't even find them tasty, but she does like killing them, but she might like elves, they have a nice earthy taste. They are softer, juicier and not so crunchy as humans."

"Then I suggest we had better hurry. I can get you well, and then you can show her where the elves are, get your meal and some revenge." Voll said smiling.

"Good idea, though I know she won't like you at all."

Voll walked around again to the back of the dragon and climbed onto the dragon. Starting at a few scales on the lower side of the dragon's neck, he pulled out the first arrow. The dragon lifted her head and jerked back and forth while bellowing out a loud roaring screech. A noise very unlike any sound Voll had ever heard, especially from a dragon. The dragon thrashed about wildly, sending Voll flying about fifteen feet sideways into the bushes.

"That hurt!" The dragon belted, and then realized that her help was missing. "Human, where are you?"

Voll sat up, made a mental check to see if he was injured. "I'm over here, you stupid beast."

'Stupid? Don't get so brave little man. Even in this condition, it will be very easy to toast your bones."

"Fine, be that way. I'm going now," Voll said as he dusted off his arms and legs, and walked back towards his horse.

"Wait. Come back. I'll be more careful not to throw you again."

The dragon still wanted his help, unbelievable though it seemed. He was very much regretting his decision to help this dragon, but something still compelled him to do just that. Shaking his head, he walked back to finish what he started.

"Good, but now I realize this is going to be a little more difficult than I expected. I need to know what is in this for me. I am no longer in the mood for good deeds for the sake of doing a good deed. I have an urgent need to catch up to those elves that peppered your back."

The dragon lifted its head and smiled. "I have an idea. How is this for incentive, you can leave me here to die and mother will hunt down and scorch you? She will find you because you left your scent all over my back. Finding you will be so very easy for her."

Voll shook his head, a little annoyed and frustrated, but managed to smile a little, realizing the fact that he was actually talking to a living, fire-breathing dragon. "Extortion will get you nowhere. I am a trained scout and can hide from you and your clumsy mother. I can blend in with my surroundings better than an elf, I can be under your nose, and if the wind is blowing away from you, and I would make sure it was, you would never find me. But, regardless, and for the life of me I do not know why, I want to help you. So, maybe you can come up for some real reward for me helping you. I will start working, and you start thinking."

Climbing back onto the dragon, hoping that his ridiculous bluff would stick, he looked at all the arrows he now had to pull, and all the scales he had to stuff to stop the bleeding. Some of the scales were slick with the black blood oozing from underneath the scales.

"So, uh, what is your name, dragon?" Voll said, breaking the silence and hoping to distract the dragon as he pulled out the next arrow.

"You probably can't pronounce it.

"Then make one up."

"Fine. Then call me Aegyn."

"Aegyn, nice to meet you," he said as he pulled another arrow out from her flesh. She squirmed some in a great effort not to toss Voll off of her back again.

Voll continued to work at pulling the arrows out from underneath her scales. After he had half of them pulled, the bleeding began to increase, so he went back to his horse and grabbed his sleeping roll and with his sword ripped it into as many pieces as he could. He ran back to Aegyn and stuffed the rags tightly underneath the scales to stop the bleeding. By this time, Aegyn was either asleep or unconscious. Either way he was able to speed up his work and not worry about being thrown off of the dragon's back again.

About an hour later, Voll pulled out the last arrow and stuffed the last scale. Jumping off of Aegyn's back, he noticed that the day was almost gone. I have got to get out of here he thought to himself, but curiosity got the best of him again. He walked in front of Aegyn to see if she was still alive. He looked at her, and her eyes were closed. He was about to lift her eyelid, or find a way to wake her up, when his horse, who had been so patient during this time whinnied and bolted at a full sprint passed him and off deep into the woods.

Aegyn's eyes popped open, and her talon claw reached out and pinned Voll to the ground. "What the . . .?" Voll squelched as his face pounded the soft dirt.

"Stay still. Play dead," Aegyn warned.

As Voll lay motionless in the dirt, and feeling the weight of her talon on his back, he saw out of the corner of his eye the shadow of another dragon. This dragon flew directly overhead, very low, and followed the path of his horse. The bushes rustled form the wind of the flying dragon.

"No!" Voll shouted. Realizing Rox was in grave danger.

"Shut-up, or you're next!"

"No, no, no, no," Voll whispered as he heard his horse whinny for the last time. Then he heard a loud popping sound of bone breaking then being crushed, followed by some thrashing of vegetation, then silence.

Within seconds, the dragon was circling overhead again. He could hear the wings beating in the air, and as it circled, it descended closer and closer to the ground. The air and bushes vibrated and shook with every beat of her wings. Then it landed on her hind legs in front of them and slowly snaked her long neck to the ground stopping only inches from Voll's face. The dragon sniffed Voll's body a number of times before it stopped. The two dragons stood very still facing each other.

Voll guessed that this was Aegyn's mother as she was larger and her head was twice the size of Aegyn's. He could tell that they were talking to each other, but he could not hear their voices. They were silent for many minutes while he lay pinned under the huge talon. His back ached and he felt a small stream of blood trickle down his ribs caused from the talon wearing into his side. He thought it ironic that the tickle from the blood irritated him more than the pain of the wound.

"Let him go," he finally heard a voice command inside of his head. The talon lifted off of his back, and Voll worked his way to his hands and knees and then arched his back from all fours before working his way to his feet.

The dragon that stood in front of him was enormous, at least twice the size of Aegyn, and was twice as frightening. Her eyes were solid black, and inset deep into the skull, like they had a black bone protruding above her eyes. The scales on her head were sleek and velvety that led to the horns on her head. Her horns circled around backwards from the head and then pointed back to the front almost even with the nose. Her teeth were jagged, sharp, and uneven. Some were missing, while others were brown and rotting. Her breath stunk as a dead carcass smells after being in the sun for many hours. She stood erect on her hind legs and tucked her wings in tight to her back. "Aegyn tells me that you saved her life."

Voll brushed the wet dirt off of his arms. "I helped ease her pain."

"You pulled the slivers that the elves wounded her with out of her back."

"Yes, I did."

"This is the first time that the elves have harmed any one of us."

Voll turned red with anger and walked a few steps toward the dragon, shaking his fist. "Well if you would spread around more of your hatred by attacking the elves like you attack us, they might have harmed you long ago."

The dragon went back to all fours and stretched her neck out so that it was only inches away from Voll's face. "We are of the same nature. The elves have not threatened us until now. Elves and dragons should do no harm to each other."

"But they have, and now you should retaliate."

"No. We will not. We are peaceful unless threatened."

"Oh, and how have we humans threatened you? All we did was reside in the land below your mountains, then you attack us, kill our livestock, ruin our homes, and murder our people."

"No! You occupy our land, you cut our trees, and dirty our rivers, diminish our prey, and shoot your slivers at us when we fly near. Your numbers grow so fast. Soon you will outnumber us so greatly that you will hunt us down for sport. We will not allow this."

Voll turned around and walked away. "There is no sense in this." Voll had only taken a few steps before grabbing his head, pulling his hair, and then spinning back around. "My horse! You ate my horse! Now what am I supposed to do?"

"Why? Are you hungry?" the dragon said smiling.

"No. I am not hungry! I need to get somewhere, and fast!"

Voll and the dragons stood in silence for a few seconds before the mother dragon answered.

"Well, you helped my daughter. So, I may help you."

"Oh, no, I don't want any tricks out of you. I know how this works. I jump on your back, you fly to your lair and then I am a tasty little snack for your little ones like Aegyn."

The dragons laughed. "Tempting as that may be I would not do that. I am a mother of many young dragons that have not yet feasted on human flesh, and they would much enjoy you."

"Oh, that's nice, yummy," Voll said as he spat on the ground. "Besides, you owe me more than a ride. The ride will only repay me for you eating my favorite horse."

"Then what do you expect in return for your gracious deed to my daughter."

"I don't know. Maybe I will call on you later when I have figured that out."

The dragon lifted her head and snorted hard. I will not be in debt to a human!"

"Then roast me now, because I am angry enough right now to not care!"

"Why do you continue to tempt me, little man?"

"Because, I am mad!" he yelled. "And you owe me more than I can demand right now!"

"You have me in a place where I am not comfortable. I do, by honor, need to repay your abnormally kind deeds, yet I am not willing to be in long term debt with you."

"Fine then!" Voll said as he walked to Aegyn, looked into her eyes and apologized, then climbed on her back and reached underneath one of her scales and pulled out a black and bloody rag and threw it on the ground. As it splattered on the ground Aegyn wailed. Voll reached underneath another scale as the blood from the first scale began to flow from underneath.

"I will fry you, little man!" the mother dragon bellowed.

"Do it then. Do it now because I do not enjoy doing this to her."

"Stop! Stop it! I will do what you want, just stop and put everything back!" The mother bellowed.

Voll jumped off of Aegyn's back, grabbed the rag, and shook it off, rung it out and replaced it underneath the scale, then did the same with the other.

"What do you ask?" the dragon asked as she lowered her head in submission.

"I will ask a favor of you later, because, as I said, I do not know what I want yet."

"Then ask anything you wish at any time."

"How?"

"You know my daughter's name. A dragon's name is sacred. As long as you know a dragon's name you have control over that dragon for life."

"For life?"

"Yes, for life, but not for you."

Voll flinched in confusion.

"I will grant you the two favors you requested. The first, to take you wherever your horse would have taken you on this day, and the second I will grant later. That is all. If you request any more in the name of Aegyn, since she was foolish enough to grant you her name, I will kill her, then in my grief, I will seek you out and make sure that you and as many humans as possible die a long, slow and gruesome death. I will roast the skin off of your body, but not so much that it will kill you instantly, but rather that you die a long and agonizing death." The dragon bent her head close to Voll's face, and smiled. "And I will watch every agonizing minute."

"You wouldn't do that."

The dragon took to the air and landed behind Voll. The ground shook as she landed.

"I hate you human! Give me one reason to kill you and other humans, or elves, and I will do it."

"Fine, then we have an agreement. You will take me to the place where my horse would've taken me as repayment for eating my horse, then all I have to do is speak Aegyn's name and she or you will come?"

"Yes."

"Good then. Take me to the elves that injured Aegyn."

The dragon snorted in disgust, and flew away, leaving Voll alone with Aegyn.

Chapter 13

The Goblin Ridge Mountains blocked the setting sun as Naemyn and the elves approached. It had been raining hard for the last few hours and the last moments of the sun shone on the leaves of the trees as the water dripped off the ends. They had been travelling at a blistering pace for eight days since they left their kingdom. Their perilous trip took them through the human territories unscathed, and they had escaped the clutches of a dragon, but were now approaching a new and equally dangerous part of their journey as they approached the goblin territory.

Naemyn had pushed his group harder and harder as they neared their destination. He had to, time was running out, and he was getting impatient to find the Shard and report its whereabouts back to King Jaerick. He also somehow hoped to find Traelyn and the Quarterstar Talisman. He found himself in relatively unfamiliar territory, as he had only been here one time in his life, and that was to bury King Keiyann Krowe 178 years ago.

Even though he was unfamiliar with this area, he still found the general area of the catacombs with ease and was relieved to find that they had also travelled through the goblin territories unscathed as well. He had led the last leg of this expedition on horseback, and halted his small force when he came to a rocky cliff face that was surrounded by tall pine trees.

His scouts led them past a maze of massive evergreen tree trunks that covered the area so tightly that the whole caravan had to find their way around at painstakingly slow pace. The trees created a canopy, and only bare earth lay beneath their feet. Naemyn halted his group and dismounted his horse. As soon as his feet landed on the soft ground, his memory served him well and clued him in that this was indeed the right place.

Facing the cliff, he paused and tried to remember where the exact entrance to the catacombs was located. It was hidden by magic to protect the entrance from intruders. A small stream dribbled over a rocky ledge high above them. Deep green vegetation grew in between the rocks soaking up the water as it splashed around it. The stream continued at the base of the rock face and continued down a gradual hillside slope.

Naemyn smiled, raised his hand, and recited a minor incantation. The water stopped moving and turned into a crack within the rocky ledge, which then split open into a large crevice. The crevice then became a path wide enough to hold two chariots side by side. A few of the elven warriors, who had never been there, gasped at the sight.

"Dismount," Naemyn commanded his warriors.

As they did so, Naemyn ordered his four scouts to secure the perimeter on foot. The elves and their hawks scattered and disappeared into the woods. They were not gone for more than a few seconds when Naemyn heard a rustling in the bushes that was too loud to be caused by the cautious elven scouts.

Five of them came back to the center of the perimeter, swords in hand, but their bodies were covered in blood. He could not make out whether it was the scouts' blood or from somewhere else.

From every direction, creatures came out of the trees. Some had crude, rusty and makeshift swords and shields in their hands while others came out shooting arrows as they ran, but many just charged Naemyn's men with their swords drawn.

Naemyn knew instantly that these were ravages, a Goblinoid creature that banded in small territorial tribes of 10 to 15. Their bodies were covered in stubbly hair, tightly woven within their skin, usually in black and tan broken stripes. They looked like disfigured creatures that stood on their hind legs, their teeth incisors extended out of their mouth and often sharpened as a weapon, which was part of their battle compliment.

They deployed tactics that could only be described as chaotically organized. Initially, they fought on their hind legs as humans until they saw the carnage of battle, but once the battle intensifies, they enter a bloodlust, lose their composure, and drop their weapons to attack on all fours like wolves.

Two ravages caught up with one of the fleeing scouts and tackled him. One of the ravages pushed the elven scout's head into the dirt while fighting off his partner at the same time. They fought amongst each other like vultures over dead prey. The scout squirmed and tried to get up, but the ravage still had his head pinned to the ground. As he concentrated on the elf, the other ravage kicked his partner in the ribs. The ravage let out a loud gasp and fell off the scout.

The scout, realizing the opportunity, began to scramble away, but the standing ravage jumped onto the scout's back before he had a chance to stand up, and then bit him in the neck ripping out the whole right side of his neck. Blood sprayed all over the goblin as the scout screamed in pain. The ravage, not liking the sound of the screaming elf, twisted his neck sharply, snapping it, and then took a bite out of the other side of the neck, severing the bone and cartilage, leaving the head connected only by a thin strip of skin on the back of the neck. This caused the ravages to enter bloodlust, drop their weapons, and attack the elves even harder.

Both ravages and elves locked into close combat, the ravages jumping on their foes from every direction. The elves screamed in terror as their throats were ripped into by the sharp teeth of the ravages, silencing them immediately as blood sprayed upon the ravage, causing it to become even more transfixed in its bloody slaughter.

Jumping to find their next victim, they scattered after the elves, herding them into a tight circle. Some ravages died before they could reach their foe as the archers hit their mark, while others continued in their attack.

A small group of elves formed a circle around Naemyn, as he stood motionless in a concentrated trance. The elves outside of this perimeter also knew the importance of protecting Naemyn, and continued to fight hard with their lives. The battle raged in the still forest morning as they fought, but Naemyn heard nothing of his surroundings as he summoned the elements from the forces of nature.

Just as he was completing his spell, a group of ravages broke through the elven defense and charged through to the circle. Eight ravages battled with six elves, leaving Naemyn now completely unprotected, but it did not matter. Naemyn raised his hands and clapped them together above his head, and as he did so, rocks from the ledge loosened and flew through the air towards their targets. Most of the ravages did not realize what was coming until the boulders struck their bodies or their heads, killing them instantly.

Within seconds, the battle was over. The elves stopped and looked around at the ravages as they lay in the dirt, dead and unmoving. Some elves sat down. Others went to one knee and surveyed the area; shocked that battle had actually ended so abruptly.

"Regroup!" one of the ranking elven warrior commanders yelled. The elves all ran to that commander and formed a tight formation in front of him. After a quick count of the living, and the dead, they broke off to collect the dead into one area, prepared them for the trip home, and put them in one of the chariots.

They regrouped again and this time Naemyn came before them. "This is what we came for. I need three elven warriors to come with me."

A few elves stepped forward. Naemyn pointed to Elsron, Paerglae, and Terson who were the first warriors at the scene when he was almost eaten by the dragon. These three elves were crucial in saving his life, and he wanted elves that he knew would do it again if needed

"I will go in unarmed, but you three may need your weapons in case there are more ravages inside."

Naemyn reached into the saddlebags of one of the pack horses and grabbed four torches, kept one, and tossed the other three to the elven volunteers.

"Let's go," he commanded as he stepped on the stone entryway and led the three elves into the crevasse.

The inner cavern was well lit from the light shining in at the entrance behind them. The walls were a gray polished stone that gave off a soft but unnatural incandescent glow. They had walked as far as they could by natural light, then Naemyn gave the command to light the torches. With this new light, they could see that the cavern was absent of any living creatures. No bugs, spiders, or rats of any kind were evident. The polished stone looked as if someone was maintaining its polish on a regular basis.

They walked forward and the cavern slowly sloped downward until they came to a set of steep stairs leading further down. As Naemyn continued to lead the way down, the air began to become stale and difficult to breath, causing each step to become a slow and laborious task that took their breath away.

Just when they thought they could not take another step, they came to an open landing with three solid walls. The four elves looked at Naemyn in confusion. Naemyn stood motionless for many minutes, studying the three walls. The elves wondered if they were going to have to return and back track, for this dead end obviously had them at an impasse.

"Naemyn?" Elsron asked.

Naemyn raised his hand, but continued to stare at the walls in deep concentration. Many minutes passed and the three other elves were beginning to groan in impatience. Naemyn let out a loud groan in frustration as he realized the obvious.

"Now I remember. This is the illusion chamber to chase away any non-elf, or tomb raider. Put out your torches."

"But, how will we see?" Terson asked, shaking his head in confusion.

"Oh, you'll see," Naemyn said smiling.

They extinguished their torches and immediately felt a small breeze blow through the chamber, followed by a shimmering blue light that ran throughout the small chamber as if a number of ghosts had been just released from their long slumber. Within seconds, the light brightened, and the three walls disappeared revealing that they were on a ledge with three sets of stairs leading down to a vast open cavern. A small stream traveled through the center of the valley, and large stone pillars and buildings were scattered along the streambed, almost looking like a small town. Terson motioned with his head to Elsron and Paerglae to look up, which they did, and witnessed in amazement and wonder the stars of the night sky above them.

"Impossible," Elsron muttered. "We are inside a cavern…"

Naemyn and the elves took a deep breath, for the air had become pure and plenty and the light breeze filled their lungs.

"The spirits have welcomed us. Only in a place of death can you feel so alive." Naemyn quoted from the ancient manuscripts as the elves were still looking to the sky. "This is how our ancestors rest in peace, my friend. Would you want it any different?"

"No," Paerglae said almost inaudibly, still in amazement.

They walked down one side of the stairs to the floor of the valley. The blue light illuminated the cavern, giving them enough light to see. When they stepped off the stairs and onto the valley floor, their step was welcomed by soft grass. Their feet sank slightly into the grassy cushion. Naemyn led them past a row of twenty stone tombs that were nestled by the stream. Some had statues erected of those entombed, standing guard for eternity. As the small group passed the tombs, he pointed out which great hero rested in each tomb.

They walked along the stream for what seemed to be an hour before Naemyn stopped again. He stepped in front of a newly erected tomb. Two statues, one in the likeness of the king, and another of an elven guard on one knee looking at the ground saddened, with his the tip of his sword an inch into the ground, were erected in front of the tomb. The stone was cleaner and newer than the others, and looked to be continuously cleaned. Naemyn stopped in front of this tomb and paused in thought as the stream rustled by.

"I remember this tomb," Naemyn said. "This is the tomb of our great King Keiyann Krowe."

The elves looked at it in wonder, silence and awe as they stood in the presence of all the great kings and heroes of their past. Naemyn turned and faced his three soldiers.

"Now we have to find the Quarterstar Shard," he said as he walked in-between them. He continued up-stream. When he was here for King Keiyann Krowe's funeral, they did not go any further than the tomb in which they laid him. It was a quick ceremony, and then they left without much fanfare or celebration, due to the sadness of losing such a great king.

Naemyn led on, he needed to get moving. Keiyann was a great king, and deserved homage, but it was time to press on. Turning to his left, he went around a series of large boulders. The boulders were stacked atop each other in a way that formed a tight inner cavern. Cautiously, he entered in between the rocks that were clumped together. They walked in between them, turning their bodies sideways and shimmying through them until they widened and formed a maze that led deeper and deeper into the cavern.

They continued walking through the maze going through many twists, turns, and switchbacks. With each switchback, they went deeper and further into the grand tomb. Oddly enough, Naemyn noticed that the deeper they went the brighter the light became, except that the blue light was fading away and was slowly being replaced with a normal white light.

Then he heard footsteps. Footsteps that were around the corner and coming towards him at a casual pace. Naemyn took a few steps back, hid behind a rock corner, and waited. Out of the light and around the corner approached an elf. A slender elf dressed in a blinding white robe. He walked at a slow steady pace, and he looked down as he walked. He did not see Naemyn as he stepped out from behind the rock. Stopping, he gasped in surprise.

The elf fell backwards and turned on his hands and knees scurrying to escape. He went a few feet before he realized that no one was chasing him. Slowly he turned and saw that Naemyn was standing in the same spot where they collided. When he realized he was not in any immediate danger he asked, "Who are you?"

"I am Naemyn, spiritual advisor to the king of elves."

"King Jaerick?" he asked.

"Yes. And I am here on a mission from him."

The elf shook his head and looked confused. "This is unexpected. What is your mission?"

"To retrieve the Quarterstar Shard," he said boldly, testing the knowledge of this elf, knowing that he could not remove the Shard from the catacombs. As a child, he learned of the prophecy and how the Shard could not be removed by anyone but a descendant of the human king.

The elf smiled. "You cannot take the Quarterstar from here. It is sacred, and the Guardian will not let you just take it from him. You should leave now."

"The Guardian?"

The elf sighed. "Yes. Surely you've heard of the Guardian."

"Well, yes, but only tales. I thought they were only tales."

"No," he said, shaking his head, looking at Naemyn as if he were a young child. "He is quite real. Well, as real as he can be for someone as old as he."

"You are not he?"

"Oh no," he laughed. "I am the caretaker of him and of this sacred place. His place is the caretaker and guardian of the shard. King Keiyann Krowe assigned me to the duty of keeping the catacombs cleaned and preserved, and to see that the Guardian's needs are well met. Do you think you can send someone to relieve me? I have been here a long time. I believe I have served my time here diligently, and honorably, but I think it has been long enough."

"Only the king can command this, but I will advise him."

"I thought I would've been relieved after King Keiyann was placed here, but I guess the new king forgot."

"I'm sorry, but we are not here to relieve you. If you would, please take me to the Guardian."

"I cannot do that either."

"Why not?"

"It is too hard to reach him. Even I cannot reach him."

"There must be a way. It is very important that I find him."

"I don't even think he will speak to you."

"He will. He is waiting for me to give me information."

"This is not the way, according to the prophecies," he said with an arrogant smile.

"I don't care. Take me to him."

"As you wish, but you won't be able to reach him."

"Go then."

The elf turned and walked back whence he came. Naemyn and the elves followed.

Chapter 14

Traegon smiled in relief as he looked up to the sky. The drizzling rain had finally stopped, and the sun peeked through the scattered gray clouds, sending rays of light onto the dripping evergreens. The drops of rain shined like tiny crystals before falling to the lush ground. Water dripped or cascaded from everything that stood, grew, or walked. Even his horse's hair was matted from the rain and sweat. Steam rose from the horse's body as it labored through the woods. Water dripped from the edges of his dirt-brown traveling hat, and it wore heavy on his head due to the saturation of the rain, so much so, that it was no longer effective in keeping his head dry. In an effort to dry it off, he took it off of his head and smacked it upon his thigh, knocking off the excess water before returning it sloppily upon his head.

He looked behind him to check on Traelyn. He pulled her behind in the wagon he made specifically for her and this journey. He used a common farm wagon and lined it with soft material for bedding, and made a strong canvas cover to keep her dry. He then attached it to a makeshift yoke, so that he could tow her behind. When he looked at her, he noticed that her face was wet, but it was not from the weather. She was crying.

"Great mother?" Traegon asked.

Traelyn turned away. "I'll come back for you," she whispered, not actually paying any attention to Traegon.

"I'll come back for you," was the last thing Jaerick had told Traelyn on that warm summer afternoon when the elven soldiers came. *So long ago*, she thought to herself, too long ago, for any human to endure.

Jaerick had taken her to the northern coast to spend a few days alone, away from the politics, royal obligations, and the responsibilities delegated to the prince of the elven kingdom. Her stay with the elves was not exactly what she was promised. Since her father was gone, she had only Jaerick to count on to come to her defense, against what seemed like the whole race of elves.

Even though he loved her dearly and showed his affection often, he still did not, nor could not, replace the love and protection her father had always given her. How ironic, she often thought to herself, that when she lived with her father, she wanted more freedom, but now with the elves, she had all the freedom she needed, but it was not satisfying to her, as the freedom the elves gave her was more of neglect than absolute freedom. They let her do her own thing as long as it did not interfere with the common population. As long as she obeyed that rule, they did not care what she did. In fact, it seemed to her that as long as she stayed out of sight, the elves did not have to worry about the problem of having her amongst them.

She remembered the day that Jaerick took her away from the castle like it was yesterday. Jaerick realized she was amiss without her father, and was feeling the isolation that the elves were giving her. Their time spent alone together, since living in the elven kingdom, had become very few and far between. The Prince always had duties to tend to and almost none of it meant spending time with his newly acquired love. Acquired love, a term she used herself to explain how the love felt to her. She felt more of a possession or a pet, than an accepted addition to the elven family as King Keiyann Krowe promised she would be.

She often felt betrayed sometimes as she was left alone amongst a race of people she knew little about. She did not fit into their customs and neither did they treat her as one of them. Sure, they were kind most of the time, but many times she would catch them whispering as she walked by. She knew she was gossip fodder for all, but there was nothing she could do about it.

If the Elven people knew that she was carrying his child, they would really have something to talk about. With all the hassle of being away from her father and living in a new home, she still loved Jaerick deeply, and hoped that their child would bring her closer to the Elven people. She was so excited when Jaerick told her about this trip. He told her that he owed her this trip, and that it was long overdue. To this, she wholeheartedly agreed and waited anxiously for the special trip.

On the day they left, Jaerick met her in the courtyard. She was dressed in simple attire, which he requested her to do so, because they would be getting "dirty," he told her with his most charming ear-to-ear grin. This prospect she liked, because even when she lived with her father, the only time she would get dirty was in her own garden within the castle walls, or when she snuck out through her secret passageway.

She stood beside the horse, her soft brown hair lay on her shoulders, and she smiled as he approached. He walked over to her, and as he did so, picked one of the lilacs from the planter and handed it to her. She smiled and immediately placed it behind her ear. Jaerick moved in close to her, grabbed her hips, brought her slowly to his, and looked into her eyes. "I have missed you so much."

Traelyn smiled, blushed, and looked to the ground. Jaerick put a finger to her chin and lifted her head to meet his gaze. "I am sorry…we will go away, and stay away as long as you wish. I long to be with you. Father has allowed me to leave my duties for as long as I want. "

"Forever?" she smiled.

"Well, no…" He blushed. "Maybe!" he then said as if making a proclamation, opening his almond shaped eyes wide.

She laughed quietly. "I know."

Without another word, they mounted their horses and left the castle. As they did so, the elven people, surprised when they saw the prince alone without guard or any procession, stared and gawked, but mostly did so at the sight of the human princess. They stared and pointed, but said nothing so loud as to be heard. Traelyn held her head high. She did not deserve the discrimination, as she was once a true princess in her own land.

Once they were free of the villages and roaming the uninhabited countryside, they both relaxed and began talking amongst each other as if they were two young lovers without worry. They rode casually, talking and subconsciously enjoying the relaxing creak of the leather saddles and feeling the horses sway between their legs. The horses' heads swayed left to right and their casual gait kept them relaxed, erasing the anxiety of everyday life.

They rode most of the day until they began to smell the wet ocean air. The overcast clouds moved slowly above from the sea, but the air was still warm and pleasant. The salty smell permeated everything, Jaerick breathed deeply as he looked over at Traelyn and smiled. "We are here. We will camp here for the night and go to the beach tomorrow."

They camped within a small grove a few miles south of the ocean. He put up a small tent for her so that she could have some privacy to herself, and still be close to Jaerick when she would want to be with him, on her terms. She found this very touching and endearing, but she needed no privacy away from him, she got enough of that on a daily basis at the castle. She was more than happy to spend every moment with him. She smiled at him as she changed out of her riding clothes and into a more comfortable and loose fitting dress, doing so freely in front of him without hesitation or shyness.

Jaerick smiled at her, excited to be with her alone, and led her outside and unfolded a blanket on the soft ground next to a large rock that he put pillows against so they could lean back, talk, and look to the sky.

As the sun was setting, Jaerick got up and made a small fire a few feet away. That evening they spent every moment together without distraction or interruption. They then stayed up late talking and holding each other under the night sky until the fire died and the stars brightened.

She waited until he was just about to sleep when she pushed him away, stood up, and dropped her dress.

"What are you doing?" he asked.

"What do you think I am doing," she responded feeling vulnerable, as she stood naked before him.

Jaerick got up to his knees, and put his hands on the bump that was beginning to show on her stomach, and then stood up and held her tight as she trembled. He then brought her back down to her blanket and kissed her repeatedly from her neck to her breasts before making love to her and releasing her passion underneath the chilly evening sky.

They cuddled tightly together and listened to each other's heartbeats as they fell asleep. The last thing Traelyn heard before she fell asleep was Jaerick whispering in her ear, telling her goodnight and that he would always be with her because he loved her more than anything.

Jaerick awoke a few hours before sunrise. He stroked a wisp of her hair behind her ear, whispered tenderly into it, and gently woke her up. He had planned the trip with full deliberation and waking in time to be at the beach so that they would be arriving just as the sun was rising. They rode silently in the dark, absorbing the mid sunrise air and crisp salty mist as they rode along. The horses also seemed anxious as they rode over the sloping hills just as the sun was rising over the Stoneridge Mountains to the east. The fog was thick as they heard the waves crashing on the beach before they could see them.

"Come on. Follow me!" Jaerick yelled as he kicked his horse to a full gallop. He charged his horse to the edge of the water. Traelyn smiled, but did not feel as energetic as he and trotted down the hill and along the beach. Noticing that Traelyn lagged behind, Jaerick slowed and let her catch up. When she did, they went back to the edge of the woods, dismounted, and tied the horses to separate trees.

"Walk with me," Jaerick said as he held out his hand to Traelyn. She took his hand and walked along the beach. Jaerick felt her soft hand in his and cherished the moment as they spent the rest of the morning talking.

"I need to sit a while," Traelyn said when their conversation ended, and they walked in silence for a few minutes.

Jaerick stopped. "Look," he said pointing, and then he took off his boots and waded in the rocky tide pool a bit until they came to a large boulder that crested just above the water. "Come on. Take off your shoes," he prompted.

Traelyn did so, lifted her dress away from her ankles, and walked to the rock where Jaerick was sitting with his feet in the water. The water was cold, but refreshing. When she sat down, Jaerick faced her and ran his fingers past her neck and through her brown hair, massaging the back of her head as he did so. "I love you," he told her.

"So you've said," Traelyn said with a smug smile.

"No, I mean it. I know the circumstances haven't been ideal since you came with us."

Traelyn put her hand on his arm, and he took this as a sign to stop. He pulled his hand away and ran it along her arm feeling her soft skin down to her hand.

"Yes, you're right," she said, looking off to the horizon, watching the seagulls fly above the water. "Your people do not like me. I know this. As much as you and your father try to deny it, they feel threatened by me. Especially now that I am carrying your child."

Jaerick waited, thinking how to answer. "They fear a half-breed. They fear that a half human will someday succeed me and rule the elven kingdom."

"I know the politics Jaerick, but this is our child. This child may not live long enough to rule past your reign anyhow. He may only live a human life span. This child may not even be a boy."

"They won't be so patient to find out. The Sorae are very powerful. More powerful than they were intended to be."

"That is exactly what I am trying to tell you. I, we, I should say now, don't belong here. We are not your people, but I love you. And that makes it that much more difficult for me."

Jaerick wiped the tears that began to flow from her cheeks. Traelyn grabbed his wrist. "Don't you love this child?"

"I do. More than you know."

"Then prove it. Stand up to your father and his Sorae."

"I will, when the time is right."

"That is not good enough Jaerick, there isn't much time left. You must tell him that this baby is not a threat, and neither am I. I do not seek to be your queen, should you become king during my lifetime."

"I know this, and father knows this, but the elven people do not share our confidence in the matter."

They were silent for many moments as they watched sea urchins within the tide pool.

"Do what you think is best, Jaerick, when you feel it is right," Traelyn acquiesced. "I trust you. And I know you have my best interest at heart."

"I do."

"I just wish father was here to help me through this."

"I know," he said, barely louder than a whisper, "I also believe that he will return."

"Well, I am not so sure, and neither are your prophets. They are so reluctant to talk to me at all."

"It will get better, I promise."

"So you've said many times, and I have yet to see it."

They sat on the rock a little while longer before wading back to the beach. They were just about back to their horses when a group of elven soldiers on horseback charged down the hill and onto the beach where Jaerick and Traelyn were standing.

"Prince Jaerick!" one of the five soldiers yelled as they approached.

Jaerick moved in front of Traelyn, blocking their approach with both hands in the air.

"Prince Jaerick!" Naemyn, dressed in his gray Sorae cloak, called out as he moved his horse in front of the soldiers.

"Naemyn? What is wrong?" Jaerick asked.

"Your father has summoned you to return. There is a revolt back at the castle. The people have demanded that Traelyn returns to her human home."

"That cannot happen. She has no home anymore. The goblins have destroyed it."

"I know, my prince, but, –"

"Have they entered the castle?" Jaerick interrupted.

"Yes. In fact, it started within the castle walls, with the lesser nobles, and their servants. It seems to have been planned and executed from within."

"Probably the Sorae."

Naemyn's face turned red, and he jumped off his horse and made a direct path to Jaerick.

"You should know me better than that, my friend," he said only inches from Jaerick's face, his face turning red with rage.

"Is anyone hurt?" Jaerick asked, feeling a little ashamed that he had offended his lifelong friend and consultant.

"No. They went straight to Traelyn's bed chambers and destroyed everything within."

Traelyn gasped and covered her face.

"But, King Keiyann put an immediate stop to it. He was able to calm them down enough to talk reasonably to them. They wish her to leave and they don't care where she goes, just as long as she is never seen again. So to appease them he sent me to retrieve you both."

Jaerick, still standing in front of Traelyn, took her hand and looked at Naemyn. "She is not going back. I do not know what they will do to her. If they are that mad, how do I know that they don't intend to kill her?"

"They won't, because your father already has a plan. She is not going back to the castle, but you are."

"Where will she go?"

"I will take her someplace safe until things calm down enough to where you can see her again."

"But I need to stay with her," Jaerick said, looking at her eyes and squeezing her hand. She returned his gaze with a worried, concerned look.

"Your father demands that you return to help him assure the people that both of you are in agreement. Once everything is back to normal we can work out away to where Traelyn can return."

Jaerick stood calm and looked past Naemyn and thought for a few seconds before turning around to Traelyn. "I have to fix this."

Traelyn nodded her head quickly, unsure of the situation.

"This may be a good thing. It now brings it all out in the open. I will fix it, just like we talked about," Jaerick concluded.

"Ok, but be careful."

"I will."

Jaerick went to the horses, untied Traelyn's horse, and brought it to her. He then took her by the waist and held her while looking into her eyes. "Everything will be alright," he said then pulled her close and held her head to his chest.

They held each other for a few moments as a light breeze shook the trees and the ocean crashed upon the beach.

"My Prince, –" Naemyn pressed.

Jaerick released Traelyn, kissed her, and then helped her up on her horse. He walked her horse over to Naemyn.

"We will take care of her."

"Where will you take her?"

"For her safety we cannot tell you. King Keiyann knows and he will tell you when you get there."

"Then go," he said to Naemyn and then reached for Traelyn's hand. Traelyn took Jaerick's hand and tried to force a smile.

"I'll come back for you," Jaerick said. "I promise."

"Ok," Traelyn said.

"Let's go!" Naemyn shouted to his soldiers as he yanked his horse around and ran back up the hill with Traelyn surrounded by the four soldiers. Jaerick watched the woman he loved and his best friend ride away. He wondered how he was going to fix this so that he would see her again. At this point, he no longer cared about being an heir to the throne. He just wanted to be with Traelyn. When they were out of sight, he climbed onto his horse and headed back to the castle, nudging the horse to run as fast as it could.

"I see the camp," Traegon announced to Traelyn, bringing her out of her misery.

"Fine, let's hurry up then. I need some rest."

"We will be with father in less than an hour."

Traelyn nodded, but could hardly care. The end was near and she only wished it could be sooner than later.

Chapter 15

The caretaker led Naemyn and the elves deeper into the cavernous portion of the catacombs. The air once again became stale, musty, and thick, making it hard to breath. He charged ahead while Naemyn and the elves labored in their breathing and struggled to keep up. As they walked farther down the tunnel they saw holes dug into the outer walls of the hallways about two feet high, three feet deep, and five feet long. There were three columns forming aisles. In these holes were the bones of elven warriors, valiant heroes, and even some lesser nobles.

The tombs within this area of the catacombs were not important enough to have their resting place marked, but still were fortunate enough to have been laid to rest within the sacred burial grounds with the kings, princes, princesses, and prophets, due to their heroic deeds or sacrifices. Most of the elves placed in these catacombs were from a time before they migrated north from this area near the Wayerman Crags. They had been dealt deadly attacks at the hands of the goblin tribes, forcing them to construct these catacombs, hiding their dead from any desecration from the goblin hordes.

Naemyn felt humbled as he walked past the remains of these ancient heroes. Among these great warriors were the ones who had sacrificed themselves in the defense of the land near the catacombs before their northern migration. These elves fell in those terrible battles that nearly broke the spirit of the elven people. Even though they were chased out by the goblin hordes, they still held their head high enough to find a few heroes from the fallen and buried them here. Naemyn and his elves lowered their heads and humbly walked passed their fallen ancestors.

After walking past countless tombs, they began to smell the fresh air moving through the cavernous home of the dead once again. A cool breeze flowed up the tunnel towards them. Their breathing, like earlier, had become easier, but this time there was moisture in the air. The breeze coming towards them was cool and wet. The caretaker put his hood over his head and pressed on. The sound of a rushing river became louder and more prominent with each step they took.

A few moments later, they came to a clearing where a wide rushing river raged before them. The noise was so loud, that if they were to talk, they would have had to yell in order to be heard. The five elves stopped at the edge of the river, where Naemyn and the three soldiers looked around them and noticed that they were underneath the stars of the night sky as before.

On the other side of the river, floating above the water was a small island where a gray haired, wrinkled elf stood in the center. He stood wearing a white cloak, almost statuesque, standing before a tall stone table reading a large book. Directly above him and high in the sky was a bright star shining light upon the elf and the contents of the island. The only items on the island were a table, single chair in the far corner, and bookshelves with volumes upon volumes of books. The caretaker pointed to the elf.

"There is the Guardian. Now you see why he cannot be visited. Even I cannot reach him," he said, nearly yelling into Naemyn's ear to be heard over the rushing river.

Naemyn looked at the caretaker. "How does he survive?"

"The Quarterstar of course."

"He has the Quarterstar? We have found it?"

"Oh yes, you have found it, that is what he is the guardian of."

"How can we retrieve it?"

"You will not be leaving here with the Quarterstar Shard."

"Watch us. We will not leave without it," Naemyn said feeling overwhelmed with having the shard so near. The power consumed his reason, and passion now ruled his whole being. The only thing that mattered to him now, was to steal the shard for himself.

He pushed passed the caretaker and stopped at the bank of the river and pulled out a pouch, withdrew a few small items and began an incantation. Within a few moments, the river slowed to almost a crawl, much like the water had turned into thick mud rolling down a gentle slope. Naemyn stood still in a concentrated trance, ordered Terson to enter the river until he was close enough to the floating island to throw a rope, hook upon it, and pull himself up.

As commanded, Terson walked toward the edge of the river, and put one foot in the river. When he felt that the water was indeed calm, he took a few cautious steps and began to run and hop in and out of the thigh deep water. He did this for a few moments, nearing the island, but then the water stiffened and turned to stone, locking Terson's legs within the now solid river. He squirmed to free himself. "Naemyn!" he yelled. What did you do?"

Naemyn came out of his trance as Elsron jumped onto the solid river and ran toward his trapped comrade.

"What are you doing?" Naemyn yelled at the caretaker, realizing the change in his spell.

The caretaker looked at Naemyn almost in as much shock as he. "I didn't do it. I told you the Guardian couldn't be reached."

"Free him!"

Elsron reached Terson and tried pulling him out of his entrapment, but could do nothing but hurt him by stretching his arms hopelessly.

Naemyn reached into a pouch underneath his cloak, withdrew a couple small items, and rubbed them in his hands. When the items were nothing but dust, he threw it on top of the solid river. The solid stone river began to form hundreds of small cracks where the dust touched it, and spread outwards finding its way to the trapped elf. The cracks moved as if they were alive and moving towards Terson with a purpose, but as the cracks reached the elf, they suddenly changed. They had changed from hundreds of small cracks designed to free the elf, to hundreds of poisonous vipers.

Naemyn saw the manifestation of his spell and looked in horror as the vipers attacked the two elves. First, they surrounded the trapped elf and covered his exposed body striking his face and torso. The other elf tried to run, but the vipers, with unnatural speed, slithered up his legs striking him until he fell, where the remaining snakes attacked his whole body, striking him countless times. He screamed as they covered his body from head to toe making it impossible to see anything but slithering snakes.

Once the two elves were dead, the vipers left their bodies and coiled upon the ground motionless, satisfied with their work. As the dead elves bled from their small bite wounds, the blood dripped onto the solid river. Naemyn grabbed the caretaker and spun him around, facing him.

"How can you do this?"

"I told you. I did not do this."

"Look!" Paerglae yelled.

Naemyn looked at Paerglae and saw him pointing toward the fallen elves where the blood was dripping onto the stone river, and where it did so, the river began to break and crumble and return to water. First, the snakes fell in, and then the bodies of the elves sank into the water and floated downstream with the remaining untransformed chunks of solid river floating downriver like logs of wood.

The river now flowed naturally, and a light breeze returned as the water once again moved the stale air. Naemyn had never seen anything like this. Naemyn shook his head, dejected at the futility of his own magic.

"Naemyn," a voice from above the returning sound of the river called out.

Naemyn looked up and saw that it was the Guardian speaking. He was standing on the edge of the floating island.

"Did you do this?" Naemyn yelled to him.

"No. I did not. You did," the Guardian answered, and as he spoke, the sound of the river died away. The river still raged on, but all sound was removed, making his voice crystal clear, enhanced now by the empty cavern.

"How? I didn't cause these elves to die."

"This sacred burial ground is ruled by the Kronn. Even you must know of the Kronn."

"Of course I do, but I have never witnessed any of its existence like I have seen today."

The Guardian paced over to an ancient textbook and picked it up. "That does not surprise me. Many do not understand its true power and meaning. What is known about the Kronn was first written in this book, and then placed in these catacombs. After that, its knowledge was only passed down through the generations through word of mouth, and I'm sure it has been mistranslated many times for many years."

"Then it is more than a magical presence of this world?"

"Oh yes, it is so much more, my very young seer prophet. The Kronn is what secures this realm to this existence. Without the Kronn, the world would die out and fade away from existence. The Kronn is the balance of life. It knows your heart, your past, present, and future. It takes your inner conflicts and desires and intensifies them. It uses the magic from the realm, the soil and inner core, if you will, and combines it with your heart and inner prophecy. I did not kill your soldiers, rather it was your Kronn that killed your soldiers."

"No," Naemyn said quietly. "I could not have. I'm not here to hurt anyone. I just want the Quarterstar Shard."

"Precisely, greed is in your heart, you may not realize it, but your heart will reveal your true intentions to the Kronn, and Kronn will intensify and expose those intentions. The Kronn, protecting the Quarterstar, used the Kronn deep inside your very being to defend itself, and in this environment, which is the home of Kronn, that power is emphasized tenfold, so what is in your heart becomes apparent.

"It is not greed that I seek the Quarterstar."

"Is that so? Let me ask you this Naemyn. Have you ever used your Kronn to heal?"

"Never, but I don't think I have ever had the chance."

"Have you ever been able to foretell the near future?"

"Yes, but only unfortunate events."

"Have you ever been able to use that knowledge and turn events around to a good or positive outcome?"

"Never, they always pass as I see them, no matter what action I take. And I have tried to change the events almost every time."

"You see Naemyn, it is evident that the dark Kronn that resides in your heart has a hold of you and is stronger than your good Kronn. Your good Kronn is there, as in all of us, but sometimes the dark Kronn, once released, becomes more powerful, and once it takes hold, it is impossible to relinquish. You will always fight your dark Kronn, and your dark Kronn will always win."

"I do not believe you. I did not come here with intentions less than honorable to my king."

"Naemyn, do not try to misguide us. We know that King Jaerick did not send you here to retrieve the Quarterstar. You and I both know that King Jaerick only sent you here to assure that the Quarterstar Shard is here and safe. In addition, I can assure you that it is here, because I am its guardian. If it was not here, well, neither would I be. I also know that your intentions to yourself are not fully clear.

"Earlier you said that you do not seek the Quarterstar out of greed. I sense that is true, or at least true, as you believe it. The question to ask yourself is 'why' do you seek to remove the Quarterstar Shard, when your king has given you explicit instructions not to do so? You know the prophecies. You know that King Jaerick cannot join the shard with the talisman. Quite simply, Naemyn, your motives are not pure."

The Guardian walked to the center of the island and lifted a transparent dome and pulled out a small, flat, jagged stone, rectangular in shape, and no larger than a finger, and held it up. "It is safe Naemyn. It is here and has been here since it fell to this earth at this most sacred spot. It must and will stay here for now. Go and tell your king what you were originally mandated. Tell him that you know that it is here, and tell him not to worry about the Shard, as it is not his concern. Tell him, no matter how disturbing his dreams, that there is nothing he can do to change his future. Naemyn, your mission is complete. Go back to your king and report your findings."

Naemyn stood dumbfounded, unsure of the meaning of the guardian's words. It all seemed so prophetic, so mysterious, and revealing at the same time. His words struck a nerve deep inside. He knew the Guardian's words were true, even if he denied it to himself. He did have motives outside of his friend and king's mandate. He spoke true about his deep confusion of his growing Kronn, which he had been struggling with all of his life. Naemyn stared at the Guardian in bewilderment and defiance. Then spoke again. "I cannot leave yet, I think the Shard will better serve the elven kingdom if I take it with us. I mean no harm to you or anyone."

"No, Naemyn this cannot be. The Shard cannot leave here without the Talisman. Don't you know the prophecies, spiritual advisor to the king?" the Guardian said condescendingly, growing tired of Naemyn's defiance.

"I know them all. At least as they were passed down to me"

"Tell me what you know of the prophecy of the first human king."

Naemyn fidgeted some, knowing his true intentions were being tested. "A period of peace will be ushered in by the sons of the first human king."

The Guardian thought about the answer Naemyn gave before answering himself. "Close enough. Interesting how these prophecies do change after time. Do you know that the true prophecy states that the Shard cannot leave this sacred place without being attached to the Talisman?"

"No."

Then, do you know that according to the true prophecy that only a descendant of the first human king may put the Shard and the Talisman together?"

"No. I mean yes…but I choose not to follow that path."

"A path as commanded by you has no bearing here. Regardless, do you have the Talisman?"

"No."

"Are you a descendant of the first human king?"

"No!" Naemyn answered in frustration. His face turned red and both hands were clenched so tight that his arms went numb. "Then what do I do?"

"I have told you already. Do as I commanded of you. Return and report to your king that the Shard is safe with me, which will be sufficient knowledge for your king."

Naemyn could not leave so soon. He was finally willing to admit that he could not retrieve the Shard. He had learned a hard lesson about that, so he planned not to press the issue. Now he wanted knowledge. He wanted knowledge that he could use to further his cause to elevate the elven kingdom to power by destroying the humans.

"Tell me. Will I find the Talisman?"

The Guardian smiled from the corner of his mouth. "Interesting question. That is a forked path. One path you will, and the other you will not. The one where you find, it will lead to the loss of many elven lives at your hand. The other will not, but the future of that path is uncertain."

"How will the Talisman and Shard be joined?"

"By a double sacrifice which will take the elven king on a westward journey. Open your eyes," the Guardian said as he pointed to the brightest star in the sky, and as he did so, they saw the veil of illusion broken down. The sky and stars disappeared to reveal the cavernous ceiling. Where the star had been was now replaced with a hole where the natural light shone through.

"A descendant of the human king will fall through this hole. He will have the Talisman and he will join it, but first the sacrifice must be made."

"What sacrifice?"

"The sacrifice of love. The love of a father protecting his son."

"Just as the Kronn forbade you to cross this river, so too will the Kronn allow the true descendant of the first human king to join the Talisman and Shard."

"I am not sure I understand, what do you mean about sending the king on a westward journey?"

"Go home Naemyn." The Guardian said in a hushed whisper, "and let destiny and the Kronn decide this fate, for you have no control of any of it, even though you will play a tremendous part in this prophecy. As far as your king goes, know that in order for you to change the prophecy to the way you wish, both events must happen, maybe not simultaneously, but they must transpire upon your hand."

"You are using doublespeak, you say one thing that I have no control and then tell me I have total control. How can this be?"

"Welcome to the realm of changing prophecies. You can always change fate, with your actions, with cause and effect, but no matter what you do, the humans will always need to be part of the prophecy to help you in your cause."

"This is not right. I will not allow humans to be in charge of our fate. Elves must be in charge of elven fate, and I intend to alter this destiny!" Naemyn shouted.

This was wrong on so many levels. Humans cannot be in charge of elven destiny. He refused to accept this notion. If only the Val elves did not hold so much power and control over the Sor elves, and if the Sor elves were not so passive as to let the Val Elves control their natural being, none of this would be happening. Naemyn wanted to only fix what the Val elves have destroyed and return the elven sanctity back to the ancient ways of the Sor Elves.

"Val Eahea has already set the path in motion," the Guardian shook his head. "Go to your king, Naemyn, and let him continue the course of events."

"I will not leave without knowing how I can alter this prophecy to make the elven kingdom powerful enough to resist the human prophecy."

The Guardian stood motionless for many minutes looking directly into Naemyn's soul.

"I have told you all, but I can tell how your king will begin his westward journey."

"Tell me! I must know," Naemyn said with a devious smile of relief, amazed that he found a fissure in the Guardian's stern prediction of elven demise.

"Betray your king. Take him as far west as you can, and leave him. Do not kill him, but only take him far away from any elves and humans and leave him there. If you do this, it will set forth a new awakening of the elven legend. However, you must understand that under no circumstances should the king ever have the talisman and the shard in his possession. If these things are done, the human sacrifice will fall into your hands, but what I believe you are most interested in is that after this is done, you will command the Sorae and the Agin-Sorae as one and will have the upper hand over the Val elves. If this is what you intend, then I cannot stop you. Once your decision is made, events will begin to unfold on your trip home. But be warned, there are severe personal consequences to you on this path." The Guardian paused. "Naemyn, listen carefully. If you choose this path, you may succeed with what you seek, but I assure you, it will mean an unwanted end to all you are!"

Naemyn shook his head. Betray his lifelong friend, and catapult the elven race to a higher glory as the Sorae has commanded him to do since he was a child. This mandate left Naemyn's stomach uneasy with both fear and excitement. He was so excited that he had found a chink in the armor that he did not pay attention to the Guardian's warning. The only thing that mattered was that he had finally found an answer he could work with. Not once did he consider the Guardian's intentions.

"Then I will find the talisman and work to join them for myself," Naemyn muttered out loud.

"It is time to go," Paerglae said grabbing Naemyn's cloak.

Naemyn looked at Paerglae with shock, as he just realized that he, as well, had just witnessed this whole conversation. There were many truths revealed that no one could know except for himself. Truths about the mission change, truths about Naemyn's heart, truths about Naemyn's true intentions. He knew that Paerglae, one of the king's best warriors, would report to his king in absolute honesty.

"I'm not finished. What severe consequences..." Naemyn started, now realizing many things all at once. All of the information and worry of his plans rushed through his head as a flash flood after a large rainstorm. As Naemyn spoke, the noise from the river returned and it was so loud that he could not hear anything but the river. Naemyn stood deep in thought as the mist sprayed upon his face.

Chapter 16

Aegyn descended, dropping a hundred feet in two seconds. Voll screamed in terror. His fingers gripped the scales of Aegyn's back, and no matter how tight he held on to her, or which scale he grabbed, he could not feel secure. His stomach flipped and turned, and with every movement, he felt that he would fall off of her back. Aegyn spread out her wings gracefully and turned in a slow arc so that Voll could see below, which only caused him to scream aloud again.

"Stop that noise," Aegyn snickered, "or the elves will hear you. Do you see them yet?"

"I can't see anything, my eyes are closed."

"I thought you were a brave warrior."

"I have never been this high before."

"Open your eyes or you'll miss the view."

"I don't care!" he yelled. "Dragons have better eyesight than humans, why can't you find them?"

"If you don't open your eyes, then I will fly upside down and drop you!"

Voll was silent before answering. "You can't do that."

"Not only can I do it, but I will do it. I will drop you to the earth, end our deal, and no one will know the difference."

Voll opened his eyes. He was getting angry with Aegyn and her games. If he was going to die, he didn't want to die watching her fly away as he fell, but rather with his sword in her throat at the same moment that she roasts him to his death.

"Ok, ok, they're open!" but before he could say another word he looked down and saw the entire valley below and saw how open and vast it was all the way up to the Goblin Ridge Mountains just east of them. It was an incredible sight, and he would have enjoyed it even more if he did not feel so nauseated from the height.

"Better?" Aegyn asked.

"No!" Voll snapped. Half lying.

"The elves are at the base of the Goblin Ridge Mountains," she continued. "They won't see us because we are flying so high, but soon we will have to swoop in."

"Swoop in?" Voll asked.

"Yes or however you choose to descend. What is your plan?"

"Land in the forest near them, I need to find out what they are up to."

Aegyn leveled her body and slowly flapped her wings, descending.

Voll began to think of his strategy. He did not expect to be scouting these elves from the back of a dragon. What could he really expect to find out? The elves were in a hurry, but why? His dilemma was to find out why, and without kidnapping an elf, how would he really find out?

"I have a better idea," Voll said just as he realized he could share his fear of heights, "Do you think you can snatch an elf in mid-flight? You know, like a hawk would snatch a field mouse?"

Aegyn laughed. "You should know better than to ask that. I can snatch a crow off of a scarecrow in a farmer's field without disturbing a single straw."

"But can you do it before they pelt you with arrows again?"

"Yes I can. We'll wait until they start spreading out, and we'll just snatch up the poor fellow taking up the rear."

"Then do it."

"Very well then, relax, and enjoy your flight."

Aegyn flew south of the elves, still skirting the edge of the Goblin Ridge Mountains and made a sharp turn west, leaving the mountains behind. As they did so, Voll could see the Rae-om Sea farther south some sixty miles away. He was astonished that he could see so far from this height. It made him feel small, and at the same time realize the perspective of the realm the dragons have. They must know so much, just from simply flying the skies. How powerful a race would be if they could control the dragons to carry them, if for no purpose other than scouting?

Aegyn leveled her flying pattern and flapped her wings only to keep a steady altitude, gliding gently in the breeze. Voll watched the sun as it began to dip below the horizon in front of them.

"It is time," Aegyn said as she turned and began to increase her speed while slowly descending. Within minutes, they were nearing the elven caravan. They had been on the move and were making haste and not bothering to stop due to the coming nightfall.

Aegyn flew directly over the caravan as they traveled single-file up the rocky road. She spotted her victim and swooped down to snatch the last elf in line. He rode on horseback, and strayed behind alone, protecting the rear flank. Just as Aegyn was about to grab him off of his horse, she and Voll came under the attack of four Hook-feather hawks. They pecked at the dragon's head knocking her off course and distracting her enough to where she snatched her talons for the elf, but only came up with air.

Voll also had his hands full of hawks, swatting at them only to have them peck and claw his arms and forehead. Voll managed to grab a hawk by the wing, but the hawk violently fluttered and tried to bite Voll making him unsure of his grip on the dragons back. He attempted to smash the hawk's head onto Aegyn's hard scales, but Aegyn turned sideways at that moment in her attempt to escape her attacks. Voll lost his balance and fell twenty feet to the ground hitting the hard ground, knocking him unconscious.

Realizing she had lost her rider, she flew straight up, reaching the apex, and then turned upside down and did a spinning barrel dive back down. As she spun in a downward spiral, she sent a blast of fire near where Voll lay unmoving. The elves scattered to avoid the blast of fire, all of them escaping the fire, but a few of them only escaped just as the fire licked their horses' tails.

Aegyn landed in-between Voll and the elves protecting him from the elves. As soon as she landed, all the elves turned around and spread out, forming a half circle in front of her. All of them had their arrows nocked and ready to turn loose. Naemyn stepped forward from behind the elves that were eagerly awaiting his command. When Naemyn recognized this dragon as the same dragon that terrorized him a few days before, he stopped.

"So we meet again," he said under his breath. "Will the surprises on this trip never end?"

Aegyn lowered her neck to Naemyn's eye level and growled, barring her sharp, jagged teeth. She then took two steps to her left, revealing Voll.

Naemyn smiled in relief. "Lower your bows!" he commanded. "The dragon has no quarrel with us. It has its prey, and it looks as if it has caught a human scout. Amazing what is crawling around in these woods. Back away. Slowly and cautiously mount your horses, and let's get away from this vile beast!"

With that command, the elves mounted their horses and rode away, leaving Aegyn alone with Voll.

"Vile beast," Aegyn snorted as she stretched her neck out and nudged Voll's torso with her nose turning him on his side. At first, he did not move, but then he groaned and turned over on his back grabbing his head. When he opened his eyes, he saw Aegyn's nose and teeth only inches from his face. Startled, he rolled away and scrambled on his hands and knees crawling off of the road and behind a tree.

Aegyn watched as he scrambled away only to watch him realize a few moments later where he was and who the dragon was. Voll sat up and leaned against the tree looking at her while massaging his head. "What happened?" he asked.

"You fell."

"What?"

"The hawks attacked me, distracted us both, and you fell. Don't you remember?" Aegyn said.

Voll sat and stared blankly at the dragon and collected his thoughts. His memory began to come back to him, but only a few seconds at a time, but then he began to remember bigger chunks, until finally, he remembered where he was and what his mission was.

"Ok, now what?" he asked.

"Well, same strategy. While you were out, I made them think that you were my prey and that I was protecting my next meal."

"How convenient. What stopped you from eating me then?" Voll said as he stood up, rubbed his neck, and walked back to Aegyn to climb on her back.

"I don't know, I did consider it though. I think the truth of the matter is that I am actually having a good time."

"Well let me on, and let's get it over with, because, unlike you, *I* am NOT having a good time."

"No. Not on my back this time," she said as she jerked her leg away from him.

"What do you mean?"

"Well, since they already think that you're my prey, I will have to carry you with my talon, make a fly by to assure them that I am not after them, then when they don't suspect anything more, I will snatch one of them and fly away so that you can question him."

"You are going to carry me as if I was your prey?"

Aegyn let out a deep rumbling growl as if she was pleased with herself. Voll turned his head, paused, and shook off the feeling that the dragon was actually purring like a kitten.

"This is more than I bargained for," he said, almost in a whine.

Aegyn lifted her left wing and leg allowing him to walk underneath her.

He began to walk toward her, but then stopped. "No. I will not do this. In fact, just take me back to my unit. I think I have gathered enough –" Voll stopped in mid sentence when Aegyn jumped up in flight, grabbed Voll with her left Talon, and was up in flight before he could protest any further.

Voll cursed as he felt the wind from her flapping wings push him downward as they ascended. Aegyn's grip was so tight that he knew he would not fall, but his shoulders hurt from her talons pinching him underneath his arms.

"Sorry Voll," Aegyn apologized. "You may be done with these elves, but I have a score to settle still. 'Vile beast,' he says, and I can still feel the pain from those arrows you pulled out."

"What? I hate dragons!" Voll yelled as Aegyn continued to beat her wings and rise higher and higher into the sky.

"No, you don't. In fact, I can tell you are beginning to grow very fond of me."

Voll looked down and saw that the ground was becoming increasingly smaller and smaller with each beat of her wings. Once again, he could see the tops of the trees below and the Dragon Cross Mountains far away to the west. He still had not become entirely comfortable travelling on the dragon's back, and now he was dangling from her talon with no control of his situation at all. Sensing the only thing he could control, he closed his eyes, but just before he crimped them shut, he saw the road that the elves were on and could feel Aegyn head straight for them.

She made her first pass and then he felt his stomach jump into his throat caused by Aegyn's sudden drop in elevation after she banked and turned back towards them. She picked up speed as she stretched out her neck and pointed her nose downward. With her wings outstretched and fixed, she honed in on the elves. Voll could not handle the speed and the rate of drop and lost consciousness.

He was awoken by a scream. He looked to his right and saw an elven warrior within the grasp of Aegyn's other talon. "Shut up you fool!" Voll yelled.

"I don't want to die like this! I don't want to be fed to young dragons!" he kept yelling repeatedly.

"Shut up!" Voll yelled at him again. "What happened to the brave and mighty elven warrior you're supposed to be?"

The elf finally stopped his yelling, looked over to Voll and spoke. "We aren't after the dragons, why are we being tormented?"

"You pelted this dragon with arrows," Voll countered.

"In self defense. And who are you, human?"

"Her prey."

"Why?"

"Don't you know? Dragons love human flesh."

"Then why is she getting her revenge on you if she wants us so badly?"

"No idea. Maybe she wants a good meal with her revenge. All I know is that I was in the woods hunting a deer when she snatched me. Kind of ironic, the hunter becomes the hunted."

"You're no hunter. You're the scout that has been following us since before the dragon attack."

Voll paused and was shocked that they have known the whole time he has been following them. "You knew. How?"

The elf wiggled attempting to free himself of Aegyn's grip. After a few moments of some painful contorted twists, he gave up and gasped. "We don't care about one human scout. We are not here for anything that has to do with you. We just want to get home."

"Home? Is that where you were going in such a hurry?"

"Yes. Where else would we be going? We completed our quick and so called simple mission and now we just need to report back to our king."

"Quick and simple?"

"Shut up human. I have told you too much already. But it doesn't matter, because you are going to die too."

"No, I'm not. Aegyn, put us down, I want to ride on top now."

"What do I do with your flying companion?"

"I don't care, let him go."

"Ok" She said as she released the elf, dropping him to fall to his death. Voll watched the elf flail his arms and legs attempting to grab the empty air.

"That's not exactly what I meant Aegyn, and you know it," Voll said as the elf disappeared in the trees below. He heard the elf scream all the way down as he fell into the evergreens breaking branches before slamming into the ground.

"Isn't he your enemy?"

"He was, but I don't need to kill every elf I see."

"Too bad, because I am pretty happy with myself."

"Fine, can you please land and let me on your back so you can take me back to my unit."

"If you wish."

"I do."

Aegyn released him, letting him freefall towards the ground, but she dropped her nose and guided gently underneath him, securing him safely on her back.

"What is wrong with you? I have had enough of this!" he yelled at her when he caught his breath.

They didn't say another word as she flew in the dark night until they were nearing Voll's unit.

"Just drop me…no set me down below that ridge before the unit. The last thing I need is my unit putting arrows into you, leaving me to pull them out again."

Aegyn descended and glided to a soft landing near a draw where a small winter stream began to show its first water of the season. Voll dismounted and patted Aegyn on the neck. "One deed complete."

"Yes. Just call when you are ready for the next favor." Aegyn stood up on her hindquarters, spread her wings, and showed her teeth. "But don't take too long, I don't like being indebted, especially to a human," she said and then jumped up and flew south, away from Voll, the humans and the elves.

Chapter 17

King Jaerick stood on top of the tallest tower that looked over the entire kingdom. The tower was so tall that on a clear day he could see for miles. To the north, he could see the Valerian Sea, and to the southeast, he could see the small calm waters of Lake Aalararae.

The vegetation smelled wet and fresh from the recent intermittent rains. However, the heavy rain clouds rolling in from the south had made Jaerick's worries feel more foreboding than normal. He could not put his finger on why, but his intuition told him that something was wrong. His son, Greynim, and Naemyn were both overdue. He had made Greynim the commander of the elven cavalry, who had taken two squads with him on a routine scouting patrol. These routine patrols were necessary due to the periodic human raids on outlying elven villages. Greynim did not always go on these patrols, but he did go on them more frequently than Jaerick was comfortable with, especially with the intensity of his nightmares of late. He was still having the recurring dream of Traelyn's betrayal and Greynim's demise, and with each dream, he felt it was more realistic, and more prophetic than a nightmare.

As he watched the dark clouds roll in, he wondered if he had actually put events into motion that would make the dreams a reality. Now, because of the dreams, he felt renewed feelings for Traelyn. Feelings that he had not felt since before she left.

"It wasn't my choice," he muttered under his breath, and then cursed his father.

"There is nothing you can do, Jaerick," King Keiyann had told him from his council chambers so many years ago. "We have to let her go."

"But I told her I would come for her."

"Jaerick, this is just as hard on me as it is for you. I promised her father to make sure that she would be safe, and it is because of that promise that I am sending her away."

"But you're the king, you can proclaim her life equal to an elf and no one can harm her."

"It is not that simple. Many, mostly the Sor elves that believe in keeping the elven race pure, do not follow or trust the prophecies of Val Eahea. They struggle with the fact that we Val elves are impure and do not belong here. Therefore, they strongly believe that the disgusting, impure humans will bring down the elven kingdom. They will do anything to refuse the humans a chance to seize even the smallest foothold, even though prophecy says that we must first endure the humans before we prosper."

"Then they should realize that we do this only so that we will rise again stronger than ever."

"Yes, but the Sorae will always remind us that there are too many forks that lead to and away from that path."

"Father, then take charge of the path you believe to be right, and make it happen."

Keiyann shook his head. "To do this will bring about Traelyn's death and you have to realize this."

"No, I refuse to believe that. I will protect her."

"How? You cannot watch her every minute of her life."

"Then I will go with her to wherever you send her."

"No! I will not allow that."

"You can't stop me from being with the one that I love!" Jaerick said clenching his fists.

"You're right. I cannot stop you, but you won't go, because if you do, not only will you lose everything, but both of you will be hunted down and killed by those who want to thwart the prophecy, fearing that a half breed baby will be born."

"She is already pregnant with my child."

Keiyann paused, his face already flush with anger from having to confront his son, turned bright red. "Who else knows?"

"You and I are the only ones who now know."

"Then we must not tell anyone else, and more than ever, she must never return."

"*We* will never return," Jaerick said taking a few steps backward to the door."

"No son. You have to realize that If you leave, both of you will die."

"I have to take that chance. I love her too much."

"You'll never find her," he said waiting for his words to sink in.

Jaerick froze in his steps then walked back to his father and pushed his father's shoulders so hard that Keiyann was forced to take a step back in order not to fall.

"You must tell me where she is!"

"To save your life and hers, I will not."

"Father! You cannot withhold this information all of your life."

"I will do exactly that, if for no other reason than the promise I made to her father and I will do this to save both of your lives, your throne, and our people."

"Father, no –" Jaerick pleaded.

"It must be this way. There is no alternative."

"No!" Jaerick shouted, and he left the room and the castle in search of Traelyn. He spent a week searching for her in all of the elven hideouts, encampments, and even the military posts throughout the kingdom, and found nothing.

Jaerick remembered how he returned through the castle gates heartbroken and disheveled, and now, centuries later, he saw his son and his squad charging through those very same gates with purpose.

He knew by his urgent arrival that Greynim had found something. Jaerick ran down the tower and through the length of the castle to the entryway to meet Greynim and his squad. They were already tearing down their horses' tack and equipment when Jaerick arrived. Greynim saw his father approach and walked briskly over to him to report. As he did so he pulled off his green tinted helm. His shoulder length dirt-blond hair stuck to his head from the sweat collected under his helm. Greynim was very slender, even for an elf, a product from his mother's side.

"Father, we found a large massing of humans just north of the Dragon Cross Mountains," Greynim said as he tousled his hair with his left hand and held his helm with his right.

"That's not too surprising. That's where their villages are."

"Not this big. We saw somewhere near two thousand men. They have never attacked with more than a few hundred."

Jaerick motioned Greynim to follow as he turned and walked away from where no one else could hear their conversation. "Did you see Naemyn, or any signs of him?"

"No. But they are near where Naemyn would've traveled."

"Or would be traveling upon his return," Jaerick concluded.

"If they haven't slaughtered him already. The humans are closer than they have been for years, especially with a force this large."

"What were they doing?"

"We watched them for two days, and they did absolutely nothing. I think they are rallying there, maybe waiting for an even larger force."

"Then I think it is time that we take the offensive."

"I can muster five hundred elves in one hour."

"Good, but we need to muster more. I will arrange for an additional thousand, and set up five hundred more for a support group and possible defensive rally station in the forest near Fort Stone-Elf. We can ambush them just south of there."

"Then I'll get busy. How soon can I lead this force out of here?"

Jaerick froze. He envisioned all of his dreams now coming true. If there was a battle south of Fort Stone elf, it could possibly occur near or at a cliff-faced valley they have strategically used for the defense of the fort. He shuddered to envision to possibility of Naemyn bringing Traelyn to the battle only to see his force decimated.

"No, you will not go on this one."

"But Father, I have started this expedition and I need to finish it!"

"No. Choose your best warrior and send him in your place. I need you here."

Greynim said nothing, turned around, and walked away in frustration. As Jaerick watched him walk away, he wondered if he was changing his dream from coming true or merely laying the plans to making them fall into place.

Chapter 18

Voll was tired and out of breath when his perimeter scouts stopped him. Even in darkness, the scouts knew it was Voll and let him pass. Voll then grabbed one of the scout's horses and was on his way to the main encampment to share the news with Commander Daegon. It felt good to be on horseback again, to feel the horse's stride, and to watch its ears change direction depending on the commands given or just by being alert to its outside surroundings.

He rode fast, but savored the moment. Even though it was not raining, he was still getting wet from rubbing against the dripping forest vegetation. This did not bother him, he knew his mission was nearly accomplished, and soon he would be able to get some rest in a dry tent and a stiff cot.

An hour later, he was facing the guards to commander Daegon's tent.

"Wake the Commander!" he ordered as he approached.

"Is it urgent?" one guard responded.

"Yes, it is. Wake him now!"

The questioning guard motioned to the other to go inside and wake the commander. He shook his head and opened the flap of the tent. Fearing the repercussion of this action, he went inside with the full knowledge that his superior was too cowardly to do it himself.

A few moments later Commander Daegon yelled for Voll to enter. Commander Daegon was tying his robe when he entered. A candle burned on his table beside his cot. Voll was impressed with the Commander's size. He always looked strong and foreboding with his studded leather armor, but he was still a large man dressed only in a robe. His long light brown curly hair matted up on one side of his head as he addressed Voll.

"What news of the elves?"

Voll saluted before responding. "They are about a day and a half southeast of us. According to one of their scouts, that was killed after giving me this information, they were on a non military reconnaissance mission for some elven artifact."

Commander Daegon put his hands in the pockets of his robe. "Is that all?"

Voll swallowed hard. "Yes, I wish there was more, but I think that is all they were after. They were even being pestered by a dragon for a while."

Commander Daegon laughed. "Now that would be a sight wouldn't it, elves being harassed by dragons? So where are they headed now?"

"They will be returning home the same way they came."

"Do they know of our force here?"

"No. They do not. Their mission as I said is purely non-military."

"And you believe that?"

"He gave me no reason not to believe him. He was in fear for his life when he gave me the information, then died shortly thereafter. Plus, they went directly to their location, spent a few hours there, and then they changed direction and are now heading home."

"You believe they are on a direct course back home?" he asked.

"Yes. They seem to be following same route they came in on."

"Non-military you say?"

"Yes, commander."

"Good. Then I intend to *make* it a military operation for them. I will not give them a chance of accidentally finding us, so we will set up an ambush."

Voll then told Commander Daegon every detail of the size, strength, and fighting capabilities of the elves, he even told him a few more details of the dragons he encountered, but did not tell him of the debt that Aegyn had promised him, because he didn't really believe in the honor of an overgrown wyrm. When he finished, Commander Daegon released him to get some much-needed rest.

As he walked to his tent, he could not help but wonder if something bigger than expected was on the horizon. Elves on a secret mission, dragons making promises to humans, and a bloodthirsty commander bent on destroying the whole elven race. Voll reached his tent, opened the flap, and walked in. As he lit a candle, he smelled the musty smell of canvas, and saw his unkempt cot in the same condition he left it, well slept in. Now he planned to jump in it and finish right where he left off.

Chapter 19

Voll awoke with a start. It was daylight outside, and the inner walls of his tent dripped from the moisture sticking to the canvas. He heard yelling outside subdued by Commander Daegon's booming voice as he walked past the outside of Voll's tent. Another voice trailed after him pleading for him to listen to reason. Voll jumped out of his cot, pulled his pants out from in between his covers, and put them on. He fumbled again in the covers to retrieve his tunic. Pulling it over his head, he smelled the odor of his sweat. He wrinkled his nose and twisted his head, and pulled it over his head anyway.

He then found his boots, buckled them, and ran out of the tent not looking where he was going. When he did, he slammed into an old woman knocking her down onto her right side. She let out a pitiful moan as she fell in the soft mud.

Commander Daegon and Traegon heard her fall and wail as she twisted over onto her back. "What in the...?" Commander Daegon yelled.

"Great Mother?" Traegon also gasped as he ran to aid her.

"Great Mother?" Voll questioned in shock and surprise as he went down on both knees and put his hand behind her neck to prop her up.

"Do not touch her!" Traegon yelled coming to her aid. "What is your problem?"

Voll faced the youth, the strong resemblance of his father showed in his facial features. Voll noticed that he was not as large as the commander, but actually was thin and scrawny compared to the imposing man.

"My apologies to the Great Mother," Voll said lowering his head in submission.

"I'm fine," Traelyn said, gaining her composure. "My hip hurts, but I think I will be fine."

"Find a healer now!" Commander Daegon shouted for all to hear, and at that command, every onlooker turned tail and ran.

"I can manage," Traelyn said as she sat up. Her shoulders slumped and her head wobbled from side to side as she did so.

"Great Mother, please," Traegon pleaded.

"Enough of the pity. Why don't you three strong men just shut-up and help me up?"

Traegon and Voll looked to each other and knew that they had to comply. As they helped her to her feet Commander Daegon stood in front of them with his hand on his hips.

"This is why, young Traegon, our Great Mother cannot go any farther and must go back home," he said, proving his point.

"It is only by her command that I follow, father," he said in defense, "and with all due respect, you should as well. How can you just simply disobey her command?"

"I do so, because I can."

"How can you do that? She is the Great Mother."

"I can do this because I am Daegon, the eldest living son in her line. And I am in command of her army, her people, and believe it or not, of her safety."

Traegon's eyes widened from hearing his father actually say what every person had suspected was going through Daegon's mind for many years now, but never thought he would hear him utter it aloud, especially in front of the Great Mother herself.

"You have no right," Traelyn said, annunciating every syllable.

"Please forgive me Great Mother, but you are old," Daegon began. "You are older than human history itself, and it grieves me to say that you are withering away. Your bones are weak, and your mind is shrinking. You being here wanting to see the king of the elves, our enemy, only proves this fact. I will not have you talk me out of it, and that is final."

"Daegon, my boy," Traelyn began as her eyes began to swell and turn red. "You are not as powerful as you think. This realm is bigger than humans, elves, and this petty war of ours. We must come together to bring ourselves to a higher state of being. You have grown overconfident and boastful. You must be humble to lead effectively."

Commander Daegon tightened his lips and shook his head. "Traegon, take her home."

"But father, –" Traegon interjected.

"Voll!" Commander Daegon yelled as he pointed to him. "Let's go kill some elves, before you knock over our supreme matriarch and hurt her this time!"

Traelyn stood still and watched Commander Daegon and Voll walk away.

"Let's go find the healer, Great Mother," Traegon said as he grabbed her elbow.

"No!" she snapped. "Follow your father. Do not let him know that you are following."

"For what purpose, Great Mother?"

"You will see. I believe this will get much worse before it gets better."

As commander Daegon and Voll walked away, they began to talk about where the elves might be next, where, and when they would be closest to their encampment.

"I want you to scout these elves again for me. This time I want one of their scouts to find you. Make sure he chases you back to our designated area so that we may capture him."

"Yes commander," Voll said, and took two steps away then stopped and turned back to face his commander. "Commander, do you think I can get a new horse?"

Chapter 20

When Naemyn was as a young apprentice to Kroejin, the king's spiritual advisor, he was a rambunctious student. It was not that he liked to cause or get into trouble, it was just that trouble had a way of finding him, but Naemyn didn't seem to mind, which made his woes that much more emphasized.

He was also ambitious and impatient. He made it known what he wanted, and since he was so ambitious in his youth, he was an obvious choice to be elevated to the spiritual advisor to the king when Prince Jaerick became king. Being the prince's best friend growing up certainly did not hurt either.

Naemyn, being so apt to find himself in trouble, often wandered out into the forest to escape his punishment for his deeds. One summer afternoon, when hiding from Kroejin and skipping his studies, he wandered into the forest and into trouble. He had actually set out to find the breeding grounds for the hook-feather hawks, except that he found them quicker than he expected and almost walked on top of them, startling himself.

Their nests were settled in the top layer of the forest canvas where he heard the babies crying for their mothers' to come back with their next feeding. Crouching down he nestled himself in the low-lying brush and watched them for many minutes and waited for their mothers' return.

Dozens of nests stretched high up in the canvas like a spider colony with massive webs stringing throughout an old barn. He began to sweat profusely and grow nauseated. He could not explain why, but a deep fear began to creep in and overtake his soul. While he hid in the bushes, he heard the hawks call and chatter. The noise seemed to increase as minutes turned to hours, until he could not take it any longer. His skin crawled, and his body twisted until he jumped out of the bushes and ran.

As he did so, the hawks saw him as a threat and exploded from their nests, taking to the air and attacking him. They simultaneously pecked at his head and back with their beaks and talons. Blood began to flow freely from his wounds as he ran. Naemyn continued to run, covering his head while they continued to pelt him.

Then, as he ran, he felt something stir from the pit of his stomach, much like a boiling of molten rock that both aggravated and excited him. Soon the boiling feeling erupted into a flood of peace and weightlessness. A bright, shady, purple haze encircled his being and cleared his vision. He sensed that nothing could touch him as if a protective shield now covered his body.

Though the hawks continued to pelt him, they could no longer pierce his skin. Naemyn stopped running and let the hawks do their best as one by one he broke their necks by doing little more than thinking about it. All he had to do was point at the bird then clench his fist and watch them fall to the ground. He did this for almost an hour until all of the hawks' dead bodies lay sprawled in a wide circle around him.

Seeing what he had done, and sensing the aura around his body beginning to disappear, he sat down and cried.

The sun slipped behind the tees and disappeared before he gained enough courage to get up and run back to the castle. He ran like a blind animal, careless of whether he ran through bushes with thorns, or barreled through the thick vines of the dense forest. By the time he regained his composure, he realized that he was lost. It did not take long for him to come to the conclusion that he would not get very far wandering around in the forest in the dark, so he found a fallen tree and nestled himself next to it, closed his eyes and began to cry, hoping to fall asleep.

At first, he tossed and turned in the soft dirt, being aware of all the nighttime insects and noises they made. Eventually, he was on his back looking at the stars as they shimmered in the atmosphere within the breaks in the canopy of the forest trees. This brought some peace to him and he finally fell asleep.

He awoke to the sound of soldiers on horseback. He actually felt the horse's footfalls before he heard them. He stood up, brushed himself off, and ran to the sound of the horses.

"Help me!" he yelled. As he ran, he pushed away branches from his face and jumped over rocks and bushes that blocked his path. He ran until he came to the elven soldiers. Kroejin was on the lead horse of twenty soldiers. When he saw his mentor, he fell flat on the ground and wept.

Kroejin pulled his hood back and commanded the soldiers to return to the castle.

"I will bring the boy back later," he said as he dismounted. The commander of the soldiers yelled the command and they turned their horses back to the castle and quickly sped off, creating a dust cloud as they did so.

Walking over to Naemyn, he noticed that the boy's light sandy hair was matted and crumpled with dried blood.

"What in the world happened to you?" Kroejin said, nervously laughing as he beheld the sad sight of a scared boy who had gotten himself into some trouble deeper than he could get out of.

Naemyn sat up and rubbed his eyes so that he could see again.

"Hawks! The Hook-feather hawks attacked me!"

"Why would they attack you? Hook-feather hawks don't attack unprovoked."

"I didn't do anything," he whimpered.

"What boy? Speak up."

"I saw them and I hid. They scared me."

"What do you mean, they scared you?"

"I was just walking through the woods when I came upon them. I saw all of their nests, heard them squawking. I just got scared and hid. When I got up to leave, they just attacked."

"Naemyn," Kroejin said firmly. "You and I both know that you could not have been just walking out here by chance. You knew this was the breeding ground for our hawks, and you were up to no good. Tell me the truth."

Naemyn looked at the ground realizing he was just caught in disobedience, and did not know how he was going to get out of this without telling the truth.

"I don't like them," he whispered.

"What were you doing?"

Naemyn looked up smiling. "I wanted to catch one."

"And do what with it?"

Naemyn looked down again, shaking his head.

"You're not going to tell me, are you?"

"No," he grumbled.

"No, but you are going to tell me what happened."

Naemyn's head snapped up and he shouted. "They attacked me I told you! What do you think happened?"

"I think you provoked them, and they attacked you in self defense."

"No! I didn't do anything."

"I find that hard to believe," Kroejin said as he grabbed the young boy's arm and began walking the direction that he was running away from. Naemyn stood his ground and snapped his arm out of Kroejin's grip.

"No! I will not go that way!"

"Oh, yes you will!"

"No," he said, crossing his arms.

Kroejin smiled at the boy. "Yes you will. You will either go with me or I will bring the king's guard out here and take you to the breeding grounds and have the soldiers set up a perimeter as you spend another night with the birds."

"That won't happen," Naemyn said boastfully with an angry smirk.

"Try me, boy, push me and I will make sure it happens."

"You don't understand. All the birds are dead, so your point will be useless."

Kroejin looked at Naemyn blankly, and waited for him to elaborate, but when he said nothing more he rubbed his forehead with his left hand.

"All of them? How?"

Naemyn stood straight as a board, now frightened of his mentor. "Every… single… one," he said with a slight pause in between every word. "Every single one, every cock, hen, and hatchling, even the eggs are crushed."

Kroejin flushed with anger. "What in the name of Raezoures have you done, boy?"

Naemyn looked to the ground.

"Take me there, Naemyn. I think I know what is going on."

"You do?" he whispered, looking up at Kroejin.

"Yes, I believe I do. Take me there."

Naemyn led Kroejin to the spot where the birds lay scattered dead and bloody on the soft forest ground. He looked in horror at all of the carcasses of the birds, noticing that none of them had any of their original shape. Feathers were strewn across the landscape, impossible to tell which feather belonged to which carcass.

Upon seeing the carnage, Naemyn began to shake and fell to his knees, then fell forward propping himself up with his elbows and forearms flat on the ground. He did not cry, but shook violently. Kroejin walked around to face him and pushed him back up to the kneeling position.

"You did all of this?"

"Yes," he mouthed, but no sound escaped his throat.

"You should not be ashamed. What happened here is not your fault."

"How is this not my fault?"

"This day has been prophesied."

"Prophesied? What prophecy?"

"The prophecy that will elevate the elven kingdom out of its current quandary of existing with these aggressive Val elves. However, for the time being it is necessary that we coexist with these impure breed of elves, but we have felt that you will be the one that will lead the next king away from this path in order create a new path, one that will bring the pure Sor elves to prominence."

Naemyn leaned back and sat on his bottom, putting his arms behind him to prop himself erect.

"Then why have you not told me of this?" he asked wiping his face.

"We didn't know for certain that it would be you. We hoped it was, but did not know, and now we do."

"We?"

"The Sorae, or more accurately yet discreetly, the Agin–Sorae. We study the prophecies and try to direct the elven kingdom to the most prosperous end. Where the Sorae believes that we can coexist, the Agin–Sorae only want the pure Sor elves to lead the elven kingdom."

"What must I do to make this all happen?"

"We don't know for certain. But we have suspected for a long time now that you were the one the prophecy spoke of. We believe that you may be the chosen one to find the heart shard of the Markenhirth, sometimes mistakenly called the fifth Shard."

"Was I chosen into this study because of the possibility?"

"Yes, you and a handful of other young children. We hoped it would be you because of your friendship with the prince."

Naemyn thought in silence for a few moments before responding. "Am I now on the path of this prophecy?"

Kroejin smiled. "Always looking forward. Yes, my boy, you are most definitely on the path, and we hope that you will be the one to find this shard, because the one who has possession of it will also be able to summon the Blue Wraeth."

"But I thought the Markenhirth and the Blue Wraeth were evil?"

"What is evil, but perspective? Choose any decisive battle. To the victor it can be seen as a glorious victory routing their enemy, but to the losing side it can be seen as a senseless and immoral massacre."

"I am not sure I understand; evil is evil. Will you explain this prophecy in detail to me?"

"Yes, my boy. All in good time, but not today. First you must do some explaining to me as to what happened with the hawks."

Naemyn, now feeling confident that he was not going to be in serious trouble for his actions, eased up on his defiance to tell the tale.

"When they attacked me, I was so scared I ran, but they kept attacking me. The fear inside of me began to boil. I don't understand what that feeling was, but it felt good."

"What do you mean it felt good?"

"At first I felt a grumbling in my chest, kind of like a hunger pain, but higher up. Then it consumed my entire upper body and warmed me up until my forehead began to sweat. After that, I felt nothing and saw a white flash followed by a bluish purple stream of smoke darting through the air. I had a strange feeling that I could command the smoke to kill the hawks, and so I did," Naemyn smiled, "and I liked it."

"You liked the killing?"

"Well, no, but I liked the power and I liked the power of killing so easily without guilt. I liked the intensity of the feeling inside me and then being able to control it."

"Do you know what that feeling is?"

Naemyn cocked his head, curious that Kroejin may know what it was that he had just described to him.

"Yes I do, but generally not in the form that you've just experienced. What you felt was your Kronn."

"I have never heard of Kronn. What is it?"

Kronn is an ancient term for channeling the magic of the land and entwining it with the magic within. Kronn is not an ability that is often used by elves, as they mostly master the craft of Wrae, not Kronn. Kronn does not belong to us, though some elves can channel it. In fact, many that can channel it don't even recognize it within them when they feel it."

"You mean those that master Kronn can do what I did?"

"No. Yours is special. The Kronn within comes from nature. It works through the earth and into your body and into your heart. It knows your heart and intensifies your desires. Many cannot control it in a lifetime, like you did on the first time."

"So my desire to kill the hawks awakened my Kronn?"

"In a sense, I guess that is correct. The Kronn also knows the future and can transpire events to ensure its passing."

"Can you teach me these prophecies?"

Kroejin smiled and put his hand on Naemyn's shoulder. "In time. In time, you will know all I know and maybe even surpass the knowledge of the Sorae."

Chapter 21

Daegon and a dozen men hid behind a cluster of jagged rocks. The humans, like the rocks, hung precariously over the pass as wolves ready to pounce upon their prey. On the other side of the road another dozen men also crouched behind the craggy cliff, anxiously awaiting their orders to kill. Their impatience seemed intensified due to the smell of another rainstorm coming. The once partly cloudy skies turned gray, but then grew dark and heavy as the clouds began to roll in. The lush green foliage that grew in between the rocks began to turn a darker hue as the light dissipated.

A soldier crawled up from the backside of the slope to the position of his commander, and waited for his superior to acknowledge him.

"Report!" Daegon commanded.

"Captain Voll is coming up the hill," the soldier reported.

"Is he followed?" the commander growled.

"Only by a scout, no others follow. He is ahead of the elves, and they are not breaking their formation."

"Then meet him and bring him here! I want him here as quickly as humanly possible. He has information for us," Daegon said without looking at the soldier.

He said nothing more and then crawled backwards down the hill, slipping away.

Daegon had been waiting years for an opportunity like this. Nasty rotten elves, he often called them. Selfish and elitist, the elves were nothing more than scrawny little overgrown children with the ability to speak intelligently, wield magic, see in the dark, and worst of all, kill humans. They are an abomination to the land they that they pretend to protect.

However, he knew if they were to be successful on a much larger scale. It was for this single reason that Daegon organized this force. If someone did not come to lead the humans, they would soon find themselves extinct.

Long before there were any assaults against the elves, the humans fought amongst themselves, usually intertribal, sometimes from within the tribe. Daegon, as a young man, with the suggestion and guidance of his Great Mother, developed a plan to align and organize them all into a single force.

Daegon understood the great fortune before him, as to be granted an opportunity such as this. After years of planning and training, the campaign would begin at long last, with the ambush of this caravan. It would be a great start to the war and he would gain great satisfaction in watching every elf in the caravan suffer.

Daegon heard someone crawling up the steep grassy hill behind him. Craning his head sideways, he saw Captain Voll crawling on his hands and feet working his way up in between the small bushes.

"Report," Daegon whispered without looking at his captain.

Captain Voll nestled himself to the right of Daegon and laid prostrate feeling the soft ground on his stomach. "A scout is following me. He should be here any second."

"Good. And the caravan?"

"They follow about thirty minutes behind."

"Did you inform the perimeter scouts as you came through?"

"Yes, I knew they would be alert, but I told them to be watchful anyway."

As the two were talking, some of the men on the other side of the ravine began pointing southward. Daegon raised his hand in acknowledgment and motioned them to stay low.

Within minutes, an elf on horseback came into view. He was off the trail, hugging the slope closest to the commander and Captain Voll. Just before he came into range of fire of the archers, he stopped. Sensing something was not quite right, he dismounted and tied the horse to a tree. He withdrew his bow and knocked an arrow as he ran into the brushy foliage.

Daegon pointed toward the elf and then pointed to his eyes to alert his men to simply watch and wait. The elf quickly concealed himself from their view. Daegon wanted to capture this elf alive, even though doing so might prove to be an arduous task as elven scouts were the most cunning and watchful of their race.

The elf then made a rare mistake by popping out of a clump of bushes and onto the open hillside and froze. Then without warning, the scout stowed his bow over his head, turned, and ran in the direction of his horse. The soldiers across the ravine began to raise their bows, but Daegon raised his hand to halt their eagerness. The elf disappeared again through the trees and bushes and reached the spot where he left his horse only to find five soldiers standing there with their arrows nocked and pointed at him.

Daegon signaled to the others to converge upon the scout and surround him. The elf turned around to run deeper into the woods, but only found more soldiers. Turning around again, he withdrew a knife and took defensive stance. He said nothing, signaling that they were going to have to take him by force. A few of the human soldiers began to close in on the elf. The elf turned, jabbed, and swung his knife in the air. He was trapped, nowhere to go, like a small animal cornered by a pack of wolves. Out of the sky came the scout's Hook-feather hawk, which wrapped its talons onto one soldier's helm, and began pecking at his forehead and eyes. The soldier screamed, dropped his bow, and tried to grab the bird.

A few soldiers took their aim away from the scout and instead gave their attention to the hawk. Seeing this, the scout charged for one of the distracted humans, and tackled the closest soldier at the same moment an arrow was loosed toward the hawk. The soldier watched the arrow disappear in the sky, missing the hawk as the elf crushed into his chest, knocking him to his back. The elf landed on his chest and as fast as a cat pouncing for its final kill. The soldier tried to sit up, but the elf jabbed his knife through the soldier's throat. Blood from his jugular sprayed onto the scout's chest and face, as one of the soldiers cracked his skull with the hilt of his sword.

"Don't kill him!" Daegon yelled as the soldiers in a blood craze were pounding the elf within the precious strands of his life.

"I command you to cease!" he shouted.

The soldiers continued with the beating by kicking him incessantly as he lay on the soft ground, now unconscious.

"I said to stop!" Daegon yelled again as he grabbed one of the soldiers by the neck of the leather armor and threw him to the ground. The rest of the soldiers, seeing their leader attack one of their own stopped and stared at him with fear and anger in their eyes.

"I want him alive!" he yelled again, his face flush with anger. He felt his forehead and ears on fire. "Pick him up and drag him to that tree."

The soldiers did as commanded, dragging the limp elven frame through the rocks and bushes some fifty feet, and dropped him next to the tree closest to the road.

"Rope," Daegon commanded, pointing to a soldier standing by a wagon that was nestled in the bushes. The soldier rushed to the wagon, rustled through a few items under a tarp, grabbed a rope, and ran back to the commander. The ends of the rope hung loosely as he handed it to Daegon who snatched it from his hands and threw it to one of his soldiers standing nearby.

"Hang him up by his feet," Daegon barked.

The soldier threw the rope over a branch from the tree. They dragged the elf to him, tied up his hands and feet, and hoisted him up so that he was upside down until his head was at even height with theirs. Daegon walked over to the elf and slapped his face. The unconscious form swayed to one side from the slap. Daegon, not satisfied, continued to slap him until he regained consciousness.

"Good morning friend," Daegon growled with a devious smile.

The elf blinked rapidly while his mind tried to grasp his dilemma. When he realized his predicament, he started to wiggle, squirm and twist his way out of the ropes. Daegon grabbed the elf's shoulders stopping him.

"You will die today, you must accept this," Daegon said, smiling at the elf's terrified brown eyes. "Knife," he said holding out his open hand.

The soldier closest to him handed him his knife. He took it with one hand, while stroking the elf's fine hair with his other as it hung down off his head.

"Don't worry, believe it or not, this won't hurt . . . much. I am going to give you the courtesy your kind does not give us before death. I will let you die peacefully."

Daegon raised the knife before the elf's eyes and touched the tip to his forehead.

"Hold him still!"

Two soldiers came around and untied the elf's hands and then grabbed his arms and stretched them outward. Without further hesitation, Daegon took the knife and sliced his neck with a small cut below and to the left of the elf's chin. The elf let out a short yelp, but made no other sound. Blood drained freely passing his ear and to the ground. The elf's eyes went wide with fear and realization that he was now in the final moments of his life. He did not move or squirm, but watched blinking as the blood flowed closely past his left eye and into his hair, matting it with the sticky warmth.

The soldiers watched the elf slowly die. All were amazed at his calm peacefulness. Some of the soldiers smiled, while others, some of the younger ones, watched in horror as the blood began to drip out of the lifeless body forming a muddy pool of blood below him.

"Take your positions; we have one more ambush to do," Daegon said, calm and firm, and he smiled with a satisfied grin when the last drop of blood hit the ground.

*　*　*

A few miles away Naemyn rode atop his horse, safely between the elven soldiers. The sky was beginning to clear and he was looking up at a patch of blue sky when he saw one of his scouts' Hook feather-hawks flying in fast. He felt a sense of trouble with his Kronn, but he did not need his Kronn to sense this. The hawk's erratic flight told the whole story. He raised his hand just above his right ear, made a fist and twisted violently. He smiled as he watched the feathers burst outward and slowly fall to the ground.

*　*　*

Rain began to drizzle into the valley where Daegon and his men prepared for the caravan to come through. The men were eager with anticipation. Daegon was confident in his men, many of these men he not only fought beside, but against. In battles against each other, they often showed great strength and ferocity, which made him proud that they had now bonded together as a single fighting force against one common enemy.

The time had come, and now Daegon would have his revenge. He smiled as the rain drenched his head then trickled down his neck. A shiver went down his spine, not sure if it was from the cold rain or just the pre-combat excitement. Daegon stood up and walked down the spur and into the draw where the road met the spur. He stood in sight of most of his men and put his forefinger to his lips to motion silence. He unsheathed his sword, raised it above his head, and circled it wildly. The men saw this, did the same, and let out quiet guttural grunts, which encouraged the others to follow in rhythm. He encouraged this near silent motivation for a few seconds before he lowered his sword and motioned with his other hand to stop with a swift palm down sideways motion under his chin.

Satisfied and anticipating a successful ambush, he ran up the hill back to his position and waited, knowing retribution was not far away. His men were ready. They were now one, awakened, and motivated for battle. This would be the first battle of many bloody, brutal, and ugly battles to come.

Chapter 22

Naemyn's head hurt. It hurt so bad he had to stop his horse to rub his head. Trouble was near. After speaking with the Guardian, he knew of all the things he had learned about his Kronn, he could always trust it to tell him when tragic events were about to unfold. Not that this was something he had just learned, but rather confirmed his lifelong suspicions, and brought out into his conscious what he had known all of his life.

His temples felt as if sharp needles were drilling into his skull just above his eyebrows. As though his skull was fracturing and would crumble from the pressure. Yes, his Kronn was screaming at him to tell him something iniquitous was about to happen. He had to ignore it, because not only did he suspect that something so utterly heinous was about to happen, he wished for it, yet that did not stop his Kronn from hurting his head.

"What is wrong?" Paerglae asked as he rode up to Naemyn.

"Nothing. We must press on. I want you to take all of the scouts away from the flanks and push forward. Ride hard now, speed is of the essence, and we need to quicken our pace."

Paerglae looked confused, but did not question his orders and turned his horse away and sped off to gather all of the scouts. Naemyn knew it would only be a matter of time, and with any luck, not too much time. After seeing the erratically flying hawk, he suspected that his forward scout had run into trouble. Fighting would soon begin, and once it did, he knew his head would stop hurting. He did not know how this would turn out, but he did know that if everyone with him today died, his plan would begin to unfold.

It did not take long before he saw a dozen hawks flying to the air in panic, a sign that their masters had been killed.

"Trouble ahead!" Naemyn yelled. "The forward scouts have been ambushed! Archers flank the swordsman, stay alert when we engage the humans, they will be in the woods just off the road!"

His elven warriors charged ahead, leaving him with two scouts flanking him for protection. Their bravery touched him, yet he felt no guilt in their ignorant obedience. He hoped for their deaths, but he did feel a slight sense of pity that they would have to die in order for him to conceal his deceit.

"Stay close to me," Naemyn said as he charged his steed down the road.

Naemyn rode for less than a mile when he heard the sounds of battle. He could tell by their death screams that they were not only dying, but they were dying a brutal death at the hands of the barbaric and cruel humans. A few minutes later, he came around the turn of the mountainside that obscured his vision of what lie ahead due the rocky hillside.

Immediately he realized the perfection of the ambush. The area was heavily vegetated around tightly clumped trees that grew out of the rocky hillside on both sides of the road. There was no way to route the attackers out of their advantage. Dead horses and elves scattered the road as more arrows flew down at the elven swordsman trying vainly to climb up to their attackers. Some elven archers hid amongst rocks on one side of the road, but had no cover from the human archers on the opposite side of the road. He watched as his small squad died in humiliating fashion.

Only four elves lived long enough to find successful cover in between the crevice of two or three boulders away from the human archers. He knew they were doomed as the humans began to inch their way out of their cover, advancing on the elves to finish them off. Naemyn dismounted his horse and commanded his two elves to stand in front of him and to shoot their arrows randomly into the hillside. As they did so, he called upon his Kronn to cover the elves trapped within the cove of the boulders.

The boulders turned black as coal and then shimmered slightly and sparkled until they appeared to fade into a black hole, covering the elves in complete darkness.

Naemyn's elven archers had no luck in hitting their targets, but once he had his elves covered, he then directed his Kronn to the elven arrows. Their arrows turned into vipers that did not go randomly into the hillside, but directly to human targets. The men screamed as these black vipers landed upon the humans and wrapped themselves around their necks, biting them incessantly upon their faces and necks.

Naemyn smiled as he watched the humans writhe in pain, the poison flowing through their veins and to their heart. The venom was quick, but painful. Feeling confident in his Kronn, he then covered himself in the same fashion as he did his elves. He walked over to the dark boulders that hid his warriors and told them to come to the center of the road. Arrows stormed upon him, but vanished as they reached the shadowy substance protecting him and his elves.

He sat down and began to cast his final piece of work. He did not want to devastate these humans, but he began to enjoy his success against them. He could not resist doing one more action to hurt these pesky, unintelligent barbarians to take away the confidence that they had gained from attacking his warriors in such a cowardly fashion.

Black clouds began to appear directly above Naemyn, forming a dark blue funnel spinning slowly at first and then faster and tighter until the tip of the cyclone touched inches above Naemyn's head. When it did so, hundreds of black lightning bolts shot out of the funnel, hitting the humans indiscriminately, killing them on contact.

Then without warning, the cloud disappeared, and began to weaken and tire. It took the humans a few seconds to gather and recollect their senses and realize that the sorcerer attacking them was now completely defenseless. They stood up and fired arrows at the helpless elves protecting Naemyn. They each took dozens of arrows in their bodies and fell listlessly to the road. Naemyn was about to lose consciousness when he heard a woman's voice screech into the air.

"Stop! All of you! Cease fire!" Traelyn shouted from the top of the mountain, holding the empty Quarterstar Talisman above her head with both hands. Traegon stood behind her holding her steady so that she did not tumble down the hillside.

Naemyn began to laugh as he lay on his back looking upwards, watching his black clouds dissipate out of the rainless overcast sky. All movement ceased at the sound of the Great Mother's voice.

Chapter 23

"Great Mother!" Daegon shouted from his vantage point on the top of the hill just a few yards away from her to his left. "What are you doing?"

"We are in need of these elves," she said.

"We need nothing from these elves!" he shouted to her, leaping from boulder to boulder to reach her before she could do any more harm.

"Traegon, take me to that elf down there. I think I know him."

"You will do no such thing!" Daegon shouted as he stood in front of her straddling two boulders.

"You will not stop me son. If you do, I will command all of your men to abandon you and go home."

"You would do no such thing, and no one would listen to you."

"Do you want to test me? You will lose, I promise you. I have allowed you so much power in my name, and you have earned the respect of your men, in my name, but remember, it is in my name that you hold your strength."

Daegon knew his men trusted him and followed his every order, so much so that he believed that if he defied her right now, they would still follow him. However, he did not want to test it just now, he had too much to lose, to end up turning back now.

"I will trust your judgment Great Mother, as always, but you are on a short leash, you are weak and need to return home. As for you Traegon, I will deal with you later!"

"Daegon!" Traelyn shouted. "You are pushing me son! There will be no such reprimand with Traegon. He has only done all that I have asked of him. Now help me down from this nasty death trap."

Daegon commanded three humans out of their positions to help Traelyn down the hillside. When they reached Naemyn, the elf had just finished standing up to meet his soon-to-be captors. Traelyn pushed Traegon to the side once she reached the road. Daegon immediately bolted toward her and jumped in between her and Naemyn.

"This is a dangerous elf Great Mother. Please do not go near him, or even speak to him," he pleaded.

"You have no idea what is going on here. I know him. I know he is dangerous. He is the person responsible for banishing me from my home and my lover."

Naemyn smiled as he looked Daegon directly in his eyes.

Daegon commanded two of his men to push Naemyn to his knees and tie his hands.

"She is right. We knew each other very well. However, Traelyn, please know that sending you away was not my decision," he said as they bound his hands behind his back.

"You lie!" Traelyn fumed. "You had everything to do with it."

Traelyn looked at Daegon and saw the confusion and rage in his eyes, then put her hand upon his shoulder and smiled the smile she gave to all of her children to calm them down. She then turned back to Naemyn and took a deep breath.

"Thanks to Daegon's powerful force here today I have you as a prisoner, and I hold your elusive Quarterstar Talisman in my possession. Now I have a secret for you. This talisman was given to me by King Keiyann Krowe."

Traelynn's hands shook. She would soon find out the truth of her exile from Jaerick, after all of these years, all she wanted to learn was why he had sent her away to die amongst the barbarian human tribes. She remembered Naemyn telling her that she needed to be with her own people, but these humans were not her own kind, they weren't as civilized as the people she lived with at the Halls of Dar Drannon. This fact alone made her hate the elves more than anything they could have done to her.

Jaerick did not even say goodbye to her or escort her himself. Naemyn was the one who gave her the news as she waited in her chambers for Jaerick to return while the king was extinguishing a revolt of the elven people when they found out that she was pregnant with Jaerick's child.

"You defile this bed with your human stink, and you have no place here in this kingdom, tainting the bloodline with this vile growth in your body. It will grow up to be a pariah that will weaken the bloodline and eventually destroy the elven race."

Traelyn said nothing, but stared at Naemyn as he looked down at her in disgust.

"However," he began again, "I have been instructed to give you these seeds. Grow them and eat the pistil from the blooms once a year and you will have everlasting life as long as you do."

"Why would you send me away, just so that I can live forever?"

"We need you alive. One day you will return to the elves, but you will bring with you destruction and devastation, and then you will die, and the gods will return to restore the elven kingdom to its proper prominence in the Known Lands."

"That makes no sense Naemyn. You send me away only to return. You would be best served to kill me now, and kill this child as well if you so believe it will destroy your race. You have been so crazed over these prophecies that you can't even think on your own."

"No, you don't understand, and I don't expect you to. I am being groomed to be the prophet that brings in the end times of this world, as we know it, and bring forth a new age of elven prominence. I alone hold the power to make all these events come to pass. You will return many years from now just as I will become the most powerful being in this realm. You and I will work together to bring about the destruction of this realm which will eventually bring in this prosperous new age."

"You are crazed! I am not here to help you bring in a new age; I am here because your king brought me here against my will. The elves killed my father, and I have been held hostage here, and now you want to discard me like old clothing."

"Must we go over this again? We did not kill your father. Your father is alive. He is merely in waiting. He is in another realm waiting for his return to this land. He left with the Sword of Valkilye, which means, even though I believe giving him the sword was a mistake that added hundreds of years to our return to power, he will return."

Naemyn then grabbed her wrist and led her down the stairs where a carriage was waiting for her and threw her in, locked the door and sent her on her way south. Without another word, they carried her away. Though she was being skirted away in the cover of darkness for her safety, they tried to make her trip as pleasant as possible to help calm her anxiety from being displaced. She was not for want of any food, blankets, or pillows. They even allowed her one of her servant girls to keep her company. Still, Traelyn did not speak a word, nor eat any of the food placed in the carriage for her.

They had only just passed the outer gates when the carriage came to a halt. She heard the elven drivers shout reverence to the king, and then the door was unlocked and opened. King Keiyann Krowe commanded the servant girl to step out, and when she did, he climbed in.

"Help me Keiyann!" she cried as she held him. "Thank you for saving me, where is Jaerick?"

Keiyann held her tight for a few seconds, but then pushed her back at arms length still holding on to her shoulders.

"Jaerick will not be here, and you still have to leave."

"Why?" Traelyn asked covering her face with balled fists. "What is going on?

"I am so sorry, young sweetling. I know I promised your father that I would protect you, and I know you may think I am abandoning that promise, but you are no longer safe here."

"That is not true! You are listening to Naemyn! He even told me I am leaving so that he can take over the elven kingdom, he plans to supplant you someday."

"That may very well happen, but I will do everything in my power to make sure that does not come to pass. Regardless, you are not safe here. I have arranged with a prominent and powerful human clan to take you in."

"This can't be happening. I want my father back, I want to go home!"

Keiyann sighed. "I am sorry Traelyn, that cannot happen. Your father may never return."

"But that was the reason you sent him away, so that he would return."

"That was true when I sent him away. I held the sword of our god Val-Eahea, and the words inscribed upon the sword predicted his return, but I have grown weary of waiting, and I fear some events have occurred that have blocked that prophecy."

"Then why must I endure all of this?"

Keiyann reached over and put his hand under her chin.

"You must endure, because he still might return. I know it may sound as if I am talking in riddles, but I am going to change events that will ensure that Naemyn cannot usurp my kingdom in the name of his religion, which has grown slightly different from mine. I believe that you and your father are the key to our elven existence, but not in the way Naemyn believes. I also believe that Naemyn and I can work through our differences to come together in an agreement with how the elven race can survive this prophecy. Someday, your father will return and he will help us, not destroy us, and I have something to give you that will help us achieve that goal as well as give you some comfort while we wait."

Keiyann reached inside his cloak and pulled out a black silk bag and from it a talisman wrapped around in woven leather and silver chain. The talisman was hardened silver and outlined in gold. The circular talisman had elven inscriptions wrapped around the outer edge leading to the middle where four empty slots to house the four Quarterstar Shards awaited the shards' return.

"Take this and keep it with you until a time will come where you are to return it to the elves."

"How will I know when to return it?"

"You will never know until the time comes. In fact, by taking this talisman you will slowly lose your memory of this day, and in time, you will lose your memory of Jaerick as well."

"Why would I want that? Why would I choose to be a pawn in your game?"

"You asked how you were to endure. This is how you will endure. This will take away the pain of your love for Jaerick. You will forget all about him, until the time comes, when your memories are returned to you."

Keiyann put the talisman back into the bag and gave it to her.

"I truly am sorry that this has happened to you Traelyn. I honestly looked forward to raising you as my daughter, a true princess to the elven kingdom, but unfortunately, that could not happen. Your father was a friend to the elven people. I am sorry."

Traelyn took the talisman, set it between her legs, and reached over to give Keiyann a hug.

"Then I will return someday?" she whispered as new tears began to fall.

"I believe so. I also hope someday you and I will see your father again and help him restore this land from the demise that will eventually fall upon it."

Keiyann then left the carriage, commanded the servant to return, and slid the bolt across the door, locking Traelyn inside.

Traelyn heard Keiyann order the driver to continue with his delivery of her. She would never see King Keiyann Krowe again.

She travelled for two days, stopping only for short breaks for food and relief. The sun had just set on the second day, but the sky was not quite dark. She heard human voices outside, at first she thought they were going to be attacked and she would die out here in the middle of nowhere, but instead the door opened and from the darkness she was yanked out of the carriage and taken away.

Someone blindfolded her and threw her on a horse, but before she lost her sight, she saw the humans loose a barrage of flaming arrows, lighting the carriage and killing all of the elves, including her young elven servant.

The human attackers took her to the tribe and made her comfortable. Before the memory of her experiences with the elves completely faded away, she planted the seeds that Naemyn had given her and was surprised that when she ate the pistil from the blooms she did not age. In doing so, she extended her life many times over. It took her fifty years just to outlive some of the leaders of influence in the human tribes. They did not treat her badly, but she was not treated with much respect either. When her half-elf child was born, they treated her and the baby as if it was diseased. Why they did not kill her outright, she did not know.

The years passed, and as she worked her way to prominence, mostly due to the fact that she outlived every single elder above her station, she found a growing mistrust and unknown hatred toward the elves. The younger generations now having grown old, realized her wisdom and dominance within the tribes and regarded her just short of being a living goddess, hence the birth of her title as the Great Mother.

During her long reign, she found that the young men were not very intelligent, but were eager to fight. She encouraged those young men to become motivated warriors to raise arms against the elves, eventually building a moderately strong force that never waged a full scale war, but rather indiscreet raids upon their southernmost stronghold, Fort Stone Elf.

Then without any known cause, she began to have the dreams about Jaerick and their love for each other. She dreamed that Jaerick was in trouble, and instead of hatred or revenge, feelings of love resurfaced. The feelings were so strong that she felt the need to find Jaerick at all costs. Why, she did not know, only that she had to do this and had to find him now. She might even be able to reconcile some of her love with him as well, though she knew that she would be fooling herself in so many ways to believe that Jaerick would accept her as she is now as she had aged so much, not to mention the political strife between human and elf relations. She had kept this skirmish war alive for near 300 years, and she knew that the elves hated her and her people just as much as Daegon hated the elves.

She saw so much hatred in her life. Elf versus human and human versus elf, and she saw that hatred in Daegon as they stood together, but Naemyn only smirked confidently, his eyes exposing no hatred whatsoever, and that not only confused her, it terrified her. He was a deceitful person. However, regardless of Naemyn's ulterior motives, she would proceed with her plan. She held up the Quarterstar Talisman by its chain so that it dangled in front of his face. His smirk immediately disappeared. However, she could not tell whether it was shock and surprise he felt, or excitement to have the talisman so close to his grasp again.

"Take me to King Jaerick." Traelyn commanded.

Naemyn smiled. "I will not do that. If I take you anywhere near the elven kingdom, you will die."

"Not as long as I have you with me they won't." Traelyn said.

"I can protect myself from my own people, but I cannot protect you." Naemyn said shaking his head.

"I have a massive force that cannot be stopped!" Daegon interjected.

"Daegon! Shut up! You are out of line!" Traelyn shouted, tired of hearing Daegon's warmongering.

"No, you are only fooling yourself," Naemyn said, laughing while rubbing his chin. "The elves are deeply imbedded into the tangle of the jungle-like forest. You will only lose yourself in the forest, and the elves will strike you, leave you, and hit you again and again until your entire force is demoralized and destroyed."

"That is not true. We have attacked Fort Stone elf with a much smaller force and have had some success. With the force I have now, we are unstoppable."

"Perhaps, I can do this. If I guide you safely north past all of the traps up to Fort Stone Elf, I might be able to convince the elves there to go farther north to grant you audience to the king."

"You fool!" Daegon laughed. "I don't want audience of the king, I want to kill the king!"

"She doesn't," Naemyn said, pointing to Traelyn. "She wants to be with her lover again. Your great, great grandfather that he is, but as you can see, we are at an impasse. Any movement forward causes a full scale war, but to not go forward means she will not see her lover."

The absurdity of the situation made Naemyn laugh hysterically, causing him to bend over to catch his breath.

"What do you propose?" Traelyn asked.

Naemyn stood up, still smiling. "I propose that you come with me to the catacombs where one of the Quarterstar Shards are, and we take that talisman to place the shard into it where it belongs and we then present the talisman to the king."

"So that you can steal the talisman for yourself?" Daegon asked.

"No, because my king is having troubling dreams and he believes that this talisman is lost, and horrible events will come to pass if he does not find it,"

Naemyn said, turning to face Traelyn and dismissing Daegon.

"You and I will be helping each other in this endeavor. You will see your lover again, and I will gain the eternal favor of my friend and king by delivering you to him with the talisman. I do not seek the talisman for myself, I only want to please my king," Naemyn finished, bowing before Traelyn with his hands still bound. Then stood up and took a knee before Traelyn and looked up to her.

"I welcome you back to the elven kingdom, and I am sorry for your absence, but it is time that you return. Please untie me and let us begin working together. I promise that I will not harm anyone."

"Do not fall for his trickery Great Mother! He is the enemy!" Daegon shouted, turning her shoulders to face him.

"Let go of me son. It is time for me to go home. It is time for me to finish this folly of a prophecy that my father is supposedly part of. I want to be with my father whether it is in this realm or another, and only Jaerick may have the answer to this end. Now untie him, but watch him closely."

"Well said my lady," Naemyn said, turning his back and extending his tied hands to Daegon. "Shall we leave immediately?"

"Take us to the catacombs Naemyn, but you will be our hostage until we see Jaerick."

"This is ludicrous! I cannot believe this is happening," Daegon shouted as he turned and left, shouting orders while looking for his top commanders. He left Naemyn's bonds intact.

Chapter 24

The dark of night fell upon Naemyn, Traelyn, Daegon, and his men two hours before they reached the catacombs. They rode non-stop in a gray overcast and warm drizzling rain the whole way southeast. As the gray clouds gradually turned darker, they considered stopping for the night, but Naemyn insisted that they press on, they had been travelling almost non-stop for over three days, and Naemyn had grown weary of the journey travelling out of the catacombs, only to travel the three days back again. Though he was excited that the catacombs were within reach, once inside, they would be clear of the gloomy weather that pressed upon their spirits.

Daegon carried his anger throughout their journey. He could not believe he was part of this folly. He was forced to take this detour away from his mission. At the height of his anger, after Traelyn made it clear that they were going with Naemyn, he assembled his commanders and put Captain Voll in command.

"Captain Voll, I am promoting you to the rank of Battle-Commander, with all of the power and conditions that I hold on the battlefield. You are now in complete charge of this force while I am away on this farce of a mission. I need to go to find a way to kill this elven mage without destroying the Great Mother's confidence in me, and if I cannot do that, I will follow them all the way to the king and kill him myself. You will clear a path for us with our force. Make it a wide path of destruction. One that I cannot miss to follow."

Battle-Commander Voll smiled and saluted. "Thank you for your confidence in me Commander."

"I have been watching your progress for many years. You have been superior in my service as Captain of the Scouts, and I am certain you will excel in your new post. However, how well you do here will determine if you will earn a spot on my council with a rank befitting once this war is over."

Daegon looked to his eight other commanders, each leaders in their own right with their own companies. Mostly tribes that he used to fight, but now won over and assembled into battle companies.

In the process of bringing these tribes together, he used their common hatred of the elves to begin their unification. It was a testament to that hatred that so many tribes with different cultures, subcultures and varying beliefs could so cohesively unite to form an effective fighting unit. This proved to be no easy task, and it took many years to come to fruition. Before any dialogue could begin, it took years of combat dominance on the battlefield, years of devastating the morale of all of the opposing tribes, years of the constant pressure of fear.

His tribe, the driving force of the constant turmoil, and barrier to peace for many years, continued to keep the pressure and chaos intact, so that no two tribes could unite until Daegon realized that the time for unity was right. All it took was to talk to the leaders of the four strongest tribes, assuring them that they must unite to end the dominance of the elves to the north.

After years of tribal warfare, the humans were ripe for new leadership, as they were tired of being defeated by the elves while fighting amongst each other. It didn't hurt that the tribes were in such fear of Daegon's tribe, that they were more than willing to jump at the chance to not only end the terror of Daegon's tribe, but to join them in a common cause. They did so eagerly, and this compelled the lesser tribes to fall in line. Daegon commanded them to disband their lesser alliances and conflicts with all other tribes and join one of the five main tribes to help unite the alliance in a stronger unit.

He then arranged an assembly with all of the tribes and informed them of the new plan to annihilate the elven race from the northern realm. They were going to swarm them like locusts to crop. Once they agreed, he then instructed them to go home, work together, build weapons, and siege tools, train brothers and sons in the art of not just war, but total destruction and annihilation of the entire elven race. In six months, they would march upon the elves and punish them for their transgressions.

Now his goal of building an army big enough to make a strategic offensive was almost complete. As he acquired new men under his command, he gave leaders of the individual tribes rank and command of his upper echelons thus giving them purpose and prestige within the force. He briefed them daily of his plans, and worked with them, teaching them, and building strong ties with each leader.

Though the tribal leaders came from near barbarian cultures, that had lived in this area for hundreds of years, they were still only slightly more advanced than the gronts of the eastern forests where Dar Drannon first called home. In the end, it was not hard to sway them into joining as he offered them a bigger prize. The promise of elven blood.

"Follow Commander Voll and march north to the Elven Kingdom. Attack their southernmost outpost that they call Fort Stone Elf along the way. We have hit that outpost a few times in skirmishes, but have never hit them with the force that we have assembled now. I want you to move the entire force out before the sun rises tomorrow. When you see the outpost, do not hesitate, do not falter, hit them hard and show no quarter!" his voice rose slightly with every word until he was nearly shouting and spitting in Voll's face.

Daegon then went back to Traelyn and kneeled before her, begging her for forgiveness for his anger.

"I should have more trust in you," he said looking to the ground on one knee.

"Daegon, my son. You are the strongest willed of all my sons, and I love you for it, but I fear it will be your end. This war with the elves must not end in the destruction you foresee."

Daegon looked up at her, incredulous. "But Great Mother, you have instilled your hate of the elves upon me from a young age."

"Yes I have," she said placing her hand behind his neck and kneeled to his level, looking into his eyes. "You must trust me in this my son. You trusted me in my hate, can you trust me in my compassion?"

"I will do as you command Great Mother, but only because you command it."

"You mistake my meaning. I am not commanding you, rather I am pleading with you, because I know that your hate, if continued, will be your demise."

Those words repeated in Daegon's head the whole trip south. All he knew was his hatred of the elves. She had made it his life mission to destroy the elves for her, since she could not do it alone. Now she wanted him to change his heart. Try as he may, he knew he would not change, nor did he want to.

He rode in the drizzling rain never taking his eyes off of Naemyn, because he had removed Naeym's bindings, but he still did not trust him. When the gray daylight disappeared, trading itself for the dark of night, Naemyn stopped the group to inform them that they were near. Traelyn had allowed Daegon to bring Traegon and five warriors for protection.

No one spoke the rest of the way. Two hours later, they reached the base of the catacombs at the exact spot where Naemyn had fought the ravages. He dismounted his horse, reached inside the saddlebag, pulled out two torches, and lit them. He handed one of the torches to Daegon and walked towards the cluster of rocks on a small hillside. With the torchlight, he exposed a dozen or so dead ravages that lay in the mud while large black crows feasted on their carcasses.

"What happened to them?" Traegon asked looking at the blood not only from the ravages, but also the dead elves that lay scattered throughout the muddied wood line.

Naemyn only grunted his response.

As they dismounted and unsheathed their swords, they heard a moaning sound coming from the carcasses. The crows immediately took flight and the only sound to be heard was the flapping of their wings as Naemyn yelled to get inside.

Traegon and Traelyn ran to tie the horses up to a tree, but Naemyn shouted. "Forget the horses, we have to get inside now!! Everyone, inside now!"

The horses were turned loose nickering, as it seemed that they could sense what was happening before the others did. First, the dead elves begin to rise, and then the ravages stood up directly onto their hind legs and stood there for a few seconds as if trying to figure out why they had been summoned back to the living. The elves were in even worse shape as they stood up and then sat back down shaking their heads, clearly confused. It did not take them long to figure out that what was happening to them was not natural, yet filled them with rage.

When they stood up, their faces still covered in mud, they showed no sign of true life except for the blue tint glowing brightly in their eyes, shining so bright that most of their faces shimmered from the glow. Some withdrew their swords while others scrambled to find their swords, knives, or bows. The ravages did not bother looking for either sword or shield but barred their teeth and ran towards Naemyn and no one else.

Naemyn, realizing both elf and ravage were coming for him raised both hands, clapped them together sending a shock wave all around his body knocking down every one, hoping that the living might recover quicker than the undead would.

Luckily, for everyone, the gamble paid off. Daegon, Traegon, Traelyn and the soldiers recovered, though their ears rung and their heads ached as if they had just been hit by a fist-sized rock squarely between the eyes.

"Follow me!" Naemyn yelled as they ran towards the rocky hillside.

"Where are you going?" Daegon yelled. "There is no where to go!"

Naemyn ignored him, stood with his arms above his head, and said a few unintelligible words before a rock on the hillside disappeared, exposing a black door.

"Inside!" Naemyn yelled as he stepped aside and let the others inside as he prepared to cast another spell.

One by one, and single file, everyone entered the entrance. When the last one scrambled to safety, Naemyn sent off another blast knocking all of the elves and ravages to their feet just as they were within inches of attacking the last human warrior that entered the entrance.

Once certain that the threat had been successfully neutralized, Naemyn stepped inside, and magically sealed the entrance. In their rush, no one bothered to grab torches, but he realized quickly that there was no need for torches as the glow inside the cavern was brighter than when they were here before.

Traelyn, Daegon, Traegon and the three human warriors stood in awe looking to the sky of the cavern seeing that there was the appearance of being outside underneath the night sky.

"How is this possible?" Daegon asked.

"The coming of Markenhirth makes it possible," he answered in a flat tone, actually surprised at the stark differences since they were last there.

The ceiling sky was dark with fuzzy stars shimmering, but the sky had a bluish tint to it as if it was an hour before sunrise. Naemyn took notes of the changes, as the clouds were flying quickly in different directions as if they were caught in an erratic wind current.

"How can there be a sky and clouds in here?" Traegon asked.

"Those are not clouds," Naemyn answered flatly. "Those are Wraeths, and something has disturbed them."

Naemyn looked to his human companions for a reaction, but received none except for awe, with the exception of Traelyn, who had been upon this realm far too long to be awed by such events.

"What has disturbed them?" Traegon asked after a long pause of watching the wraeths scatter and flit in the sky as if they had no purpose other than bats chasing insects in the night air.

"I cannot say for sure, other than maybe it is because the Markenhirth season is nearing."

The old elven kings had always considered this area sacred, so they began entombing their dead deep within the mountains. It was not until many years later that they discovered these mountains contained one of the Quarterstar shards. This led them to sanctify this area as the most sacred place in the whole realm. They soon learned that the spirits laid to rest within the catacombs were not completely resting. These spirits could not leave this entrapment and journey to their final resting place with the elven gods, instead a part of them remained to communicate truths to those left behind. This caused the catacombs to become a sought out destination for adventure seekers or scholars of the prophecies. However, most of them ended up becoming trapped and tortured wraeths themselves.

"We need to keep moving," Naemyn said, taking Traelyn's hand, looking down as he kissed the top of her hand. Surprised at how soft her hand felt, he paused to look closer, and noticed that her knuckles were large yet her fingers were frail and bony which matched her long scrawny jaw line. This was the first time that he realized just how old she had become. The last time he saw her she was still a young beautiful woman just out of her teenage years.

He took her hand and led her down the steps into the lower expanse of the entrance. As they walked, Daegon, Traegon, and their three warriors continued to look up at the open cavernous ceiling and the moving wraeths that were still floating about.

As soon as Naemyn's foot touched the soft bottom of the grassy expanse the wraeths disappeared and the ground began to shake violently. The shaking only lasted a few seconds, but when it stopped, everyone had lost their balance and was on the ground. Before they could stand up, long, skinny, over-stretched arms began to come out of the ground and grab their arms and legs.

Traelyn began to sink into the ground quicker than anyone else, as she did not fight as hard as the others. Naemyn was the first to stand up, as he was familiar with the source and the type of magic that was being used. His Wrae and Kronn were much stronger than anything within these catacombs. Daegon, Traegon and the others struggled fiercely, but were not making much headway with the multiple arms that were holding them down, attempting to pull them underneath the mud.

"Naemyn's body began to shimmer blue and fade in and out of the blue light and darkness until the attacking arms no longer had anything to hold onto. Taking a shadowy ethereal form, he then floated near the humans picking up their swords that they had dropped while struggling to free themselves, and put them into their owners' hands, before returning to solid form.

"You must fight them yourselves, I cannot touch them, I can only evade them."

Daegon reacted first by taking his sword and swung about wildly. On his second swing and every swing after, he sliced the arms into pieces that fell to ground wiggling like bifurcated worms.

Once he was free, he then charged over to Traelyn, dropping his sword and landing on top of her, grabbing her left arm, as her arm and her head were the only things exposed out of the muddy ground.

"Traegon, help me!" he yelled as he pulled in vain, helplessly holding her as she continued to slip under the ground. Traegon still battled the arms that were pinning him down and could not free himself to help his father.

"You cannot let her slip away!" Naemyn yelled, showing real fear in his voice, realizing that if he lost her, he would not be able to steal away the Quarterstar talisman from her.

Muddy arms snaked their way around Traegon's throat as he slashed the two that were at his feet, though he could not move any more than the sitting position that he managed to get to.

The more he struggled to stand up, the more pressure the arms pulled upon his neck, choking and blocking his airway. Then arms wrapped around his chest, and he was about to give up when he realized that the arms were one of Daegon's warriors. Traegon dug his heels into the ground and pushed while Trapper, another one of the human warriors, encouraged him to push hard. As Trapper pulled, Traegon pushed, but the arms around his neck tightened as he did so.

"Keep pushing!" Trapper yelled as he strained to pull Traegon away.

Push he did, but the more he pushed, and the harder Trapper pulled, the less he could breathe. Then, without warning, the arms around his throat turned loose. He flopped on his back and allowed Trapper to pull him free of the dozen or so arms looking for new victims.

"Father," Traegon said as he grabbed Trapper's arm and pointed to him to help Daegon and Traelyn. As they ran to her, they saw the fingers of one of the warriors hands slip beneath the surface and seconds later the foot of another warrior.

When they reached her, Naemyn guided each of them to grab her left arm and pull. Daegon, during the time Traegon and Trapper were freeing themselves, had managed to pull her out passed her shoulders.

"Can you bring out your right arm?" Daegon asked her.

"No, something has it and is pulling it down. Hurry, it hurts!"

"Naemyn, what can we do? She is too old for us to be playing tug of war with her! You have to be able to help!"

"I cannot help without hurting her further. The only help I can offer is to sever any body part that the wraeths have a hold of, and I know you do not want me to do that. Just keep pulling, they will turn loose, they are not that strong."

"But they are so strong, I can feel their strength pulling against me."

"They will tire, just hang on."

Hang on they did, for nearly an hour they fought, only gaining an inch at a time while Naemyn shouted encouragement. Though his encouragement wasn't helpful for all the good he thought he was doing, he was merely reminding them that they needed to get moving, for he feared that the longer they took, the more intense the peril they were going to face when traversing deeper into the catacombs.

They did not quit, even when Traelyn begged them to let her go. They pulled as hard as they dared and rested frequently by holding their position. They continued in this fashion, until finally, with a whimper and a cry, Traelyn passed out, which gave the men a little more encouragement to pull harder without fear of hearing her crying out in pain.

Inch by inch, minute by minute, they gained ground and eventually pulled her free. When all that remained held by the ghastly hands was below her knees, the wraeths released their grip and Traelyn's company pulled her out and rolled over in exhaustion.

Naemyn gave them no time to relax. "We have to move. Let's go!" he shouted picking Daegon up off the ground.

"Let go of me elven scum!" Daegon shouted as he planted his hands squarely into Naemyn's chest and pushed him back. He then bent to a knee and placed his arm behind Traelyn. "Great Mother…" he whispered. "We have to go. Please wake up."

He repeated that to her as he gently shook her. After the fifth time, her eyes opened, blinking quickly.

"Oh, no," she said, realizing that she was not in a safe place.

"We have to go now," Daegon said, bending over to help her up to her feet. Once she was on her feet, she looked around to get her bearings, straightened her blouse, and regained her composure the best she could.

"What attacked us?" she asked, still stunned.

"Not good beings, and not entirely of elven nature, but rather beings placed here not of their own will. Even though this is a place of respect, and reverence, it is also prison to the dead that do not die. I do not know why or how they got here, but they are here." Naemyn explained. He had studied about these malevolent wraeth's under Kroejin's tutelage. He learned that their activity increased with the coming of the Markenhirth when the Sippling tree's roots loosened their tight grip upon the realm, thereby allowing the cold frozen dark season of Markenhirth to take place.

"Do you know where the shard is?" Daegon asked impatiently. "If you do, let's go, before more of these things come."

"Precisely my intention. Follow me," Naemyn said as he walked toward the center of the expanse. The soft grass squished beneath his feet, but began to harden with every step. Daegon, Traegon, Traelyn, and Trapper followed him. They crossed over many shallow two-foot wide streams as they wandered through the open expanse. Naemyn did not speak a word, but they trusted him that he had their best interests at heart and was not setting them up for another attack like the one they had just escaped from.

After twenty minutes of walking across the expanse, they came to a solid rock cliff that stretched before them to the left and to the right as far as they could see with each side running into the darkness, fading out of sight. Naemyn did not stop and showed no signs of confusion as he turned to their left and walked another hundred feet until he found a seam and walked in between the wall.

They found themselves in another section of the cavern that also had the appearance of no ceiling, and as Naemyn had predicted the wraeths were increasing in number. There were so many above, that instead of wispy clouds, it looked as if a storm was creeping in, covering many of the stars.

They stood upon another precipice that overlooked another section of the catacombs. Stairs led down many flights into a maze of walls and twists and turns. Naemyn didn't not waste any time looking at the maze below. Once again, he never spoke and expected the others to follow, which they did without question.

Naemyn knew where to go and where not to go, he searched his memory from his tutorship with Kroejin when his master made him scour the maps of the catacombs and commit every angle to memory.

Now he just needed to get there as quick as he could without running into any of the troublesome wraeths that could hinder their progress. Traversing through this maze would not be the quickest way, and he needed to go above the Guardian's chamber in order to accomplish his goal. In order for him to secure the Shard to the Talisman that Traelyn holds, the Guardian specifically told him that only a direct descendant of the first human king, Dar Drannon, which Traelyn and her two sons were, would be able to take it out of here. He only needed one of them, and by his stroke of good luck, he had both sons.

Right now, all he wanted to do was secure the Shard and Talisman and take it for himself. The maze below was not somewhere he wanted to be. If wraeths were flying above as well as coming out of the ground, it would not be long before they would be coming out of their crypts.

The last time Naemyn was here, the Guardian made it clear to him that his Kronn did not always bring about the best of him or those around him. He had to be cautious in using his Wrae and his Kronn, especially in these catacombs where both exist. Both Wrae and Kronn have existed here since the creation when their gods defeated the Markenhirth sending the star of creation through his heart and separating the star into four shards, and one of them landing here.

He looked behind him and saw the others obediently following him. He lifted the hood of his cloak over his head and walked on. He knew his way around here, but he had to make a few extra turns to avoid some of the crypts. The Tombs of Kings was one in particular, and he did not want to run into the wraeth of King Keiyann Krowe. He did not know why, other than the guilt he carried that he might eventually betray the entombed king's son, who was also his friend, Jaerick.

Naemyn and the others walked into the maze but skirted the edge by staying to the left, hugging the wall, and taking every left turn. Daegon murmured his disgust many times, as he grew ever more impatient and distrustful following Naemyn, which Naemyn ignored and kept leading. After nearly an hour of wandering through the cavernous maze, they came to stone steps that looked to be painstakingly carved with a fork. The stairway went straight up for hundreds of feet at a sharp incline.

"I can't climb that," Traelyn gasped.

"I will help you Great Mother." Traegon offered.

Traelyn smiled and touched his chin. "I know child. I know you mean well, but I am not going to let you carry me."

"Then how are we going to get you up?" Daegon asked.

"I will stay here. Traegon and Trapper can stay with me. You two will go."

"Then give me the talisman," Daegon said holding out his hand.

"I would no sooner give you the talisman as I would Naemyn."

"Then what are we going to do?" Daegon asked shaking his head while putting his hands on his temples.

"It is going to be ok Traelyn. We are not in any hurry at this point. We will go one step at a time," Naemyn said with a warm smile.

Traegon and Daegon each took a hand and walked her up the steps, one step at a time, while Naemyn led and Trapper took the rear. Trapper took each step one at a time as well, but he let himself fall behind a few steps so that he could keep a close eye on the others as they advanced up the stairs. They had only traversed fifty steps when one of the wraeths came down from the sky, floating down onto the stairway about ten steps above them, and then materialized into an elf in full leather with leaf style imprints and silver ring mail battle armor. He wore a helm and held a shield in his left hand and a silver sword with a jeweled pommel in his right. Naemyn instantly recognized him as one of their greatest warriors.

"Naemyn," he spoke, as his eyes glowed the same blue hue that the dead ravages and elves had outside. "Do not continue in this endeavor."

"Why do you want me to stop?" he asked, removing his hood. "I recognize you. You are Eranon, and the Eranon I knew would not want to stop me."

"Indeed, I am Eranon, and though I have passed out of the living realm, I live in a more powerful realm, and I aim to retake elven power using this realm and yours."

"But I am trying to restore elven purity and dominance," Naemyn said trying to convince this once living defender of elven purity.

"Then you are on the wrong path. This woman is a descendant of Dar Drannon. Dar Drannon cannot return, and she will bring him back, so she must die here and now, and you, if you insist on pressing forward, you will disrupt our plans to nullify all that we are attempting to do."

As he said that, Traelyn's body began to raise and spin with her hands outstretched. Naemyn felt something grasp his ankles and looked down, seeing his ankles held fast by muddy hands that came out from the steps. Daegon, Traegon, and Trapper each had a wraeth materialize behind them and wrap their arms around them as well, holding them so tight that all three of them gasped to breathe as they felt their chests were crushing from the pressure.

Traelyn screamed in fear as six more wraeths dropped down from the sky and floated in front of her. Looking into their faces, she saw only skeletal figures that glowed blue and white flickering back and forth from boned skulls to full-fleshed elven form. They did this as they circled around her and began to scream louder and louder as they closed in tighter.

Then, as if by some command, they stopped, and when they did, their form materialized into a solid form and all six wrapped their arms and legs around her. When they did so, the weight of their bodies dropped her to the ground and she came down hard, twisting her ankle and shattering her left shin.

"Stop this!" Naemyn yelled at Eranon.

Naemyn struggled to get free from his wraeth captor by using his Kronn, even though he knew doing so was dangerous in this place. He began to reach deep down inside to send out an explosion that would send the wraeths back to their sleeping tombs when he felt the air become thick. So thick that he could see the air floating in front of him like shimmering water.

Then it happened. Everything went black, followed by bright orange light. The wraeths that held Traelyn screamed in terror and pain as their forms caught on fire. The fire wrapped around their bodies but was extinguished after a single burst of flame, which was immediately replaced by a solid block of ice around them. Their bodies flew to the air and then fell to the ground frozen. When their bodies hit the ground, they shattered and turned to water which was quickly absorbed into the ground.

Traelyn stood up, and when she did, she was young. Naemyn stopped calling his Kronn and saw Traelyn as he remembered her when she left: young and agile, soft skin and long brown hair. She looked terrified, but he also saw rage and anger in her face.

Sensing the change in her, Traelyn felt a renewed sense of commitment. She looked at her hands and felt a new invigoration to her soul. She would take her mission in her own hands.

"I am here to find my father!" she shouted to Eranon walking up the steps pointing at him. "Your kind took him from me and you will bring him back to me."

"I will not and I cannot. Your father is imprisoned. Keiyann Krowe was fooled into thinking he was helping him, but know this, we have your father, and we will not let him go."

Chapter 25

In a furious rage, brought on by a new flood of memories that came to her with her youth, and by the revelation that she and her father had been betrayed by the elves, Traelyn charged up the stairway towards Eranon. Her anger fumed so strongly inside of her that she had no time to notice that her ankle and leg were no longer broken.

Along with this youth came the feelings of justified rage against the elves, but at the same time, her feelings of love for Jaerick were becoming increasingly stronger with every step up the stairs. She wanted to see him, and see him now. She needed to get at this elven spirit and dispel his being whence it came. She did not know how she was going to do it, but she was going to get a hold of him and throttle him to death if she had to.

Eranon did nothing but open his arms as if she was his long lost love.

"Traelyn, stop!" Naemyn yelled.

She did not stop, but Daegon, Traegon, and Trapper bolted behind her and was only a few steps behind when she felt a tug at her back. She could not lift her feet another step forward, but she could turn around, and when she did so she saw that Daegon, Traegon and Trapper were three solid blocks of obsidian black ice, smooth and tight against their bodies. They floated trapped in frozen blocks over the stairs, dripping as they were already beginning to melt. Naemyn stood behind them also frozen, but in fear and not ice. Traelyn was about to unleash her rage on Naemyn when he spoke first.

"I am so sorry," he pleaded in earnest as if he were a child apologizing to his mother.

"What have you done?" she screamed in fury, raking her fingers through her hair from above her ears to the top of her head.

"My Kronn doesn't always work the way I intend it to."

Eranon began laughing as he turned around to walk up the steps, took two steps up, but stopped and turned back around.

"You cannot control your Kronn Naemyn, because your heart is not pure anymore. You are not the Sor elf that you think you are, you are now neither Sor nor Val. You are a part of this puzzle that connects the two races, Val and Sor, in order to destroy everything."

"I am not here to destroy anything! I am here to bring power back to the elven race!"

"Then why are you here with this daughter of Dar Drannon, if not for selfish desires?"

"I want what she wants, she wants the Shard."

"If that is that what you want? Then I will not stop you."

Eranon turned around again, walked up two steps and then changed into his wraeth form and swirled into the air and flew away down the hallway at the top of the stairs.

"What do you plan on doing do with my sons?" Traelyn asked.

"I can help them," Naemyn said, but as he said that, they heard Eranon's voice in the chamber echoing out. "There is little you can do, that I cannot undo."

Naemyn was able to adjust his Kronn to release her, and when she was free, she looked up the steps to make sure that Eranon was gone, and once she confirmed that, she ran down the steps to her sons, and as Naemyn had promised, they began to melt out of their confinement.

The ice block melted within minutes, and the three men fell to their knees. Traegon and Trapper rolled over to their sides, straddling on top of three steps and shivering out of control. Daegon however, stayed on all fours and began cursing, then stood up still shivering and pointed to Naemyn.

"This is the last time you will betray us!" he yelled to Naemyn. "I may have been frozen solid, but I could hear every word you said. If your own people do not believe your motives why should we? And now this elf-wraeth is giving you the go ahead to move on. I do not trust you, and why should I?"

"Daegon, you are right," he said, holding up his hands as Daegon approached.

"Please don't touch me as I cannot guarantee your safety as far as my Kronn is concerned."

Daegon stopped, looked at Naemyn, and then turned to his son and Trapper, and saw them slowly rising to their feet. He turned back around to Naemyn rubbing his arms for warmth.

"We want the same thing," Naemyn began. "We may want it for different reasons, and I realize that you don't want any of this at all, and are just doing it because Traelyn wants it, but we can get this shard and get out of here."

"Naemyn, you have us in a bind, and I don't know why I allowed you to get us here. I devastated your force at the ambush, and now you are here telling us what to do."

"Daegon, I understand your hatred for us, as I feel the same hatred for all humans, but together we can get your mother what she needs and then we can continue with our hatred for each other."

"I don't trust you, and I…" Daegon started.

"Where are we going Naemyn?" Traelyn, tired of their fighting, interrupted. "Lead us out of here, before I let my sons kill you now, and I will figure out my own way out of here."

"Traegon, Trapper, get up!" Daegon shouted. "We're moving."

Traegon stood up first and picked up Trapper. When Trapper stood up, he found his legs were a bit wobbly and took him a few moments to regain his balance. Naemyn urged them to follow him up the stairs, without seeing if they would follow, but they did. Traelyn followed behind Naemyn showing a bounce in her step from her newly invigorated youthful legs. Traegon and Trapper followed her while Daegon took the rear. They climbed the stairs for many moments until they reached the top that opened up to a corridor that no longer had the illusion of sky, but rather a solid stone ceiling with an opening through the top that flooded the entire corridor with sunlight.

"This is it," Naemyn announced, sounding surprised that he had found the exact spot he was looking for.

Naemyn picked up his pace to almost a run until he found another hole, but this one was a three-foot hole in the center of the floor. Naemyn went to his knees and stuck his head through it. He smiled when he saw the Guardian down below sitting at his table reading books. He heard the river rushing in the cavern. Even though it brought back bad memories of when the Guardian informed him of the deception of his own Kronn, he could not have been happier to find him.

He pulled his head out of the hole and signaled to the others to gather around.

"Get down here. Each of you take a look inside."

Daegon looked at Naemyn with distrust, as if by sticking his head through the hole, he might lose it.

Everyone did as he asked, Traelyn was the last and when she pulled her head back out she looked incredulous.

"Who is that?" she asked.

"That is what we call the Guardian. We have called him the Guardian because he guards the Quarterstar Shard. No one can remove the Shard. I tried the last time I was here, and failed, but he did give me one important piece of information. He told me that a descendant of the first Human King Dar Drannon would remove the Shard from the catacombs."

"Which one of us should go?" Daegon asked.

"They way I see it," Naemyn said. "It doesn't matter, three of you, including Traelyn are descendants of Dar Drannon. Traelyn is the closest, so I think she should go."

"She is NOT going down there," Daegon protested.

"Then it makes no difference to me. Descendant is descendant; I only need someone from the bloodline. You choose."

"I will go," Traegon volunteered.

"Then give him the talisman," Naemyn said.

Traelyn removed the talisman from the bag she held inside her blouse, and handed it to Traegon.

However, I must tell you something more," Naemyn said as he leaned back, still on his knees.

"There will be a sacrifice in order for us to remove the Shard. I do not know what the sacrifice requires."

"Then I will go," Traegon said. "Father, I am no use for you as a warrior, let me do this. This may be the only way to make a name for myself."

Daegon stood up and looked down upon his son. "I may not have a use for you as a warrior, but that is not what is important to me. You are my son, and I still love you. You will not go down there, I will."

"No father, listen, I want to do this. I can help the Great Mother achieve what she wants with the elven prince. That will be enough for me to know that I did something in a grand scale and be remembered for it. I *want* to do this. Look at the Great Mother," he said pointing to her. "She is young again. Something big is happening here, and I want to be a part of it."

"By sacrificing yourself? No, I won't have it, and you have no choice. Besides, he is an elf, and elves die!" he said with a devious smile.

With that, he leaned over, kissed his son on the forehead, snatched the talisman by the chain, and jumped into the hole.

Daegon fell next to the Guardian. He landed hard on his feet and rolled over his shoulder, but the fall had been too far and both of his ankles snapped as he landed. He rolled away in pain grabbing his ankles.

The Guardian stood up and walked over to Daegon, looked at him as if he knew he was coming, bent over, touched his ankles, and rubbed them. Daegon watched him as the Guardian's warm hands massaged his ankles. As he did this, he looked around at the cavern he was in and felt the coolness of the river rushing by as it moved the air, removing the stale cavernous stench he had been breathing since they entered the catacombs.

Daegon sat up, rubbed his ankles, and felt that there was no pain, soreness, or tightness to his ankles.

"How did you do that?" he asked.

"There are many things I have learned to do here. With the help of these books and with the help of the Shard and its Wrae and Kronn attributes, I have learned so much of this realm, and you will as well."

"What do you mean?"

"Are you not my replacement? I have been waiting for the king to replace me. I have served well over my required time."

Daegon shook his head. "No, I think you misunderstand, I am here to take the Shard. Naemyn said it would require a sacrifice, so I am here to make sure you make a proper sacrifice, so that we can take the Shard from here."

The Guardian looked at him confused.

"That is impossible. Even if you kill me, or even if I was to give it freely, neither you nor Naemyn will be leaving here with the Shard," he said.

"You lied!" Naemyn roared from above and jumped through the hole, but instead of landing, he stopped in mid air five feet above them, and was held motionless under the Guardian's power.

"You do not understand. This cannot happen because he is not the one."

"But he is a descendant, and he can be the sacrifice. Do not listen to his threats. I will assure that Daegon will be the sacrifice that you require."

"Prophecies can be tricky," the Guardian started, as if explaining a difficult lesson of life to a child, "especially the ones written in these books, some are false, and some are not. We will find out which ones are true in time."

"I followed your mandate, here he is, give me the Shard."

"It does not work that way, Naemyn. Even if I give you or him the Shard you will not be able to remove it, because he is not the one."

"Then what do we do?"

"Simple, you can just leave. I will allow you and Daegon to leave. However, if Daegon leaves, you will lose the first of your double sacrifice."

"And what if I choose to leave Daegon here, and take the talisman, what does the prophecies say then?"

Daegon stood up incredulous. "Why would I even want to be your sacrifice if we aren't going to get what we came for?"

"Listen to me now. Daegon may not have had pure intentions to relieve me, but if he stays here in my place, he will help you, Naemyn, accomplish your goal and at the same time, he will know that he will be helping the elves. He will, in essence be helping you crush the elven kingdom."

"I do not want to crush the elven kingdom, I want to restore it!"

"You will restore it, but all things must be destroyed before they can be rebuilt stronger."

"I do not want to help them in any way!" Daegon protested.

"Then the human race will become extinct," the Guardian whispered to Daegon. "Naemyn," the Guardian continued, pointing to Naemyn, still held suspended in mid air, "you will not receive any immediate benefit to Daegon's sacrifice, however, in time, a descendant of the human king will indeed fall through that hole and release Daegon from his bond. However, if Daegon does not stay, and his descendant falls through the hole, nothing will happen, just as nothing for you is happening now. Daegon must stay in order for the prophecy to continue on its path."

"Won't I die down here?" Daegon asked.

"No, you will live until relieved, by your descendant, or the elven king."

"But you said they have forgotten about you, what makes you think they won't forget about me?"

"I am confident that you will not be relieved by the elven king. One of Traegon's offspring will relieve you. Either way, right now, it is up to you to be part of, or to thwart prophecy. The choice is yours."

"What are we to do then?" Naemyn roared back again, struggling to decide if he should continue on the path to betray his king in order to gain power and prominence within a new age of elven rule, or to stick beside his friend and find another way.

"You must decide. Your decision will affect the prophecy one way or another. Do nothing, and to tell you the truth, I do not know what will happen. The prophecies are not written for that choice."

Naemyn twisted in his bind in an attempt to free himself, but could not.

"Do not struggle Naemyn. Make your decision and you will be free. I will tell you one more thing that may help you in the short term." The Guardian then pointed at the talisman. "The talisman has properties that when a shard is placed upon it, the user can travel throughout the realm. Even though the shard is not combined with the talisman, but because of the close proximity of the two, you can benefit from that power for a one-time trip out of here.

Use it well and leave to a place where you will be most beneficial."

"Then he is staying," Naemyn concluded.

"No, I am not, I will not have any part of this elven mysticism. Get me out of here, now!"

"Turn me loose! We are leaving," Naemyn announced.

"As you wish," the Guardian said, and in a flash of orange light Naemyn, Traegon and Trapper disappeared. Daegon felt a tug at his hand and noticed that the talisman also disappeared.

"I want to leave," Daegon said after they left, and realized he was alone with the Guardian. He held out his hands as if looking for the talisman. "Now get me out of here, I need to leave, I cannot stay here."

"You are where you belong. I will not and cannot help you out of here."

"Why not?"

"You have been placed here as a sacrifice by Naemyn. Now that he has done so, Kronn will not release you from here."

"So, I am to die here," he stated.

"Not for quite some time, but yes, you will die on the day that you are relieved. Until then, you will live here as the Guardian of the Shard at the Catacombs."

"What about you?"

The Guardian smiled. "There can only be one Guardian."

"What will happen to you?"

"The elves have reserved a special place for me here in the catacombs, I will become a wraeth and wait for a time when the prophecy states that we will be released to return to our god Val-Eahea."

"Then I will be here by myself?"

The Guardian looked at him as if to say, what did you expect, but instead said, "It is not as bad as it seems. Not only will you have books to read, you will learn how Kronn works, and how Wrae magic works, and how the two are polar opposites, yet attract and need each other to survive. You will also hear tales from some that enter the catacombs, and you will learn from the wraeths that visit you from time to time, especially during the Markenhirth extension. It is not without its surprises."

"What do we do now?"

The Guardian turned around, walked to wall opposite side of the river, near his table, and grabbed a stone cup off of a carved out shelf imbedded into the rock wall. He walked to the river, threw the cup into it, and within seconds it reappeared in his hands full of the water. He walked back and handed

Daegon the cup.

"Drink from the cup and tell me your name."

Daegon looked curiously at the water in the cup. The liquid inside had the substance of water, but it was streaked with blue, orange, and purple ribbons. He inhaled deeply and the ribbons lifted out of the cup and into his nose. He then raised the cup to his lips and drank.

"My name is Daegon."

"My name is Rogeuin the Everlasting, and you are now Daegon the Everlasting, the first non-elf Guardian of all of time."

Then the Guardian smiled, and changed into a purple mist that held his form for a few more seconds, and then became a wraeth as he drifted towards the river, lowering into it where he became one with the water and disappeared downstream.

Daegon watched him go. He felt no less human than he did before he drank the liquid, but he did have a sense of peace about his predicament. He no longer felt a deep hatred of the elves. He did not particularly feel a love for them either, but war and hate was no longer in his heart.

Feeling oddly satisfied, he looked up to the ceiling and saw no top to the cavern, but only black sky with a brightly shining star where he had just fallen through. He wondered which one of his great grandchildren would be the next one to fall through, and what would he say or do when that time came.

Chapter 26

Moving over two thousand men through the thick-forested tangle proved to be harder than Voll could have ever imagined. He would not have been able to do it without the help of Daegon's other top commanders. They traveled north along the road as long as they dared, but the commanders talked him into proceeding off the path and into the tangle after the scouts reported having seen traces of the elves, and suspecting that they were watching their advance.

Voll's scouts said that they first noticed movement in the trees, but when they looked up, they admitted to only seeing large, broken spider webs hanging down from the limbs. They never once saw any elves, but all in the scouting party admitted that they heard abnormal movement.

"If the elves are in the forest and watching us, why would we leave the road, and into unknown territory that only they know best?" Voll asked.

"I know commander, it may sound like the wrong thing to do to you, but Daegon would take action, by using the forest as cover," Commander Urish said.

Commander Urish was once the leader of Daegon's rival tribes. Since his tribe was the first to align with Daegon, he was rewarded with the highest command under him by making him commander of all of the rival tribes that followed thereafter. Commander Urish knew Daegon's tactics better than anyone as he had seen Daegon on both sides of the battlefield.

"We will end up spreading out our force," Voll protested.

"That is not necessarily a bad thing. Our scouts have not been able to draw out the elves, but a large force might, and if they do, then we will know where they are, and as long as we keep the distance between us short, we can easily strike them with the remainder of the force."

"Or they can hit and run us all day long, as we have done to them in the past."

"I will not let that happen. Let me lead the forward force with a few horses and archers flanked by light spearmen and two companies of infantry. Let me do this and I will draw them out to a fight."

Voll agreed to the plan, but told him that they would keep a few companies on the road, for flanking security, along with a company farther down the road to provide a rear guard. If there were to be any fighting it would be farther north, and he insisted that he would ride with Commander Urish. To which Commander Urish protested, stating that they do not need to have two commanders together, so Voll acquiesced and agreed to let the commander lead. They traveled for most of the day amongst the forest keeping out of the thickest tangle so as not to become trapped and boxed in.

The thick forest frustrated the scouts at every turn as they navigated through the forest when they could and switching back to the road when they hand to. This caused for even slower movement, as they had to twist, turn, and backtrack through and around numerous draws and spurs. Large sentinel pine trees towered into the sky in large clumps, sometimes so tightly that not even a small boy could fit between the openings. The ground foliage also prevented travel as large horse sized ferns and bushes crowed the hillsides around the trees.

The sun began to set and cast dark shadows upon them through the thick canopy when Voll heard shouts. He turned on his mount and shouted at his men to be prepared for battle. He listened and waited, but the longer he did, he realized he was losing the morale of his men, for the sounds they were hearing were not the sounds of battle, but the sounds of fear, death and destruction of his men and horse.

The dying horses set off some of the worse sounds he had ever heard as they nickered and screamed just as loud, if not louder than the men. He knew if he waited any longer, his men might be paralyzed with fear, and would lose confidence in their fighting abilities.

"Follow me up this spur, we will come around the top of the hill and pin them between Commander Urish's men!" Voll shouted, not certain if that is how it would work, but he could only hope.

He kicked his horse to charge up the small hill that rounded around the draw. His twenty mounted archers followed while the spear and infantry ran behind them just below the tip of the spur on the backside of where the sounds were coming from. The closer they came to the battle, the more they could hear the men screaming in fear and agony as they approached. *What could cause that much fear,* Voll wondered as he crested the hill and looked down into a valley.

As he rolled over the top, he could not believe his eyes. The hill where they stood upon did indeed provide higher ground against the elves, but the elves had Commander Urish pinned in a large deep crevice. In the ravine attacking his men were swarms of spiders large and small. Large spiders attacked the men one at a time, while some men were being consumed and covered by hundreds of smaller spiders.

Elven archers, in dark green and black leaf patterned leather armor surrounded them on three sides of the upper edge of the ridgeline. Only the northern side remained uncovered as that side of the depression ended in a solid cliff face that made traversing impossible. In between every archer was another elf kneeling with large buckets on their backs filled with long 4-foot arrows that had large black bulbous arrowheads.

The archers nocked, set, and loosed each arrow at a rapid pace, and as soon as the arrows hit their mark, the black arrowheads turned into large spiders. Whether it was a human target or just on the ground nearby, the spiders were released from the arrow and attacked the humans. If the arrow hit the human directly, the spiders came to life inside the body cavity, and worked their way out of the body climbing out of their throats or ripping their way out through their chests.

The elves shot arrows that had different types of spiders that were magically sealed within the arrowhead. While some were aimed directly at the warriors, others were shot into the air and exploded into a webbed air assault of thousands of the smaller spiders dropping down upon their prey, biting them, poisoning and killing them in a painful, but quick death. The warriors that found themselves covered in these little black spiders ran in confusion, their skin turning purple, and the veins in their face turning black.

Voll witnessed all of this confusion, and none of it he would consider a battle, but rather a tortured slaughter. Men ran in fear swatting their bodies and faces, while others tried to kill the spiders as they crawled on their fellow warriors, and others died grisly deaths as the spiders climbed their way out of dead body cavities.

He had seen enough.

"Captain Droe, take one spear company and two archer companies to the north of both ridges and force the elves to the south of that ridge, from there we will meet them and either crush them or push them into that valley and see how they like that treatment."

Captain Droe rode away barking orders. Voll could not stand there watching his men being slaughtered without doing something. He risked losing the morale of those able to fight. He had to act now, as the men that were witnessing the slaughter were more angry than fearful, so he thought to take advantage of that anger before it turned into fear.

The elves were so engrossed in their malicious spider butchery that Captain Droe took them by surprise. The elven archers began dropping from the barrage of arrows of Captain Droe's cavalry. The first barrage came from his archers on foot followed by his cavalry as they rode along the ridge first taking out the elves, and then knocking the remaining elves off of the ledge with the horses as they powered through their line.

By the time the spearmen came up, there wasn't much left along the ridge except for unarmed basket carriers whom most either jumped to avoid the charge or fell to their stomachs to avoid the spears. After the ridge was mostly cleared, the spearmen dropped their spears, unsheathed their short swords, and fought back the remaining elves on the ledge.

Once Voll realized that the tide of the battle had turned in his favor, he ordered the remainder of his force to hold tight while he went to regroup the rest of the force. When he returned, he was met with a new force. This new opposition must have been alerted to Captain Droe's attack and had come out of hiding for support.

They charged towards Voll's warriors on horses with lances and swords. Voll yelled at his cavalry and speared infantry to charge into the fray, which they did, quickly and obediently. He was actually surprised at just how obedient they had been, and it gave him a small sample as to the power that Commander Daegon held.

The elves and humans crashed at each other with a loud clash of sword and shield. Horses nickered, reared up, and died under the human spears, causing the elves to fall off of their horses and succumb to the brutality of the human swords. A few were able to recoup in enough time to take to the fight on foot. Voll continued to monitor the battle and bark orders to his sub commanders who followed each command flawlessly.

During the battle, he also noticed a group of elves on the northern side of the ravine monitoring the battle. These elves looked to be the commanders. They wore the same green and black armor, but he noticed their banner was the same as their shields that were strapped to the side of their mounts. When he studied the banner, the style of this attack made sense. It was a large black spider with all eight legs touching the edges of the standard on a dark green field with a black cross background.

Then he heard a voice inside his head. A voice he recognized as eerily familiar, and a voice he was neither receptive to right now, nor immediately discarded. It was Aegyn, and she flew directly overhead surveying the battle, causing almost everyone to stop fighting if only for a few seconds to see what it was. Fearing their death by the distraction, they refocused on the battle, forsaking the danger from above.

"Help me Aegyn," Voll asked.

"I have told you before that I will not hurt the elves."

"Then help me without directly hurting them."

"How?"

"See those elves over there," he said pointing to the commanders on the northern side. "Get them to lead their forces into that ravine."

"I am not sure if I should."

"Aegyn, do this…please, for me."

Voll did not wait to see if she would help him, but he barked orders to another company of archers and infantry to follow him to the western side to outflank the elves on the north and west. He noticed that Aegyn flew away to the west and did not return. It did not matter, he felt the tide was turning in their favor and he needed to push harder to route the elves. He wanted to do nothing more than give these elves a taste of their own medicine by trapping them in the ravine.

Voll and a dozen of his mounted warriors raced through the forest slashing the foliage so that the archer and infantry companies could follow. They made quick time of it, rushing through a mile of hacking their way down spurs and back up the draws, until he came headlong into the northwestern side of the elven force.

They did not take them by surprise though, as Voll did not worry about how loud they were. Speed was of the essence in this charge. Voll hacked away at the elven ground forces as he charged his way to the elven commanders on horseback. When they realized that they were in trouble, they turned and scattered, fleeing alongside the eastern edge of the ravine. He mounted a chase, feeling excitement as everywhere he looked the humans were routing the elves.

"I guess we don't need Aegyn after all," he said aloud as he chased the commanders, but as he said that Aegyn flew over his head, and just three feet above him before landing with a thud in front of the elven commanders.

At the exact moment that Aegyn landed, the elven forces were skirting along the east side as Voll's forces and were chasing them towards the open end of the ravine. They had intended to escape the battlefield by turning into the woods just south of the ravine and circle back north, but instead saw the dragon as she arched her back, spread her wings, and mimicked that she was about to spew fire on them.

The elves stepped back in fear and turned to run away from her, only to be met with Voll's infantry that were right on their heels, leaving them no choice but to run into the ravine. The elven warriors scattered into the ravine like ants that had their scented path disrupted, including the commanders that Voll was chasing.

Voll looked at Aegyn in a form of thank you and she lowered her head to the ground and looked up at him, then stood back up, straightened, and beat her wings a number of times before she took flight and headed north.

Voll then rode back through the forest to the road and announced that they needed to follow him back to the ravine and off of the road in case more elves were coming. He also commanded one company on the road with instructions to announce with their horns if any elves arrive. Once he returned, he gave orders to surround the ravine.

"Take good aim, take your time, pick them off one by one!" Voll commanded.

His archers happily obeyed.

Chapter 27

Jaerick sensed Greynim was in trouble. He knew his son had disobeyed him when he heard the horns calling to muster. The sentry blew the horn from the tallest tower and within an hour, Greynim charged out of the castle with five companies of his favorite Spider Battalion. They marched out wearing their black and green leather leaf patterned armor with dark green mailed sleeves. Two of the companies were the Spider Archers, and the other three were the Spider Infantry. Jaerick was very proud of his Spider Battalion, and he rarely got to use them, so it did not surprise Jaerick when Greynim marched out of the gates with them.

He waited until the next day days for his son's return, but could not wait any longer. He had to find his son, for this sensation that he was in trouble was just too strong. Now it was Jaerick's turn to sound the muster. He assembled three battle companies of mounted cavalry to come to his son's aid.

Jaerick would have found the day invigorating, to be able to stretch his legs outside of the castle had he not been so worried for his son. His heart pounded in his throat, and his chest felt heavy all day, even as his servants helped him put on his light combat armor. He wore his green leather mail and breastplate, covered by his green and yellow hooded leaf cloak. He did not don the hood though, as he wore his darkened silver crown with the dark green emerald rubies etched into the needles of the pine trees that extended out of the crown. This was his favorite crown to wear when he did not want to be too obvious, but still wanted to announce that he was the king.

He marched out into the staging area after his companies had mustered. His servant helped him onto his mount, and then just as his son had done the day before, he led his newly mustered battle companies out of the main gate south into what he hoped would not be a battle, and definitely not the battle that his dreams were predicting.

They rode south along the main road knowing that Greynim had to have made a stop at Fort Stone Elf along the way. He also knew that the humans wouldn't be north of the their southernmost outpost, so they rode hard until they reached there.

When they reached the gates of Fort Stone Elf before sunset of that day, the elves at the post had his banners of the Elven Kingdom raised. The banner was of a star falling through the sky, split into four pieces by a smaller red star on a purple field. It rose high as they approached and the horns blared that the king was near. The Elven Kingdom Banner on the battlement rose higher between the two towers on the main gate followed by another flag raised just below it displaying a crown lying on top of the Sword of Valkilye overlaying a purple and white field. This was the banner of the king to signify that the king was now in residence. Jaerick did not see the banner of the prince, so his heart sank a little further, realizing that he still must be south of the outpost.

Jaerick commanded that his companies eat, and immediately find their billets and get some sleep, as they would be rising in four hours to continue south. Jaerick went straight to the King's Tower and summoned the commander of the post. Within minutes, he heard a knock at his door before he even had a chance to get fully settled in.

"Enter," Jaeirick said.

"My King," Kaesting said, bowing before his king.

"What do you know of Greynim?"

"He left here yesterday very anxious to meet the large human force that our scouts reported had finally started moving north."

"How large?"

"Over a thousand as far as they could tell. They have been mustered for weeks just north of the Dragon Cross Mountains, and last week they started moving north."

"Why didn't anyone send word to me?" Jaerick asked, feeling his neck redden in anger and fear.

"My king…" he said bowing in supplication. "Prince Greynim said he would inform you personally when he had the head of the human commander."

Jaerick turned his back on Kaesting, and walked to the window overlooking the southern forest. "Of course he would." Jaerick's worst fears were beginning to come to fruition. The only thing he could not foresee at this point was what part Traelyn had in the dream.

They rose again an hour after midnight, assembled in the darkness and borrowed a squad of scouts from commander Kaesting. Jaerick sent the scouts out thirty minutes before their main force even began to assemble in the yard.

Jaerick was impressed with these elven warriors. They had been well trained. Greynim took great care in the training of the entire elven force by taking an active role in as much training as possible, but more importantly, he supervised the entire training personally. As a result, the morale of their fighting force was extremely high, as Greynim loved combat, and especially in the use of his decorated Spider Battalion.

They had been travelling south for many hours by the time the sun rose, warming the forest and causing the dew to evaporate, creating a steamy fog as they weaved their way through the forested foliage. Two of the scouts led the way as they had been through this forest many times on patrols and knew every section of the forest in darkest of night as well as they did in the daytime. By midday the rest of the scout squad returned, their horses were lathered and exhausted from running so hard.

"My King, there is a big battle in the ravine south of here," The scout commander reported.

"Could you tell the status of the battle? Are we winning? How is the prince?"

"We did not stay too long, we could not tell if they were winning or not, both forces were surrounding the ravine in full combat, mostly hand to hand."

"Did you see the prince?"

"Yes, but he and his commanders were scattering to join the fight, we could not tell if it was to route or be routed."

"Then we need to ride hard!"

Jaerick kicked his mount and ordered his forces to ride hard and not fall behind.

They ran their horses hard for two hours, and were nearing the ravine when a dragon flew over their heads.

"What is a dragon doing this far north?" Jaerick asked rhetorically loud enough for everyone to hear. "This cannot be good."

Jaerick turned on his mount and watched the dragon continue northward towards Fort Stone Elf. Dragons had never flown this far north before, and he was not about to have his fortress under a dragon attack while he was away rescuing his son. He turned to one of his lesser commanders and yelled at him to return to Fort Stone Elf.

"I want you to go back and keep an eye on that dragon. Capture it if it causes you any problems. The Castellan will know what to do, we have the harpoon that can take one down. We have never had to use it, but now would not be a bad time."

The commander did not wait for further orders, turned his steed, and headed back north.

●●●

When Jaerick came out of the clearing on the north side of the ravine, he saw human forces attacking the elves that were now trapped within the ravine. The human archers were picking off the elves one elf at a time. Jaerick sent his forces to attack on the left and right sides of the ridgelines to stop them from killing his warriors and hopefully his son.

Then he saw him. He was not mounted on his horse and he had five elves encircling him, as he lay wounded with three arrows in his lower torso. This cannot be happening. Panic filled his heart as he looked on the ridge to see if he could find Traelyn, but did not see any sign of her. It wasn't until he glanced down at his son and then back to the ridge that he saw her standing there. No one was there only a few moments before. He had no idea how she could've just appeared like she did. To make matters even more confusing, he saw that Naemyn and two other humans were standing next to her.

Just as she was in his dream, she was cloaked, but instead of a baby in her arms, she held the Quarterstar Talisman. From this distance, he could not tell if the Shard was imbedded in it, but when she lowered her hood, he saw that she looked exactly as she did the day she left. She then took the talisman, held it over her head, and yelled for someone named Voll to stop firing.

The humans stopped first, then Jaerick commanded the elves on the ridgeline to stop, and the battle ended. Jaerick immediately sent a small squad of healers from the rear to go into the valley to begin healing Greynim and any other elves that needed help.

●●●

Voll, incredulous at the cessation of fighting, began to issue orders to continue attacking, but Traelyn walked over to him and put her hand on his shoulder.

"Where is Daegon?" he asked, confused as to what was happening, especially to the fact that they arrived out of nowhere. Was he that immersed in the battle that he just did not see her arrive, or did she really just appear over the ridge without warning? Not to mention his confusion at seeing this woman who sounded like the Great Mother, composed herself as the Great Mother, but clearly did not look like her, as this was a young and beautiful woman.

"We will explain later, but right now, we need to talk to the elven king."

"Talk? You are not serious?"

"I am very serious. It is time we stop fighting, if only for a moment."

Voll continued to look at her with dismay, and as she spoke, he noticed that the King was already on his way leading three of his commanders on the opposite side of the ridge.

* * *

King Jaerick Krowe rounded the south side of the ridge and entered into the crevice to see his son, while his three commanders watched from horseback atop the entrance to the valley.

"Will he live?" Jaerick asked the soldiers tending to him as he approached.

The soldiers that guarded him saluted as he rode up, but the healers continued to apply aid.

"He is badly injured, and has lost a lot of blood already my King, but he will live. He is unconscious now, but if we return him to Aalararae, with lots of care and rest he should pull out of this," the healer responded as he applied dressing to the wounds where the arrows had already been removed from his body.

"Then return him quickly. He needs to live!" Jaerick said as he spurred his horse and returned to the top of the ridge. He was angry with the humans, but he could not blame them as much as he blamed his son. He took actions into his own hands and attacked the human force without proper reconnaissance. He would deal with him much later, but right now, he wanted nothing more than to confront these humans, Traelyn, and especially Naemyn.

Jaerick charged his horse up the ravine where they stood, stopping only inches in front of Traelyn and Naemyn.

"What is going on here Naemyn? I sent you on a mission to make sure the shard was safe, not to come back here and attack your own people with these humans!"

"I am responsible for this, Jaerick," Traelyn said stepping forward in front of Naemyn. "Though, I am not responsible for the attack, I am responsible for Naemyn's actions."

"How can any of this be? Where have you been all these years, and why do you return now?" he said attempting to hide his anger, hurt, and confused feelings.

"I know you have a lot of questions, as do I, but many of them are going to have to be unanswered for a little while longer, at least long enough for us to end this war between the humans and the elves. My aggressive son is now held captive by your spirit ancestors at the catacombs, so now we can work on making peace and returning Daegon back to me, and maybe, just maybe, this whole endeavor has been started so that my father can return from his imprisonment."

Jaerick dismounted his horse and his three commanders followed his lead. He walked over to Traelyn, wrapped his arms around her, and buried his face into her neck. He remembered her scent the minute he nuzzled into her neck. Traelyn did not return the embrace, but stiffened. Jaerick realized his embrace was not returned, so he put his hands on her shoulders and pushed her away, outstretching his arms, but still held on to her shoulders. "I don't understand," he said.

"Naemyn has been our hostage, my son killed every elf that was with him. Daegon must have sent Voll ahead to command this battle without my knowledge. I specifically told him not to attack, but rather to wait for us. Regardless, the fighting must stop."

Traelyn grabbed Jaerick's arms and forced them off of her shoulders, and then slid her hands down to his and held them. She looked into his eyes and saw hurt and confusion in them. She began to wonder if he had known she was even alive all of these years. She wanted to ask, she had so much she wanted to talk about, but now was not the time.

Jaerick put his right hand under her chin and smiled. "Naemyn, take Traelyn back to Fort Stone Elf."

"Are you not coming with us?" Naemyn asked.

"No, I am going to escort my son back home to Aalararae, and I will take the majority of the forces I brought with us. Traelyn, we are done with hostilities here. I want you to tell your warriors to go home as well, and no longer fight us."

"Great Mother..." Voll interjected, "you cannot do this. Commander Daegon has given me orders to advance, and not to stop until they are defeated."

Traelyn's neck turned red, and in her renewed youth, she felt the anger rage inside her in a form that she had not felt in years. She turned to face him, pointing her finger at him. "Who leads us? My son or me?"

"Forgive me, Great Mother," Voll said looking at the ground, "you command us. I will do as you wish as always."

"Mother…" Traegon spoke, but Traelyn snapped her head back to Traegon interrupting him with her glare.

"You, my son, are in total command of this force. Voll, you will advise my son, but you will not deviate from my command. I want you to take these brave warriors home."

Then she removed the Quarterstar Talisman from her neck and placed it over Traegon's head amidst the shock of all those present. Incredulous and confused to her purpose they gawked and stared at Traegon.

"What do you want me to do with this?" Traegon asked holding the talisman in his hands.

"You cannot give that to him," Naemyn objected, speaking at the same time as Traegon.

"I can and I have. King Keiyann Krowe gave it to me and he never said I had to return it, but rather to use it to my advantage. Now that I have done so, I no longer need it."

"Then give it back to the elves," Naemyn pleaded, then turned to Jaerick. "King Jaerick, please explain to her the importance of this talisman."

"I no longer find it important to us, Naemyn. It has been nothing but a vision in a nightmare I had. Now that we have found it and now that I have found Traelyn, it means nothing to me."

"But the prophecies?"

"They are the creation of the Sorae anyhow…I do not need it."

Naemyn turned to Traelyn and tried again. "Give it to me," he said looking at her, but holding out his hand towards Traegon.

"No, we will not," she said spitefully. "Traegon, take these brave men home."

"Yes mother," Traegon acknowledged and walked away, taking Voll with him back to the force to spread the word.

"My King," Naemyn interjected. "Allow me to walk with Traegon and Voll so that our two forces can separate peacefully."

"Then go, Naemyn, but hurry back so you can escort Traelyn to safety."

"I will return shortly." Naemyn bowed and left.

Satisfied, Jaerick grabbed Traelyn's hands and smiled. "You are so beautiful, I am so happy that you have not aged in all of this time. How did this happen?"

"It is not as it seems. There is something happening that I am not controlling. Your father sent me away and had me forget everything about you, but then, only recently, all of my memories returned, and I now am not sure why I hated you for so many years."

"I missed you Traelyn. I looked for you for years, but could not find you, but then something happened and I forgot about you. It was as if you never existed. Now I have been dreaming about you. My dreams predicted this day. What is happening?"

"I think we are near the point where all of the prophecies will come true or change, but right now, I need to find answers to where my father is."

"I agree, something beyond our control has brought us together again, and we may just be on the cusp of something enigmatic, but first we need to get out of here, all I want to do right now is take you back to safety and never let you go again."

"That is fine, Jaerick, but I don't want things to go back to the way they were. I have spent five lifetimes fighting you, and to be honest, I don't think I can feel for you the way I did so many years ago."

"I can live with that, but it wasn't our fault that we were separated, it was my father, Naemyn and the Sorae that did that to us."

"I know that Jaerick, but I am not certain as to what is happening here, and I am very old. I may not look it right now, but I fear it won't last long, and I know you are not going to love the old, frail, and bitter woman that I really am."

"Traelyn, I am not going to worry about that right now. What is important is that I have you back and I am going to take you home and keep you safe as my father promised so many years ago. We will find out together what is going on and we will make it work to our advantage."

* * *

"Traegon!" Naemyn shouted when he caught up to him and Voll. "I need to talk to you before we leave."

Traegon and Voll turned around. They were talking to their commanders under a thick grove of majestic pine trees and were just about ready to finalize their plans to retreat. The commanders had been red faced and upset as they had the elves beaten and wanted to finish them off. They wanted, no, *they needed* their victory that Commander Daegon had promised them. Their rage increased even more when Naemyn approached them, so much so that Naemyn felt the hate from their eyes searing into his soul.

"May I approach?" Naemyn asked, timidly genuflecting, emphasizing obedience with an over-exaggerated bow.

"Do so at your own peril," Commander Urish said.

"It is ok," Traegon said putting his hand on the shoulder of the commander.

"But keep your distance," Voll said trying to keep his rage under control.

"This won't take long," Naemyn began. "I just need to tell you how imperative it is that you do not take your forces home."

"What are you talking about?" Traegon asked, obviously very confused.

"Do you want to see your mother again?"

"What is this trickery? Do you see what they are doing? We beat them militarily and now they take advantage of us by taking our supreme leader as a hostage!" Commander Urish yelled in frustrated rage, and continued his rant, "This is your fault Traegon! Your father never would've let them live, he would've killed every single elf."

"Naemyn, what is this, why are you doing this?" Traegon asked.

"I respect your commander, and he is right in thinking as such. It was foolish for you to stop the attack when you had your enemy pinned down."

"Why are you telling us this?" Voll asked, equally as angered as Commander Urish. "You are merely insulting us for the weakness of our Great Mother."

"He is setting us up for a trap," Commander Urish said at the same time.

"No, I assure you, I am not setting up a trap or an ambush. I am telling you that you need to continue north with your force and continue with the attack."

Everyone looked to Naemyn in shock and confusion.

"Why would you tell us this?" Traegon asked.

"Because our king is going to take your Great Mother away from you, and I alone cannot stop this."

"Why would you not want that? Without our leader, you hold a great hostage, and have a powerful advantage that keeps us from attacking you, lest you kill her," Voll added.

"You are correct in that assumption, but there is a bigger picture that you do not see, and one that I am not going to reveal to you. Just know this, you need to go after her, or else you will never see her again."

"This is a trap," Voll said, pleading with Traegon to see through the obvious deception.

"I assure you it is not a trap. However, the elves will not allow you to follow them, there will be a fight, but the question you need to ask yourselves is, whether or not you think the fight is worth it. Trap or not, you must press on. I will leave you three to discuss your fate. I will do nothing to learn of your plans. You must decide on your own. And now I will leave you to decide your fate."

With that, Naemyn turned, raised his hood, and left, disappearing out of the thicket, leaving the three commanders shaking their heads in their uncertainty as to what had just happened.

"Do we attack as he said?" Traegon asked.

"It doesn't make sense to do what our enemy tells us to do, even if it sounds traitorous on their part, but I don't see where have much of a choice." Commander Urish cautioned.

"Commander Daegon would jump on this opportunity and attack. In fact, I don't think he would be too happy right now, if he knew that you let the Great Mother just walk away with the elves without trying to stop her. You should not have even brought her here Traegon," Voll Reprimanded.

"What would you have me do? It was her decision to come here, and her own decision to leave with the elves. Even my father could not stop her from doing anything once she set her mind to it."

The three of them looked north as if visualizing their forces moving forward and attacking the elves. The sun began to set over the western horizon, the tall-forested pines casting dark shadows upon the three men.

"We attack north," Traegon said with shaky conviction.

Chapter 28

Aegyn flew over Castle Stone Elf a dozen times before she hit them with the first blast of fire. She knew that the elven beings were made from the same creation as she, and attacking them would be akin to attacking her own being. Her mother had often impressed upon her to shirk her impulse for curiosity, but more often than not, she could not ignore that impulse. Today was no exception. The elves and the humans were more active than normal, and more importantly, she spotted her friend Voll with the massive cluster of humans.

Humans and elves fighting amongst each other made her not only very apprehensive but excited as well. Oh, how she enjoyed a good fight. The humans for many years fought amongst each other in small clans, but lately they had joined forces and migrated north. Sometimes the elves and humans even fought each other, but never had she seen so many humans moving this far north, this had to be a precursor to a large fight, and she was not about to miss it.

All she had done was fly over the elven castle looking and waiting for some fighting to start. Many elven archers were massed atop the castle's battlements and many more elves were mustered in the yard just behind the gate mounted on horses, and even more in full battle armor were mulling around the yard behind them.

She then flew back to the humans to look at them and even to see if she could see Voll again, which she did, but he did not even look up at her. Many other humans saw her and scattered into the tree line. Then she flew back to the castle and that is when they attacked her. A large bolted harpoon tied to a long rope cut the air close to her just missing her left wing as she banked around the castle.

Why were they attacking her? They had seen her before, and never feared her then, and in return she had never attacked them, or given them any reason to fear her, until now. They did not attack her outright, but when the elves opened up their gates and charged out of the castle, their composure became tense. Arrows flew towards her at the same time the gates opened, but all of the arrows fell short as she flew higher than any competent archer could reach.

Feeling the tension, she stayed far away, but watched the elves scatter into the tangled woods and disappear as if they became part of the forest. When she lost sight of them, her curiosity got the best of her so she flew directly above the canopy to get a better view.

Not very far away, she could also see the human force charging through the tangled forest. Swordsmen hacked away with swords that were longer than they were tall and blades twice as wide as a normal broadsword. As they hacked away, soldiers on foot and on horseback followed also hacking away at any left over tangle protruding in their path.

Behind them, the large force followed. Then the elves came out of the forest first, attacking the human forest hackers. First, they sent out a barrage of arrows from archers hidden within the canopy, destroying the front line of the hacking force on the left and right flanks. The center of the force kept hacking away as the human cavalry began sending arrows of their own into the forest knocking many of the elves out of their tree posts.

The humans behind the vanguard were then commanded to scatter within the woods and press on. They stayed in groups of twenty and traversed through the thick forest foliage individually and hacking only if they needed to as they were commanded to get to the fort as quickly as possible. This command seemed to be successful as Aegyn saw the trees shake, as though a massive beast were moving through the trees. The elven archers that remained in the trees were not enough in number to stop the force as they scattered throughout the forest. It did not take long for the elven archers to realize that they were outnumbered, outflanked, and surrounded when the human force clashed with the elven cavalry.

The elves on horseback knew the forest very well. They had pre-carved out trails in the forest for just such battles, for hit and run tactics, but when the humans found those paths, they devastated the elven cavalry. The elves put up staunch resistance, but the human numbers were too great and the elves soon retreated with less than half of their force intact. The humans trampled over the dead archers and dead horses that scattered the trail.

The elves had no choice but to retreat to Fort Stone-elf, passing by a large statue of one of their most celebrated warriors, Eranon, also known as the Stone-elf. A name given to him because of his glorious battles with the humans, of whom he once said had the combined intelligence of a single stone.

It was his job to eradicate every stone from the forest.

He was also found to have said that for every human he killed, they would be transformed back into their original form of a stone and he therefore collected stones as if they were prized jewels. The elves then erected this large stone statue to symbolize that he did indeed become made of all of the stones he collected in his life.

The statue stood next to the front gate reaching twenty feet tall and was dressed in full battle armor with his sword pointing south towards the human tribes. As the elves passed by Eranon they lowered their heads in shame, but Eranon still stood tall as if he was now asking his elves to stop and make a stand that he would proudly lead in the defense of the fort of his name.

It did not take long for the human force to realize that the elves had retreated and sped up their attack even more. Within an hour they came out of the tangled forest and into a small clearing, surrounding the fort on three sides. They could not surround the northern side of the castle as the forest climbed up the battlements on the backside of the fort, completely sealing it from any known approach. The human force stopped short of the clearing, staying hidden in the forest as they stared at the statue of their known and hated enemy, Eranon the Stone Elf.

Aegyn made another pass over the fortress, and that is when she felt her wings sticking to her body, disabling her from flying. The spider battalion had fired a large harpoon that turned into a spider web substance upon impact, and surrounded her whole body. Panicking she wiggled and turned trying to free herself from the sticky substance. Her attempts to free herself only caused her to go into a headfirst corkscrew spiral to the ground. She closed her eyes as she saw the ground coming towards her at breakneck speed. The ground was coming up fast, but she was able to direct her fall just slightly enough that her tail caught the top of their prized statue shattering his head into thousands of pebble sized pieces.

Before she hit the ground headfirst, she heard her mother's voice reprimanding her as she had done many times about never trusting the humans or the elves. Elves she had told her often, were part of them, but they had their own agenda and did not care for dragons, but humans were bred from the evil side of creation and would only destroy the land. Aegyn knew her mother was right as she landed head-first, destroying a dozen majestic pines with her tail and body as she rolled out of the forest and into the clearing unconscious.

The humans saw the dragon fall to the ground and cheered so loudly that it seemed that the air shook louder than the ground did when the dragon first crashed to the earth. Then before the cheers ended, the humans witnessed over two hundred elves appear out of nowhere. They quickly realized that the spider battalion had fired the harpoon, snaring the dragon with the intent of capturing it. Their cheers turned to fear and trepidation as they watched the elves roll out a large crate with a crane-like arm that surrounded the dragon with a large chain mesh.

They worked with the crane and dragon for nearly an hour as the human archers attempted to pick them off as they worked. The elves responded in kind by outflanking the humans and counter attacking them from the trees. Commander Voll had decided that elves were more interested in the dragon and now was the time to take advantage of the situation to organize an attack of a larger scale.

First, he commanded Commander Urish to take one third of his front line archers to the west side of the fortress and begin hammering them with everything that they had. He decided to have Traegon stay in the center and hold and wait with the main force. He would take command on the eastern side where the dragon was and begin to attack the elves.

Voll could not believe that the elves had actually taken down not only a dragon, but had taken down Aegyn. He still did not have a love for dragons, but he did feel that he understood this one very well, having ridden on her back and actually spoken with her. How he could feel compassion for a large murdering beast he had no idea, but he did, and watching the elves take her down and work on capturing her infuriated him in a way he could not explain.

Voll's attack happened close to the same time as Commander Urish's barrage with his archers. The two attacks did not do much to the elves, other than causing the elves on the front face of the fortress to take cover. Since the elves providing cover on the fortress wall were now taking cover, they could no longer protect the elves working on the dragon. This softened their force as they transferred some of their archers to the south and west walls. This is what Voll hoped would have happened, and when he saw that he had achieved this, he had a force of three hundred maneuver through the woods and pop out of the tangle and into the clearing just as the majority of the archers left the east side.

Voll sent a first wave of fifty humans to attack the elves with a foot charge of swordsmen and spearmen. The spearmen hit first and then backed off behind the swords as they hacked the elves off of the dragon one by one. To his surprise, the attack, and the loss of a few archers, did not distract the elves from their mission. Like the disciplined unit they were, they continued attaching ropes around the dragon's wings and muzzle.

The elven archers near the dragon responded with a barrage of arrows that exploded above the humans, dropping little spiders from the air which landed on top of the humans, causing them to drop their weapons and retreat. Voll watched his warriors run back into the woods either swatting at their bodies or stripping off their armor as they ran.

"Damn spiders!" Voll cursed as he watched his first wave return having only killed a handful of elves.

"Send the second wave!" he yelled to his captain, and within seconds, a second wave ran into the fray of terrified retreating warriors. The second wave attacked with swords forward in one hand and their shields covering their head with their other hand. Archers lined the wood line and sent a barrage of arrows into the tangle in an effort to have the spider elves take. This allowed the human warriors to again hack at the elves as they worked on securing the dragon.

The humans had knocked off and killed a few dozen elves, and then without warning they stopped what they were doing and jumped off of the dragon and disappeared into the woods. The humans began to follow, but the elven archers launched another barrage of spider arrows that again exploded tiny little venomous spiders above them. The humans, not having anyone left to fight, turned and ran back to the forest before the spiders landed on any of them.

As they ran back, the humans heard commands from the handful of elves that remained as the crane lifted the dragon off of the ground and onto a large multi wheeled cart. Within minutes, the cart began to move, and as it did, the elves launched another barrage of spider arrows that went above the forest canopy dropping into the trees. Within seconds of the arrows landing, spiders began dropping from the canopy on hundreds of long webs reaching to the ground searching for new victims. The human warriors, seeing this, fled deeper into the forest.

Voll saw them running back towards his position and he cringed at his failure. He was experiencing a double defeat by turning out to be an ineffective leader and losing Aegyn to the elves in one single battle. Voll cursed, turned on his horse, and then commanded his warriors to follow him to a safe rally point out of range of the elven spider archers.

Commander Urish did not fare any better, as an even stronger force of the spider battalion hit them. As the human forces neared the wall, the elves hit them with a larger force of spiders that were launched from a catapult from behind the fortress walls. A large black ball sailed across the sky and exploded directly above his force. Instead of small spiders, the ball broke up into five smaller pieces that then floated down to the ground using webbing to slow their descent. Five separate spiders that stood slightly taller than a man glided to the ground and began to attack the humans.

A handful of humans dropped their weapons and ran back into the woods while the rest attacked the spiders as soon as they hit the ground. The spiders in return spread out and sprayed a web around the first humans that charged near them, immobilizing them with their sticky web. They fell to the ground, swords and shields in hand, squirming and trying to escape the sticky webbing. The second wave of humans hit the spiders in a rush so large that the spiders could not do anything except a futile attempt to knock down the warriors with their spindly legs or grab a warrior and bite them with their large teeth. One spider managed to grab a warrior and landed a bite into his chest, and then webbed him up and dragged his lifeless body into the woods.

The remaining four spiders did not have a chance against the massive rush of humans that attacked them. The humans attacked and hacked at the spiders long after they were dead as if they feared they would reassemble their body parts and rise again to attack.

As they were doing that, the elves sent another barrage of arrows that exploded the little black venomous spiders directly above them. Knowing what was coming, the humans did as Voll's force did earlier, and turned and ran back into the woods. Seeing all of the humans run in fear, the elves defending the fortress cheered and sent out taunts for the humans not to return to their fortress or else experience much more of the same thing.

Voll returned from his side of the battle just in time to witness the retreat and wanted to yell at his warriors to get back into the fray. They had the numbers to overwhelm this fortress, and the elves could not produce enough magical spiders to stop this large of a force. Daegon built this force to be so large, that if they encountered a fortress such as this that they could attack and occupy it with no siege engines other than simple ladders. Yes, the casualties would be high, but Daegon was willing to accept that in exchange for speed.

Voll charged his steed into the clearing and yelled at his men to get back into the fight. As he did so, he witnessed the small spiders attacking thirty of his men as they jumped and swatted at their bodies, some were taking off their armor in a feeble attempt to rid themselves of the poisonous attackers. The elves on the battlements took advantage of the confusion and began to pick the defenseless warriors off one at a time.

Voll looked up and watched them as they laughed amongst themselves in the slaughter. They did not need to make a sport of it, the men would die from the poisonous bites soon enough. Though, he did find it a slight relief in the fact that the elves, in their sport, were inadvertently putting them out of their misery. He was beginning to fully understand the core of Daegon's hatred for these elves.

He realized that there was nothing he could do to stop this retreat, so as the last unaffected warrior ran past him, he turned around and charged back into the woods and commanded his men to sound retreat and to fall back to their rally point. Voll grabbed one of the bows and a quiver of arrows from one of his archers and charged back into the clearing. He dropped the reigns, took aim, and knocked out three elves unawares as they were still intrigued in taking out the suffering humans. The rest of the elves realizing that they were under attack again took cover, giving Voll enough time to change his target from the elves to his own warriors. He was not going to allow the elves to take his men out of their misery; he was going to do it himself.

By the time he emptied his quiver there were only five men on the ground still alive. Their faces were turning black as they had twisted and turned in pain. Voll unsheathed his sword from his saddle, jumped off of his horse, and ran to the men stabbing each of them in the chest killing them instantly. The last man alive saw what was happening and climbed up on all fours exposing his neck to allow a swift execution. Voll shook his head, feeling the man's pain as he raised his sword above his head and came down with a swift and powerful swing, severing the head from its body. Blood sprayed to the ground as the body fell flat in the hard dirt.

Anger filled Voll's chest as he turned to find his steed, but noticed that the metal door of the main gate dropped with an earth-pounding thud. He turned around as he mounted his horse just in time to see the elves charging out of their fortress towards him. They had them on the run and they were planning on finishing them. Voll smiled, as this was too unreal. Why would they leave their defensive position in attempt to route their opponent? The elves had to know they were still outnumbered and did not have enough troops to overrun his force. Voll hurried to reach back to the rally point in hopes that they could still defeat this force while the gate lay on the ground exposing their castle.

***

"What are you doing?" Traelyn yelled at Naemyn, grabbing the back of his cloak as he looked over the battlements, watching the catapult shoot the large spiders over the wall. "Your king ordered you not to fight us."

"What do you expect me to do, your forces are attacking us!" he barked without turning around, watching the launch above the human soldiers break up and turn into five large spiders. He smiled as the warriors closest to the spiders turned and ran like the cowards that they were, but cringed as the second wave of humans crashed into the spiders, killing them within minutes.

Now angry, Naemyn turned to Traelyn. "What would you have me do?"

"Do as your king commands and stop fighting!"

"And let these humans of yours take our southernmost outpost? We are merely defending our post from your own people. If anything, your commanders are betraying *your* orders. If you want the fighting to stop, you might as well go out there and tell them to stop."

"If I do that, I will be thrown in the middle of a dogfight and killed. You would let me do this?"

"No, I would not. I see your point," he agreed, rubbing his chin.

"Make your people stop the fighting," she pleaded.

Naemyn looked over the battlements again and saw the spider archers let loose another barrage of the small spiders that drifted down above the hapless humans.

"I cannot make them stop," he said, "look at them, if I told them to stop, they would rebel and ask the king for my head. I am not their leader. I am merely the spiritual advisor to the king."

"You are trying to tell me that you have no say in matters of the state?"

"That is exactly what I am telling you. The commander of this fortress is only defending it against your people."

"I don't believe you Naemyn. You have been whispering in the king's ear back when Keiyann was the king. That may have been many years ago, but that I do remember."

Naemyn ignored her last comment and walked off of the battlement catwalk, down the stairs and onto the inner bailey where a force of seventy elves were mustering for a possible breach. He stood and watched them mingle for a few moments until he spotted the captain. He raised his hood and walked over to him.

"How does it look out there?" the captain asked as he saluted.

"Greynim's Spider Battalion is terrorizing them and they are now in retreat."

The captain smiled. "What will you have us do now?"

"I want you to open the gates and attack their retreat."

The captain's smile disappeared and was replaced with slight fear. "Their force is so large, is that wise?"

"It is, because we are also going to retreat. We will not be able to hold this fortress for very much longer. Eventually their leaders will regroup their numbers and then they will regain their morale and attack and overrun us. Your force will go out there to give us time to escape so that they will not follow us."

The captain saluted. "We will do as you command!"

Naemyn turned away as the captain yelled at his troops to prepare for battle. He picked up his pace, as he needed to talk to the castellan and inform him of his decision to abandon the fortress. He knew the castellan would not be happy, but he also knew that he would not dare to interfere with the decision.

•••

The gate dropped and the elves charged out of the fortress, passing at the feet of their headless hero. Many of them noticed the statue having been beheaded and in a rage picked up the pace and charged after the humans into the forest. The humans were caught unprepared for such an impromptu defensive tactic, but Voll and Commander Urish were able to pull up their forces and turn them around for a counter attack.

The first line of defense clashed with the attacking elves to the roar of shouts from the humans, then the clang of swords and shields smashing into their foes. The elves fought valiantly for an hour, but the humans continued to come in waves. Twenty or more human soldiers would fall and twenty more would replace them. Despite their disadvantage, the elves continued to press on, even though they began to lose ground and were almost back to the fortress gate.

Only twenty elves remained by the time they were pushed back to their hero. Almost as if Eranon gave them inspiration from the grave, the elves pressed forward killing another twenty humans without losing a single elven life. Heeding the call to help their fellow elves, archers from the battlements rained down a barrage of arrows, taking out the next line of reinforcements.

The elves, feeling a sense of hope, charged again, gaining back some of the ground that they had lost.

The battle continued with neither side gaining ground for another thirty minutes. The elves fought with their backs against the fortress while the archers continued to pound down every wave as they were being replaced. Then, without warning, the arrows stopped coming. The elves on the ground continued to fight, but it did not take long for the swarm of humans to overcome the remaining handful of brave elves dying for their people.

Fearing a trap, Voll sent only a handful of men into the fortress, but within minutes, they came out shaking their heads.

"They're gone!" one of them shouted as he crossed over the gate.

"What do you mean they're gone?" Commander Urish shouted back.

Voll spurred his mount and charged into the fortress to find out that his scout was correct: the fortress had been abandoned. All of the battlements were unmanned, all of the inner buildings were eerily silent, there wasn't even any horses left behind in the stables. It was as if all of the people had been magically removed, for there was evidence of recent habitation, including fresh footprints in the dirt, tools, and equipment dropped in place. Then it became clear that the elven ground attack was only to give them time to abandon their keep.

"We have won!" Voll shouted when he returned.

The humans cheered, as this was their first major victory against the elves. For many years Daegon had attempted to find this fortress and attack and occupy it, but had been unsuccessful in doing so as the forested tangle inhibited them from getting anywhere close to the fortress. Voll wished Commander Daegon were here to take part in this victory, so he did the next best thing and called Traegon to come forward with his force behind him.

Traegon spurred his horse and galloped up to the smiling Voll.

"We did it! Your father would be proud," Voll said to his commander's son.

"We should regroup and advance farther north." Traegon suggested.

"We will, but not you. You need to inform him of what we are doing, so I want you to go back to him. Return that cursed talisman to him and bring your father back here so that he can join us and attack the elven capital. Will you do that?"

"Yes, I will," he answered, a bit hesitant of being sent on another mission to help someone else.

Voll then shouted to the rest of the force, raising his sword and making his horse turn a tight circle. "You have won this battle for Daegon, father of Traegon, now we will charge north to finish the battle!"

Traegon also raised his sword then kicked his mount and charged southward back to the catacombs.

"Follow me!" Voll shouted as he led his force into the fortress. He ran through the staging area and then found the elven standard as it flew above the Keep Tower. He ran to the flagpole, grabbed the rope and ran it down and then replaced it with the human standard of the Great Mother; A red flag with a black iron crown. Voll went to the inner gatehouse up the stairs and continued up to the top tower, seeing brave happy warriors in the inner bailey and he then looked outward and saw many more of his battle ready and untouched warriors.

"Fort Stone-Elf is now ours!" he yelled as loud as he could, knowing that it would be impossible for everyone to hear, but he knew the word would get out. "I now proclaim this fortress Fort Traelyn!"

Chapter 29

"Why did we leave?" Traelyn shouted at Naemyn as she rode in the back of a covered carriage as it speedily bounced along the road to the elven capital. "You were supposed to stop the fighting and make peace, not retreat!"

"You don't know the king like I do, my lady, I have known him for the many years since you have been away, and I assure you that he is not the same person you once knew," he said leaning back, giving her the impression that he was bored and that her view was insignificant.

Traelyn took the hint and stayed quiet for the rest of the trip. She would talk to Jaerick. She could not be confident that Naemyn was not wrong in saying that Jaerick was a different person, but she also knew that she and Jaerick were connected with this prophecy by the dreams she had. Though she was not looking to rekindle her love for the elven prince, now king, she was looking for answers to this calling.

She looked at her hands and marveled at the soft new skin she had, soft skin that had left her many years ago. She had to force herself to remember that her appearance was youthful again. She had not looked at her reflection yet, but she could tell by her skin and feel of her soft hair that she had her youth back.

Naemyn sat across from her looking out the window. She had never trusted this elf, but now she mistrusted him even more. Was she now his captive, and he was misleading her into thinking all was well? Was Jaerick also part of the plan to capture the leader of the human forces? Her mind began to spin many different possibilities, all coming to horrible conclusions. She wanted to jump out of the carriage, but the curiosity for answers kept her in place.

As hard as she tried to come to any certain conclusion, she could not. She did not understand how she could come so far in this whole affair and still not have the answers. Her memories were now completely restored, yet she still did not know how they were restored to her, and according to Jaerick, his memories of her were restored for the same unknown reason. However, she felt Naemyn knew all of the answers, yet was not going to divulge them to her.

The more she thought about it, the more she brewed in her anger towards the smug elf that sat across from her. The sun began to set upon the land, and so too did her thoughts as she drifted off to an uncomfortable sleep. When she awoke it was morning. She had slept through the whole night in the back of the carriage. To her surprise, she found herself laying down on the bench seat with a blanket that had been placed over her by Naemyn.

"Good morning," he said with a pleasant smile that she found oddly comforting.

She sat up grabbing the blanket and wrapped it around her as she brought her knees to her chest. "How much longer?" she asked groggily.

Naemyn looked out the window briefly. "Only a few more minutes. I see the familiar cedar trees that surround the lakeshore. We have been on the western side of Lake Aalararae for many minutes, so we should be arriving very soon. You should prepare yourself."

"Prepare myself for what?" she asked, slightly unsure of his intent.

"We are on the cusp of a civil war," he answered. "Look out the window."

Traelyn unfolded her legs and leaned over to look out the window. They were now travelling down a large main road through the city. Elves were running through the street, all of them male, and in a panic as if running for cover.

"Why is this happening?" she asked.

"I have sent word ahead that you were returning. The Sor Elves do not want you here, the Val Elves trust their king, but the Agin-Sorae have threatened to severe the peace ties between the two factions of elves if you are to return."

"Why would you tell the people of my return knowing it would cause this turmoil?"

Naemyn smiled. "Because this is just the perfect amount of turmoil I need to finish my mandate."

"And what is this mandate?"

"I am going to sever the peace of the Val elves and the Sor elves and rule the elves in the purity that they are meant to be. We cannot have the likes of half-breeds weakening our race. We have used the aggressive war-like Val elves that worship the warrior Val Eahea to exhaustion. It is time to use the peaceful Sor elves that worship their god Raezoures to bring back peace to the land and unify our race, as it should be."

"It sounds like you are taking an aggressive route to make this happen," she said flatly.

"You have figured out the sole purpose of the Agin-Sorae. That is something your lover king hasn't figured out yet. We are a secret faction made up of both Sor and Val elves. We are made up of the purest of the Sor and the most aggressive of the Val elves. That is what the Agin-Sorae is for. Since we are Sor elves with the aggressive nature of the Val elves, we no longer need the Val elves' protection. We will eradicate them just as I will dethrone your lover, my friend and elven king."

Naemyn leaned over to move a lock of hair away from her face. Traelyn flinched as he did so. "Sleep my child," he said as he slipped his hand behind her neck and squeezed, coursing his Kronn through his hand and into her being, causing her to slump over fast asleep. Naemyn gently leaned her down on the bench seat and covered her up with the blanket just as the carriage came to a stop.

After a few seconds, the door opened and two elves dressed in battle armor helped him out of the carriage. "Take me to the king," he said as they closed the door behind him.

The carriage was inside the palace. It was no more than a fortified and elaborate living quarters for the king and his family. Servants and soldiers also lived inside. The inner bailey where the carriage had stopped was a large open expanse layered with grass and decorated rock. Massive trees jutted into the sky, towering over the battlements that towered over the bailey. Every square inch of the walls were covered in ivy. Naemyn took a deep breath, taking in the sight of his home. Things were about to change, he thought to himself as he walked underneath the inner curtain and up the stairs to find the king.

He found the king with his son in the infirmary. The guards at the open door stepped closer together blocking him, but did not raise their swords as they recognized the king's closest advisor.

"Let him through!" Jaerick yelled, after glancing behind him as he watched two elves attending to his son.

"My king," Naemyn genuflected, looking down at the ground, "How is the prince?"

"He will survive. His wound is severe, but he is past the worst of it. We arrived just in time. Is Traeyln safe?"

"Yes, my king, she is here now."

"Thank you Naemyn, for bringing her here safely so that I could save my son."

"I not only serve you my king, but I am here to help you as your friend."

"Yes, Naemyn, you have always been here for me," he said, finally looking up.

"Where is Traelyn? I thought you said she was here."

"There is a slight complication. Yes, she is here, but she is in the carriage in the inner bailey. She will not leave the carriage until you come to her. She has become fearful after witnessing the chaos in the city."

"Has it become that bad?"

"The Sor elves are preparing to attack you very soon. It appears they have gained the upper hand in the city. I would suspect that they will be breaching these walls before nightfall."

"How has this happened? How did anyone receive word that Traelyn was coming?"

"I do not know. It seems we have a traitor in our midst."

"It seems we have always been dealing with someone in the Agin-Sorae attempting to thwart us at every turn, haven't we my friend?"

Naemyn did not respond, but turned around and left the room. Jaerick followed as they went downstairs.

"I must ask, where is the dragon?" Naemyn asked as they headed down the spiraling stairs that led out of the infirmary.

"The dragon that you foolishly captured? Well, I have been informed of this foolish decision. I have ordered it to be taken to the the Aestfallia Keep. Right now, it is in a cavern west of here. We will be keeping it there until we can get our dragon speakers to communicate with it and find out why it attacked us. If we find it to be hostile we will take it to the Aestfallia keep and send it away using the Triestones."

Naemyn smiled and said nothing.

When they reached the inner bailey, Jaerick saw that half a dozen elven soldiers surrounded the carriage.

"Is that really necessary?" Jaerick asked as he approached.

"It is a dangerous time, I prefer to err on the side of caution, my king," Naemyn said.

"Step aside," Jaerick commanded as he approached the carriage. The two soldiers closest to the door stepped aside and allowed their king to open the carriage door. Naemyn approached as well, keeping close to Jaerick.

When Jaerick opened the door, Traelyn was still sleeping peacefully underneath the blanket on the bench. "Traelyn, I am here," Jaerick said softly, but she did not respond.

"What is going on?" Jaerick asked turning to face his friend.

"You will find out soon enough, go inside and wake her," he said calmly, smiling back at his king.

Jaerick stepped inside, placed his hand on Traelyn's forehead, and kissed her cheek. "I don't understand, why is she sleeping?" he asked, looking at his most trusted advisor, but began to fear that something ill was about to befall him. Naemyn stepped inside the carriage, grabbed his friend's hand, and sent his Kronn into Jaerick causing him to fall into a deep sleep, slumping over in between the two benches.

"Sleep well my friend." Naemyn said as he stepped out and closed the door. The soldier standing next to him walked behind him, placed a lock on the door, and took his place in the drivers seat on top of the carriage.

"Take them southwest of here until you come to a large lake. There you will receive further instructions as to what to do with our king and his vile mistress."

As the carriage moved out of the inner bailey heading on its long journey to the wild forested mountains southwest, Naemyn waked back to the top of the battlements.

"We must prepare for war! The humans are coming!" Naemyn shouted and as the warriors scrambled in preparation.

Naemyn then headed back inside the castle and walked directly to one of the sanctuaries. Entering the sanctum of Raezoures, he passed by two guards who obediently allowed his entrance and found one of the Sorae, as he was deep in prayer to his god Raezoures.

"Please forgive my intrusion, but I must interrupt your prayers," he said, just louder than a whisper.

The elf stood up from the steps in front of a statue of the ancient god. "What can I do for you Naemyn?" he asked, humbly looking to the floor of his leader.

"The king has betrayed us. I need you to go spread the word throughout the land that the king has abandoned us with his human mistress! I will assume the role of king until the prince recovers from his wounds. I will lead the defense of the elven nation. Spread word throughout the city to cease fighting each other and prepare for the humans that will be here before nightfall!"

As he obediently left the room, Naemyn looked at the statue of the god that he too had once worshipped, and began to contemplate the new path he had set himself upon. His guilt began to get the best of him and he struggled to find his resolve. He had sent away his king, his friend that he had known since childhood, the man he had sworn fealty to. He walked over to the window and looked upon the soldiers below readying for war. The war he had been preparing for had finally come to fruition. The civil war that had been brewing just under their skin for years had finally come to a boil at the same time that they were preparing for the onslaught of the human war machine.

"I have done as you asked!" he yelled out loud to the Guardian and the empty stone walls. "I betrayed my king and my friend as you suggested, now it is your time to come through with what you promised. I have now combined Sorae with the Agin–Sorae to finally be rid of these impure Val elves."

Naemyn shrugged. He felt awkward yelling to an empty room, but it also felt good to get his frustration out into the open, even if no one heard it. He looked at the statue again and shook his head in frustration, wondering if this god was too weak to deal with his own people. Slowly, he walked over to the hearth to warm his hands when he heard a crack that sounded like wood popping in the fire, except the sound came from behind him. He turned around, slowly at first, but then snapped around quickly when he saw a black shadow out of the corner of his eye.

"What are you doing here, and what are you?" he asked in exaggerated boldness to hide his startled fear.

The black shadow spun like a miniature tornado sucking the air around it and eventually turned blue. It briefly turned into the horned demon Markenhirth, but then transformed into a blue faceless shadowy figure, that for a brief second, Naemyn thought he was looking at a distorted figure of himself.

"You called me, so I came," the voice said as its shape flickered from its misty form to its icy dark blue shaped horned monster.

"I don't understand the meaning of this." Naemyn whined. "I did as instructed by the guardian. I sent my friend and king, my king that I have been loyal to my whole life, away, and possibly to his death."

"You cannot lie to me Naemyn. I know you and I have and will become you as you will become me. You were never loyal to your friend and king. You despise his weakness to the elven race. You and your Sor elves want to return the elven race to their purest of beginnings. I am merely here to help you and we are here to help each other.

"I will help you return the elves to purity and you will help me escape my imprisonment in the frozen underworld. You have done as promised and will be well rewarded. I leave behind a token of this promise, but use this power wisely, a sacrifice will always be required as payment of use."

Before Naemyn could respond, the image sparked and crackled loudly and then disappeared, leaving Naemyn alone again in the dimly lit room. He turned to face the statue of his god one more time, but his thoughts were interrupted with shouting from outside the room. He ran to the door, opened it, and found one of the guards tending to the other guard who had fallen to the ground.

"What is going on?" he asked, disgusted at the intrusion.

"He just passed out," the guard responded as he checked his pulse. "He is dead."

"Get him out of here, we cannot have this kind of distraction right now."

The guard grabbed his fellow soldier by the ankles and dragged him down the hallway and out of sight. Naemyn was about to go back into the sanctum, but became distracted by a popping sound where the dead soldier had once stood guard. A blue substance swirled on top of the stone floor. Naemyn bent over to reach into the swirling mass, and just as his hand was about to touch it, the swirling stopped and formed into a solid blue shard.

He picked it up and stared at it. As he did so, he could see the black and blue swirling inside the shard. He could feel its power. Instantly he knew what this shard was. He was holding a broken off piece of the fourth Quarterstar, the dark heart shard. A portion of the Markenhirth's dark Kronn heart as it was separated at the time of the realm's creation. He could use this dark heart to summon the spirit of the Markenhirth, and something told him that this would eventually be a force of power to help him achieve his goals.

Naemyn smiled to himself, put the shard in his pocket, and walked down the hallway to prepare for the human siege that would only be a few days away.

Chapter 30

Voll and Commander Urish stood on top of the highest hill amongst a cluster of thick and large deep green-needled evergreen pine trees. Just five miles away on a large forested hill on the opposite side of the valley rested the fortress of the elven capital. They might not have even seen the fortress sitting atop the hill; it was so discreetly covered by the trees and foliage. The fortress, blending in with its surroundings, lay largely obscured. Any pathway to move the forces up to attack the fortress equally lost.

They watched the elven people hard at work on their farms and ranches below. The serene valley below had given Voll a false sense of peace. He knew that he would be bringing death and destruction to these people. Though in his mind they deserved every ounce of terror he could deliver, he still felt pity for what was about to come.

They left a small detachment at fort Stone Elf and now they were only a few miles south of the elven city of Aalararae. Their forces had marched north for five days to reach the city. They moved over two thousand men, horse, and equipment slowly and laboriously until they were just a few miles short of this valley. They did not stop until sunset and were up again just before dawn. They did not dare travel at night, as they would be clumsily travelling through the thick enemy forest. They stayed on the road, and their scouts immediately captured or killed any travellers that they encountered.

At one point, Voll's scouts reported that they were on the trail of the dragon that the elves had captured, but somehow they lost their trail.

"How can you lose the trail of dragon that is tied up upon a wagon??" Voll yelled at his scouts.

"They went into a hillside and never came out."

"What do you mean they went into a hillside and never came out? The dragon is huge. Did they go into a cave or around the backside of the hill? I don't understand what you are saying."

"That is just it commander, we don't know. The wagon, the elven soldiers, the dragon just went straight into the side of the hillside and disappeared," he said, looking straight into Voll's eyes, pleading for understanding.

Voll turned his back on his scout leaving him to contemplate his failure to provide adequate answers to his commander. Voll burned with anger against the elves that aggressively attacked and captured Aegyn. Aegyn was not his friend, however, he did feel the bond between them. He could not quite describe it, but he did feel connected to the dragon.

The Elves stood idle as the dragons destroyed the human villages south of the Dragon Cross Mountains. It was this attitude that caused Voll and his tribe to hate the dragons and the elves, but this relationship with Aegyn changed his view of the dragons slightly. He still hated what the dragons did, but Aegyn's compassion for him during that time helped him feel a shared compassion for her.

He wanted to find a way to help her, but it was more important for him right now to get his forces to the elven capital, attack, and take it over. Lying on his stomach next to Urish, he focused on the elven farmers peacefully working their crops. It made no difference that these elves had never been a part of the force that attacked the human tribes – he did not care– he wanted revenge on all the elves.

"How do you suppose we get to their fortress?"

"How soon can we get a force down there to burn that village to the ground?" Voll asked his sub commander.

•••

The elven farmers screamed in terror as the massive army rolled over the hill. Five hundred ragged men in leather armor ran down the hill waving their swords and shields yelling at the top of their lungs. The peaceful farmers had never seen an invasion of any type in their lives as no human force had ever come this close to their beautiful elven capital. Voll had sent the first force down to harasses and terrify the people, but as the elves scattered they soon found that their western flank was blocked by human spearmen. Nestled in the woods, the spearmen jumped up from their prone positions when the elves approached. With a loud grunt, they stood firm with their spears affixed toward the enemy, blocking their escape to the west.

The elven villagers turned and ran north up to a hidden path to what they hoped would be safety. They clearly did not want to expose the hidden path, but the fear for their lives superseded their need to keep their secret safe. A solid green wall of ivy that wrapped itself tightly amongst a tight cluster of pine trees slipped away and separated itself from the trees exposing a tunnel like trail leading deep into the tangle.

Voll saw the vines unwrap themselves from the trees allowing the elves to escape to the north. Voll seized the opportunity and commanded the bulk of his army to charge down the hill and follow the fleeing villagers through the tangled forest.

The cavalry charged down the hill followed by five hundred more screaming swordsmen on foot. The horsemen spurred the horses, charging them to sprint directly through the opening before it could close upon itself. A handful of cavalrymen followed through the opening just as the last of the elven farmers crossed into the forest. Their swords gleamed in the filtered sunlight as they swooped down upon the fleeing villagers, slaying them inside the forest path just when the elves thought they had escaped. As the last elf lay dying, the vines began to untangle and charge after the horsemen as snakes looking for mice ready to satisfy their hunger.

The vines sealed the opening behind the handful of horsemen that made it through. Voll first heard his men yelling at each other, then heard swords slicing through vines and hardened wood, followed by terrified screams of men and horse. The screaming only lasted a handful of seconds before they were silenced by loud crunching sounds of wood and bone.

"Burn it down!" Voll shouted. "Burn it all down, the village, the forest, all of it, light it up!"

Even before Voll finished his command, his sub commanders were ready for the call, and had their archers light their arrows and send them flying through the sky. The forest on the north side of the valley was out of reach, but the village was not, and within minutes, homes, barns, and dried crops were beginning to burn. The remaining elves that still lingered in the village began to scatter and run for their lives.

"Charge to the forest! I want the forest on fire, let's choke out, and burn the vile pointy-eared vermin!" Voll commanded as the smoke began to rise out of the valley.

The humans charged into the valley, disappearing into the smoke. Voll heard the screams of elves dying by sword and arrow. Voll felt his horse shift its weight underneath him. He reached over and patted the horse's neck suspecting he was feeling the anxiety of his actions. He had just commanded his men to destroy and execute innocent beings. The screams of what he was certain included women and children made him very uneasy.

The screams of terror and sounds of death only lasted about thirty minutes. Voll waited for the smoke to clear before moving into the valley. He could see through the clearing smoke that most of the buildings burned down quickly, leaving only a smoky haze from the smoldering fires. Voll found his commanders giving orders to the warriors as they searched the unburnt buildings for survivors. They had already found a handful of mostly elven woman and children. It seemed that in the killing frenzy even his most hardened warriors steered clear of at least some of the women and children. Even though he had given the command to kill them all, he felt relieved that many had disobeyed that order.

Voll watched a handful of his warriors round up the survivors, placing them in one of the small barns that remained untouched by the fires, when Urish spotted him and spurred his horse towards him.

"We could not light the forest on fire," he said as he approached. "It must be protected by magic. Every arrow that fell into the forest would not light it. I even had torches made and we attempted to light the forest where the elves escaped through, but it still would not catch."

"Then it is good that we have survivors, we can use them as hostages, because I am certain that the elves will retaliate for what we have done today. Post men around the barn with torches ready to light, if the elves attack we will light the barn on fire."

"We had better have an escape plan if you do that, because they will have no reason to hold back," Urish cautioned.

"I have a better plan that that." Voll countered. "We will be ready for them when they come. If my plan works out right, we won't need the hostages, but if we do, I will have a plan for that as well.

"We will prepare for an attack and set up a defensible perimeter here, but more importantly, I have a hunch that we are going to have an angry dragon mother on our side before any fighting starts," Voll said, not smiling, but looking toward the forest where the elven capital was safely nestled deep in the tangle.

Chapter 31

When Naemyn entered the king's council room, he was already in a foul mood. He had heard the reports that humans had made their way north to the borders of their capital and had destroyed the southernmost village in the kingdom. He should have expected as much, he had encouraged their commanders to follow them north and rescue Traelyn, but he did not expect them to be so destructive so quickly. Now he was being summoned to give order on what to do with the dragon that they had just captured.

He had just left Greynim's quarters with news that the king's son would recover from his wounds. He was assured the prince would need to stay in his quarters for at least a month and was in no condition to be making decisions, as he was barely staying conscious for more than a few minutes at a time.

Naemyn knew that he had to work quickly if he was to achieve his goals of retaking the elven kingdom and returning the power to pure elven hands. The passive Sor elves that lived here did not deserve to rule beside the aggressive impure Val-elves. Only the purest of the Sor with the aggressive nature of the Val that make up the Agin-Sorae were worthy of ruling the elven race.

When he entered the king's council chambers, all members of the King's Sorae were sitting erect, showing an air of confidence and hubris. He made eye contact with two of the members that were a part of his secret sect, the Agin-Sorae. He now knew how King Jaerick felt when he entered, knowing that his Sorae aggravated him dearly. The king had mentioned to him many times that their smugness and arrogance irritated his core being. Now standing before them he saw firsthand exactly what he meant.

"What is happening Naemyn? Why are the humans at the footsteps of our capital? How did you let this happen?" One of them asked, placing both hands on the table, leaning forward with his elbows pointing outward. Others mumbled in agreement, as he settled down in his chair.

Naemyn sat down in the king's large stone chair, placing his feet on the edge of the table just as King Jaerick often did. "You know, I could get used to this," he said looking at one of his Agin-Sorae members. He wanted to give a confident wink, but he did not want to look to overzealous, but he did like the feeling of throwing some hubris back at the arrogant so-called advisors to the king.

"The humans are falling into my trap," he began after looking at each member's eyes for a few seconds before moving on to the next. "We fought them at the Stone Pit and then at Fort Stone-Elf. We captured a dragon and then strategically retreated here. I purposely urged them on to come and attack us."

"Why would you do that?" one of them interrupted, "You have just caused many elven farmers to die by their hands, and we have lost one of our most productive villages."

"A minor sacrifice to achieve our end game," Naemyn stated, showing no intimidation.

"Please explain yourself then," one of them demanded.

"I planned on informing you right now," he said, leaning back in the chair, keeping his feet on the table. "As you know, the prince was severely wounded at the Stone Pit. Unfortunately, he will not recover for many weeks, and the king in his grief has urgently left the kingdom to seek help from elven spirits." Naemyn smiled, as he almost believed the lie himself.

"The king is gone?" another asked.

"Yes, the king has left with the human queen and now the humans feel he has kidnapped her and they attack us for her safe return."

"What is the truth, Naemyn? Did the king take her or is he seeking the spirits?" another asked.

"Where is he going to find these spirits? Back to the catacombs?"

"Why did he take the queen of our enemy?" two of them asked at the same time.

Naemyn lifted his feet, stepped down from the chair, and walked to the large window, looking out to the west briefly before turning to face them.

"He is seeking an ancient breed of elven spirits to the west, and he is taking his once lover to them as a sacrifice for their favor to return with these spirits to win this war once and for all," he lied.

"That is not possible! Those spirits cannot be spoken to, they will destroy him."

"Which is why we must assume our king will not return, and in his place, and until Greynim recovers, I will assume responsibilities of king and commander of the elven defense."

"Do you think that is wise?"

"I don't see why not. I have known the king all of his life, I have been named his personal advisor, and head of the Sorae. I don't see what could be better."

They all mumbled amongst each other leaning to one direction or another attending to different conversations for many minutes, before a member of the Agin-Sorae spoke up, "We will allow this, Naemyn, tell us your plan."

Without a word, Naemyn returned to the chair, but did not place his feet on the table. "The dragons are going to win this battle for us, they will attack the humans before our forces meet on the field of battle."

"And how do you propose to get a dragon to do our bidding?"

"We have captured a young dragon at Fort Stone-Elf and the mother will come and kill the humans in order for us to return her youngling to her."

"This is madness!" many of them yelled, standing up. "You cannot do this. The dragons are a part of us as the land is a part of us! You cannot defile the bond!"

"It is this bond that will bring all the elves together in victory!" Naemyn responded. "This act will strengthen our bond and annihilate the humans once and for all."

"Look at our faces. Can't you see that we all do not agree?"

"I don't care. You need to trust me on this. I have been in touch with a higher calling, higher than the elven gods Raezoures and Val-Eahea. You need to trust me on this, when this is done you will all agree that the elven race will be stronger, more powerful and more pure than it has ever been."

"You have lost your senses Naemyn! You cannot be in communication with gods higher than our two elven gods," one of them responded.

"No, I have not. On the contrary, because of this, I have not seen our agenda more clearly. Soon you will see that the two races of elves will finally be united as one race. We will no longer need the Sorae to intermediate to the king assuring the two races work together. This has been necessary for far too long. This whole ordeal with the human Dar Drannon has plagued the elven races for far too long. We will finally control our own destiny."

Naemyn sat down in the chair and looked at the council. He waited to see the reaction. When their only reaction was silence, he stood up, straightened out his robe, and walked out of the room.

•••

Naemyn watched Aegyn as she lifted her head and roared. She released a breath of fire that filled the lower end of the cave where she was chained down. She could only move her head as her legs were clamped and chained to unmovable solid rock, and metal mesh netting wrapped around her body held her wings tightly against her back. She struggled for hours trying to free herself, but was unsuccessful in every attempt. She thrashed and roared fiercely, but every movement only made the bindings on her wings tighter.

Naemyn stood next to three very skinny elves dressed in worn and smoke infused protective dragonscale armor. They were dirty and disheveled from travelling with the dragon and then securing her to the cavern. They watched the last fireball work its way nearly to the top of the narrow rocky precipice that had a small overhang overlooking the dragon. They felt the smoke and heat rise as the angry dragon squirmed and thrashed her neck back and forth.

"This is beautiful," Naemyn admitted.

"We don't understand the reason behind this," one of the elves admitted. "The dragon is so angry, what do you intend to do to her?"

"I intend to release her during the battle to destroy all of the humans."

"But you don't understand dragons. She is so angry she will destroy everything. Humans, elves, the forest. Everything!"

"You are correct, that is what I am hoping she will do. Mass destruction of the humans and elves."

"But…" was all that the elf could get out before Naemyn grabbed him by the breastplate and threw him into the pit. Aegyn's quick eyes saw the elf fall and quickly sent another fire blast towards the elf, immediately scorching his exposed skin. He screamed only for a second, but was silent by the time he crumpled to the ground in a mass of burnt flesh.

Before the other elf could respond, Naemyn grabbed him by the arm, swung him to the ground, and pinned him down on his chest with his chin over the ledge looking down at the dragon. Aegyn watched from fifty feet below waiting for a little more revenge on the elves. Naemyn saw the dragon's eyes watching and saw fear and hate in her eyes. It made him pause to see emotion in such a great beast.

He grabbed the hair on the back of the elf's head. He was about to scoot his weight forward enough to drop him over the edge when a dark blue mist swirled in the crevice below. The blue and black mist swirled until it formed the shape of an elf wearing a long black hood. Naemyn could barely see the features of the elf. He recognized it as the same apparition that came to him in his chambers, but then the features were obscured. There in the cavern, he was beginning to see more facial details of this dark elf. What he saw began to terrify him.

"I am waiting," a voice echoed eerily throughout the chamber. Naemyn thought he was the only one who could hear the voice, but the elf he had pinned to the ledge strained his neck to look back at Naemyn in confusion, obvious that he heard the voice.

"Waiting for what?" Naemyn spoke slowly.

"To finish your betrayal to your king and kingdom."

"What if I don't want to complete this?" Naemyn asked, beginning to doubt his purpose.

"It is too late. You cannot turn back. You started this with the killing of Terson and Elsron back in the catacombs. You have proven yourself worthy. This is what you and the Agin-Sorae have been waiting for and now I will guide you with every step to complete your destiny."

Naemyn cocked his head and patted the back of the elf underneath his knee. "I am sorry. You have been loyal to the king, and for your loyalty, you will pay the ultimate sacrifice. Your death will be remembered."

Naemyn stood up and without any hesitation propped his foot between the elf's legs and shoved him off of the ledge. The elf tried to grab the ledge to save himself, but found nothing that he could take hold of. His body followed his head all the way down to the bottom of the crevice. His armor crashed loudly, subduing the sound of his neck snapping.

Aegyn lifted her head, and pawed at the elf, as a cat would do a dead mouse attempting to wake it up and play with it. When she realized that the elf was dead, she exhaled a puff of flame and smoke that incinerated the body inside of the armor, leaving an empty shell full of bone and ash. Aegyn, bored, lowered her head down, and gave up any more effort to escape and fell asleep.

Naemyn looked over the ledge at the dragon and searched for the apparition, but he must have been satisfied with that action, because it had disappeared. Naemyn straightened his robe and left the cavern with his head down, deep in thought as to how he was really going to carry out his new mandate. He had always wanted the Agin-Sorae to succeed, but this was not quite the way he envisioned. However, he did smile to himself when he realized that even though this wasn't how he realized it would come about, he knew the elven kingdom was about to go through a massive transformation that would have him on top and in control.

As Naemyn exited the cavern, the sun was beginning to set, and he smiled an anxious smile as a trail of dragon smoke followed him out. As the smoke left the cavern, it first made the form of a dragon and then took the form of a human skeleton before disappearing into the air.

Chapter 32

Traelyn awoke first. She had no idea how long they had been travelling. Her neck ached from sleeping in such an awkward position, but she was amazed how different this ache felt in her young body compared to the aged and decrepit old body she had become accustomed to during the passed two hundred years. Their carriage bumped and bounced along a forested road lined with large pine trees. She looked out the window and had no idea where they were going.

"Jaerick," she said reaching over and shaking his shoulder.

Jaerick opened his eyes and snapped awake once he realized he wasn't necessarily in a safe place.

"Where are we?" he asked as he sat up and placed his head out of the window.

"I don't know. I have never seen evergreens this massive before," she said.

Jaerick looked out the window again and realized that they were in the western forests of the Molydenum Woods. He had never been there, but he had heard tales of a small population of an ancient race of wood elves that inhabited the forest.

"Where are you taking us?" Jaerick yelled to driver pounding on top of the roof on the carriage. When there was no response he grabbed the handle of the door and shook it violently, hoping to break it free, but it held tight.

"I guess we are just going to have to wait," he said calmly, looking to Traelyn and expecting her to be rattled, but she leaned forward, laughing silently while shaking her head.

"The elven king is no longer in control," she said smiling.

"No, you are right, I am not used to being a prisoner." Looking at her, he felt his anger subside. Her beauty brought back fond memories of their short time together, "I missed you so much," he said, not being able to control his emotions for her.

"No you didn't," she countered. "You forgot about me just as I forgot about you. How can you miss something or someone you cannot remember?"

"You know what I mean?" he said.

"No, I don't. Why don't you explain," she said, feigning anger, but covered her mouth when she giggled like a little girl.

"That! That is what I am talking about. Your feistiness, it drove me crazy back then, just as it is driving me crazy now. All I wanted to do was be with you. I was willing to give up my position on the throne. If given the chance I would have convinced my father to name Naemyn the heir, but sadly, they didn't give me that chance. They took you from me. No, they ripped you from me.

"You have to believe me Traelyn, I had no idea what was happening that day on the beach. They took you from me without a chance to defend myself, or even to accept our fate and say goodbye. I will make Naemyn pay for that, for everything, now that I am coming to see the truth in all of this."

Jaerick paused to reflect some more and then went to his knees in between the two benches. Traelyn pulled her knees up to her chest keeping him from getting too close. "Still you tease," he laughed.

"Yes, I do," she said as she dropped her knees and leaned forward off the bench and wrapped her arms around him.

Jaerick held her tight and felt her tremble as she did so many years ago. When he pulled away, he saw that she was crying and he wiped the tears off of her cheek.

"What are we going to do?" he asked, but no answer came. "I think I have allowed this to become quite a mess," he said, pulling away slightly to look into her eyes.

"It has been a mess for quite some time, Jaerick. You allowed your father and his advisors to control you into this. You should have made your father keep the promise that he made to my father and me. You were weak, and you paid the price."

"You are right, I was weak, but I was just too young and afraid."

"I had your child, a child you never saw, a child that has long since lived a full life and passed away. No wonder I was filled with hate for all elves. Even though I couldn't remember anything by the time the baby was born, I was still filled with a rage, a rage that I could not place until now."

"I am sorry. Traelyn. I wish this could have worked out better."

"So do I, but it didn't and now we are paying the price for it."

"I will get us out of this, and we will finish our life together. You are so young and beautiful again. We can make it right for the rest of our lives."

Traelyn grabbed Jaerick and held him tight while he kissed her neck. "I do not know how long this form will last Jaerick. I am feeling weak already."

"We can fix this. I will find a way to make it permanent. I will get us out of here and we can finish our lives."

As Jaerick finished speaking, the carriage came to a stop and a few seconds later the door was unlocked and opened by an elven warrior. After the door was opened, he took two steps back and went to one knee. "Forgive me, my king," he said looking to the ground.

"Forgive you for treason? I cannot forgive this. What is wrong with you?"

"Naemyn is our leader, not you," he said, head hung low in shame.

"Give me your sword," The warrior stood up without a word, unsheathed his sword, and handed it to Jaerick hilt first. "Kneel," Jaerick commanded as he lifted the sword to take the head of his disloyal warrior.

"Jaerick no!" Traelyn screamed, stopping him before he brought his swing downward upon the warrior's head.

Jaerick turned around and looked at her incredulous. "What?"

"Do not do this. It is not necessary," she pleaded.

"He is a traitor, but I will do as you ask."

Jaerick lowered the sword and for the first time he looked around at his surroundings and saw that they were at the fabled Lake Quarterstar, where legend told was the landing place of the 4th Quarterstar. He looked at the calm deep blue water as it lapped at the soft dark brown soil and was in awe of the beauty and splendor of the area. The lake was bigger than he had imagined as its shores stretched out far beyond to what he could see and the massive evergreens towered to the sky from massive peaked mountains.

"I had no idea," he said as the warrior got up from his knees and ran away.

"Let him go," Traelyn said after Jaerick took two steps to chase him.

"I suppose you are right. Where can he go?" Jaerick laughed. Shaking his head, he went to Traelyn and helped her out of the carriage. As soon as her feet touched the ground, the earth began to shake violently. The carriage bounced up and down and side to side. Jaerick grabbed Traelyn and ran away from the carriage and towards the lake.

The shaking became increasingly violent. The water on the lake jumped straight up into the sky, but then without warning a beast flew out of the water and hovered in mid-flight fifty feet above the water.

"A dragon?" Jaerick mused aloud, shocked, as he watched a massive dragon with green and yellow scales spread its wings, covering the entire lake. As it flapped its massive wings, the trees swayed from the gusts, and the lake water roiled underneath and splashed upwards.

Traelyn walked to the edge of the water as if in a trance. "I know you," she said staring at the dragon.

"Yes you do. I am a manifestation of your Kronn. I have been by your side all of this time. I am also a manifestation of your father's Kronn. I protect the Quarterstar Shard that rests in this lake from harm, by using your Kronn. I will continue to protect this shard until the time comes for their rejoining. However, your time here is almost complete. You have put into motion the part of the prophecy that will combat the fire witch from taking this realm for hers. Your children will fight her, but the future is yet unwritten. The only thing that is certain is that you have now initiated the Quarterstars Awakening."

Jaerick, hearing this conversation, stepped up next to Traelyn, and took a knee before the great beast and then stood up. "Will I bring the elven people to this land?"

"You will begin the process very soon, and I will welcome you. If you succeed in your endeavor, your race will build a beautiful floating palace above this lake. However, there is still much to be done before you move forward."

As the dragon finished speaking, Traelyn felt a sharp pain in her back. When she screamed, Jaerick turned and saw his traitorous warrior behind her with his dagger in her back. Traelyn fell forward, but before Jaerick could respond, a spray of water hit all three of them, knocking them down, followed by a sucking sound. The elf dropped his bloody dagger as his body lifted off the ground and continued through a stream of water leading to the dragon's mouth. The dragon opened its mouth slightly and swallowed him.

"What have you done?" Jaerick shouted.

"I am completing the prophecy for you," the dragon said.

"She will die!"

"Yes, she will, but she is not completely done yet."

"What do you want us to do?"

"Go home, go back to your kingdom and she and I will do the rest."

"I don't know how to get back." Jaerick said as he put his hand behind Traelyn's neck, propping her up.

"It's fine, Jaerick. It is time," she whispered.

"No it isn't. I love you! We can fix you," Jaerick said and then looked at the dragon. "I need to get her back, we can help her."

"As you wish," the dragon said before turning into a massive tornado above the lake that quickly sucked up Jaerick and Traelyn into its midst.

Chapter 33

The men hacked and slashed at the tangle for hours to no avail. At times, they felt that they had penetrated some of the thick forest jungle only to watch the vines, trees and foliage grow back thicker and stronger than before. Voll and Urish grew weary of watching their soldiers' futility and moved down from their hill to get a closer look. Voll jumped off of his horse and walked over to the cluster where it had once opened and grabbed one of the vines. As he did so, it wrapped around his hand and thorns began to grow out of the stalk. Voll ripped his hand out of the vine before it was able to take a strong enough hold.

"This is magic. I think the only thing that can beat this is magic," Voll said, clearly frustrated.

"We have nothing to counter this, yet we cannot quit and leave now. There must be another way," Commander Urish said.

Voll mounted his horse and the two commanders had just rode away to look for another way, when the vines began to move quickly and noisily until they opened up. Voll was about to issue a command to rush the opening when elves, mounted on horseback, charged through the opening. They slowed their horses as they rode into the meadow without attacking, spotted Voll and Urish and then formed a half circle in front of them as hundreds of human warriors ran to the defense of their leaders.

Voll saw Naemyn, raised his hand, and spun his mount around, signaling to his warriors not to attack. The warriors saw the signal, but pressed forward, itching to attack and decimate such a small force. Once they calmed down, Naemyn nudged his horse forward and stopped just in front of the two commanders.

"What do you want Naemyn?" Voll shouted when he stopped his approach.

"It is now time for you to leave," he said shifting his weight in his saddle.

"We are not leaving. Our forces outnumber yours, and we will storm your city, your fortress, and kill every elf if we have to."

Naemyn smiled at the threat. "There is no need. Our king and your Great Mother have left us. I do not know why, but they abandoned us just when both of us needed them the most."

"Where did they go? I think you killed them and are trying to throw us off."

"I am employing no such tactic. They went west. I do not know why. Perhaps you can take your force, follow them, and ask them. There are elves crawling around an ancient forest near a lake. Maybe you can satisfy your wanton lust by killing them instead. They are merely a barbarian and crude race of elves, very similar to you humans. Your men will enjoy the senseless slaughter."

"I don't have time for your games Naemyn." Voll spun his horse sideways and pointed to the end of the meadow at the barn that his men had under guard. "See that barn? We have a few dozen elves hostage inside. If you do not open this forest we will burn it down and kill everyone inside."

Naemyn feigned shock and then shook his head. "That is unfortunate. However, it is within reason to accept a handful of innocent deaths to save thousands within the city and fortress. However, I do beg mercy for their lives," Naemyn said with spitting hubris.

Naemyn's smug and arrogant attitude angered Voll. Daegon did not entrust him with his army only to stop short of the elven capital. "Kill them, kill them all!" Voll commanded.

Within seconds, swords, spears, and arrows were clashing and flying throughout the battlefield. Naemyn turned his horse and headed back towards the tangled forest. Voll began to chase, but the elves charged forward and engaged him, blocking his path. Voll, Urish and their men could only watch as the forest again opened up, allowing Naemyn to escape before closing behind him.

The elves were outnumbered and had no defense to protect themselves from the massive onslaught of angry war-hungry men overwhelming them. Each one fought valiantly and took a fair number of humans with them before they died. Voll turned around and saw that Commander Urish was already in trouble being attacked by two elves on horseback. Voll charged his steed back towards them. The two elves were on each side of Commander Urish's mount slashing to penetrate his armor or knock him off of his horse.

Voll spurred his mount and took the arm of one of the elves as his arm was extended cracking Urish's skull. The elf screamed in pain as he fell off of his horse. The other elf, still engaging Urish, plunged his sword in the commander's side and Urish went limp and slipped off of his horse. Seeing one of their commanders die, two spearmen broke their engagement and plunged their spears into the elf's side. When the elf fell off of his horse the spearmen took turns stabbing the elf leaving him a pool of blood.

Voll spun around to look for another target, but his men were surrounding three more elves that were no longer on their horses. He smiled and let them take their frustrations out on the last of Naemyn's small guard.

Their small victory was short lived, as before the last elf of the squad took their last breath they all heard a loud thump coming from the north. Voll feared the worst. There was no mistaking that it was a catapult shot, but what would be raining down from the sky upon them?

It did not take long to get his answer, and his worst fears were confirmed.

Flying high above them was a gargantuan sized black swirling ball. The ball landed directly behind him in the middle of the valley, with a loud thud as it hit the ground. The swirling stopped and eight long spindly legs popped out of the black circle and a giant spider the size of a dragon finished materializing.

Smelling human flesh, the spider took a few steps towards it prey. The skin on the bulb and back of the spider looked to be forming still as it crept one leg at a time towards the humans. They did not immediately run as they looked upon the creature in fear and awe. When the spider got within a hundred feet of them, they could see the movement and shimmering upon its back was not the spider still forming from the spell, but rather thousands of baby spiders coming to life.

The giant spider shook its body and its small offspring took to the air. At first, it looked like a puff of dust was shaken off of the back of the spider, but now the small pumpkin sized spiders crawled towards the men with great speed. The men then realized their fatal error in hesitating and ran back towards the hill to escape the spider onslaught.

When the spiders caught up to the men, the spiders crawled up the backs of the men and wrapped their spindly legs around the head and neck of their victims, and punctured their exposed necks with their poisonous fangs. To catch the men that were further ahead, the spiders shot webs at their feet, knocking the men to the ground so they could catch them. Men screamed in terror as the poison coursed through their veins.

Once the small spiders were released, the giant spider stretched its legs and shook again. This time, giant dragon-like wings sprouted off of its back and it jumped up into the air and took flight. It took two low flying passes of the valley before it started spitting venom out of its mouth, splattering its victims below it. The venom ate through the leather armor as if was melting butter. The men screamed in agony as the venom worked its way from their armor to their skin, eating it to the bone and beyond.

Voll ran his horse past them and up to the top of the hill to somehow protect the remaining force from becoming consumed by this terrible enemy.

"Aegyn now is the time. I need you now!" he shouted into the air as he rode, hoping that she could hear his thoughts from afar.

"I cannot. The elves have me prisoner," she responded.

"Call your mother then. We need help!"

"She will not be happy with us."

"I do not care. She needs to free you so you can save me."

"As you wish," Aegyn responded. "You will not like the outcome."

•••

Naemyn entered the lower side of the cavern on horseback. Aegyn rested, curled up in a tight ball. The cavern smelled of acidic smoke as he approached her. Her breathing was erratic and she twitched showing her anticipation for revenge. He could sense her stress, and it was where he wanted her. He wanted her to be angry at everyone, he knew by releasing her she could take out her anger out on the elves, but he wanted her so angry that she would attack more humans than elves as the humans would be easy targets in the open field.

"It is time to go," Naemyn said as he raised his hand and twisted the four fingers on his right hand, braiding them together and then snapped them apart. The metal mesh fell off of the dragon's back and Naemyn charged his steed out of the cavern as fast as he could.

•••

Voll was amazed as to how quickly the mother dragon arrived. She made two passes over the valley making an obvious survey of the damage and looking for her daughter. Voll instantly questioned his decision to have Aegyn call in her mother. His actions would soon become fate, as he would now have little control as to what would happen next. The spiders were down below, consuming and webbing his forces and he could not bear to watch any more.

On her second pass, the flying spider saw the dragon and flapped its large wings rapidly to catch up to the dragon. The two massive beasts maneuvered high in the sky above the battleground looking to manipulate the other into a favorable position. The spider rose above the dragon and then dove in front of her causing The dragon fly past the spider before the dragon could react.

The spider then flipped over upside down in flight, and shot a large web towards the dragon. Aegyn's mother dove to the ground as the fired webbing missed its mark. She flew underneath the spider, and then turned upwards blasting a large breath of fire encompassing the spider. The spider's legs curled up as it burned and fell, splattering to the ground in burning spider waste.

The dragon made one more pass from east to west, torching the lower valley and killing the spiders that were feasting upon their human prey. Upon reaching the end of the valley she flew straight up, stretching her wings using all of their force and power to raise herself so high above that she was a just a small speck in the sky. She floated at the apex for a few seconds and blasted a victory burst of fire, before descending back down to the valley.

With great speed, she flew through the valley, then banked hard to the left, and flew straight towards Voll stopping just in front of him. She flapped her wings; slowly hovering just above him as he sat mounted on his horse watching in awe the whole scene. He was thankful for her actions in killing all of the spiders, and even his men, as he knew she had done them a favor by putting them out of their misery.

"Where is my daughter?" she asked, her voice booming inside of his head.

"The elves have captured her and are holding her somewhere. I do not know where."

"Why would the elves do this? You are lying to me?"

"No, I am not. Talk to her yourself," he pleaded.

"I sense that she is in danger, but I would not expect the elves to be responsible," she said as she lifted high in the sky. Voll watched her circle the area as she searched for her daughter from high above. He watched her and was fascinated as the beast flapped her wings gaining altitude and then corkscrewed back down to earth. She was only a hundred feet off of the ground when Aegyn appeared.

"The moment of truth," Voll whispered to himself as Aegyn found him and landed to his right and walked over to him. She walked on four legs until she reached him and turned around facing the valley next to him. Voll could hear his men behind him stir in anticipation unsure if the dragon was now going to attack them. Swords, spear and shields raised as the dragon came close. Voll spun around, raised his hand, and lowered his arm to signal them to be at ease.

"Why did the elves attack me?" Aegyn asked as she approached.

"I do not know. Maybe they thought you were with me, which in a way you are."

"But I was not going to attack them. I was just curious to watch."

"I know, but they didn't know that. You and your mother tend to forget that you are frightening."

Aegyn's Mother then came into sight and landed directly in front of Voll. She eyed her daughter, but he could not hear the conversation that he knew they were having.

"My mother and I agree that it is time for me to finish our bargain so that we can leave this place before it erupts into chaos," Aegyn said to Voll.

"Well, it just so happens to be that is exactly what I was hoping for," Voll said with a grin. "I am in need of your help and I am also expecting a fair amount of chaos after you help me."

"Then speak your need," Aegyn's mother snapped, clearly growing impatient.

"I need entrance through that thick forest so that we can storm their fortress. It is magically sealed and we cannot break through," he said, pointing to the spot of the forest that had given him so much consternation.

"And you think dragonfire will clear a path for you?" Aegyn's mother asked.

"I am certainly hopeful. Can it be done?"

"You are asking us to destroy and dispel this magical forest so that you can kill countless elven lives?"

"Well, yes, that is precisely that is what I ask. The elves have captured your daughter and held her prisoner. Don't you think they deserve some retribution?"

The two dragons spoke again to each other silently for a few seconds before they both took to the air and flew south. Aegyn landed in front of the tangled forest of trees and vines and arched her head back and blasted the edge of the forest with a fire so hot that Voll could feel the heat reaching him as he watched from the hillside. At the same time, Aegyn's mother came in from directly above the tangle and shot a huge blast of fire torching the tangle from above.

The impassable tangle erupted into a massive forest fire, but it only lasted a few minutes, as the fire was so hot that everything in their blasts were incinerated to ash. When they were finished, they took to the air and circled above twice, inspecting their work. Aegyn's mother roared and Voll knew she was not happy with her actions.

"Charge!" Voll yelled to his men, wanting to take advantage of the open passageway before there was any chance of the magic repairing itself and closing up the path. He charged his horse to the rear of his forces, shouting at all of the sub commanders to charge and take the fortress. They now had a clear path, and even though the elves and spiders had taken down a large amount of their force, they still had the numbers to finally win this battle and destroy the elves.

Voll watched with great satisfaction as the large force of humans crowded through the smoldering forest that had once blocked their way. Within minutes, he heard the sub commanders giving orders as they began to meet resistance at the fortress. The final siege had begun. With the last of his force charging through the forest, he then began to work his way down the hillside when he saw Aegyn and her mother watching the fight just above the fortress.

Aegyn's mother turned around and headed back towards him. "This is far more than we bargained for!" she said as she flew, circling above him.

"Call it revenge against them for capturing and holding your daughter prisoner."

"So be it. I regret agreeing to allow Aegyn to make that bargain with you in the first place. I should've toasted you when I first saw you with her."

"I saved her life!" Voll shouted shaking his fist at her.

"That is why I agreed, but now we are done with you!" she shouted to Voll, clearly angered at the whole situation. She then gained altitude and swooped down, opened her mouth and a sent a large blast of fire over the elven village, catching what remained untouched by the human torches on fire, including the barn that contained the elven survivors. The dragon watched in horror as a handful of elves scrambled out of the burning barn, their bodies completely engulfed in fire.

"What have I done?" she roared. "This is not what I bargained for."

Aegyn witnessed what her mother had done and flew south to escape her wrath.

Voll watched the dragon now fly towards him and saw her open her mouth just seconds before a large blast of fire encompassed his body.

Chapter 34

Naemyn returned to the castle just as the human forces were breaching the walls. The human force was massive and it would not be long before their defenses were overrun. The elven archers expended most of their supply of arrows attempting to take out the men as they climbed up the walls with their ladders, but there were just too many men. As they crested the walls, the humans, realizing their victory close at hand, attacked with such vigor and rage that the elven defense could not rally against the coming onslaught.

He heard the human force work their way through the castle, killing every elf in sight as they picked their way from room to room behind him. It would not be long before they would reach the king's chambers where he sat on King Jaerick's throne. He sat stone-faced looking straight ahead wondering how he had been so wrong. He had done everything the Guardian had told him to do if he had wanted the result he sought.

The fighting was getting louder as he could hear the humans working their way up the steps to the throne room. He would not die by a human blade, or possibly be subjected to their torture. He had made his decision; he decided that he would walk to the balcony and throw himself down to the inner bailey.

Realizing that he needed to hurry, he stood up, straightened out his robe for no purpose other than habit, and walked upon the balcony. As soon as he opened the glass doors, he heard a sucking sound coming from behind him. He turned around and saw again the black and blue swirling mist. His need to jump was immediately replaced with the sensation of being pulled into the mist.

"Come to me, Naemyn," he heard a voice whisper from inside the mist as he could see a body forming inside. Its form shifted in and out of visibility as he neared it. "Come and become one with me Naemyn. You cannot accomplish your goals in your present state," the voice continued.

Naemyn no longer cared enough to fight the urge or even question it. Without any hesitation, he stepped inside the swirling mist. Immediately he felt a presence that would change him forever. His body swirled within the mist and he could feel his old body melt away and become replaced with a new dark, but powerful form. This new form made him feel invulnerable, unstoppable, and completely invincible.

***

Jaerick and Traelyn transported back to the throne room. Jaerick looked around and realized where he was. Looking down, he saw that he stood above Traelyn as she lay on the stone floor. Her bleeding had stopped, but she was still in pain. She writhed in agony as her skin wrinkled upon her face and her soft brown hair turned from the beautiful silky brown to gray.

"Jaerick," a voice echoed throughout the chamber alerting him that they were not alone. Taking his gaze off of Traelyn, he looked up, recognizing the voice of Naemyn. Except what he saw was not his friend. What stood before him was a black figure that towered above him, standing twelve feet tall. He had black wings unfolding out of his back and bright blue eyes shone out of a dark face that had sharp black horns upon its head. A blue mist rose off of every inch of his skin looking as if the body had just walked out of an icy tundra landscape and into a warm environment.

Jaerick looked at the creature and somehow knew it was once his friend.

"I am going to destroy these humans for you," he said to Jaerick as he spread his dark leathery wings and smiled, showing his jagged and sharp teeth.

"No Naemyn, you will not," Traelyn said, exerting effort to stand on her own power, first from all fours and then painfully standing erect.

The door to the throne room crashed down, sending splinters of the solid oak door flying upon the polished floor. The human force charged in expecting to meet a stout defense, but paused when they saw their Great Mother, the elven king and a demon apparition standing before them.

Traelyn raised her arms and walked towards them. "Stop!" she shouted. "The fighting is over and you have won. This kingdom now belongs to you!"

"Kill the elven king and his demon!" one of the men shouted.

"No! Kill no more elves. They will leave peacefully. I will take care of this demon."

"What are you doing?" Jaerick said to her, rushing to her side.

"Leave me Jaerick. It is time that I finish this. The spirit at the lake has told me what to do." She smiled at Jaerick, giving him a look with her eyes that told him this would be her final act in life. With incredible speed for an ancient woman that had just struggled to stand up, she charged for the black beast, grabbed his chest, and pushed him onto the balcony and over the edge.

They fell, and Naemyn laughed as he wrapped his arms around Traelyn and started to unfold his wings. He tried to make the wings move to fly away, but something stopped him from doing so. He struggled and just before they hit the ground, his black form turned back into a blue and black mist, consuming Traelyn. When they hit the ground, it was in the form of a solid black and blue shard.

The green dragon from the lake appeared from the west. He swooped down out of the sky, landed in the bailey, picked up the shard, and took flight. Jaerick watched the dragon disappear, heading north.

•••

The dragon flew north passed the coastline and miles over the northern sea until he came to an island, landing on the highest peak. He waited a few seconds and then a large crevice opened up before him exposing a massive hole where nothing could be seen except darkness and shadow. Taking flight again, he dropped the shard into the crevice, watching it fall inside. As the shard fell, he saw the bodies of Traelyn and Naemyn reappear and flail about as they fell. Before he lost sight of them, he saw their bodies return to the shard and then the crevice sealed them in.

Satisfied, the dragon flew back to the western lake.

•••

The elves left their fortress home and began their journey to the west. Jaerick had gathered them together and told them of a beautiful lake deep in the forest that they would soon make their home. The humans were gracious in their victory and allowed the elves to leave in peace. Before they left, Jaerick commanded a handful of his most trusted elves to go to the Aaestfallia Keep and remove the Triestones. The humans could not be trusted to have control of this magical portal, so they would, in essence, neuter its power so that it could not be abused.

As they filed out of the burnt forest, they came upon the valley and saw for the first time the battle that had waged there. Blackened and bloody bodies littered the field of battle. As they crested a hill, they saw one body that was

226

still alive. Two elves slowly approached the body and heard him moan. The hair on his head was gone, his eyes had melted, leaving two large gaps where they had once been, and his skull could be seen in several places.

The two elves looked at each other and placed their hands upon his head. Within seconds, his eyeballs returned to the sockets, and the man screamed as soon as he regained consciousness. Voll looked at the elves and could not believe he was alive.

"You will live out the rest of your life as this ugly creature," one of the elves said.

"Let this be a reminder of your horrible deeds to the elven kingdom," the other elf said as they stood up and walked away.

Chapter 35

Traegon entered the catacombs again, this time alone. To his surprise, the magically sealed entrance opened as soon as he neared it. It seemed to him he was welcome. There were no ravages, wraeths, or goblins, nothing hindered his progress as if it was his home and all of its inhabitants welcomed his arrival. The stars in the sky opened up on him as he entered just as they did the first time he entered, but this time the cavern did not have the bluish purple haze, the wraeths, floating above. They seemed to have either calmed down, or simply had gone back to sleep.

Whatever it was, he only cared that they were gone, as they had scared him terribly the last time he was here. He pulled his torch out of his backpack, lit it, and then walked down the steps as quickly as he could. When he reached the bottom of the steps and into the open expanse where the long undead arms attacked them from the ground, he hesitated, took a deep breath and then stepped forward and stopped. When nothing happened, he walked as fast as he could, eventually breaking down and running. He ran all the way to the wall that led to the tunnels that would eventually lead to his father.

Surprisingly, he remembered the way, though he had to admit to himself that he felt as if he was somehow being guided by some unknown entity rather than his keen intuition, which he knew was not really all that sharp. He could not explain how he knew where to make each turn, but every time he did, he rounded a corner that not only seemed familiar, but felt as if he was indeed going in the right direction.

This continued for nearly an hour when he began to hear the sound of the river rushing through the cavern and the air began to move stronger and stronger with each corner he turned. He knew he was close and began to feel the excitement and anxiety of seeing his father. He really wanted to see his father, but he feared that he might not even be there, or he might be eternally trapped in this creepy elven crypt.

He was still deep in thought when he rounded a corner and his path was blocked by an elf in a bright white robe with his hood covering his face and his hands crossed in front of his waist. His head was down as he was sleeping standing up. Traegon stepped slowly to the elf, stood directly in front of him, and waited for a response that did not immediately come.

When the elf did not stir, Traegon walked around the elf, continually facing him and keeping a close eye on him. He had just rounded to his backside and had only taken one step backwards while still keeping his eye on him, when the elf spoke.

"You are welcome here today."

"Why am I welcome here?" he returned.

"You are of the Guardian, and I, as the Caretaker welcome you."

"What is going on?"

"Your father is waiting."

Without any further response, Traegon turned around and headed down the final corridor where he found the rushing river running through the cavern. His father stood on an island in the center of the river as if he had been waiting there for him.

"Do you have something for me?" Daegon asked as he removed the hood from his head. He wore the same white robe that the Caretaker was wearing. Traegon had only been gone a short while, yet his father had looked slightly older and more wizened.

"The talisman, yes, I have it," Traegon said as he pulled it out of his pouch, and as soon as he did, it disappeared from his hands and reappeared in a blue flash into the hole in the wall on the far side of the room. Both Daegon and Traegon stared in wonder as it seated itself in the hole. It floated in place, illuminated by a magical light as if on display. "It is time to come back to the battle father, we need you. Naemyn has taken the Great Mother with him and they have left us behind to battle the elves."

Daegon looked down upon his son and frowned. "I cannot. My place is here. Besides, the battle is already over."

"But you still have to leave here. I don't know what has happened to the Great Mother!" he protested clenching his fists like a child moments before throwing a tantrum.

"No son, you don't understand. I cannot leave, I am no longer who or what I was."

"Are, are you dead?"

Daegon laughed. "No, not really. In fact, I am very much alive and have been granted eternal life, or at least until certain events transpire, and I am no longer needed."

"What do you have to do?"

Daegon laughed again and scratched his growing facial hair, that was turning whiter than the usual salt and pepper color Traegon had been accustomed to seeing on his father. "Really, all I have to do is wait. Wait until the prescribed time," he said.

"So you are a prisoner here?"

"I guess you could say that. Technically yes, I suppose so, but it really is more complicated than that. I am to wait for a few generations to pass, until one of *your* offspring return to take this talisman away from me."

"But this is an elven sanctuary. How is it that you are to stay here and help the elves?"

Daegon laughed at his sons predicted response. "Yes, I admit that I am not thrilled about being so close to these elven spirits, and sometimes my human nature wants to kill them. However, I am now enlightened and see life and the workings of this realm from a different aspect. In the short time that I have been here, they have shown me many things. I have seen many things: the big picture of things, if you will. I have seen the future, the past, and have come to see the connection in all things. The elves play a big part in the end of this world as we know it, and your son, grandson, great grandson and so on down the line will each play their role in restoring the realm as it should be, as it once was before the great disruption."

"I don't understand. I don't know why you have to stay. We need you, Voll needs you, and we need to get the Great Mother back."

"No, that is no longer important. The Great Mother is where she needs to be. It may not be a happy-ending for her, but her part in this prophecy is almost complete."

"Then the more reason for you to help us."

"No, son, it does not work that way."

"Yes it does," he said.

"The talisman will wait here with me. It not only waits for the one who will take it, but the one who takes it will restore all of the four shards of the broken star known as the Quarterstar. When that child takes the talisman with the first Quarterstar Shard, the events will begin to move very quickly. It will begin with a short awakening of the Time Keep. For a brief moment, the spirit of Dar Drannon in the future will be able to travel to the past and communicate to his daughter, our Great Mother, Traelyn. In fact, he has already done so. He has given her information to start this prophecy. All time lines are now interconnected, even if for the briefest moment.

"This child will have to be very careful at first. He will not realize who he is, and many will want him dead. Those opposed to Wrae magic, and those opposed to Kronn magic, both will want him dead. Only the gods of Wrae can save him, but he will resist, as Wrae is of elven gods and elven magic, and he will have the imprint you and I both share to destroy the elves. So, you can see his dilemma, but the Markenhirth will rise in his new form, created by Naemyn. He will be called the Blue Wraeth, and he must be defeated.

"If the Blue Wraeth is not defeated then the Markenhirth will arise in solid form, crawling from the icy prison below. During this time, the first human king, Dar Drannon will return as well. The one the prophecy speaks of, the one who will fall through this hole, will need the help of a goddess named Fyaa, whom he will not trust, nor should he. He will need the help of Kronn, which he will be attracted to, but that power will be dangerous for him, and he will need the help of elven gods to control it. With all of these actions needing to be in play, he may not succeed."

"This cannot be real. You are deceived by the elves into thinking that you are what you are not. You will die down here if you don't leave."

"I can see where you might think that, but I have been here nearly two months since you first left, and I have had no food and no water since then. I should be dead, but I am not. In fact, I do not crave food or water, or any other cravings that mortal men need to survive. I merely exist, and I am satisfied with that."

"Father, please."

"Traegon, go. You must forget me. Forget the war with the elves, as it is already over. Go hide in a quiet village and with a peaceful clan in the south, by the ocean in the Val-Ron Bay, find a woman and have son, and begin the next stage of this prophecy."

"I cannot leave you father."

"You must and you will. You must never return. It will do you no good to do so. Consider me dead to this world and move on. Your role is crucial to the future. Traelyn's father, Dar Drannon will return to this world, and restore this realm."

"I am not leaving without you!" Traegon shouted, and as soon as he did so, he felt hands from behind grab his shoulders, forcing him to his back and he felt incredibly sleepy.

"You have worn out your welcome, forever," the Caretaker told him just as Traegon's vision turned foggy and black.

***

He awoke hours later outside. The sun shone in his face and warmed his body as he opened his eyes and looked up to a blue sky with wisps of puffy clouds moving swiftly to the east. He rolled over and pushed himself up and stood rubbing his face as if to rub away any ants or insects that had been crawling on him.

Now he just had to decide if he was going to head north and help Voll and the others, or if he would follow his father's advice and head south to a quiet village and forget what he had just told him about the end times, and forget everything he had learned about hating elves and destroying the race.

He found his bearings; he was not far from the nearest road that led east to the Valelands. He decided to walk and think. By the time he reached the Valelands he had made up his mind, he would head south to the Val Ron Bay and find a new home, and see if he could find other humans with elven descent just as himself and start anew.

The Weathered Old Man

The children watched the old man finish his tale. They were seated along the edge of the cliff as he floated above the rocky shoreline below. Now that he was finished he glided back to the edge of the cliff where they were seated and started to walk back to the crumbled remains of his home that once was a prestigious school of sorcery and prophecy.

"What happened to the elves?" One of the children asked.

"They migrated west and found their true home – where the fourth Quarterstar Shard was found."

"What will become of Voll?"

"He will wander the land as a monster and will be shunned by all."

"That is terrible," another one gasped.

"But there is a more important question you are not asking," the old man said smiling baiting the children to ask.

"Dar Drannon!" the eldest child stood up and shouted while grinning expecting praise.

"Very good," the old man said as he straightened his beard. "What do you think is going to happen to him? Where do you think he went to?"

"I do not know," the boy admitted, sitting down.

"I will tell you some, but not all. Dar Drannon is indeed a prisoner of Wrae magic, but he is also bound by Kronn magic, and when he returns, or rather escapes, he will attack the realm with a vengeance."

"Is he evil?" one of the girls asked.

"No, not necessarily so. He is merely a being of circumstance created by the three gods that entered this realm. You could almost say that they created him, even though it was not their intention to do so. The Quarterstar Prophecy has demanded action, and Dar Drannon will be at the center of it before this tale is over. Now you must realize that there will be many more terrible events to transpire before any sense of calmness will ever come to this land. This tale will not come to a happy ending, but it also will not be all bad. In the end, the hermit will get his way, but it will come at a great cost for everyone in the realm. Therefore, it is our place to make sure we go forth and accomplish what we must for this realm to make it a better place."

"When can we start wise one?" the eldest boy asked.

"Soon," he said smiling, "very soon."

Acknowledgements

My first thanks goes to Black Rose Writing for believing in my work.

I would like to express my eternal gratitude for my loving wife who has helped me grow in so many ways. She is my rock and foundation and this book would not have been possible without her.

I also thank Robert Cano for his amazing insight on story structure and continuity.

I thank all of the beta readers who gave me their input and advice along the way.

A big thanks goes to my friend and mentor Stephen Oppenheim.

Thank you to my Aunt Linda Graham and Gary Stoppenbrink for their support.

To my mom who believed even when I did not. I miss you mom.

I would also like to thank all of the people who have helped me along the way Tom Hunt, James Tucker, Loganpaul Eickhoff, Mitch McDaniel, Chris Black, Evan Allen, Sue Allen, Allessia Cowee, Elle Lewis, Robert Cano, Aaron Steinmetz, David Ketcham, and to all of the members past and present who have sat with me at the D&D table.

My love goes to my family. I love every single one of you.

Note from the Author

Word-of-mouth is crucial for any author to succeed. If you enjoyed the book, please leave a review online—anywhere you are able. Even if it's just a sentence or two. It would make all the difference and would be very much appreciated.

Thanks!
David

About the Author

David L. McDaniel has a love for words and storytelling. He wandered the halls in high school dreaming up fantastical stories to share with his friends. Now he lives in Northern California putting these tales onto paper as mandated to him by the Rager's House of Renegades as Word Blade.

Thank you so much for reading one of David L. McDaniel's novels.
If you enjoyed the experience,
please check out where the Quarterstars Prophecy really begins...

The Warrior's Bane
War for the Quarterstar Shards Book One

"...an entertaining journey." **–KIRKUS REVIEW**

"…delivers on its intent to both entertain and intrigue." *–IndieReader*

View other Black Rose Writing titles at
www.blackrosewriting.com/books and use promo code
PRINT to receive a **20% discount** when purchasing.